THE LONG JOURNEY HOME

With best wishes
Jenny Whitfield.

The Long Journey Home

A YOUNG WOMAN'S SEARCH FOR HAPPINESS

JENNY WHITFIELD

Cover design by: Lisa at The Art Partnership

Matador
9 Priory Business Park,
Wistow Road, Kibworth Beauchamp,
Leicestershire. LE8 0RX
Tel: 0116 279 2299
Email: books@troubador.co.uk
Web: www.troubador.co.uk/matador
Twitter: @matadorbooks

ISBN 978 1785893 483

British Library Cataloguing in Publication Data.
A catalogue record for this book is available from the British Library.

Printed and bound by CPI Group (UK) Ltd, Croydon, CR0 4YY
Typeset in 11pt Aldine by Troubador Publishing Ltd, Leicester, UK

Matador is an imprint of Troubador Publishing Ltd

I would like to thank everyone who helped and encouraged me with this book. From small pieces of valuable information to the massive help from my daughter-in-law, Steph and my stepdaughter, Lisa. Lastly, I simply could not have come this far without the help of my darling Husband Martin.
Thanks to you all.

PART 1

CHAPTER 1

1982

Grey clouds scudded across the sky and the occasional drop of rain began to fall. Only the strength of the wind was keeping heavy rain away. Josie slumped down on the low wall surrounding the car park. It was November and late afternoon, and very few cars were coming into the service area now that the holiday season was over. Just a few tucked up close to the building, which probably belonged to staff, and one other parked some way off. Behind her and to the side, trees and shrubs grew, and further over were a deserted picnic area and a children's play area. A sharp gust of wind blew the last few leaves from the trees and hurled them across in front of her. Sweet wrappers, screwed-up receipts and an empty Coke can came to a halt in the corner of the car park, amongst the leaves. *So near and yet so far*, she thought. *It may as well be a million miles away instead of fifty. But I just can't go any further.*

A family came back to their car; a father, a mother, a boy of about twelve or thirteen, and a skinny girl three or four years younger. Their voices floated across to her on the wind. Even after a year in France she still struggled with the language and could only pick out the odd word here and there, but what did it matter? The girl skipped around the car, full of energy after food and drink, until her mother spoke sharply to her and she climbed into the car. It brought back memories of Josie herself as a child, tall and skinny and never still, driving her teachers mad. Car doors slammed, the car started up and moved away, the sound of the engine fading away in the distance. Then there was just the wind and the leaves and the litter blowing around her feet.

CHAPTER 2

1968

Josie stood in front of Mrs Reynolds' desk, pulling at her pigtails and hopping from one foot to the other.

"Josie, you are eight now and old enough to understand what I am saying to you. It's about respect. Respect when you are in God's house and respect for the people around you. Just for that hour, once a week, could you not sit still and behave yourself?"

"But I dropped my penny and it rolled under the seat." Josie's face was a picture of innocence.

"You have been told to keep the money in your pocket till the collection plate comes round." Mrs Reynolds held up her hand to silence any more arguments. "You will wipe the tables in the dining room after lunch and sweep the floor, and consider yourself lucky that's the only punishment. You may go now and have your lunch."

Josie left the room and frowned in annoyance.

"It's not my fault the stupid penny ran under all those seats and ended up at Lady Mary's feet."

She began to run towards the dining room; then remembered they must walk, not run. She walked sedately into the room where twenty girls, ages ranging from five to eighteen, were already eating. There was only one child under five at the moment, and she was being fed in the nursery. Josie went over to the servery where Cook put food on the plate for her, then sat down next to her friend Stella.

"Tell you about it later," she whispered.

Meanwhile, Mrs Reynolds was still sitting at her desk, a small smile playing around her lips. She was fond of Josie, but she knew she would never be tamed, and could only hope that her spirit would carry her through life. Josie knew that she had been left on the doorstep of St. Anne's when only a few hours old. But she had also been told that she was warmly wrapped up as though someone had really cared for her, but was unable to keep her. She had been told this on her eighth birthday and had accepted it in uncharacteristic silence. Life could be tough for the girls when they left the home. Some made a good life for themselves, and some fell by the wayside. Mrs Reynolds sighed and stood up, tidying her desk quickly; then went to join her colleagues for lunch.

Josie and Stella were sitting under a tree in the local park. This was a regular outing for all the girls on a Sunday afternoon, providing the weather was fine. Two teachers would be keeping an eye on them to make sure they didn't get into mischief.

"So did you get told off?" Stella asked.

"Course I did, but I don't take any notice. They are always telling me off anyway," Josie muttered.

Stella looked at her. "Why are you always naughty? Things would be nicer for you if you tried to be good."

Josie leapt up and glared down at her friend. "Just because you're nine, you think you can boss me about, and anyway I don't want to be a goody-goody like you." She kicked at the grass. "And one day, I'm going to be an important person, and then I'll be telling people what to do!"

"That's not going to happen. You don't try in class and Miss Wetherby says if you want to succeed in life you have to try hard in your lessons."

"Oh, pooh to Miss Wetherby," was Josie's response.

Stella looked at her "OK, if you're going to be horrible I'm going over to Margaret and the others."

She got up and walked over to a group of girls standing near the swings, and Josie was left on her own to think about what her pal had said.

St. Anne's had once been a private residence. Built early in the reign of Queen Victoria, it had large rooms with high ceilings. Prior to being a childrens home, the last person to live in the house was the granddaughter of the original owner. Having lost her fiancé in the First World War, she had remained a spinster, and a very wealthy one. During World War Two she became acutely aware of how many children were being orphaned by the bombing, and had decided to give her home to be used as a pleasant place for girls to be raised and educated. She financed any alterations that needed to be made and made sure everything was legally sound. Sadly she passed away several years after the war ended, but left the money in trust for the upkeep of the home. Any girl who found themselves at St. Anne's was lucky indeed. The staff were kind and usually stayed for many years. The girls were given a good education to the age of eleven, when they would go to an outside school, either a high school or a secondary school, according to their abilities. They would continue to live at St. Anne's till they were at least sixteen, but by eighteen they were expected to have found somewhere else to live, or they could go to a council-run hostel.

CHAPTER 3

Three years had passed and Josie's schoolwork had improved. In the July exams she had done well, but she knew she would never be as clever as Stella. Only a year to go and then she would be going to an outside school, and she just couldn't wait. Stella, at nearly thirteen, had grown into an attractive girl, with smooth, dark hair cut in a shiny bob. Josie was just as tall, but skinny, and to her dismay she had no 'bumps' at all! Now she wore her hair in bunches, which made her feel more grown-up and controlled the curls.

It was a Sunday afternoon in September and the two girls were sitting under 'their' tree in the park. Stella had just finished her first week at the local high school and was telling Josie all about it. It all sounded exciting, but rather hard work. Still, she was enjoying it and had already made new friends. Josie was silent for a few minutes.

"Am I still your friend as well?" she asked.

"Of course, silly." Stella hugged her. "You'll always be my best friend, even when we're grown-up."

The girls looked across the grass to where three of the older girls were standing close together. Stella drew in her breath sharply.

"Oh look, Margaret is crying! I wonder what's the matter? Perhaps she's worried about getting a job – I heard her say she doesn't want to go to college. She just wants to earn some money and be independent. After all, she is sixteen now."

"But will she still live here, or do you think she'll be allowed to go to the hostel? Perhaps she's got relations she can live with," Josie said. "But I wonder why she's crying? I thought she was clever like you and looking forward to college."

"Well…" Stella hesitated. "I heard something horrible about Mr Shenstone."

"What, the school governor?" Josie asked.

"Yes. He… he sometimes hurts the older girls."

Josie stared round-eyed at her friend. "What do you mean?"

"I'm not sure," Stella said, although she did have a vague idea.

"Well he'd better not hurt me or I'll thump him," Josie hotly replied.

The girls looked at each other, then burst into giggles at the thought of skinny little Josie thumping the fat, red-faced Mr Shenstone.

He was one of the three school governors, Lady Mary being another and Mr Brown from the council being the third. The girls were familiar with them as they met once a month at St. Anne's, where they would discuss matters relating to the running of the home with Mrs Reynolds. This was the only time a door was closed –

well, almost closed – in the building, apart from the bathrooms. Mrs Reynolds had an open door policy. All doors must be left open at all times. So classrooms, bedrooms, leisure rooms and her own office were always open, but the governors wanted the office to be closed during meetings. A compromise was reached, and the door pushed up but not closed. The girls were all taught to knock before entering any room except for the leisure rooms and it was soon second nature to them.

Mr Shenstone was a big, rather loud man, full of his own importance but with money and 'connections'. He owned a large farm a couple of miles away, where he lived with his little mouse of a wife and two strapping sons.

Lady Mary was a sweet lady in her fifties. With her husband often away in the city and her two sons and a daughter married and living their own lives, visiting St. Anne's gave her great pleasure. She adored the girls and would often drop in just to chat and see how they were.

Mr Brown was quite the opposite of Mr Shenstone, rather pale and thin and as quiet as Mr Shenstone was loud, but with a determination to do the best he could for the girls.

That evening before the girls had their meal, Mrs Reynolds clapped her hands for silence and said, "I have an announcement to make. As you know, Margaret is sixteen now and is leaving us. She has managed to get a job in Woolworths and is going to live in the hostel.

I have tried to persuade her to stay here with us, but she is determined to be independent." Mrs Reynolds paused and smiled at Margaret. "We shall miss you and we wish you all the best, and please do come back and see us any weekend."

Margaret gave a shaky smile and a small nod, but it was obvious tears were not far away.

Josie's birthday fell in July, and on her twelfth she was given a gift from St. Anne's, as all the girls were on their birthday. Josie's was a book about gardening with sections on how to grow vegetables and flowers, and in the back a few simple recipes. Two months earlier eight girls of around the same age had been taken out for the day in the home's minibus. The destination was Riversview Manor, a large country house with huge grounds some ten miles away. They were greeted by a very nice lady who took them around the house and told them its history, and about the people who had once lived there. It was very interesting, and the girls marvelled at the old furniture and ornaments. Then they were taken to the huge kitchen, where copper saucepans hung on nails around the walls, some of them so large it must have been difficult to lift them once they were full of food. Finally the girls were led outside and given a tour of the grounds. This included flower beds at the front and parkland at the back, with huge, ancient trees dotted about. There was also a woodland walk with sweeps of bluebells as far as the eye could see.

Josie was bewitched, but even more so when they were led into the walled kitchen gardens. Josie watched a young lady hoeing between rows of tiny seedlings and a man putting supports in for peas. *I want to be a gardener when I grow up*, she thought. That night, as she lay in bed, she thought of the majestic old trees – could they really be five hundred years old? Were those tracks in the woods really made by rabbits, foxes and deer? And the banks of flowers just beginning to come out in the herbaceous borders – how wonderful, but best of all, the neat rows of vegetable seedlings just coming in the walled garden.

The next day the eight girls were asked to write an essay about their day at Riversview Manor.

Later Miss Wetherby called the girls to order and said, "I have read all your essays and they are very good and all quite different. It has reminded me that we all have different interests. What fascinates one person, another may find boring. I have picked out two which illustrate this point, and I would like to read them out to you. First, Marie, who obviously enjoyed the tour of the house." Miss Wetherby then proceeded to read out Marie's essay. As she came to the end she added, "And very neat too, Marie, and no spelling mistakes."

The girls clapped politely, which was something they were encouraged to do when any pupil had done particularly well.

"Now for the second essay. The content is good and rather humorous, but spelling and writing leave a little to be desired." Miss Wetherby looked pointedly at Josie, but her glance was not unkind. She picked up Josie's essay and began to read. "*I found the house quite interesting, but it was rather dark in there and a bit spooky.*" There were a few chuckles from the girls, and then Miss Wetherby continued. "*One of my favourite things was the main bedroom with the old bed. Fancy having a roof over your head; then drawing curtains all the way round. It must be like sleeping in a cardboard box.*" Miss Wetherby paused while the girls giggled again. "*But the best bit of all for me was the garden. The way the grass had been cut in lovely straight lines was the first thing I noticed. I loved the walk through the woods with the bluebells and other wild flowers, and the bright green leaves of the beech trees. The flower beds were lovely too, although not many flowers were out. When we went into the walled garden I wished I could pull a carrot up and eat it, but I realised they would be too small. This was my favourite bit of our day out, and I would like to go back one day in summertime so I can see all the flowers out and the vegetables ready to be harvested.*"

Now it was her birthday, and she had been given a book about gardening. She thanked Miss Wetherby and gave her a big smile.

"Right, girls, off you go now. Josie, will you stay and help me tidy up, please?"

When the room had emptied of girls, Josie got the broom out and began to sweep up, but Miss Wetherby called her over to her desk.

"Now, Josie, it seems to me that you are really interested in horticulture – that's gardening, of course. A plot in the allotment has just become free. Margaret had one and of course she is leaving. We only have

14

six plots, so would you like one while you've got the chance?"

"Oh yes, please!" replied Josie eagerly.

"Good. I know you are going to secondary school in September but it shouldn't make any difference, you'll still have weekends and holidays. Mr Copcut has agreed to help you and give you all the information you need, and he will explain about tools and how to take care of them. Now, tomorrow is Saturday and Mr Copcut has kindly agreed to come in for two hours in the morning to start you off. What do you think about that?"

Josie could barely contain her excitement. "That will be really good, Miss Wetherby. Thank you, Miss Wetherby."

The next morning at 9.30 Josie ran across the lawn and joined Mr Copcut at the allotments. They walked across to what had once been Margaret's plot.

"Now, young Josie, you've got some hard work ahead of you. Margaret lost interest in her plot this year and it's full of weeds and not much else. I think you'll find it fairly easy to turn over because we had that drop of rain last week and nobody's been walking on it to make it hard. I'll help you for a while, but if I'm late home my missus will give me what for! Come to the shed first and I'll show you the tools."

The shed had a certain aroma, a mix of soil, fertiliser and other mysterious things.

"We look after our tools because they are good

quality and cost a lot of money. So clean them off when you've finished and put them back where you found them. Then lock the shed and give the key to Mrs Reynolds straight away." He looked at Josie sternly. "That's very important."

Josie nodded, and the two of them chose a fork each, a big one for Mr Copcut and a smaller one for Josie.

Over the next hour the two of them loosened the soil and pulled out the weeds, throwing them into the wheelbarrow. Josie was shown where to empty the wheelbarrow and where and how to store it when she had finished. Each plot was only ten feet by fifteen feet. It was all that could be spared, but was enough for a few rows of veg and maybe some flowers. Some of the other plots had strawberries, and this appealed to Josie. The girls were all given a little pocket money each week (Mrs Reynolds believed it would help them to manage their money later on), but each new allotment owner was given a little extra to start them off; maybe to buy seeds, plants or even gardening gloves. Any product could be sold to Cook, and one of the girls always put flowers in Mrs Reynolds' office.

Mr Copcut left for home and Josie continued, completely absorbed in her work until Miss Wetherby hurried over and announced with a smile that it was lunchtime, and that perhaps it was enough gardening for her first day. Josie hurriedly emptied the barrow on the compost heap and stood it on end behind the shed. After cleaning her fork and putting it away, she ran indoors and gave the key to Mrs Reynolds before washing her hands and joining Stella for lunch.

During the five and a half weeks of the summer holidays, the plot gradually became neat and tidy, its edges neatly trimmed with the edging shears. It was a bit late to put anything in the garden but Josie had bought some strawberry plants and these were looking healthy, although it would be next year before she had any fruit. But now it was time to prepare for her first term at Kingsacre Secondary School.

The winter was a hard one and the girls hurried home from their respective schools each day, glad to be back in the warmth of St. Anne's. Josie had settled down well and was finding the work fairly easy, although history would always be a problem for her. She made new friends and sometimes they would come and see her at St. Anne's. As soon as spring arrived she began to spend several hours a week on her plot. She put in carrot and radish seeds and a few lettuce seeds in a pot to prick out later. Mr Copcut allowed her to put the pot in his greenhouse, along with another pot with tomato seeds in. As the days warmed up she carefully pricked out the tomato seedlings and put them in individual pots, and put the lettuce seedlings in the ground.

Mr Copcut sprinkled a small amount of slug pellets round them for her. "Else there won't be anything left in the morning," he said. "But you mustn't touch those things on the top shelf 'cause they're dangerous."

As June arrived and then July, the strawberries began to ripen and Josie felt a rush of satisfaction. Over a few days she managed to pick enough to sell to Cook, who decorated a trifle with them, and very soon she was able to supply Cook with lettuce and radish, and then tomatoes. Stella could not understand Josie's fascination with her allotment but was only too happy to eat the strawberries and enjoy an ice cream Josie treated her to from her earnings.

CHAPTER 4

1974

Another two years had gone by, and Christmas was approaching. At fourteen and fifteen and a half years old the two pals were given permission to walk into the town and do some Christmas shopping. Plumbford was a small market town nestling in a valley some thirty miles from London. It had a good variety of shops, and as it was late November the Christmas decorations were up and everything looked bright and cheerful. The girls linked arms and wandered from shop to shop.

"We'll have to part company soon and do some secret shopping," Stella said with a grin.

"I've got a few ideas," Josie replied, "but let's go and have a cup of hot chocolate first."

The girls found a seat in the corner of the café and Stella went to buy the drinks, while Josie kept the seats safe from other shoppers. Soon the girls were sipping the delicious hot chocolate.

"That Mr Shenstone is up to his tricks again," Stella whispered. "He was being horrible to Marie. You know he waits till somebody is nearly sixteen; then he starts on them. Marie is two months older than me and that's good enough for him. Course, when girls are sixteen, it's legal, and then he can say they asked for it."

Josie looked at her in shock. "What do you mean?"

"Oh come on, Josie, you can't be that innocent. He touches them and tries to get them to touch him."

"But why doesn't someone report him?" Josie insisted.

"Because nobody would believe them, it's his word against theirs," Stella said. "I make sure I am never anywhere alone with him, but I must admit he does scare me."

"He doesn't scare me," Josie retorted. "You let me know if he touches you and I'll report him even if you don't, or I'll use the garden shears on him."

The outburst was followed by uncontrollable giggles, till the girls were red in the face and mopping their eyes, and getting disapproving looks from other tables.

"Come on," said Stella, "or we'll never get our shopping done."

The girls arranged to meet outside Woolworths in half an hour and set off separately to get gifts for each other. Josie also wanted to get a birthday present for her pal, who was sixteen the following week. It would only be something small in each case, because they only had a little pocket money each week. But it didn't matter. The pleasure and anticipation was just as great as any teenager might experience, rich or poor. The girls met up again and went into Woolworths to say hello to Margaret and finish their shopping. There was no chance to tell Margaret about recent events as she was too busy with customers, but they arranged to meet next day in the park; then they hurried home for lunch.

The three girls sat on a bench in the park. Margaret was staring wide-eyed at Stella and Josie as they told her about what had happened to poor Marie.

"Just how long is he going to get away with this?" she said. "And what's Marie going to do?"

"I don't know, she's not very brave. I think she'll just put up with it and try to avoid him."

Stella managed to escape Mr Shenstone's attentions till after Christmas. Josie found her crying in the bedroom they shared.

"He grabbed me before I could get away, and started to touch me," she sobbed. "He pushed me up against the cupboard in the cloakroom. I was really scared. Then someone walked along the corridor and he let me go."

Josie was furious. "Right, that's it! I'm going to report him."

Stella grabbed her arm. "No, don't, I shall move to the hostel straight away and get a job."

"But what about college in September? You're so clever and you enjoy learning about things," Josie said. "You can't give it all up."

But Stella was determined. "Don't you see? If we report him all the other girls will be dragged in and it will really upset them. It doesn't matter about college; I've just got to get out of here before something even worse happens."

Next day Stella went to see Mrs Reynolds, and although she did her best to persuade Stella to continue with her education, in the end she could see it was no good.

"If you want to throw your chances away, I can't stop you, but I am surprised and disappointed. I thought you were looking forward to college."

"I was." Stella paused; then said, "I just want to get a job and be independent."

"Well you can get a job, but still live here," Mrs Reynolds suggested.

"No, no," Stella blurted out. "Sorry, Mrs Reynolds, I mean no thank you. Do you think they will have room for me at the hostel?"

Mrs Reynolds looked at her for several moments. "Is there anything else I should know about, Stella?"

"No, Mrs Reynolds, I've just changed my mind, that's all."

"Very well." Mrs Reynolds sighed. "I don't think there is a room at the hostel but the hotel two doors up will take you till a room becomes available. But you must eat at the hostel so they know you are all right. I'll phone them later and I suppose I'd better phone the hotel as well. I really cannot let you go unless one or the other has room for you. I'll phone the employment agency as well and see what jobs they have." She pursed her lips and sighed again. "All right, Stella, off you go."

She picked up the phone and made the call to the hostel, but as she thought, there was no room. The hotel could have her, although the room was tiny and up in what was once an attic.

The next day was Saturday, and Stella and Josie were given permission to go into the town.

"I don't want Mrs Reynolds to choose a job for me. I want to choose my own," Stella declared.

The girls walked all the way down the high street on one side and then back along the other side, looking in all the shops and business premises hoping to see a sign saying *Staff Required*, but there was nothing.

"Don't give up," Josie said. "We'll go down all the side streets now."

Nearly half an hour later, when the girls had almost given up, they went down a small road on the edge of town and there on the window of a small supermarket was a sign. *Staff Required, Apply Within*. Josie stepped back and gave Stella a little push.

"Good luck!"

Stella seemed to be gone for hours, but in fact it was forty-five minutes later when she appeared with a big smile on her face.

"I got it!" she said. "I start Monday. It's 8.30 to 5.30 Monday to Friday, and sometimes Saturdays as well if they are short. Mr Khan showed me round the shop and warehouse and I met his wife and daughter, whose name is Farah. His wife doesn't usually work in the shop, but somebody left quite suddenly so she is helping out. He wasn't very happy I'm only just sixteen, but I think they were desperate."

"Oh, well done, Stella." Josie gave her a hug.

"I'll be filling shelves and putting away deliveries and things like that to begin with. Then after a couple of weeks Mr Khan will train me on the till." Stella's eyes sparkled with excitement. "They are ever so nice, Josie; I think I'm going to enjoy working there. Now I've got to go and tell Mrs Reynolds what I've done and I'm hoping I can move to the hotel tomorrow."

"Oh, it's all happening too quickly. I'm really going to miss you." There were tears in Josie's eyes. "Promise me we can see each other at the weekend."

Meanwhile Mrs Reynolds had contacted Lady Mary and asked her to call in for a chat. The two ladies were sitting upstairs in Mrs Reynolds' flat drinking a cup of coffee.

"What can I do for you, my dear?" Lady Mary said.

"I've just got this feeling that something not very nice is going on. It suddenly occurred to me that possibly half a dozen or more girls, who I expected to stay till they were eighteen, have quite suddenly decided to leave at sixteen. All of them have seemed rather unhappy, and almost desperate to leave. I don't understand it."

"Maybe when the first one left, the others were envious of their freedom, and to be able to go out and buy clothes and records whenever you want – well, it must seem wonderful. I'm sure it's nothing more serious than that," Lady Mary said.

"Then why are they so unhappy?" replied Mrs Reynolds.

24

"Yes, I see what you mean. We must keep our ears to the ground and see if we can find some answers."

Lady Mary patted Mrs Reynolds' hand and prepared to leave.

It was only a short walk from the supermarket back to St. Anne's, but the girls had so much to talk about that it took them ages.

"So what are they paying you?" Josie asked.

"£15.20 a week," replied Stella. "When I've paid for my board I should still have lots left. I feel quite rich."

She grinned at Josie, her ordeal with Mr Shenstone temporarily forgotten in the excitement of finding a job. Josie gave her a thoughtful look.

"Mrs Reynolds is not going to like this. You've got a job without her permission. I bet she'll phone them up and say you can't do it."

Stella gave her a horrified look. "I know you think I'm a goody-goody, but there's another side to me, you know. I'm going to do this job no matter what she says, and if I have to rent a room somewhere instead of the hostel, I will."

There was a short silence; then to her consternation, Josie burst into tears.

"What am I going to do without you?" she sobbed. All of a sudden the events of the morning were too much. "I've got a year and a half before I can leave. Please will you come and see me at the weekends?"

Stella hugged her. "Course I will, and you'll be fine. We can meet in the town sometime. It will be fun."

They arrived back at St. Anne's and Stella went to find Mrs Reynolds and face the music, and Josie went to the bathroom to rinse the signs of tears away.

Later that day the girls met in the library, where they knew their conversation would be more private, and Stella related how her chat with Mrs Reynolds had gone.

"I really thought she would have a go at me, but she just said she was sorry I was not continuing my education and she actually said well done about the job. I couldn't believe it. But I've got to stay at the hotel for now till there's a room at the hostel, and I'm going tonight because of my job."

"Tonight?" gasped Josie.

"Yes, and I've already packed most of my stuff. I'm going after dinner – I just can't wait."

All of a sudden, Stella looked very grown-up. As with most of the girls at St. Anne's, she had a sad past. Her mother and father had been killed in a car crash when she was four and she could barely remember them. She had a photo of them by her bed and said goodnight to them every night, and if she thought no one was looking she kissed them as well. Her only relative now was her maternal grandmother, who was elderly and in poor health. She had taken Stella after the accident and they had been a comfort to each other as they came to terms with the tragedy. But after a year it all became too much for the old lady and she had placed Stella at St. Anne's. Stella went to see her most weeks as she lived only a mile away, but she was becoming increasingly frail and so neighbours and the District Nurse called on her morning and evening. Stella helped her too, doing jobs around the house and picking up a few bits of shopping for her. Josie would go with her sometimes, and had become fond of the old lady.

Josie watched from her bedroom window as Mrs Reynolds' car, with Stella inside, pulled away and disappeared through the gates. It was 7pm and had been dark for a couple of hours. Mrs Reynolds would see Stella settled in her room at the George Hotel, and had promised to come and have a chat with Josie when she got back. She was well aware how upset Josie was, and how strange it would be for them not to see each other every day. When she arrived back an hour later, she called Josie into the lounge.

"Well, I think she'll be fine. She's got a dear little room right at the top, under the eaves. The views are wonderful even at night, the lights of the town spread out all around, and in the daylight, I would think you'll see for miles. She wants to meet you next Saturday at your usual café at 10.30am, so that's not so bad, is it? Tomorrow, I'm going to move Gillian in with you. She's a bit squashed where she is now. She's a nice girl as you know, and you'll have company."

Josie just nodded; she was too upset to say anything. Mrs Reynolds squeezed her shoulder and left to catch up on some paperwork, and Josie wandered up to her room. Gillian was there, putting her things away and hanging her clothes in the wardrobe.

The girls smiled at each other, and then Josie said, "I'm sorry, I'm a bit of a misery tonight. I'll be better tomorrow, I expect."

"That's all right," Gillian replied. "I know Stella was your special friend, but she's not far away, is she, and I expect you'll see her soon."

The next Saturday was cold, windy and wet, but Josie donned her raincoat, pulled on her wellingtons, borrowed an umbrella and set off to meet her pal. Stella was waiting outside Carol's Café, and the girls flung their arms round each other, which wasn't easy with two umbrellas.

"My treat this time," Stella said. "What cake shall we have?"

"Anything chocolaty," Josie replied.

As they sat sipping their hot chocolate, Stella told Josie all about her week. "My room's very small, but I love it. I can see the river and the woods on the hill. I have to go down to the next floor to the bathroom, but that's OK. There are just two rooms up at the top, and one of the staff is in the other and she's nice. I have a lovely breakfast in the hotel but I have my evening meal in the hostel, and of course Margaret's there so there is somebody I know."

"Yes, but how's the job?" Josie eagerly enquired.

"It's OK. They are very kind to me, but I get lonely."

"How can you be lonely in a shop?" Josie was puzzled.

28

"Well, most of the customers are Pakistanis and so they speak Urdu all the time, and I feel left out. It's such a relief when someone English comes in and I can have a quick chat. Don't get me wrong, the Pakistanis are very friendly and they smile at me and say hello, but they would rather Mr Khan attended to them. By the way," she continued, "I've signed up for a course on shorthand and typing. Mrs Reynolds helped me to sort it out. I've already been to one lesson on Wednesday night. It's ever so hard, but I must keep trying. I don't think working in a shop is for me, and I think I'll earn more in an office and maybe get a promotion."

"Well, you're clever enough to, Stella."

The girls finished their drinks and went into Woolworths, because Stella wanted to buy some lipstick and it was always nice to see Margaret. Then Stella asked Josie if she would like to see her room.

"On the way, do you mind if I pop into the hostel and see if they have a room for me yet?"

Josie didn't mind, and they waited while the lady looked through her book.

"I don't think anything is going to come up for a week or two," she said. "Come back in three weeks. Aren't you happy at the hotel?"

"Oh yes, I've got a nice little room," Stella said. "I'll come back and see you in three weeks' time."

At the hotel, Josie gazed out of Stella's window. "Wow, what a view. You are lucky."

"Yes, I know, but I wish you were here with me." Stella gave her friend a hug.

Most Saturday mornings, Josie and Stella would meet at Carol's Café and have their usual hot chocolate and sticky bun. In the middle of February Stella had news for Josie.

"I'm moving to the hostel this afternoon."

"Are you pleased?" asked Josie.

Stella looked thoughtful. "Well, in some ways I am. I shall have company. I've been a bit lonely in the hotel, although I love my room. I've got to know all the girls at the hostel and they are a good crowd. I've got more stuff to move this time, 'cause I've got more clothes now and more bits and pieces. But it is only a few yards anyway. I'll soon have it done. They are letting me share with Margaret because we're friends."

"It all sounds really good," Josie exclaimed. "I'm really envious. How are the evening classes going? Are you finding it easier now?"

"Well," replied Stella, "I'm getting the hang of it. I've just got to speed up, I'm so slow and you have to do umpteen words a minute. Still, I've only had six lessons so far and you'll never guess – I can speak a few words of Urdu! Mr Khan has tried to teach me 'good morning', 'please', 'thank you' and 'goodbye'. But I'm hopeless, and it makes Mr Khan laugh. Still, I'm quite happy to stay there till I've got qualifications."

CHAPTER 5

As spring arrived and the weather improved, Josie asked permission to have all day Saturday out with Stella. The girls wanted to walk along the River Plumb and take a picnic. Mrs Reynolds agreed and Cook made up a picnic for both girls. The day was pleasantly warm, with sun and a few light clouds. The path was well used and maintained, and ran some four miles along the banks of the river. There was an alternative route back through woods and fields. Mrs Reynolds had loaned them a map of the walk so they wouldn't get lost, and the girls set off through the town to the river. To begin with there were a lot of other people walking, taking advantage of the lovely spring day. Some were walking dogs, and there were families keeping a careful eye on small children because the river was high and flowing well after a rather wet couple of months. Soon, however, fellow walkers became fewer and the girls had the path to themselves most of the time. It was fascinating to look back towards the town and try to see Stella's room window at the top of the hotel, and Stella spotted the cinema.

When the riverside path ended the pals decided it

was time to see what goodies Cook had packed up for them.

"Yummy," said Josie. "There's cheese and pickle and some ham sandwiches. Gosh, and crisps as well. What a treat, and look, Cook's put in two flapjacks each, and an apple."

"And a big bottle of squash," added Stella. "There's some seats over there, let's sit down. We shan't have so much to carry when we go back."

"You mean I won't have so much to carry," said Josie with a grin. "My good old faithful rucksack comes in handy, doesn't it?"

After the girls had eaten everything except for two flapjacks and drunk three quarters of the squash, Josie hoisted her rucksack onto her back and the girls set off once more. The first half-mile was through a wood, where bluebells were just beginning to show colour. Birds sang and chased each other, and the sun shone through the branches of the trees. It was truly enchanting. The path then skirted a farm, and suddenly Stella grabbed Josie.

"It's Shenstone, don't let him see us," whispered a frightened Stella. They watched as the hated Mr Shenstone climbed into his Land Rover and drove off, and then sighing with relief, the girls set off once more. Without the need to say anything, they both walked faster until they had left the farm behind. They passed through a tiny hamlet where they rested on a seat on the green, overlooked by several old cottages. The last two flapjacks were soon gone, as was the rest of the squash.

It had been a lovely day out, and they were almost sorry as they arrived back in Plumbford. It was good to catch up on all they had been doing. Josie to talk about her favourite lesson at Kingsacre and her dislike of history, and Stella actually said, "Good morning, and how are you?" in Urdu. Her shorthand and typing were coming along in leaps and bounds and she was hoping that by the time she was seventeen she would be able to get a job in an office. The girls hugged each other outside the hostel and Josie walked back to St. Anne's, where Mrs Reynolds wanted to know all about their walk when Josie returned the map.

CHAPTER 6

Josie was still thoroughly enjoying her gardening, but Mr Copcut had retired and two young men came along one morning every two weeks and hurtled around mowing the grass, weeding and pruning. It wasn't the same, and Josie really missed Mr Copcut. However, she had been to tea at his cottage on the edge of the town and met his wife. She had been able to ask advice about growing something different, and Mr Copcut had shown her around his garden, which was lovely. He had flowers and lawn at the front and near the house at the back. But his garden was very long, and he had a greenhouse and a large vegetable garden, and right at the bottom, half a dozen fruit trees.

Josie's fifteenth birthday came, and then in the winter Stella turned seventeen. At the end of the year, she took her exams and passed with flying colours. As soon as Christmas and New Year were over, she started to look for another job. It was several weeks before she was successful. She would be a junior in the office of a local building supplies company. Mr Khan was not surprised when she gave her notice. He knew she had been going to evening classes, and he and his wife Parveen wished her luck and gave her a box of chocolates as a leaving present. Farah was at university, so was not able to say goodbye.

So on the second Monday of February, Stella started work at J. Brown & Son building suppliers. She was not sure how she would get on in what was essentially a working man's environment. But apart from a bit of teasing, she found it a welcome change from her previous job. Everyone, from the boss down, treated her in a warm, friendly manner, and very soon she felt like a member of the team. The only problem was that she had to work Saturday mornings, so she would have to see Josie some other time. In the end the girls arranged to meet on Sunday afternoons, sometimes in the town, sometimes at St. Anne's.

One very wet, cold day in March, the girls were in the leisure room at St. Anne's.

"I really love my new job," Stella told Josie, "and the pay is good already, although I'm only a junior. It's very busy, but I like that. I get to go out on errands, to the post office mainly, but sometimes to the shops."

"Well," replied Josie, "I hope I can find something I like. I might try the garden centre on the other side of town, or maybe a nursery where they grow plants and trees. And I'll do evening classes like you did, only mine will be in horticulture."

"Have you started gardening yet?" asked Stella.

"No, it's too early and too cold, but I'll start in April. Cook is keen to have some of my lettuce." Josie chuckled. "Mind you, I think she's just being kind."

The girls settled down to a game of Monopoly, which would keep them busy for the rest of the afternoon.

During April and May, Josie was busy in the garden, planting seeds in the ground and in pots in the greenhouse. She now kept the shed tidy as well, and looked upon it as her domain. All dangerous chemicals had been removed when Mr Copcut retired and there were now just slug pellets and greenfly spray. In June she put tomato plants in the garden and began to pick a few strawberries.

One afternoon, when lessons were finished for the day, Josie went out to check the garden and found a few holes in her lettuce leaves and also in the strawberries, so went into the shed to find the slug pellets. As she was lifting them down from the shelf, she noticed with horror that Mr Shenstone was walking past the window. Taking a deep breath, she pushed down her fear and replaced it with anger and determination, thinking to herself, *well this is it, and he's not getting the better of me.* She picked up her fork and lifted down the greenfly spray, as Mr Shenstone's bulk filled the doorway. He gave a startled look when he realised fork tines were pointing at his stomach, and the look Josie gave him would have stopped an army.

"What are you doing, girl? Put that fork down. Don't you know you could injure someone, waving that about?"

"Yes, Mr Shenstone, I do know." Josie had already

decided to say as little as possible, but she needed him to know she was aware of his previous activities and was not going to become another of his victims. He tried to grab hold of the fork, but found himself being prodded in the stomach.

"Leave the shed, Mr Shenstone," Josie said through gritted teeth. He retaliated by pushing further into the shed, a horrible glint in his eye. Josie snatched up the greenfly spray and pointed it at his face. "Leave the shed," she repeated. To her relief Mr Shenstone backed away.

"I'll be reporting you to Mrs Reynolds," he said.

"Then I shall report you, Mr Shenstone. It's up to you," Josie challenged him. Mr Shenstone glared at her for several moments, then turned and walked away. Josie didn't move till she saw him go past the window and back across the lawn. Then she sank to the floor, where she buried her face in her hands and tried to stop her body trembling.

When she felt calmer, she picked up the hoe and went outside to her plot and began hoeing between the seedlings. She didn't go into the building until she saw Mr Shenstone leave. She felt a huge surge of adrenalin as she ran up to the bathroom. She bolted the door and made plans, her heart pounding and her mind racing. She glanced at her watch. It was five o'clock, an hour before dinner. With a bit of luck Gillian would be downstairs doing homework, which she was, so Josie went through her drawer and took out all the important things and put them in the smaller section of her rucksack; then in the middle section she put underwear. Best not to pack her clothes yet or Gillian might notice, but she put the things she didn't intend to take up one end of the wardrobe. She'd have to do the rest when Gillian was brushing her teeth.

Not for one moment did she waver from her plan to run away. It was something she had always known, at the back of her mind, that she would do in this situation. She smiled to herself. Mr Shenstone had proved to her that he was guilty by not reporting her to Mrs Reynolds. She tucked her rucksack back on the top shelf of the wardrobe, then picking up a small, half-empty bottle of shampoo that someone had given her for Christmas, she went into the bathroom again and topped it up from the big one everyone used. Grabbing a half-used bar of soap, she went back into the bedroom and tucked it in her rucksack.

Now, a towel – what am I going to do about a towel? I don't want to steal one. Then she remembered the old bits of rag in the shed. Suppressing the urge to run, she wandered back over the lawn to the shed. There were two bits of rag which had once been towels. Grabbing these, she locked the shed, stuffed them in her pocket and took the key back to Mrs Reynolds.

"Hello, Josie, been gardening?"

"Yes, everything is coming on well; Cook can have another couple of lettuces tomorrow."

"That's good, Josie. Now, you had better tidy yourself. Dinner will be ready in five minutes, and with this heat wave we're having, washing is even more important."

Certainly in this year of 1976, the whole country had been sweltering since the end of May. The lawns were parched and going brown, and Josie had been watering every evening.

"You're quiet," Gillian said later. "Do you feel OK?"

"Yes, I'm fine," Josie replied. "It's just the hot weather."

When they had finished their meal, Josie ran upstairs, and glancing over her shoulder to make sure she was alone, she unlocked the landing window and gently eased it up and down. To her relief it moved easily and silently. She then closed it, but didn't lock it.

It was almost impossible to sit in the leisure room, trying to relax and pretending to read a book. At 8pm she went upstairs and had a bath and washed her hair and the old rags, then took her book into the bedroom, climbed into bed and tried to read and rest. Later Gillian came in and got undressed and went off to have a bath. Instantly Josie leapt out of bed and packed her clothes in her rucksack, and just managed to squeeze in a spare pair of shoes as well.

By the time Gillian came back to the bedroom, Josie was curled up on her side with her eyes closed. It seemed hours before she could be sure Gillian was asleep, but the gentle snoring ensured she was well away, and also covered up any noise Josie might make. She crept out of bed and rescued the two damp, but considerably cleaner rags, picked up her rucksack and coat from behind the bed and carefully pulled open the door. Then she crept down the hall, paused and listened, then slowly raised the landing window. Heart pounding, Josie leaned out as far as she dared and dropped her rucksack onto the porch roof, where it landed with a soft thump. Her coat followed, then easing herself over the windowsill, she landed beside her possessions.

The porch roof creaked and complained, and reaching up on tiptoe, she pulled down the window, then moved carefully to the edge of the roof. She was suddenly aware that even in the dark night, her pale pyjamas would show up like a beacon. Hastily she put on her navy anorak, and then carefully dropped the rucksack onto the grass below. This time the drop was a little further, and for several seconds she hung suspended from the edge of the roof, then let go and landed rather heavily, losing her balance and falling in a heap, half on the grass and half in the flower bed. But she seemed to be unharmed and snatching up the bag she ran across the lawn to the shelter of the bushes at the edge of the property. Climbing over the wrought iron gate or the six-foot wall at the front was not an option. She made her way towards the back, stopping behind the shed to take off her pyjamas and put on a t-shirt and jeans. Packing her nightclothes away, she did up the laces on her shoes and walking undercover in the shelter of the trees, she made her way to the rear of the garden. She knew there was a small gap in the hedge at the back, but wasn't sure she could get through. Taking off her rucksack, she tried to push it through the gap, without success. But after removing her shoes and a thick sweater, the bag went through fairly easily. Then twisting and wiggling, she managed to get through herself. She was now in a field, and was able to walk fairly easily to a five-bar gate, which she climbed over to the rough track on the other side. This led from the road to a farm, so it was quite easy to make her way to the road.

She hesitated and listened, but all was quiet, so she ran across the road to a footpath on the other side. Here she paused, trying to steady the beat of her heart and hoping she had everything she needed.

Leaving without a note for Mrs Reynolds seemed rather unkind, but it was hard to know what to say, so in the end she had just written:

Please don't worry about me, I will be perfectly all right.
Love Josie xx

Then across the bottom she had written in large capitals *MR SHENSTONE*. She had slipped the piece of paper in an envelope, sealed it and written *Mrs Reynolds* on the front, and laid it on her pillow as she left.

She set off once more down the footpath which led eventually to the river, but a few hundred yards along she turned left through a kissing gate and into the cricket field. Just visible in the dark was the wooden pavilion where she intended to spend the next few hours. She climbed the steps onto the veranda and flopped down onto the wooden planks. After a few minutes she lay down, resting her head on the rucksack, and tried to relax and hopefully fall asleep. But it soon became obvious this was not going to happen, so standing up, she walked down the steps and slowly began to circle the pavilion, hoping that a gentle walk might calm her down. Round the back was a grass-roller covered by a tarpaulin, and peeping out from under the tarpaulin was an old-fashioned deckchair. *Ah*, she thought, *that might be more comfortable*. She opened it out and cautiously sat down, hoping the canvas wasn't rotten. But it held, so resting her feet on her rucksack and covering herself with the anorak, she prepared herself for a few hours of rest until dawn, when she could move on.

Sleep did come, fitfully, and in the end the dawn chorus woke her. There was a tap behind the pavilion, so she slaked her thirst and freshened her face. She blessed the hot weather and checked her towels, which were now dry and could be packed away. Her first priority was to write to Stella, buy a stamp as soon as possible and post it, because they had arranged to meet Sunday afternoon and she didn't want her best pal to worry.

> *Dear Stella,*
> *Well, it's happened, but I am all right. Forks can be used for other things besides digging the garden! I have left St. Anne's and I will contact you when I have an address. Look after yourself.*
> *Love Josie xxx*

She put the letter in her bag, slung it on her shoulder and set off.

Going back to the footpath, she followed it to the river and soon found herself in the area where Stella and she had walked six weeks earlier. She stepped out briskly along the riverside path, hoping to get as far as possible before the heat of the sun slowed her down. It surprised her, however, how quickly she got to the end of the footpath, and now instead of turning back she took the other path, which went on in generally the same direction away from Plumbford. She glanced at her watch and smiled when she saw it was only 5.45am. The days were long and it would be the longest day next week, so it was light by 4am.

This was all unknown territory to her, but keeping an eye on the position of the sun and some hills in the distance, she managed to keep going in roughly the right direction. Her first stop was going to be the village of Brigton, about eight miles from Plumbford, where she hoped she could stop and buy a stamp and post Stella's letter. Also, she now realised she was very hungry and thirsty, and with the hot weather it was important to drink plenty of water. She only had a few pounds, so it would be water and something very cheap to eat.

She bent down and picked a few wild strawberries from the grassy bank at the side of the path. Delicious, but not nearly enough to satisfy her hunger.

Looking up, the hills appeared to be just as far away, but at that moment the path came out onto a narrow lane and ahead a few cottages stood in the morning sun. An elderly man clad in old clothes and wellington boots was just coming through the gate with a dog at his heels. He looked surprised to see anyone up as early as he was.

"Good morning, miss, you be up and about early. I thought only cowmen like me were about at 6.30 in the morning."

"It's cooler to walk now," Josie replied. "I wonder if I could bother you for a drink of water, please? I seem to have left mine somewhere way back."

"Of course, just wait there a minute." He turned back and went into the cottage, and Josie heard his voice as he spoke to someone. Then he came out with a woman who was probably his wife, and she beckoned to Josie and told her to sit on a wooden bench under the window.

"I've just put the kettle on, would you like a cup of tea?"

"Oh yes, please," Josie eagerly replied.

Five minutes later the two of them were sitting side by side drinking tea and eating toast. Josie repeated her little white lie about losing her water bottle, and when she left twenty minutes later she had a large plastic bottle full of water and a chunk of fruit cake tucked into a carrier bag in her hand. She thanked the lady several times and then strode out once more.

She had been told the village was just beyond the hills, and where to leave the lane and join another footpath. This would take her to the top of the hill and from there she would be able to see Postwaring. It was becoming very hot walking along the lane and she was glad she had her sun hat with her. Once she left the lane and joined the footpath, there was more shade.

It was 8am when she began to walk up the hill and another forty-five minutes before she got to the top, hot and wet with perspiration and breathing hard. Plonking herself down on a rock, she surveyed the view. Below her nestled the village, surrounded by green fields and areas of woodland. It was a clear day and the view was breathtaking, stretching away many miles into the distance and on the horizon there appeared to be the tall factory chimneys of a town.

Once Josie had got her breath back, she walked the last mile downhill to the village. The path came out by a church and then ahead the village green, with a pub and several shops. She made her way to the village store and post office, bought a stamp and posted her letter. She wandered round the shop several times before deciding on some bread rolls and a tube of cream cheese and then picked up two apples as well. When she paid she asked the lady very politely if she could top up her water bottle for her, then left the shop and headed in the direction of the distant town, looking for a possible footpath. She was aware that by now she would be missed at St. Anne's, and there was a possibility someone may be looking for her.

Gillian awoke to bright sunshine and birdsong. She stretched and yawned before glancing over to the other bed. At once she realised things were not as they should be. A letter rested on Josie's pillow, with Mrs Reynolds' name written on it. She leapt out of bed and opened the wardrobe for her dressing gown, then opened the other half – Josie's half. It was almost empty. She dragged on her dressing gown and ran along the landing and down the stairs. Sounds of activity came from the kitchen, but everywhere else was quiet and deserted.

Pushing open the kitchen door, she ran up to Cook. "Please, Cook, can you get somebody? I think Josie's run away."

"What make you think that, young Gillian? She's probably just in the bathroom."

"No, no, all her clothes are gone and there's a letter." Gillian waved the letter in the air. Cook reached for the telephone and seconds later was informing Mrs Reynolds that Josie appeared to be missing.

Mrs Reynolds came down and ripped open the envelope and read its contents. "All right, Gillian, go and get ready for breakfast and try not to worry. I'll soon have this sorted out." She went out into the hall and then accompanied Gillian back upstairs into the girls' shared room. In silence she looked in the wardrobe and the small chest of drawers beside the bed, then went back to her flat.

It was only 7.30am and too early to ring Lady Mary, but she must speak to her soon, perhaps in another half an hour. Hurrying back downstairs and into the kitchen, she made a cup of coffee and sat in a corner out of Cook's way.

"Elsie, I must ask you not to mention this to anyone. I am going to contact Lady Mary shortly, then the police. I will announce at breakfast that Josie's unwell and staying in bed for the day." She leapt up and rushed towards the door. "And I must tell Gillian not to say anything."

Ten minutes later, she rang Lady Mary's number and spoke to her housekeeper. "I must speak to Lady Mary as soon as possible, something urgent has cropped up."

"I'll get her to ring you back," the housekeeper replied.

Soon the two ladies were speaking, and Lady Mary said she would be there in half an hour. When she arrived she sat in Mrs Reynolds' lounge, a cup of coffee on the table beside her and the letter in her hand. She seemed to be lost for words, and shocked and upset.

"A rather strange thing happened yesterday," Mrs Reynolds began. "Josie was out doing her gardening and Mr Shenstone went out to see her. Five or six minutes later he came back and something had clearly upset him. He rushed off mumbling something about an appointment, then ten minutes later Josie came in and she was pale and noticeably shaking. When I asked her if she was OK she just said the heat had made her feel a bit funny, but she wouldn't let me give her anything and just ran off upstairs. Between you and me, Lady Mary, I think Mr Shenstone has been interfering with my girls. I know it's a terrible thing to accuse someone of, but it all adds up now: the other girls leaving suddenly and seeming upset, and all of a similar age. With your agreement I shall phone the police immediately and say Josie has gone missing and I need to speak to someone as soon as possible."

"Yes, you must do that straight away. It's going to cause a dreadful upheaval but we must think of our girls. The ones who have moved on and the younger ones here."

"Have you had breakfast, Lady Mary?"

When the answer was no, Mrs Reynolds contacted Cook on the telephone and asked her for some toast when she had a minute. Then she phoned the police.

"Hello, this is Mrs Reynolds, matron of St. Anne's girls' home. We have a young lady who has run away overnight. She is almost sixteen and I realise there's probably not much you can do, but it's the reason for her running away that I must talk to you about. We believe that a visitor to the home has been molesting the girls."

"That's a very serious accusation you are making, madam," the duty officer said. "Someone will probably be round to see you later. Will you be there all day?"

Mrs Reynolds assured him she would and thanking him, she put the phone down.

A little refreshed after eating a roll and drinking some of her water, Josie set off again, but it was getting hotter by the minute and she really needed to sleep. She decided to walk till about 11am and then find somewhere to rest. However, it was 10.30 when the footpath took her along the edge of a pine wood. It was cooler here, and where the conifers clustered together there was deep shadow. Josie left the path and walked some way into the wood till she found a spot that suddenly looked very inviting. Laying her anorak on a soft bed of pine needles, she lay down, covering herself with her thick sweater, more for comfort than warmth, and resting her head on her rucksack, soon fell into an exhausted sleep.

Chattering magpies woke her much later, and she was surprised to see it was 3.45pm. Her mouth was dry and unpleasant. Reaching into her rucksack, she rummaged around and found her toothbrush and toothpaste, then hesitated. *Might as well have a couple of bread rolls before I brush my teeth*, she thought. Half an hour later, fed, watered and freshened up, she set off again. What she needed now was a high vantage point to try and discover where she was, but the way now was mainly flat, so the next best thing would be a road and signpost, hopefully pointing to Sandacre, the town she had seen on the horizon.

As the sun sank lower in the sky, the heat became more bearable. Eventually the footpath came out into a lane. Josie paused, and then decided to turn right. In the distance she could hear traffic, so guessed that before long this lane would lead to a larger road, where hopefully there should be a signpost. This proved to be the case, and it seemed that Sandacre was still seven miles away by road and probably much further by footpath. She had to walk several miles on the grass

49

verge, until with relief she saw a footpath sign. At this point she was desperate to leave the busy road in case, amongst the homeward-bound traffic, there might be someone who recognised her. Not caring where the path might lead, she started to walk along it, and when after some way another path crossed it, she turned right, hoping she was now heading roughly in the direction of the town.

By now it was virtually dark and she desperately needed to rest. To her left were open fields, but on the other side a bank led to an area of bushes and trees, which would give her enough shelter as the weather remained hot and dry. Scrambling up the bank, she laid her anorak down with the rucksack as a pillow and prepared for sleep. Already she was becoming used to sleeping under the stars and on hard ground, and she was soon asleep.

On waking early the next morning, the first thing she did was climb a nearby tree and scan the horizon. To her relief she could just see Sandacre over the top of the trees several miles away, but she was off-course and would have to try and turn right again if possible. After much twisting and turning at exactly 6am she came to the edge of the town. The church clock struck the hour as she walked past the first few houses. Finding a park with seats, she sat down and waited until a nearby paper shop opened, then bought some food for the day and cadged some water. Thanking the shopkeeper, she asked if there was a public swimming pool in the town, and when he nodded and gave her directions, she set off again to find it. The charge was very reasonable and stowing all her worldly goods in the locker, she leapt in with relief. Only two other people were in the pool this early on a Saturday morning, so it was very pleasant to swim up and down. Feeling much refreshed, she collected the necessary items from her bag and went into the shower area, where she was able to have a good wash and wash her hair as well. Whilst in the shower she washed through a few bits of clothing before drying off and dressing.

Walking back to the paper shop, she bought a bar of chocolate, and then asked the man if he knew of any jobs going in the area.

"No, nothing that I know of," he said.

Then a voice came though from the back of the shop. "What about the King's Head? Don't forget Betty broke her arm yesterday, and with the weekend here, I bet they're desperate."

"Oh yes, hang on and I'll give them a ring." He glanced at his watch. "Just after 9am. They should be up and about." He picked up the phone and dialled a number. "Hello, Bill. Hope I didn't get you out of bed." The landlord obviously came back with a witty retort, because the shopkeeper chuckled. "Guessing you're probably a bit short-handed, I thought I'd let you know I've got a young lady here very keen to get a job." He grinned and winked at Josie. After a short conversation he put the phone down and taking Josie's arm, led her to the door. "Right, follow this road for another fifty yards or so, then turn right down Albert Street and you'll see the King's Head about a hundred yards down on the right. Bill said he's happy to have a chat with you if you go along now. Just go round the back to the car park and rap on the back door."

"Thanks ever so much." Josie smiled gratefully at the man and left the shop, walking briskly down the road and round the corner, and there was the King's Head within sight.

Rapping on the back door, she waited some minutes before it was opened by a short, rather dumpy middle-aged lady.

"Gosh, you were quick. Please, come in. Just go down the corridor. My husband is in the bar and we'll have a chat."

Her husband Bill was sitting at one of the tables, and they joined him.

"Hello, I'm Bill and this is my wife Doris. I don't know whether Jim told you what has happened to our kitchen helper?"

"Yes, he did. She's broken her arm, hasn't she?"

"Yes, that's right, and likely to be off for some weeks, I'd say, so we need someone as soon as possible to help prepare veggies, keep the kitchen clean and possibly wait at tables and clear away. There will only be you most of the time, and it's hard work, but as you can see, we've only got a dozen tables, so it's not too bad. We would need you to start promptly at 11am and finish about 3pm. That can vary. Then start again at 5pm and finish about 10pm. Once again, the finish

52

time can vary, but extra time is added up and you will be paid for it. Now, have you any experience?"

Josie had to say that the only experience she had was at school, where they had been taught basic housekeeping and cooking.

"Well," Bill said, "I'm willing to give you a try. How soon can you start?"

Josie, who had never been shy and retiring, said, "How about eleven o'clock today?"

Doris put both hands in the air and exclaimed, "Wonderful! I'll make a cup of coffee and Bill can talk to you about wages. Do you drink coffee?"

"Yes, I do. Thank you."

With three coffees in front of them and the wages sorted out, Bill asked, "Where are you living?"

"Well, actually I only arrived in Sandacre this morning, so I haven't found anywhere yet. I have to admit I've only got a few pounds, so I just need someone to loan me a settee or a piece of floor till I get some money. I'm able to sleep anywhere so it's not a problem. I swam this morning and showered at the swimming pool and I can always do that again."

Bill scratched his head. "Well, I don't know, that's not much good, is it? We haven't got anywhere here, I'm afraid."

"Not even an attic room or something. Or even a shed?" begged Josie.

Bill and Doris thought hard, made suggestions and then discussed them.

"The trouble is," Doris explained, "we do have

an attic with a proper staircase, but it doesn't have a window and it's going to be unbearable up there with this hot weather. And it's filled with clutter. I just don't think it's good enough. Let's go and have a look anyway before we discuss it."

Josie followed them up some stairs to the first floor, where Bill and Doris had a flat. Then Doris opened a small door, behind which were some narrow wooden stairs. There was a small landing at the top with a door going off to the right. She switched on a light and stepped inside. There was no room for Josie and Bill to get past the doorway.

"See what I mean?" Doris ran her hand through her hair.

Josie looked around. "What about if I tidied it up and stacked it, and then just cleaned this area here by the door? It would do me just fine. And if I left the door open perhaps it won't be too hot. It will only be for a short time, anyway, and I can use the loo downstairs and swim every morning."

"There's no need for that," Doris said. "We've got a separate loo which you can use in the night if you need to. Bill always showers in the morning, so you can bathe or shower at night."

"That'll be great." Josie suddenly found her eyes filling with tears. "You are so kind. I'll never be able to thank you enough."

"Don't be silly. Now come on down and I'll find you a broom and duster. And there's an old Z Bed up there that might still be OK, so there's no need for you to sleep on the floor." Doris glanced at her watch. "I'm going to make a drink and some toast, then we can sort out the attic and then it will be time to start the veggies. It can be busy on Saturday, so there's plenty to do."

Back in Plumbford, Mrs Reynolds had arranged to meet Stella and Margaret at the hostel. They greeted each other fondly, then Mrs Reynolds suggested going to the park where they would be more private.

"I have to tell you that Josie has run away," she began.

"We know," replied the girls. "We had a letter yesterday." Stella handed the brief note to Mrs Reynolds. There was a short silence while she read it, then Mrs Reynolds told them of the interview with the police and warned them that they may be interviewed as well.

"I'm really sorry about that, but I couldn't let it go on any longer. Once I realised what was happening I had to do something about it. I hope you understand."

The girls nodded silently, but gripped each other's hands and hoped it wouldn't happen.

"Now, girls," Mrs Reynolds continued, "everything I have said must not be repeated, and especially what I am going to tell you now. I believe that a certain gentleman may also be interviewed today, but until I speak to the police again I won't be able to tell you any more. Now, will you both promise me you won't breathe a word about all this to anyone?"

"Yes, you can rely on us, we won't tell anyone," the girls promised.

Mrs Reynolds stood up and beckoned the girls to follow. "Come on, I'll buy you a coffee and a cake at Carol's and we'll try and talk about other things and cheer ourselves up."

It was 3.30pm, and Josie flopped down in the pub kitchen. "Phew, that was busy. Is it always like that?"

"At the weekend it is, but during the week it's quieter. We'll give you Monday off, and Thursday till 5pm. Can we see what you've done in the attic?"

The pub was now closed till 6pm, so all three climbed up to the attic. Josie had swept and washed an area of floor close to the door. The Z Bed was opened and ready and she had draped her clothes over various items of spare furniture, hoping some of the creases would fall out. She had stood a cardboard box by the bed to put her watch and a drink of water on. Doris said she could use the iron if she wanted and she would find her some hangers. After another very hot day, the temperature in the attic was probably 100°F and Doris said Josie could borrow the fan from the bar after closing time to help make it more bearable.

They trooped back down the stairs to the flat and Doris set up the ironing board near an open window. While Josie did her ironing, Doris and Bill chatted about the evening routine. Josie was relieved she wasn't being asked too many questions. She had told them she was from Oxford and had decided to move to another town for a change of scene. It was difficult to know whether they believed her, but they seemed to accept this information.

Josie was up fairly early on Sunday morning because she was worried about all the veggies that needed to be prepared. The menu for the day was pinned to the noticeboard and so she knew what was needed. After some toast and tea, she set to, and by the time Doris and Bill came down from the flat, she had two large saucepans filled with potatoes and carrots, keeping fresh in water.

"There was no need for you to do that, my dear," Doris said.

"Well, I'm just so slow, I thought I'd make a start."

Doris looked in the saucepans and nodded. "Well done. Now sit down and have another cup of tea before you do any more."

By ten o'clock that night, Josie was so exhausted by the hectic day and the heat that Doris sent her upstairs for a bath and told her to go straight to bed afterwards.

"And you can get up whenever you like tomorrow, because it's your day off."

Josie woke the next morning feeling much refreshed. Despite the heat in the loft she had slept soundly all night, and now it was 9.30am and the rumbles coming from under the sheet told her it was time for breakfast. Bill was in the kitchen and busy cooking bacon and eggs.

"This is about the only time I cook," he said. "I don't suppose you'll say no to a cooked breakfast. Sit down; Doris will be down in a few minutes."

All three tucked in, then Josie cleared the table and ran water on their plates, squeezing out the cloth and wiping the hob down.

"You are a good girl." Doris smiled in gratitude. "It's nice to be spoiled. What are you going to do today?"

"I'm going to write to my friend Stella, so she knows I'm all right, and then I'll go for a walk to post it, and explore Sandacre."

"Good idea. There's a nice park and quite a good selection of shops. But don't waste your money on food. There's plenty here and I know you are a bit short till payday."

Dear Stella,

I hope you are well. I have been so lucky. I have a job already in the kitchen of a pub. The people are very nice and they are letting me sleep in their attic. But there are no windows and it's SO HOT! I have today off, so I shall look for lodgings. Keep your fingers crossed for me. I am going to explore Sandacre as well today, and then I'll go back to the pub and cool off in the garden. I may even offer to tidy the garden. I noticed it was a bit messy. I think Bill mows the grass and that's it.

Please write soon. My address is: The King's Head, Albert Street, Sandacre. My name has changed from Josie White to Jo Black. And I'm seventeen next week, not sixteen!

With lots of love from Josie xxxx

She put the letter in the envelope and sealed it, wrote the address on it and then realised she didn't have a stamp. Never mind, she'd get one from the post office. Picking up her rucksack and sun hat, she went into the kitchen and filled the water bottle. Doris thrust a pack of cheese sandwiches at her and gave her a warm smile.

"You have a lovely day now, and don't get lost."

Josie walked back up to the main street and turned right towards the middle of town. Her first stop was the post office, where she bought a stamp and sent Stella's letter. Then she found a newsagent and bought a local paper. Sitting on a seat in the square and under a shady tree, she scanned through the paper until she came to the accommodation section. Here a few houses and flats were listed, but as the paper had been out since Friday, they had probably been taken. However, there were a couple of phone numbers, so nothing ventured, nothing gained, she found a phone box and dialled the first number. There was no reply; the person was probably at work. On ringing the next number, a sleepy voice answered.

"Hello?"

"I'm phoning about the accommodation. Is it still available?"

"Yes, it is. Do you want to see it?"

"Yes please. Could you tell me where it is, please? I'm new to this area."

"Just ask anyone where the swimming pool is. We are the second road on the right after that. It's called School Lane because there used to be a school here years ago. We are number 26. When do you think you will be here?"

"Well, I would think about half an hour, if that's all right?"

"Yes that's fine, see you about one o'clock, then."

Josie found the house without any problems and knocked on the door. A dark-haired young lady of about twenty-five or maybe a bit older opened the door.

"Sorry, I was a bit dozy on the phone, but I'm on nights this week and I didn't get to bed till 7am this morning."

"Oh, I'm so sorry."

"It's OK, you weren't to know. Come and see the room."

She led Josie straight up some stairs and along a landing.

"This room is the smallest, I'm afraid, but you're only a skinny little thing so it should be big enough. What do you think?"

"It's lovely, and it looks out over the garden. That's nice."

"Come down to the kitchen and we'll talk about it. Would you like a cup of coffee?"

Josie followed her into an extremely untidy kitchen, where she cleared some magazines off a chair and indicated that Josie should sit down.

"Before we go any further," Josie began, "I know it's the usual thing to pay a month's rent in advance, but I've only just got my job and I can't afford to do that."

"Oh, I don't worry about things like that. If you can pay for just one week in advance, that will be fine. It's a small room, so I don't charge as much."

She named a sum and Josie agreed, although she didn't have anywhere near enough money. But it was very reasonable, so fingers crossed; her first week's wages would cover it.

"By the way, my name is Maria, and this house is mine but I can't afford to keep it unless I let the rooms. My bedroom is next door to yours, and the other room is taken by Kathy and Kirsty, who are twins. We all get on well together, which is important, as you can imagine. When would you like to move in?"

"Would Monday be all right? It's my day off, or are you all working?"

"Yes, I'm afraid so – the weekend would be better."

"OK, well I start work at 11am, so if I come round about 9am on Saturday will that be OK? Then I'll be back for 11am easily."

This was agreed, and Josie made her way back to the King's Head where she plopped down on the grass in the garden.

At 3.30pm Doris came out with a cold drink and eased her aching body down on the grass beside Josie.

"It's been busy today, for a Monday. I'm glad we've finished for now. Have you had a nice day?"

Josie told her all about her new lodgings and where they were, and Doris was pleased for her. She had been worried about her sleeping in the attic and was relieved she had found somewhere better.

Josie looked around the garden, taking in the brown grass and the untidy shrubs and pots with dead flowers in them. "I love gardening. It's what I would really like to do, you know, as a job. I'd be happy to help you keep this tidy if you like."

Doris didn't seem to know what to say for a minute or two. "Well, don't you think you work hard enough already? Do you really like gardening? Bill and I certainly don't!"

"Yes, I've done a bit in the past. I don't want to be paid; I'll just do it for fun. It's cool in the mornings; I'll do it before I start work."

Doris still looked doubtful, but she said she would have a word with Bill.

Mrs Reynolds tidied her office and went upstairs to her flat. It had been a ghastly day, and one she would never forget. Just after lunch Inspector Crombie had phoned and told her he must see her as soon as possible. So when classes were finished at 3.30pm, the two of them had gone up to her flat and the inspector had told her to sit down and prepare herself for a shock.

"As you are aware, we invited Mr Shenstone to come to the station for a chat on Saturday."

Mrs Reynolds nodded, and the inspector continued.

"Well, I'm afraid Mr Shenstone has taken his own life."

Mrs Reynolds gasped and put a hand to her mouth. "When... how, can you tell me?"

"He shot himself yesterday. His sons found him, thank goodness, not his wife. I can't imagine how she would have coped with it. She's a rather nervous woman."

Mrs Reynolds was silent for several minutes, her head down and her face pale and drawn. Then she looked up and met the inspector's eyes.

"So is this going to be the end of it? Please tell me those poor girls won't have to go through any investigation and we can put it all behind us."

"If that's what you want, yes, and for all concerned I think that's the best thing to do. I will leave it to you to break the news to any young ladies who were involved."

They stood up and shook hands, and Mrs Reynolds saw him out. After returning to her office to finish a few pieces of paperwork, she then tried to decide the best thing to do. The most important was to speak to Stella and Margaret, so as soon as she thought they would be home from work, she rang the hostel and asked to speak to Margaret.

"I need to have a chat with you and Stella," she said, as soon as Margaret came to the phone. "Come to St. Anne's this evening and ring the front doorbell. Anytime will be all right, just whenever you are ready."

An hour later, two stunned girls were trying to absorb the news. Shocking though it was, neither of the girls could be sad.

"Stella, I know you are probably in touch with Josie. Could you tell her, please, and perhaps she will come home."

Stella promised she would, and the girls said goodbye and walked back to the hostel, silent and with their heads full of the news.

As soon as they got in, Stella asked to use the phone and dialled telephone enquiries.

"Could you give me the number of the King's Head in Sandacre, please?"

There was a pause, and then the lady gave her the number and offered to connect her. A deep voice answered the phone.

"Hello, this is the King's Head, can I help you?"

"I'm very sorry to bother you, but it's important that I speak to Jo. I promise I won't keep her long. It's her friend, Stella."

A few minutes later a breathless Josie came to the phone.

"Stella, it's a good job it's my day off. I was outside in the garden. What's so important you had to phone me?"

"Josie, prepare yourself for a shock. Oh, I don't know how to say this. It's Mr Shenstone."

"What's he done now? Don't tell me he's abused someone else, so soon after he tried with me."

Josie looked cautiously over her shoulder to make sure she wasn't overheard, but Bill and Doris had gone back into the bar.

"No, nothing like that. After Mrs Reynolds got your letter with *Mr Shenstone* written on the bottom, she suddenly realised what had been happening and she called the police. They took him down to the police station on Saturday afternoon and interviewed him, then yesterday…" Stella paused. "His sons found him in one of the barns. Do you know what I'm trying to tell you, Josie?"

Josie collapsed into a chair. "Has he killed himself?"

"Yes. Are you all right, Josie?"

"Yes, just shocked. How did he do it?"

"He shot himself. Oh, Josie, doesn't that prove to everyone that he was guilty? Anyway, the whole thing's over now, thank goodness. We won't have to all be questioned. I can't tell you how relieved Margaret and I are. And Josie, you can come home now. We all really miss you, especially me."

"I'll think about it, Stella, but at the moment I feel a bit dazed. I'll let you know when I've made up my mind. But I know one thing: I'd really like to see you, but it's so difficult. There's no bus between here and Plumbford and I can tell you from experience, it's a long way to walk."

"You walked all that way?" Stella was amazed. "It's got to be twenty miles."

"Well, not quite, about seventeen by road, but when I think about it, I used mainly footpaths, so I probably did at least twenty miles. Anyway, to get back to meeting up, it means getting a bus to Oxford, then another one here, or the other way around, and that would take ages, and Stella, you have weekends off and I have Mondays and Thursdays, so I don't know what we're going to do. Look, I must go now, but I'll write tomorrow because I've got loads more to tell you."

"OK, Josie. I don't want to get you into trouble, so I'll say bye for now."

"Cheerio," said Josie, and put the phone down, before wandering out into the darkening garden.

She picked up her cardigan and went back in to say goodnight to Doris and Bill. She thanked them for the use of the phone and assured them she was all right, and then went up to the attic to sit on her bed and try and take in recent events.

The next morning after breakfast, she sat in the cool garden and wrote to Stella, telling her all about her new lodgings and her work at the King's Head. Then she walked back into town and bought two stamps this time, stuck one on the envelope and dropped it in the postbox. As she walked back, her mind dwelt once more on the events of the last few days. Was it really only five days since she stood in the shed at St. Anne's, defending herself with a fork against the advances of that horrible man? It seemed weeks, even months ago, and now he was dead.

When Josie came down for breakfast on Thursday morning, Doris and Bill were just finishing theirs.

"Morning, Jo, any plans for today?"

"No, I think I'll stay here if you don't mind. I've only got 45p to my name, so I couldn't do much if I went out." She grinned at the couple. "Would you let me tidy up the garden? I'll enjoy doing it and it's fairly cool out there at the moment."

When Josie had finished her toast and tea, the three of them went out into the garden. It consisted of a small patio outside the door with a table and two chairs on it, and two tubs with dead flowers from last year. The rest was mainly grass, with shrubs and herbaceous plants in beds down each side and across the bottom. The weeds in the beds were nearly as high as the shrubs and these were straggly and untidy. Not wanting to appear too pushy or rude, Josie kept quiet and waited for the older couple to speak.

"Well, if you're sure you would enjoy it," Bill said. "There's tools in the shed and rubbish sacks, but don't overdo it. It's sure to get hot later because according to the forecast, there's going to be no break from the hot weather."

Josie rummaged around in the shed and found some pruners and a fork. Mr Copcut would be horrified at the state of these, she thought, as she struggled to open and close them. Then she noticed some 3-in-One on the shelf. Squeezing some oil onto them, she soon had them moving more freely. For the rest of the morning she toiled away, pulling the dead plants from the pots and loosening the soil in the beds and pulling out the weeds. There wasn't much she could do about the shrubs as it was summer and hot, but she tidied them up as best she could. There was still lots to do, but satisfied with her morning's work, she went to the shed to put the tools away, then stopped and wondered whether, if she tidied the shed, it might be cooler to sleep in there for the next two nights. No, it wasn't worth the fuss and she didn't think Bill would agree anyway; at least she was in the house and safe where she was now.

She was awake early on Saturday morning, and crept downstairs for some breakfast. She had already packed her few belongings and tidied the loft. The folding bed was tucked away, the hangers on a table on the landing and the linen in the washing machine. Doris had been horrified at her scraps of towel and had given her an almost-new towel, which she claimed didn't match her bathroom. Josie took a few items of clothing from the utility room waiting to be ironed, and then she was all set to go. She looked at her watch. It was 8.30am, and just as soon as Bill and Doris appeared she could be on her way. Fifteen minutes later she heard their footsteps on the stairs and she was able to say a quick goodbye and assure them she would be back in time to start work at 11am.

When she got to her new home, all three girls were up and ready to welcome her. Maria introduced her to the twins, Kathy, slim and dark, and Kirsty, blonde and curvy – obviously not identical twins.

"Gosh, is that all you've got?"

They looked in amazement at her two carrier bags. After putting them in her room, she came downstairs and the four girls sat in the kitchen. Maria made coffee and explained how they managed with one bathroom and an extra toilet downstairs, and the hours everyone worked and the times everyone left in the mornings and came back at night. She explained how they each had a shelf in the fridge and a basket in the freezer, and how they mostly washed everything together, not worrying what belonged to whom, only that dark and light things were kept separate.

The twins then disappeared upstairs, and Maria and

Josie were able to sort out the money. Bill had paid Josie the previous evening. £13.50 seemed a huge amount of money, but £7 was going on the room. Still, she guessed that she would get something to eat at work and would only have to buy breakfast food, and something for her days off. She was fully aware that money was going to be tight, but by shopping carefully she felt sure another couple of towels and more clothes wouldn't take long to acquire.

It was very busy all day at the pub, and although Doris had planned to let her off early that evening for her first night in her new home, it was not to be. But at 10.30pm, Bill insisted on taking her home in the car.

"I'm not having you walking home in the dark, there's bound to be some drunks about. There always is on a Saturday night."

So although Josie felt guilty for being a nuisance, she was very relieved. The twins were out at a party, but Maria was in and sitting at the kitchen table in her dressing gown. Although Josie was exhausted, they sat for a while and chatted. Maria told her how she had married at twenty and she and her husband had saved for the deposit on this house, but two months after moving in he had left her for her best friend. He had borrowed money and given her a lump sum to help out, but it was not enough, so the answer was to rent out the spare bedrooms. After two years, it was working well and Maria was able to meet the bills. She had a boyfriend, but nothing serious. Her job as a nurse kept her busy and she loved what she was doing. At the moment she was in the maternity unit working two weeks on days, then two weeks on nights. This was followed by a long weekend. Josie talked about her job but explained that it was only temporary and in five weeks' time she would be looking for another job. Then yawning widely, she said goodnight and went up to bed.

Snuggling down, twenty minutes later, she just had time to think how lovely it was to be in a proper bed, with cool air coming in the window, before she fell into a deep sleep.

Josie woke quite late the next morning, went downstairs and joined Maria for some breakfast. The twins were still sleeping after their very late nights, and were still asleep when Josie left for work at 10.30am.

Sunday lunchtimes were always busy, but as things began to quieten down a couple came in and walked over to the bar.

"The usual please, Bill," said the man, and his wife gave Bill a kiss on the cheek and went and sat down. Josie was clearing tables and noticed the lady had her arm in a sling. She wondered if this was Betty whose job she was doing, and straight away Bill called her over and introduced her.

"How's the arm?" Josie asked.

"Oh, it's still a bit painful but improving. I'm already bored at home; I can't wait to get back to work."

Josie felt a little uncomfortable, as it was obvious that Betty wanted her to know she would be back as soon as possible. There was an awkward pause; then Josie said, "Are there any plant nurseries or garden centres around here? That's what I would really like to do: work somewhere like that."

Betty seemed to relax. "Yes, there's a garden centre on the Oxford Road, about a mile out of town, and I believe there's a nursery on the other side of town, but it's a bit further away and it's not on the bus route."

Josie thanked her and went back to clearing tables, then helped tidy up the kitchen. Sunday nights were quiet and Bill only served a limited menu, so they could all relax a bit.

When Josie got to work on Tuesday morning, Doris handed her an envelope.

"There's some post for you."

Josie knew straight away what it was. She had said nothing to the girls or Bill and Doris, but it was her birthday today and this would be a card from Stella. She opened it and smiled. Stella had written *Happy 17th Birthday*, when they both knew it was only her sixteenth. Still, she could now put it on the windowsill in the kitchen for the rest of the day and it didn't matter who looked at it; her secret was safe.

Bill and Doris insisted on giving her a £5 note, which was very generous of them, and Josie said, "Now I can get some more towels. Thank you very much."

She told them what she had been doing on her day off.

"The kitchen in School Lane is really grubby and

terribly untidy, I spent the day cleaning and scrubbing. I wondered if Maria might have been offended but she was thrilled to bits, and it gave me something to do."

"Oh Josie, what a workaholic you are, keeping our garden tidy and cleaning your new lodgings! Why don't you relax when you get the chance?"

"I'd rather be busy doing something and at least I'm not spending money when I'm doing that. I want to buy a few more clothes; then I'm going to save a bit in case I don't get another job straight away."

"Very wise." Doris was pleased her young helper realised that Betty would be back in a few weeks and then Josie would have to move on.

Betty's return was delayed by another two weeks because she had to do exercises with her arm, but during that time Josie had been busy. On her days off she had used the time looking for another job. She had caught the bus to the garden centre to be told that at present there were no vacancies, but they took her phone number and said they would contact her if anything turned up. The following Monday, she set out early before the heat of the day, along the road to the plant nursery. She had her trusty rucksack on her back, with sandwiches and water tucked inside, and her sunhat, ready to put on as it warmed up. She had no idea how far it was going to be or how long it would take to get there, but she was well prepared. Having always enjoyed walking, it was no hardship to her and the day was just perfect. Warm sunshine and a gentle breeze stirring the leaves added to her pleasure, and there was little traffic as it was still early in the day.

She had been walking for an hour and a quarter when she came to a few houses, and then what was obviously the nursery. A wide driveway led to buildings and greenhouses, and to one side there was a bungalow. A man was moving shrubs about, and a young woman was moving around in one of the greenhouses.

"Can I help you?" The man put down a shrub and smiled at Josie.

"I'm looking for work, and this is the sort of thing I would really enjoy. Any chance of full or part-time work?"

"Well, I don't know, I'm fully staffed at the moment, but there may be a job coming up at a later date. Hang on a minute." He turned to the greenhouse and called out, "Kate, can you spare a minute?"

As Kate walked toward them it was obvious she was pregnant. "Yes, Bob, what did you want me for?"

Bob grinned. "I'm not trying to get rid of you, but when were you planning on leaving?"

"Well, in about a month's time – I'll be seven months by then and that's when I ought to stop as it's such a physical job. Why do you ask?"

"This young lady is after a job." He glanced at Josie. "She doesn't look very strong, but you can never tell. I'll take her indoors and have a chat. Can you hold the fort for half an hour?"

"Course I can. I'll keep my eyes open for any customers."

Josie followed Bob to the bungalow, where a dark-haired woman was sweeping the kitchen floor.

"This young lady is after a job, so I thought we'd come in for a chat. Pop the kettle on, love."

They sat down and Josie told him that she was seventeen and had some knowledge of gardening, and that despite being skinny, she was in fact fit and strong. She told him where she was working at present and that she was only standing in, and where she was living.

Bob listened; then said, "So how did you get here? We're a bit off the beaten track."

"Oh, I walked, it was no trouble."

"You walked?" Bob said in astonishment. "That's got to be a good four miles; you wouldn't be able to do that every day, especially in the winter."

"I'm going to get a bike." Josie had already decided that as she walked along.

"Well, I'm prepared to give you a try. When could you start?"

"My job finishes in three or four weeks, so I should be OK when Kate leaves."

Bob turned to his wife. "Sue, could you write our name and phone number down and take Jo's details as well? I must get back outside and finish off what I was doing."

He walked back outside, and Josie was left with Sue.

"Sorry, Bob doesn't think sometimes and he hasn't introduced us properly. I'm Sue, and I'm Bob's wife, as you probably gathered. We manage our nursery with help from Kate in the week. We've got two sons: Richard is twenty and at university in Oxford, and Nigel is eighteen and at college. The boys and Kate take it in turns to do Saturdays, so you would be doing one Saturday in three. Is that all right?"

Josie assured her it would be and Sue told her she would be earning £15 per week, but of course there would be stoppages. Also, drinks would be supplied throughout the day, but she was to bring sandwiches. Then Sue asked the same question as Bob.

"How did you get here?"

When Josie told her she looked even more surprised and offered to take Josie back to Sandacre, but Josie said she was fine and left soon after for the walk home. She couldn't resist a little squeal of delight as she reached the road, thinking how lucky she was to get the job of her dreams. As she walked back, slower this way, as it was now another hot day, she made plans. She would need a bike and working clothes, but hopefully nothing else. And the first task when she reached home would be to write to Stella and tell her the latest news, and that they would now be able to meet in a few weeks' time as her weekends would mainly be free, although of course Stella worked Saturday mornings.

Josie managed to get a second-hand bike and a pair of working trousers, and then waited impatiently until she could start. It was August by then, and the weather remained hot and dry. Nobody could remember anything like it. Everything was parched and brown, and water restrictions were in place. Betty was back at work, her arm almost back to normal, and Josie bid Bill and Doris a fond goodbye and promised to come now and again to tend the garden. She had bought Doris a big bunch of flowers with a tag attached: *You saved my life when you gave me a job and the attic. Thank you a million times xx.*

Dear Stella,

I've been meaning to write for at least two weeks, but I've been so busy. I've got another job! This time at a plant nursery, which as you can imagine, I'm thrilled about. I start tomorrow (Monday). It's about four miles from Sandacre along a country lane, so I have bought myself a second-hand bike to get me there. It won't be much fun in the winter, but I'll survive. I'm well settled in my lodgings and I get on well with everyone. It's very reasonable, which is good because I haven't many winter clothes and I expect one day it will cool down!

Write soon.

Lots of love, Josie xx

PS: We'll be able to meet now. If you ring me one evening on Sandacre 12983 we can arrange a day.

CHAPTER 7

Josie's first day went well, but she realised she had a lot to learn. Kate was staying on for two more weeks, mornings only, to help Josie familiarise herself with the work and where things were. There were two large greenhouses, one now empty and the other one being used to bring plants on for Christmas. There was a shed which was called the shop, because the till was in there, and wrapping paper and empty boxes and also garden tools and seeds for people to buy. Another shed housed the tools and spare stock and another smaller shed held chemicals and fertilisers. The bungalow was in its own small garden, mainly grass and a few rose bushes, and at the rear a small vegetable garden, which Sue took care of. Josie got on with Bob and Sue, although Bob was rather quiet and as he stated, only spoke when he had something worthwhile to say. He was tall and slim and his hair was showing signs of grey. Sue was his opposite: bubbly and chatty, short and shapely; she seemed to really enjoy it when Josie went in for a coffee or tea. Josie was still using Jo as her name and still claimed to be seventeen, but had decided that once she felt secure in her employment she would come clean and tell the truth.

She cycled home on her first Wednesday and put her bike away. As she was inserting the key in the lock the sound of the phone reached her faintly through the door. Hurrying in, she snatched up the phone.

"Hello?"

"Josie, it's Stella, I just got your letter. Sounds like everything is really good for you."

"Yes, it is. I'm getting on well at work, although I've only done three days, of course. I'm free this Sunday if you are. We could meet in Oxford, or I'll cycle over to Plumbford if you like."

"No, let's meet in Oxford; say at the bus station about 11am. I've got lots to tell you too, but I'll tell you on Sunday."

"OK, see you Sunday, then. I just can't wait."

The pals said goodbye and Josie went up to her room with a big smile on her face. Things seemed to be working out well.

The buses to Oxford ran every two hours from Sandacre on a Sunday and Josie caught the 10am, which meant she would be in Oxford by 10.40am in plenty of time to meet Stella. It took her a few minutes to find the area the Plumbford bus pulled into, and then almost straight away the bus arrived and Stella waved through the window, before jumping off. The girls hugged and walked from the bus station arm in arm.

"I like your new hairstyle." Josie looked at Stella admiringly. Her hair was shorter still, and suited her. "It always looks so smooth and shiny." Josie's hair was still pulled back into bunches, but curls would still escape, much to her annoyance.

They found a café and bought a coffee, then found a seat near the window. Josie discovered she wasn't the only one on the move. Stella and Margaret were moving into a flat together, just a short distance from the town centre. Margaret was now a supervisor at Woolworths and Stella had received a rise on her seventeenth birthday, so they could well afford to be independent. They had a wonderful day together, eating a sandwich in a park and looking round all the grand old buildings. The day flew by and it seemed no time at all before they were saying goodbye at the bus station. They felt they had caught up on all the news, and it was decided that Josie would cycle over to Plumbford in two weeks' time.

Over the next few weeks Josie got to know her employers' son Nigel well. He was a quiet young man, but very kind and helpful. He was usually home from college by 4pm and would sometimes help out at the nursery if there wasn't too much homework. The only time she saw Richard was on Friday evenings, when he would come home for the weekend. He usually arrived between 4pm and 5pm so Josie didn't see him for long. He seemed very sure of himself, and Josie was uneasy in his presence. However, their paths crossed rarely, so it didn't matter. The hot, dry summer came to an end in September, and everyone breathed a sigh of relief and looked forward to cooler days and more comfortable nights.

Autumn passed and November arrived. Josie had been at the nursery for three months and her trial period was at an end. Bob called her into the bungalow and said they were pleased with her and would like her to stay on. She would be given a bonus at Christmas and a rise on her birthday the following July.

"You'll be eighteen and an adult," Sue said with a smile.

"Well actually, I have a confession to make," Josie began. "You don't know much about my past, but I think I should tell you now. I was brought up in an orphanage, that much you do know, but there were problems over the last few years I was there. One of the governors was abusing the girls."

Sue gasped and looked horrified.

"He would wait until his victim was sixteen or almost sixteen, and then start on her. When he started on me, I was in the garden shed and I defended myself with a fork and an aerosol of greenfly spray, then later that night I ran away, but I left his name on a piece of paper. Just his name, I didn't actually accuse him of anything. Anyway, Matron realised then why the girls always seemed in a hurry to get away and she called the police. I can't tell you the details, but that put a stop to it. I had already gone by then, and I wasn't quite sixteen. I had to lie about my age otherwise I would never have got a job, so I added a year. I'll be seventeen next July, not eighteen." She paused. "Are you going to sack me now?"

For once Sue seemed almost speechless. "Well,

what a story! No, we are not going to sack you, but is there anything else we should know?"

"Well, yes. I'm Josie White, not Jo Black, but that's everything."

"I remember something in the local paper earlier this year. Some farmer was interviewed by the police, then he committed suicide," Bob said. "Would that be him?"

"I don't really want to say." Josie was wary of saying more. "But I just wanted to tell you everything. It didn't seem right to deceive you."

After Josie had gone back to work, Bob and Sue discussed things but decided that they were willing to keep her on. She was a good worker and learning fast.

Josie and Stella continued to meet every two or three weeks; sometimes in Oxford, and sometimes in Plumbford. It took Josie over an hour to cycle there, but she enjoyed the ride. One Saturday in October she had plucked up her courage and visited St. Anne's with Stella. Everyone had been delighted to see them and she need not have worried. They had a cup of tea with Mrs Reynolds, and although she said Josie was welcome to come back, the young lady's life was far too good now for her to want this. Mrs Reynolds accepted this decision with a smile, then listened amazed as Josie told her the events of the last four months. Yet she could see, in her mind's eye, Josie climbing out of the window, walking and sleeping under the stars. Her feisty spirit had seen her through, and Mrs Reynolds could believe that she would work hard to keep a job and make anyone pleased to employ her.

"So now you are doing exactly what you wanted, working in horticulture. How do you like it?"

"Oh, I love it, and the owners are really nice. I've told them the truth now." Josie looked a little ashamed. "I had to lie about my age, but when they seemed pleased with me, I told them the truth."

"I do so wish you girls had told me what was going on with Mr Shenstone. If just one of you had confided in me, maybe we could have avoided a lot of unhappiness. I'm thinking back five years or more to when all this started."

"Well we didn't think anyone would believe us. They would say we were just making it up."

"Well, maybe. Anyway, it's all in the past now, and by the way, the farm has been sold and Mrs Shenstone and her sons have moved away to make a fresh start."

When it was time for the girls to leave, Mrs Reynolds stood at her window and watched them walk arm in arm down the drive, the short, dark hair of Stella beside the golden brown bunches of Josie, their heads close together as they discussed the day.

November progressed and the nursery received deliveries of Christmas trees, and later on, holly and mistletoe. The shed began to look quite festive, and sales were good. Towards the end of the week, Josie went into the covered area to tidy up the Christmas trees. With only two weeks to go, they were expecting the next day, a Saturday, to be busy, and hopefully a lot more would be sold. It was already quite dark outside, and a cold wind was blowing from the east. Josie was not looking forward to the cycle home. Straightening up the last few trees, she was taken by surprise when the light flashed off; then on again. Startled, she turned to see Richard coming towards her, a smile on his face… and a sprig of mistletoe in his hand.

"Hello, Josie, how about trying out this mistletoe?"

Josie backed against the wall, her heart thumping. "No," she said, and as Richard came closer, "don't. Leave me alone."

"Come on, Josie, just one little kiss."

He grabbed her arm and tried to reach her lips, but was stopped by a fighting, struggling, determined young girl, and found himself on his back in amongst the Christmas trees. Josie took the opportunity to run from the covered way, across the yard and into the outside toilet, where she bolted the door and collapsed against the sink. She began to cry with the shock of Richard's actions, and couldn't seem to stop. She sank down onto the floor and buried her head in her hands, sobbing bitterly. *He's spoilt everything. I can't possibly stay here now. I just won't come in to work on Monday. I'll have to move right away and start again – and I don't want to.* She began to cry even harder, and at first didn't hear her name being called.

"Josie? Josie? What's the matter? Open the door, Josie."

It was Sue. Bob had seen her run across the yard

and into the toilet, and when she didn't reappear he had gone into the bungalow to find Sue.

"Something has upset her," he said. "I don't know what, but I think Richard might have an idea. He was under the tree area as well. You go and see if you can sort out Josie and I'll have a word with Richard."

Josie blew her nose and opened the door to a concerned Sue, who took her arm and led her into the bungalow.

"What's the matter, dear, are you ill?"

Josie shook her head and struggled to control her weeping.

"Then what has upset you so much? Come on, Josie, surely you can tell me?"

When there was no reply, Sue filled the kettle and plugged it in and dropped a tea bag into a mug with sugar, because it was clear Josie was suffering from shock. Then she placed it in front of Josie and waited while she took a few sips and blew her nose again.

"Josie, I need to know what happened out there in the tree store. Did you see a rat? Or have you had a mishap with the trees? It doesn't matter what it is, you can tell me and we'll sort it out."

Josie looked up at Sue for several minutes before starting to speak.

"You won't like this... well, I don't suppose you will believe me." She hesitated. "You'll probably think it's a fuss over nothing."

"Let me be the judge of that," Sue replied.

"Well, it was Richard, you see," Josie whispered.

"He tried to kiss me and he wouldn't take no for an answer, and he tried to force me." She began to cry again. "I shall have to leave, because I'm scared he'll try again."

Sue stared at Josie in horror, and then pulled her close, stroking her back and trying to calm her.

Bob followed Richard into the shop, where thankfully they were alone.

"What's the matter with Josie then, is she ill?"

"I wouldn't know. Why ask me?" Richard glared at his father.

"Well, you were in the tree store with her; you should know what's happened."

"Look, Dad, she just rushed out suddenly; I assumed she'd been taken short."

"Well, she'd hardly be crying because of that, would she? Did something happen that I should know about?"

"I don't know what you're talking about," Richard snapped.

Bob could tell he would get nowhere with Richard in this frame of mind. He went over to the bungalow and slowly opened the door, not sure what he would find. Josie and Sue were sitting at the kitchen table, talking quietly. Josie's hand was enclosed in Sue's, and she raised her tearstained face to look at Bob.

"We need to talk, Bob," his wife said. "Sit down, love."

She related what Josie had told her, and a look of anger flashed over Bob's face.

"I think the best thing I can do is take Josie home, and then have a chat with Richard."

"No, love, I'll take Josie home. You lock up and then you can sort Richard out."

Bob saw Sue and Josie off, putting Josie's bike in the back of the pickup, then locked up. He sent Nigel into the sitting room to do his homework; then pointed to a kitchen chair and waited while Richard hesitated, then sat down.

"Right, lad, there's two sides to every story. We've heard Josie's side, now I want to hear yours."

"I told you what happened, Dad."

"Do you want to add anything to that, son?"

Richard shook his head. Bob stared at him for a few moments; then said, "According to Josie, you tried to kiss her, even when she asked you not to."

"It was only a bit of fun, Dad. Any other girl would have just given me a kiss and not made such a fuss about it."

"What gives you the right to force yourself on a young lady?"

Bob put up a hand to silence his son, who was about to argue.

"Now you just listen to me. What you did is assault Josie, yes, I mean assault. She could go to the police and report you. Just think about that. You need to treat girls with a little more respect."

Richard was silent as he absorbed this information.

"And I am going to tell you something else, which

must be just between you and me. I get a feeling something like this has happened before to Josie, and it's made her frightened of men. It's a shame it's happened again. I should think it will put her off men for life. She's talking about packing in her job and never coming here again; even leaving her lodgings and moving to another part of the country, that's how scared she is. I want you to go up to your bedroom and have a good think about your behaviour, and I think you owe Josie an apology. Off you go, son."

All this was said in Bob's usual calm, measured way. And as Sue knew, it was far more effective than ranting and raving, which only served to antagonise and worsen the situation. Richard disappeared upstairs and Nigel came through from the lounge.

"What's going on, Dad?"

"Nothing for you to worry about, Nigel, just a misunderstanding between Richard and Josie. I think it's all sorted out now. Best not to say anything to Richard though, OK?"

"Yes Dad. Any tea in that pot?"

Josie and Sue were silent driving back, but as they pulled up outside Josie's lodgings, Sue patted her knee and told her not to worry, that everything would be all right and she would see her on Monday. Josie thanked her, lifted her bike out and let herself in. Only Maria was home. Josie called out that she had a headache and was going straight up to her room. She certainly didn't need to explain to her why her face was all red and blotchy.

Over the weekend, Josie's thoughts went one way and then the other. The Josie that was scared wanted to pack her bags and run far away. The feisty Josie thought, *why should I give up the job I love? Bob, Sue and Nigel will make sure I'm OK. I'm not going anywhere!*

Come Monday morning she was on her bike, riding to work, happy in the knowledge that Richard would be back at university and not around till Friday evening. Sue gave her a hug and said how relieved she was to see her, and when Josie went indoors for her coffee at 11am, Sue told her that Richard was truly remorseful and there was no chance of anything like that happening again.

It was now into December, and Sue was spending quite a lot of time helping at the nursery, as it was very busy. Then she would rush off and do some Christmas shopping or hurry over to the bungalow to push the vacuum cleaner around. As Josie was tidying up the poinsettias on Friday evening, she was aware that Richard would be home for the weekend. Even so, when he appeared at the door of the greenhouse, Josie gave a frightened start. Richard came no further, but looked at Josie and noticed, with a sinking heart, the fear on her face.

"Josie, I want you to know I'm really sorry about last week. I know now I was out of order. I give you my word that nothing like that will ever happen again."

There was no response to this.

"Do you think you can forgive me and be friends?"

Josie stared at him for a few minutes; then replied, "We'll have to see, won't we? But I can tell you, I will do more than push you over if you so much as touch me again. I can be quite… defensive if I'm backed into a corner."

"Don't worry, it won't happen." Richard hesitated; then turned and left the greenhouse.

Over the next two weeks leading up to Christmas, things did improve between them. Richard came home for the Christmas break and helped in the nursery so that Sue could do last-minute shopping and baking, and so he and Josie quite often found themselves working together, and this helped.

On Christmas morning, Josie cooked egg and bacon for Maria and the twins, and then they sat in the lounge and exchanged presents, giggling and exclaiming with pleasure as each parcel was unwrapped. Kirsty had a wicked sense of humour, and the presents she gave reflected this. A floppy clown for Josie (to cuddle in bed, Kirsty told her), for Maria, a book with jokes and funny pictures, and for her sister, a hat with rabbit ears. Then they all set to and tidied up the wrapping paper and the kitchen.

"You are not to wash up, Josie; you do far too much for us." Kathy rolled up her sleeves. "We'll do it while you have a shower and make yourself beautiful."

Josie didn't argue, but couldn't resist popping the salt and pepper away on her way past. The girls grinned at each other in complete understanding. They were all completely different characters, but got on famously together.

An hour later, Josie set off for the King's Head, where she was to spend the day. Doris and Bill's son David and his wife Diane would be there with their two sons, Kevin, who was six, and Geoffrey, only two years old. Doris and Bill also had a daughter, Janet, who was married to Steven. They had a baby daughter, Sara, born in the summer. They were having Christmas dinner with Steven's parents and then coming to the King's Head for tea. Josie had not met any of them before and she was a little nervous. But she need not have worried as they all made her welcome. She chatted to the grown-ups, played on the carpet with the boys and nursed the baby, thoroughly enjoying every minute of it. At 10pm Steven took her home, tired but happy. Her three housemates were all staying with their families for several nights, so she had the house to herself. That was good for a while, but by Boxing Day evening she was beginning to feel a little bored and lonely, so she was relieved when the phone rang and it was Sue inviting her for lunch and tea the following day. She eagerly accepted and went to bed much happier.

After an enormous lunch the next day, the five of them piled in the car and drove up into the hills. It was a lovely day, cold but sunny. They walked in the woods, down footpaths and across fields, coming back two hours later to the car. Afterwards they played games until finally Nigel ran Josie home.

"See you in the morning. Back to the grindstone," he said with a grin as her dropped her off.

The following weekend, Josie, Stella and Margaret went to a New Year's Eve party in Plumbford. Josie did the journey earlier in the day, bussing to Oxford, then on to Plumbford. Stella had borrowed a Z Bed and Josie would stay for a couple of nights because there would be no buses on New Year's Day. She had been given the 2nd January off, so there was no hurry back to work. It was so good to see Stella and Margaret and catch up on all the news. Margaret had a boyfriend but was already getting tired of him, so she was quite relaxed about making an excuse and not seeing him for a few days.

"I'm never going out with boys." Josie pulled a face. "They're all right as friends, but I don't want all that other stuff."

Stella threw back her head and laughed. "You're not going to be very happy with me then, 'cause I've got a boyfriend."

Josie stared at the two girls. "I don't understand how you can have anything to do with men after what happened."

"Josie, we've got to forget it and get on with our lives. Most men are OK, and we don't want to end up bitter old maids," Stella replied.

"Well, it's all right for you two. Something else happened to me. You didn't know that, did you?"

Josie then related what had happened between her and Richard, while the girls listened with concerned faces. Stella hugged her.

"Oh Josie, you poor thing. No wonder you're completely off men. Is he all right with you now?"

"Oh yes, he's fine, although I'll never be relaxed with him like I am with Nigel. Nigel's really nice, but only as a friend," she added hastily. "Anyway, Stella, you're eighteen now; I'm still only sixteen so there's plenty of time before I become a bitter old maid."

The girls chuckled and then changed the subject to clothes – much more interesting!

For the next month things were quiet at the nursery, and Bob was taking the opportunity to have a new building put up near the entrance. This was to be a much-improved shop. The old shop would be used for more storage. Then once February arrived, there was plenty to do. Bob had decided they needed to do more bedding plants, so seeds were sown, seedlings pricked out, cuttings potted up and shrubs outside tidied up. Nigel had left college at Christmas after much argument and was now working at the nursery full-time.

Spring passed and the nursery was doing well. In July, Josie had her seventeenth birthday and was taken out for a meal by Bob, Sue and Nigel. Bob had given her a rise on her birthday, which as it turned out, was just as well. Maria had been going out with a young man called Ian for some months, and now they were engaged and were hoping to marry in the autumn.

"I'm going to have to ask you to find somewhere else in the next two or three months," she told her lodgers. "I've enjoyed having you around but I don't think Ian fancies living here with four women."

So Josie found herself looking for a flat. Now

she was seventeen, she hoped renting her own place wouldn't be too difficult. She had been thinking about learning to drive and buying an old car, but now this would have to wait. For several weeks she scanned the papers, but flats went quickly and those she went after were either too expensive or too far from work.

Finally after a month, Sue spotted one in the local paper.

"How about this, Josie? *Small, one-bedroom flat in a convenient position in Sandacre. For more information telephone Sandacre 25886.* Phone now, Josie, before someone else takes it."

When Josie came back from the phone, she had a smile on her face. "It's still available and I can go and see it this evening. Oh, I'm so excited."

The reason the rent on the flat was so low soon became apparent. It was very small and above a fish and chip shop, so one had to live with the smell of fish and chips every day. It also badly needed decorating, and there was a damp patch on the living room wall. The man showing her around was the owner of the fish and chip shop, and although he apologised for the state of the place, he made no offer to sort it out. Josie, never a girl to hold back, told him he ought to sort the damp out because it would only get worse if he didn't, and then she would be prepared to decorate out of her own money. But if she made it look nice, she informed him, she wouldn't expect him to raise the rent, at least for another year.

"My, you're a sharp young lady. OK, we'll have it

all down in writing and you're right about the damp, it's beginning to come through into the shop. I'll get a roofer in. Hopefully it's only a couple of loose tiles."

It was agreed that Josie would have a key straight away so she could start to smarten the place up, and her landlord, whose name was Charlie, accepted her advance rent, gave her a receipt and promised to get on to a roofer the next day.

The two weeks flew by and included one of Josie's Saturdays at work, so when she moved in, very little had been done to the flat, apart from a thorough clean. True to his word, Charlie had employed a man to fix the roof and gutter and the damp patch was already beginning to dry out. The flat was reached by metal steps at the rear of the shop. At the top of the steps there was an area of about four by six feet, just about big enough to put out a chair and sit in the sun, or an airer of washing and maybe a pot with flowers in. The flat was long and narrow, with a living room at the front, a small kitchen area in one corner, and then a tiny bathroom, with a bedroom at the rear. As it came unfurnished, Josie had borrowed Bill and Doris' Z Bed, a couple of old dining room chairs and a coffee table from the loft where she had slept those first few nights. She bought some very basic bits of kitchen equipment: one knife, fork and spoon, one plate and mug, a saucepan and an iron.

Fortunately she had saved hard while at the nursery and there was still a little money left, but she was keeping that for emergencies and bills. Doris had also loaned her some bed linen, a blanket and some pillows, so on her first night she was snug and fairly comfortable in the rather lumpy Z Bed. It was a Saturday, but Josie was too exhausted to be kept awake by smells and noise, which fortunately were not so bad in the bedroom at the rear.

Josie was up bright and early the next morning. After some toast and a mug of tea, she wandered through her flat, still undecided about which room to paint first. It made sense to leave the living room till last because of the damp. Having never done anything like this before, she decided to start with the smallest room. Sitting on the floor in her small hallway were tins of white gloss and undercoat, a large tin of white emulsion and two large tins of magnolia, with various sizes of brushes and a bottle of cleaner. She had also been advised to buy some sandpaper, which she now picked up and took into the bathroom. The morning was spent rubbing down and undercoating the woodwork in the bathroom, then painting the ceiling with white emulsion. Then she had to clear everything away and tidy herself because Bob, Sue and the boys were coming at 2pm to look at the flat. She opened the windows as far as she could and put the fan on in the bathroom, then sat down with a sandwich.

Promptly at 2pm there was a knock on the door and Josie went to let them in.

"Oh yes, Josie, this is just perfect for you," Sue exclaimed. "You'll soon have it looking really nice."

Josie put the kettle on and got out the mugs. She

now had six matching mugs, but still only one plate, on which she placed some chocolate biscuits. She had no carpets to worry about if crumbs fell on the floor. It was vinyl tiles from front to back in a rather dull dark grey. But she didn't mind. She was just so proud and happy in her first home.

Bob inspected her decorating in the bathroom. "I'll come and put new sealant round the bath for you and show you how to smarten up the tile grouting, then it'll look really nice in here."

"Has your friend Stella seen it yet?" Sue asked.

"No, Stella and Margaret are coming over next Saturday. Margaret has just passed her test and bought a car, so they can drive over. It'll be so much quicker than going via Oxford – about twenty minutes instead of about two hours. While it's still light in the evenings, I might be able to do a bit more painting before they come."

"What about your driving, Josie? I know you were keen on starting lessons," Bob said.

"I can't afford it now. This flat is twice as much as the rent of the house share. Anyway, Stella and I thought we might go on holiday to Spain next year, so I'll be saving up for that."

"Spain, you say?" Sue pulled a face, but there was a twinkle in her eye. "Well, that sounds nice; it's something I've never done. I'm envious!"

After Bob, Sue and the boys had left, Josie felt restless. She wandered from room to room; then glanced at her watch. It was only 4pm. She ran into the bedroom and changed into her old clothes, got out the white emulsion and started to paint the living room ceiling. It was slow work and made her neck ache. She wished she had some music to spur her on, but a hi-fi was right at the bottom of her list. However, she got quicker as the work progressed and by 6.30pm she had finished. She stood back to admire her handiwork and was relieved to see it would only need the one coat.

Every evening she toiled away, and by Friday evening she was about halfway through the decorating. Sue had brought over a lovely pair of curtains she didn't need anymore and these fitted the bedroom window perfectly. There was a jumble sale on in a local church hall the next day and Stella and Margaret would have to tag along. There was no way Josie was going to miss some possible bargains!

After Josie had admired Margaret's car and the girls likewise Josie's flat, the pals bought some of Charlie's delicious fish and chips and tucked in with enthusiasm. Then they set off for the jumble sale just a few hundred yards away. There was already a queue forming, as jumble sales here were always good. As soon as they walked through the door, Josie saw some colourful curtains which would do very well for her living room, and by the time they left an hour later, all three were well laden with bargains: clothes, kitchen equipment, pictures, ornaments and a bedside table. Also, some hardly used bed linen.

"This calls for a celebration," Josie said. "How about a cup of tea and a cream cake?"

Both Stella and Margaret had dates that evening, so they soon left after their refreshments, with plans to meet up in a few weeks' time.

CHAPTER 8

Autumn passed, and then winter set in. Stella turned nineteen in December and the three girls celebrated. Stella no longer had a boyfriend, and all she could talk about now was a holiday in Spain.

"If we go in May it won't cost as much and the weather will still be good."

"How do you know?" Josie asked.

"Well, I've been making enquiries in the travel agents. The girl said it could easily be in the 70s in May, especially if we go to the Costa Blanca or the Costa del Sol."

"Oh, listen to you, you'll be talking in Spanish next," Josie teased.

"*Si*." Stella used one of the few Spanish words she knew, which set them all giggling.

Margaret looked at Josie and Stella. "I wish I could come, but somehow I don't think Alan would think much of that. Maybe he might take me there for a honeymoon."

Josie had dug into what little savings she had and bought a convector heater for the hall in her flat. She left the bathroom and bedroom doors open, and as the whole flat was so small, the heater and the gas fire in the living room kept the flat at a reasonable temperature. She would put them on when she got up in the mornings and turn them off again before leaving for work. Then the two heaters would see her through the evening. She was managing with her few bits of furniture, but would have bought more things if it weren't for Stella's nagging about Spain. When Josie was being honest with herself, she had to admit that she was excited about going abroad. It was something she had never imagined would occur and when their passports arrived she realised it was really going to happen.

After Christmas she spoke to Bob and Sue about it and they stressed straight away that the last two weeks of May were out of the question as they would be too busy with bedding plants. A couple of weeks later Josie and Stella came out of the travel agents, hardly able to contain themselves with excitement.

"We've done it!" Stella beamed at Josie. "Let's go celebrate in the coffee shop."

Josie looked at her, suddenly serious. "Listen, Stella, I don't earn nearly as much as you and there's only me to pay the rent and bills. I'm afraid if I'm to find the money for this holiday, visits to coffee shops and nights out just won't be happening."

Stella looked contrite. "I'm sorry, Josie, I just didn't think. I've bullied you into this and now it's too late to stop it. But I'll help you a bit with the cost if you'll let me."

"You may have to," Josie said. "But I'll pay you back when I can."

It was late April when Josie found herself booking in at Luton Airport with an excited Stella beside her. Everything went smoothly and the plane was only ten minutes late taking off. Josie found the whole thing exhilarating; the power of the engines and the speed at which they left the ground behind. She wasn't aware at first that Stella was petrified. She was clinging onto the arm of the seat, her face pale and trembling like a leaf. Josie took her hand and gave it a squeeze.

"Didn't you like the takeoff, Stella? I thought it was great. Come on, it's not like you to be scared, just relax and enjoy it."

Stella slowly calmed down but when the stewardess came round with drinks, she ordered a glass of wine and drank it with indecent haste!

They had a smooth flight except for a bit of bumpiness going over the Pyrenees, when once again Josie took Stella's hand and tried to take her mind off it by talking about what they would do when they arrived. It had been an early morning flight – Bob had taken them to the airport – and so they touched down at 11.30am. Stella seemed much more relaxed during the descent and couldn't hold back a little cheer when they touched the runway. They taxied in, and after a few minutes the doors were opened and everyone filed out. Josie would never forget that moment as she stepped out of the door. Warmth hit her, and the smell of aircraft fuel as the breeze wafted it across. It was just magic! The girls waited for their suitcases, piled them onto a trolley and walked towards the exit.

Alicante airport was small, and they didn't have far to go. A coach waited outside to take passengers to various hotels. Theirs was called the Paradise and about ten people got out there. It was overlooking the beach and on the edge of the city. A tall, modern building ten storeys high, it looked nice from the outside and they were not disappointed as they entered. The reception area was huge and beautifully tiled. A lady stepped forward and smiled a welcome.

"Hello, everyone, I hope you had a good journey. My name is Belinda and I'm your courier. The first thing we are going to do is sort out the keys for your rooms, all of which are on the third floor. If you would like to unpack, then meet me down here and we'll have a cup of coffee and I can tell you the activities nearby and in the hotel and the trips you can take if you wish. So shall we say 2.30pm here? Does that suit everyone?"

Everyone nodded or said yes, and satisfied, Belinda went to the desk and collected the keys, which she handed out to the guests.

"The lift is over there." Belinda waved her hand vaguely in the direction of a seating area and a bar. "See you over there at 2.30pm."

"Look." Josie dangled the key under Stella's nose. "Room 333 – that should be easy enough to remember."

The room was spacious, modern and beautifully clean, with its own facilities. There were twin beds, a dressing table and a small hanging area; also two chairs and bedside tables. But best of all, the most amazing views from the small balcony. The girls stepped outside, and for several minutes they were speechless. It was just blue sky and blue sea, with a few boats going in and out of the harbour. To their right the beach stretched away into the distance, and as they stood there they could see a plane coming in to land at the airport. To their left, the city of Alicante, a mix of old and new, and to the girls wonderfully exotic. Stella reached into her bag and pulled out a camera.

"I've simply got to take some photos of this, Josie, in case it rains tomorrow. Stand over there, against the balcony with the beach behind you. That's good, smile please."

Josie dutifully smiled, then they swapped places and took more photos.

"Come on, we'd better unpack, then freshen up. Gosh, I hope there's food, that nibble on the plane won't keep me going." Josie patted her stomach.

Coffee and delicious little pastries awaited them in the bar area. Belinda explained that there was an outdoor pool at the rear of the hotel, but as it was unheated and early in the season it would be rather cool, as would the sea. The forecast for the next few days was good, with only the odd small cloud. She talked about the city and the surrounding area, and then went on to trips.

"There will be a trip up the coast on Tuesday, I will be there to explain what things are and give you as

103

much information as possible. Then on Thursday we are doing a tour of the city, which will include a visit to the castle. Think about whether you would like to do either or both of these and let me know in the morning. Now, as you may or may not know, the Spanish eat at different times to the English. Breakfast is normal, between 8am and 9am; lunch is down to you, but be prepared if you want a proper meal: most restaurants won't be serving until at least 1.30pm. Then the evening meal back here in the hotel is at 8.30pm. Both meals are buffet style, so just grab a table and leave a cardigan on the chair, not your handbag, and queue up for your food. The food is very good and I'm sure you will enjoy it. Any drinks or snacks from the bar will have to be paid for, of course. Any questions?"

"We don't speak any Spanish," Stella said. "How will we get on?"

"Oh, don't worry about that. Most waiters speak at least a little English, so you'll be fine. Now, just a few words of advice. If you go into Alicante or you are visiting a street market, it's best to leave expensive jewellery in the hotel and only take the money you need for the day. Crime is rare, but it's better to be safe than sorry. And finally, don't forget to use your sun cream. It may only be early May but the sun is very strong here and bad sunburn could ruin your holiday. If there are no more questions I'll leave you to enjoy the rest of the day and I'll see you at dinner tonight."

Josie and Stella went up to their room, and taking Belinda's advice, put sun cream on; then made haste out into the glorious sunshine. They walked down to the beach and took off their sandals. The sand was warm on their toes and a gentle breeze ruffled their hair.

"Let's go and dip our toes in the Med." Josie tugged her friend towards the sea. The shock of the cold water made them both shout out.

"It's freezing, I thought it would be warmer than that." Stella ran back up the beach to the warm sand, and Josie swiftly followed her.

"Well, Belinda did warn us," she said. "Let's walk towards the city, and perhaps we can get an ice cream. I really fancy one and it's a long time till dinner."

They bought their ice cream and continued walking, passing more hotels, shops and offices. Suddenly they were aware that the sun was low in the sky and the air felt cooler, so they sat on a wall and brushed the sand from their feet and put their sandals back on. Linking arms and climbing some steps back to the walkway, they set off at a brisk pace back to the Paradise.

"We must remember that the evenings are cool and take a cardigan with us," Stella suggested, and Josie agreed.

They took it in turns to bathe and then put on fresh clothes for the evening. The dining room was already filling up and the people from the earlier meeting were gathering around Belinda.

"OK, is everyone here now? The procedure is quite simple. It's a buffet, as I said earlier, and you can have as much as you like." She pointed out two men and a girl standing by the buffet. "This young lady is Anna and the other two are Manuel and Jose. They will help you, and also bring wine round the tables. They speak good English so you'll have no problems. I advise you to join the queue straight away."

She set off and joined the queue herself, and everyone followed.

The food looked and smelled delicious, and soon the girls' plates were loaded and they found a table and sat down. The younger of the two waiters, Manuel, came over and smiled at them.

"Would you like red or white wine?"

The girls opted for white and were given a generous measure, and then Manuel moved on to another table.

"Gosh, he's gorgeous." Stella's eyes followed the young waiter as he moved from table to table.

"Yes, he is rather handsome," Josie agreed. "Now don't you go falling for him, will you? Or are you hoping for a holiday romance?"

"No, I'm not; anyway, he seemed more interested in you, Josie."

"I don't know how you can say that. He was only at our table about thirty seconds. Anyway, you know I'm not interested in men."

Stella didn't reply. She was sampling each food on her plate, and so far everything was good.

"I'm not sure what this is." She pointed to some pieces of white food. "I'll ask Belinda later. It's a bit tasteless, actually."

"Yes, I agree, perhaps it's some kind of fish."

The girls finished their food and went back for dessert. Belinda was also looking at the desserts and explained what they were. When Josie asked her about the white fish, she told them it was squid, and the smaller white circles were octopus.

"Well, I think we'll give it a miss tomorrow if it's on the menu," Stella said with a smile.

"Yes, it's an acquired taste. It's cooked in different ways and I love it now."

Belinda went back to her table and the girls were left to decide which dessert to have. Later, coffees were brought round by the waiters and waitress.

"I love the way they make their coffee." Stella looked around, hoping for another cup. Manuel came over to their table and said he would bring them two more cups. "We won't sleep tonight after all this coffee," Stella giggled. But of course, they did! After an early start and all the excitement, they were soon asleep, the sound of the waves gently ebbing and flowing like a lullaby through the partly opened balcony door.

The next morning found the girls down in the dining room, studying all the food on offer for breakfast. There was egg and bacon especially for the English guests, Belinda told them, and cold meats and slices of cheese; also fruit and fruit juices. To finish off, there were croissants, rolls and even small squares of cake.

"Oh gosh! Where do we start? I want it all!" Josie laughed.

Later, as they left the hotel for the beach, Stella patted her stomach.

"We're going to be so fat by the end of the week. The plane will have trouble taking off."

They walked in the other direction along the beach, sandals hooked over their bags. They had towels with them, and their bathing costumes. They found a nice area on the edge of dunes and sat down on the towels and watched the boats, large and small, going in and out of the harbour. Then they lay back and enjoyed the sunshine. As the morning progressed, the sun got hotter and they decided to brave the cold sea. They couldn't possibly come to Spain and not swim in the Mediterranean. But there was much screaming until their bodies got used to the water and then they swam around for half an hour. Stella came out first and wrapped herself up in her towel and Josie soon followed. Then after drying off, they helped each other to put more sun cream on. But after a short time, Josie stood up.

"I'm a bit worried I might burn. I'm very fair-skinned. Do you mind going back to the hotel? We can have a drink and a snack in the bar, or we can go to one to the bars on the beach."

"Let's go back to the hotel," Stella said. "We can have it inside or outside by the pool."

When they got back to their room, they hung their towels and swimsuits out on the balcony to dry, and then went down to the bar. Anna was on the bar and served them with a nice cold drink and a long crusty roll, filled with tuna and salad.

"This is called a *bocadillo*," she said. "It is very good." And it was!

That morning at breakfast they had booked both trips. Now as they sat by the pool, munching their way through the *bocadillo*, Belinda came and sat down by them.

"I was hoping I'd find you. I've got another trip which I'm sure you will enjoy. It's great fun. We will be going inland to a hacienda – that's a farm. We will be in a huge barn and a meal will be served, followed by Spanish singers and dancers. I can promise you a good evening. Have a chat between yourselves and let me know tonight. Oh, and it's Wednesday evening, by the way."

"Oh, that sounds fantastic!" Stella's eyes sparkled with excitement.

Josie sat thoughtfully as she watched Belinda walk away. "Well, you go, Stella. I don't mind staying here. I really can't afford any more trips."

"Oh Josie, you must go as well. It won't be the same without you. I'll pay and you can pay me back sometime."

"Well, I am tempted. Are you sure you don't mind lending me the money?"

"Of course not, that's what friends are for. How about a walk now? We could explore the area around the hotel."

That didn't prove to be very interesting. One little street looked much like another, and all very quiet as it was still siesta time. But they did find some public gardens with exotic plants and flowers, and in one corner an aviary with brightly coloured birds.

That evening as they queued for their evening meal, they told Belinda they would do the trip, and she told them that most people were going so it should be a good evening. The girls filled their plates and sat down. After a few minutes Manuel came to their table with a smile.

"Would you like white wine again?"

"Yes please," they replied.

"I see you have the fish. The white wine will be good with that."

He looked at them when he had poured the wine. "What are your names?"

"I'm Stella and my friend is Josie."

"Stella, I have not heard that name before. It is pretty. But Josefina is a Spanish name; I will not forget that. I will come back soon with more wine. Enjoy your meal."

Stella looked at her friend with a twinkle in her eye. "This fish is delicious, Josefina. Don't you agree?"

"Oh shut up, you'll never let me forget that, will you?!"

The next day being a Monday, all the shops were open and Stella said she would love to look round the big supermarket just down the road. It was fascinating.

"Oh look, Josie, Brussels sprouts in a jar. Yuk! And can you smell the fish. Let's go and have a look."

They gazed in amazement at the huge display of fresh fish. Big fish, small fish, ugly and pretty, white

110

and colourful, and all neatly laid out on a bed of ice. They moved on to the chilled section.

"Look, Stella." Josie laughed and pointed. "It looks like you see in a cartoon, just the bones of a fish with the head still on. What on earth would anyone do with that?"

"I have no idea. We'll ask Belinda tonight."

Inevitably the girls ended up at the bakery section, where they bought some rather interesting savoury pastries for later. After leaving the supermarket, they wandered along the front until they found a kiosk selling postcards. They decided to send one jointly to Margaret and to St. Anne's. Josie got one to send to everyone at the nursery, and Stella to her workmates. They sat on a seat in the shade and wrote them out, stuck stamps on them and went back to the kiosk. The lady soon realised they were looking for a post box and directed them to the post office a few streets away. Close by was a square with shady trees and seats where they were able to eat the pastries they'd bought earlier.

"I think its tuna and tomato puree." Josie licked her lips.

"Yes, I think you're right. Mm, yummy," Stella said.

They bought a coffee at a nearby café and sipped it with the sun shining through the trees and the sparrows chattering busily to each other. Arm in arm they wandered back to the hotel where they found a seat by the pool. Stella disappeared to freshen up, and whilst she was gone Belinda came and sat by Josie.

When Stella came back ten minutes later, Josie was

sitting once more on her own. She turned to her friend with a smile and said, slowly and carefully, "*Dos bocadillo con atun y ensalada por favor.*"

Stella stared at her in astonishment. "Where did you learn that? What does it mean?"

"It means 'two sandwiches with tuna and salad, please.' Are you impressed?"

"Yes, but how did you learn it?"

Belinda taught me just now, while you were upstairs. I would really like to learn Spanish. It's a nice language, don't you think? I wonder if I could get evening classes when I get home?"

"What, in Sandacre? I doubt it! Still, you could try I suppose."

That evening, one of the dishes in the dining room was paella and the girls decided to try it. As they sat down, Manuel appeared.

"Good evening, Stella. Good evening, Josefina. Have you enjoyed your day?"

Josie frowned, but Stella gave her a little nudge and she smiled and said, "Good evening, Manuel. Yes, we had a lovely day, thank you."

Manuel poured their drinks and moved on to the next table.

"What would you do if he asked you out, Josie?"

"Oh, for goodness' sake, Stella. He won't ask me out and if he did I would say no."

Stella shrugged, gave up and began to eat the paella, which was delicious.

Manuel came back later and topped up their glasses. "Tomorrow I am not working. Would you meet me in the Plaza Iglesia and I will buy you a coffee?"

When he was met with blank stares, he continued. "How you say in English? Iglesia is…" He put his hands together and tried to look angelic, which had the girls in fits of laughter.

"You mean church!" Stella exclaimed.

"Yes, *si*, church, would you do that?"

"Sorry, we are going on a trip tomorrow, so we won't be here."

"Oh, I am unhappy. Maybe another day?"

"Maybe," the girls agreed – *but not if I can help it*, Josie thought.

As the girls left the dining room, Belinda stopped them to say the coach would be leaving at 8.30am and so breakfast would be earlier at 7.30am.

"Don't be late; it's going to be a long day."

Josie paced up and down the bedroom. "Stella, do hurry up. I want to sit at the front of the coach, not the back."

"It's my hair. It just won't go right this morning."

"Oh, it's perfectly all right. Don't be so fussy."

"It's all right for you. You don't care what you look like."

Josie glared at her. "Well thanks, Stella, now I know what you think of me. I'm going down. Don't forget the key."

She walked through the door and closed it none too quietly behind her. The first seat had been taken by an elderly couple, but the one behind them was empty, so Josie quickly sat down and made herself comfortable. It was another ten minutes before Stella climbed aboard, and by then the coach was almost full. Josie ignored her and looked out of the window.

"I'm sorry, Josie. Please don't be cross with me. I didn't mean it to come out like that; I was just cross with my hair."

"Stella, you and I are different people. That's why we have always got on, I think. You always look smart and do the right thing and you're clever. I'm not clever and I say what I think. My style is old jeans and a t-shirt and hands covered in mud. But I shower every day and when we go out I'm respectable. Don't tell me I don't care how I look because it's not true."

"I really am sorry, Josie. Please, let's be friends again."

"I'll think about it."

At this point the coach pulled away and headed out of the suburbs and on to the motorway. Belinda picked up a microphone and began to speak.

"Good morning, everyone."

Everyone called a cheery 'good morning' back.

"Well, we are on our way. Benidorm is a fairly direct route and we should be there in about one and a half hours. We will stop there for an hour, time to get a coffee and use the facilities and have a look around. Take note of where the coach will be picking you up and don't get lost! Then we are heading for Guadalest. I will let you know when we are approaching it, because the view is quite something. Actually, I'll get our driver to stop so you can take photos. The small white tower you will see is part of Alcozaiba Castle, built in the 11th century by the Moors. There are also the remains of El Castell de Guadalest, built later in the 12th century. The village itself dates back to 715 AD. Over the centuries the village and the castles have been damaged by earthquakes, but restored. There is also Our Lady of the Assumption Church, which was built" – Belinda smiled – "comparatively recently in the middle of the 1700s, and also a prison. The area is surrounded by mountains and it's very beautiful. While we are there, see as much as you can, get something to eat and drink and make the most of the souvenir shops. There are also some nice clothes shops where a lot of the garments are locally made. We will be in Guadalest for three hours, then head off back to the coast road. If we have time, we will stop in El Campello on the way back. Enjoy the day, and remember I am here if there is anything else you would like to know."

This was greeted by an appreciative round of applause. As Belinda was talking, Josie felt her irritation with Stella slipping away, and she smiled at her friend, patted her hand and said, "Friends." Nothing more needed to be said.

Some time later, Stella looked to the front and could see skyscrapers on the horizon.

"Look, Josie, I wonder if that's Benidorm?"

Belinda heard what she said, and picking up

the microphone, informed everyone that they were approaching their first stop.

"You may leave your coats and cardigans on the coach, but take your bags with you, please."

Ten minutes later the girls found themselves standing on the pavement on Benidorm front. They laughed out loud when the first people walking past were British.

"Come on, Fred, I'm dying for a cup of coffee."

"Oh stop nagging, woman, I'm coming."

That happened several times, and they could only assume it was a popular place for Brits. The girls found a bar and Josie slowly asked in halting Spanish, "*Dos cafes con leche por favor.*"

"Two coffees with milk, ladies," the Spanish waiter replied in perfect English. "Two hundred pesetas, please."

Josie's face dropped a little, but not for long. They took their coffees outside to drink and watch the world go by. Then they wandered along the front and up some of the side streets, always staying within sight of the sea. As they walked back to the coach, they posed in turn and took photos, then climbed aboard.

"OK, is everyone here?" Belinda walked up the coach, counting heads on the way to the back and checking once more on the way back. "Right, as the crow flies Guadalest is not really that far, but it is a very twisty, turny route, so it will take about an hour. We will be going to a height of about three and a half thousand feet. To give you some idea, that's about the same height as Snowdon."

Josie and Stella looked at each other and gasped.

Fifty minutes later the coach pulled into a lay-by and everyone got out, cameras and binoculars at the ready. It certainly was a magical sight.

"Do you know, Josie, I had no idea Spain was like this. I thought it was all high-rise hotels and sandy beaches. It's spectacular. I could take photos all day long."

"OK, everyone, back on board." Belinda ushered the passengers back onto the coach and they soon covered the next few miles and pulled into the car park at Guadalest. She once more picked up the microphone.

"Right, folks, I will just say that it's quite a climb to the top, but well worth it. Please be back here at 3pm. See you later."

"What shall we do first, Stella?"

"Go right to the top and look at absolutely everything."

The girls smiled at each other and set off. They resolutely passed all the shops and climbed the steep path to the very top, where they stood silently and took in the breathtaking views.

"I think I've fallen in love with Spain." Josie sighed.

Stella got a great photo of Josie gazing at the view with the mountains behind, and then Josie took one of Stella with the castle behind. Eventually they began to make their way slowly down, stopping after a short while to have a tortilla and a cold drink.

"I like the way they do their omelette," Josie said.

"It seems to have potato and onion in it. I'm going to try this at home."

They looked in the church and the prison and continued downwards, finally arriving at the shops. Stella treated them both to a t-shirt with *Guadalest* on the front. Josie's was green, a colour which suited her, and Stella looked best in the red one. They bought small gifts for friends at home. By the time they got back to the coach it was 2.30pm.

"Just time for a cup of coffee." Stella headed for a café.

"I fancy a cup of tea for a change," Josie replied.

They sat down with their drinks at an outside table. Josie took a sip of her tea.

"Yuk, this is horrible, it's nearly all milk and the milk has been boiled. I just can't drink this, Stella. You try it."

Stella did, and shuddered. "I think I'll stick to coffee in the future."

They wandered back to the coach and climbed aboard. Once everyone was back and settled, Belinda told them what a great crowd they had been, getting back at the appointed time and making everything so easy and enjoyable.

"Right, off we go, back to the coast road and El Campello."

On the way back to the main road, everyone sat quietly, enjoying the view and concentrating on the twists and turns of the narrow road. As they turned south, Belinda gave them some information about their next stop.

"El Campello is a small coastal resort, very pretty and quite select. There are some lovely villas amongst the trees on the hillside. The promenade stretches for about half a mile, that's all, but it's a pleasant stroll. If you feel you've done enough walking for today, there are seats in a pretty garden where you can relax. We'll stop here for just forty-five minutes, and then head back to Alicante."

She sat down, and very soon they arrived at El Campello. The girls decided that an ice cream sitting in the gardens was a perfect end to the day.

"Gosh, I can't believe it's Wednesday already." Stella set down her towel and made herself comfortable. They were back at their favourite stretch of beach, suntan cream and sun hats at the ready, because the weather forecast for the next day was cloudy with possible rain later. "Got to make the best of this." She looked at Josie. "You look really well, Josie. I know you're not very brown, but you look gorgeous."

"Oh come on, Stella, nobody has ever called me gorgeous, just healthy will do! Course you look like a native with your colouring. I keep thinking you're a local señorita."

The girls chuckled; then decided to go for a quick dip before settling down to sunbathing. Later they made their way back to the hotel for a cold drink and a snack. Belinda was in the coffee bar and they sat together and chatted about the forthcoming evening's entertainment.

"I don't want to tell you too much, but I've been to lots of these evenings and I never get tired of them, they are just so much fun. We'll be eating while we are there, but not till late, probably nineish. The coach will be leaving at 7pm, so I'll see you then."

She got up and left them to enjoy the rest of their snack.

That evening, Josie wore a pretty gypsy blouse and flared jeans. Stella wore her best navy and white dress, and her hair was freshly washed and shining. She tried to persuade Josie to wear her hair loose, but after trying hard to tame it, finally gave up and tied it back in the usual bunches.

When they boarded the coach, Josie was annoyed and Stella amused to see Manuel on board. They arrived at the hacienda and the driver parked next to several other coaches. They headed for a huge outbuilding and were met by a barrage of chat and laughter and music. Seven musicians stood on a stage at one end, with a space in front for dancing. The rest of the barn, about three quarters of the whole area, was taken up with long tables with benches to sit on, already half-filled with people of all ages. Very soon it was completely full, and the noise was deafening. A pretty young lady climbed onto the stage and announced in perfect English that the evening would begin with some flamenco dancers. A couple in traditional costumes came out on to the dance area, the music began and the next half-hour was filled with stamping feet, hand-clapping, the swirl of the colourful dress and exciting music. The girls were entranced, and as each dance ended it was met with a roar of approval. Then as the dancers rested the musicians played Spanish music, some familiar and some unknown to the rapt audience. The waiters came in with huge bowls of large potatoes, boiled in their skins, and waitresses brought in bowls of salad and platters of cold meat. Jugs of wine were placed along each table, and baskets of crusty bread. No butter was offered, but oil and vinegar to go on the bread and the salad. Everyone tucked into the food, while in the background a man played Spanish guitar music. After the food had been devoured the tables were cleared and the dancers came back for a grand finale. As the coach made its way back to the hotel, everyone agreed it had been a fabulous evening with a wonderful atmosphere.

The girls were rather late down to breakfast the next morning, and somewhat bleary-eyed after a very late night. They were greeted by a bright-eyed Manuel.

"Good morning, ladies, did you enjoy last night?"

"Oh, it was wonderful," they enthused.

"I was hoping there would be dancing for us, Josefina, and I would dance with you, but no dancing and I am sad."

This was met with a tight little smile as Josie moved along the buffet to choose her breakfast. Stella didn't dare make any comment and risk upsetting Josie as the two of them sat down at their table with laden plates.

"I've just got enough money left to buy a small

memento for the flat," Josie told her mate. "Shall we do that this morning? It's cloudy and a bit windy so it might be a bit cold for swimming. Or shall we get something in Alicante this afternoon when we do the tour?"

"I think I'm going to get something in Alicante," Stella replied. "It's already 10am and the coach leaves at 11am – don't forget!"

There were only about a dozen people going on the city tour, so it was a smaller coach that picked them up an hour later. Belinda didn't need a microphone as her voice reached easily to the back.

"Hello, everyone. First of all, would you mind moving forward so that I don't have to shout? Then we'll be on our way."

Everyone dutifully did as they were asked, which left a few empty seats along the back.

"We will be driving into the city, where our driver will drop us off. I will take you on a tour for approximately two hours, maybe a bit longer, then we will have a tapas lunch before being picked up again and going to the Castillo de Santa Bárbara. The weather forecast is dry but with some cloud and some sun."

Twenty minutes later, they all piled out of the coach and gathered round Belinda.

"You will see I have an extended car aerial, with a nice bright chiffon scarf tied on top, so you won't lose me. It's nice there are only twelve of us. It will be easier to answer any questions and keep close together."

Belinda started the walking part of the tour, chiffon

scarf held high and twelve obedient 'chicks' following close behind. She led them into plazas, down wide streets with tall, modern buildings and narrow streets with very old and ornate buildings; through gardens and through more squares where people sat enjoying coffees in the dappled sunlight.

"This road leads into another small square where sometimes weddings are held—" She broke off as a deafening series of explosions had everyone screaming. They looked into the square as bride and groom and guests left the building and stood to one side, watching a display of firecrackers going off in quick succession around the four sides of the square. The volume of noise was multiplied by the tall buildings on every side. In a few minutes all was quiet again except for a spontaneous round of applause from the guests and tourists.

"Well, that was a little extra I wasn't expecting," Belinda said with a smile. "Now, we'll slowly make our way towards the seafront for our tapas lunch."

As they walked along, they became aware of another noise, this time much more pleasant. Turning another corner, they came across a string quartet, smartly dressed in black and white, playing on a street corner. The group stopped for a while to listen; then dropped some coins into an upturned sunhat and continued on their way.

"Everything is going our way today." Belinda smiled at her 'chicks'. "Those musicians are very good but unable to find work, so we are lucky indeed to hear them."

By now it was 1.30pm and everyone was hungry, but the sea was in sight and tasty food not far away.

"For those not familiar with Spain, I will explain what tapas are." Belinda beckoned for everyone to gather round. "*Tapa* literally means a small bite. Food is served up in small dishes or plates, so if you are not very hungry you can have just one or two, or if you are very hungry, as many as you like. Some dishes can be heated up, if they are not already hot, and others are salad-type dishes. Eggs and tuna are used in a lot of these. There will also be Spanish omelette, or tortilla in Spanish, which is nice hot or cold. Can I suggest couples or families who are together try a good selection? Right, follow me and I'll explain what everything is."

Josie and Stella chose mainly cold dishes and some tortilla and sat down near the window, looking forward to the meal. Belinda had phoned in advance and ordered wine and water to be brought to the tables. Everything was delicious, and soon all gone. The waiters cleared the dishes and brought round a selection of simple desserts to round off the meal. Crème caramel, mousse, ice cream or rice, then coffee for those who wanted it. After nearly a week at the hotel the guests were all familiar with each other and quite happy to chat and drink more coffee while they waited for the coach to pick them up and take them to the castle that dominated the city.

The road wound round the castle and dropped them a short way from the top. From there they could walk up to the top quite easily, which is what most people did. There were gasps as they looked from the battlements out over the city. The assortment of roofs, all shapes, sizes and colours, slanted this way and that and exaggerated by the shadows of the late afternoon sun, were a photo opportunity. Cameras clicked away and people posed with the view behind them. Slightly to the right in the distance, the remains of another castle caught people's eyes, and to the left the sun glinted off the sea. Slowly, people began to drift downward.

"Oh Stella, look at those poor cats, they look half-starved."

Belinda was standing nearby. "Don't worry about the cats; they are not as thin as they look. Because of the hot weather in Spain, cats do not have thick fur and that makes them look thin. Probably by British standards they are a bit neglected, but it's not as bad as it seems."

Slowly everyone made their way back to the coach after another enjoyable day.

"I can't believe this is our last day, Josie, but the sun is shining so we can have a last swim."

"Yes, and we didn't get any bits of shopping yesterday. There was so much going on we forgot. Shall we shop first, and then swim late morning when it's hotter?"

"Good idea. Come on then, grab your handbag and let's go."

It certainly wasn't difficult to find a memento as there were several places along the front only too happy to oblige them. Josie chose a plate with the castle painted on it to hang in her living room and Stella decided on a Spanish donkey condiment holder.

They strolled back to the hotel, enjoying an ice cream and every moment of their last day. Dropping their mementos back in the room and picking up swimming costumes and towels, they headed for the dunes.

"Oh Stella, I don't want to go home."

"Neither do I, 'cause I don't think I'll ever come back."

"Why on earth not, you've enjoyed it, haven't you?"

"Yes, but I'm dreading the flight home and I don't think I'll ever fly again."

"Course you will. You'll get used to it in time. I know I'll be back, next year hopefully. And I'll come on my own if necessary. I just feel I belong here, Stella. I can't explain it."

Stella made no response, but dashed off and leapt into the waves for the last time.

Later, as the girls made their way back to the hotel, they saw a familiar figure sitting on a seat looking out to sea.

"Hello, Manuel," they chorused. "I need the bathroom," Stella whispered. "I'll see you in a minute."

"Come and sit with me for a few moments." Manuel patted the seat beside him. Josie hesitated; then decided it would be churlish to refuse. She sat down, keeping some distance away.

"I was hoping we would get to know each other a bit better, Josefina, maybe have a date. You could have met my mama and my *hermana*."

"*Hermana*?" Josie asked.

"*Si*, my sister Angelina. She is about the same age as you and she speaks good English."

"What about your father, Manuel?"

Manuel was silent for so long, Josie wondered if he had heard her.

"My father… he has a problem. He drinks too much. He's an alc… What do you call it in English?"

"An alcoholic, you mean?"

"*Si*, he drinks and then he comes home and beats my mother."

Josie gasped. "Oh, that's awful. Does he hit you and your sister as well?"

"No, he has never done that, and he wouldn't dare to hit me now."

"Can't you protect your mother from him?"

"No, he waits till we are not there."

"Why doesn't she leave him?"

"We are Catholic, and we don't do that. She just has to put up with it and try and keep out of the way." Manuel looked up and their eyes met and held, his full of sadness and Josie's full of shock. They gazed at each other for a long time, and then Manuel took her hand.

"Thank you, Josefina, for listening to me. I wish you were staying here and not going home tomorrow."

"I'll probably come back next year, so I'll see you then."

"It's too long." Manuel lifted her hand to his lips and gazed at her with his dark eyes. Josie gently pulled her hand away.

"I must go now, Manuel. I have to pack because we leave early in the morning."

She stood up and smiled at him, then walked back to the hotel, her feelings confused.

I really like him, she thought. *It's a good job I'm going home.*

Stella looked up questioningly as she came into the room, but said nothing.

"I don't want to talk about him, Stella. Do you mind?"

"No, that's OK. Have you got room in your case for a couple of my presents?"

The girls set to and after an hour everything was stowed away ready for the morning.

Manuel was not on duty that evening, and they only spoke briefly the following morning. Everything was a bit of a rush and in no time at all they were on the coach and heading for the airport.

"Ladies and gentlemen, we will shortly be beginning our descent into Luton airport, where I'm sorry to say, it's cold, wet and windy. Would you please return to your seats and fasten your seat belts?"

Josie dragged her hand away from Stella's and rubbed her bruised knuckles, but Stella grabbed hold of it again.

"For goodness' sake, Stella, relax. We're nearly there and I'd rather not have my hand in plaster, if you don't mind."

"Sorry," croaked Stella. "I'm just so scared."

It was with much relief that they soon touched down, and picked up their cases. Sue was there to pick them up and hustled them quickly into the car and out of the ghastly weather.

"Welcome back to England." She laughed. "Did you have a good time?"

On the journey home the girls never stopped talking, and it was obvious they had thoroughly enjoyed themselves.

It took Josie a long time to settle down. Everything that she had enjoyed before the holiday – her work at the nursery, relaxing at home in her little flat, meeting friends – all seemed suddenly so mundane, so boring. It was very busy at the nursery and this helped a bit, but there seemed a big hole in her life. It was as though she had left her heart in Spain with the sunshine, the way of life and maybe a tiny bit with Manuel. Gradually she began to enjoy the routine of her life, but always there was the thought that one day, possibly next year, she would go back.

Margaret and Eric were getting married in September and Josie and Stella were to be bridesmaids, so the weekends were often spent looking at dresses and spending hours going over arrangements. Eric was quite happy to let them get on with it. As Margaret was an orphan, Eric's mother was sorting out the reception and checking with Margaret every step of the way. She had grown very fond of Margaret and didn't want to step on her toes.

Stella had a new boyfriend, so Josie didn't see her that often. So she decided to help Doris and Bill again, working in the pub and keeping the garden tidy. The extra money she put to one side for her next holiday in Spain. Stella had warned her she would not be going again, but Josie was quite happy to go on her own. She had seen some lovely photos of inland Spain with its snow-capped mountains and miles and miles of olive trees, and made up her mind that next time she would try and see more of the country.

"Wake up, Josie, are you back in Spain again?" Bob grinned at her. "There's a delivery of pots out front, could you check it off and give the driver a cup of tea?"

Josie smiled back sheepishly and walked towards the lorry parked out the front. The driver, a young man in his twenties, was just taking the last few boxes off.

"Morning, Josie."

"Morning, Dave, cup of tea?"

"Yes please. I'll have it all off in five minutes; then we can check it."

Ten minutes later they sat down with a mug of tea each, after counting and ticking everything on the delivery note.

"I've been meaning to say to you, Josie, how about coming to the pictures with me? Michael Caine is on at the Odeon and I've heard it's a good film."

Josie hesitated. "Well, I don't really go out with boys. I like them as mates, but not all the other stuff."

"Yes, I know that, but I'm talking about just going as friends, nothing more. You'd be quite safe with me."

"How do you know? Has someone been talking about me?"

"Well, sort of… but I'm not saying who, so don't ask me. I gather you've had an unpleasant experience, but as I said, we'll just go as friends. What do you say, Josie? Do you think you could put up with me for one evening?"

"Well, OK."

"We're not all brutes, Josie. Some of us are quite decent. See you outside the Odeon then, at 7pm. OK?"

As she cycled home that evening Josie thought, *What have I done? I can't believe I agreed to go out with Dave.*

Even though she had told Sue and she had thought it was a good idea, she still wasn't sure. In fact she was plain scared. Still, she decided she would go through with it, telling herself it was no big deal and she would be all right with Dave.

When she got home she rang Stella.

"I know you'll be getting ready to see Brian, but can you spare me five minutes for a chat?"

"Oh Josie, you make me sound horrible! Of course I can spare you five minutes – half an hour if you want! What's the matter? You sound really worried."

Josie told her about Dave and how nervous she was. Stella was quick to reassure her.

"I'm relieved actually, Josie. You should get out more and have some fun; otherwise you'll grow into a boring old maid. Now, phone me and let me know how you get on. I shall want every detail."

131

She chuckled, and Josie had to laugh with her.

As Josie got ready later, she realised she was quite looking forward to the evening. The churning inside was a mix of nervousness and excitement. She pulled on her best jeans and apple green t-shirt – it had a red apple on the front with a big bite out of it – smiled at herself in the mirror and set out for the Odeon.

Three hours later as Dave walked her home, she felt much more relaxed. The film had been good and Dave had behaved like a gentleman, buying her an ice cream in the interval and insisting on seeing her to the door.

"I wouldn't dream of asking you out, then expecting you to pay. I've enjoyed it too, and maybe we can do it again sometime. Now, am I going to shake your hand, kiss your cheek or pat you on the head?"

"Oh Dave, you are funny." Josie laughed, then stood on tiptoe and kissed Dave's cheek. "See you next week. Thanks again, goodnight."

She turned and walked up the outside steps to her flat. She didn't see Dave gazing after her, one hand touching his cheek where Josie's lips had lightly kissed him, and a look of affection and longing on his face. To her it had just been a good night out with a pal.

Autumn passed and winter began with early snow and icy winds. By the end of November Christmas trees and decorations were beginning to sell, and the display of poinsettias just inside the shop looked magnificent. Josie and Dave were still seeing each other, but Josie kept it at once a week, despite Dave trying to persuade her otherwise. True to his word, he was still treating her with respect (much to her relief), and they had arranged to go to a Christmas dance in the middle of December. Stella accompanied Josie to the shops to buy a nice outfit.

"You must wear something nice, Josie. You've got nice legs; please buy a dress for a change."

To her surprise, Josie agreed, and they spent the next few hours going from shop to shop. Stella was just running out of patience when Josie slipped into a simple cream dress with gold thread running through it round the neck, cuff and hem. They looked at each other in delight.

"This is it, Stella. It just feels right."

"You look wonderful, Josie, what a transformation."

"It's a bit expensive."

Josie hated to dig into her precious savings. But when Stella rolled her eyes in exasperation, she quickly reassured her that she would buy it and even suggested that some gold sandals or shoes would look nice with it.

Half an hour later Josie twirled in her bedroom and admired herself in the mirror. She even allowed Stella to pile her hair up and into a plait.

"If Dave doesn't already love you, he's going to when he sees you next Saturday."

"I don't want him to love me, Stella, but he can tell me I look nice if he wants to."

"You could do worse than Dave. He's a nice chap and he would take care of you."

"I know, but actually, Stella, I don't love him. I'm fond of him but not in a romantic way, he does nothing for me I'm afraid. If he starts to get serious, I shall stop seeing him."

For such a well-built man, Josie thought, *Dave's remarkably light on his feet.*

The two of them were enjoying the dance, and whether it was a slow number or a lively one, Dave did well and obviously enjoyed it. When Dave had picked her up earlier, he had been stunned into silence by how lovely Josie looked. When he eventually found his voice he left Josie in no doubt that she looked good.

"You look amazing. You'll be the most beautiful one there tonight, Josie."

From then on the evening had gone well. They danced and paused for a cold drink, then danced some more. The evening flew by, and finally it was the last slow dance. Dave held her very close and his cheek rested on her hair. Josie resisted the urge to push him away a little, not wanting to spoil the evening.

Dave drove her home and pulled up outside. He switched off the engine and gently took her in his arms.

"It's been a great evening, Josie, and you *were* the most beautiful girl there. Please can I kiss you goodnight? I want to so much."

Before she could say no, his lips were on hers and his arms tightened around her. Josie struggled and he let her go.

"Why did you have to do that? You know how I feel." She glared at him.

"I did it, Josie, because I love you. I've been very patient, but we need to move on in our relationship. I can't wait forever. Don't glare at me like that; it was only a little kiss."

"We're supposed to be just friends, but you've spoilt it now." Josie paused and drew in a shaky breath. "Thank you for a lovely evening," she said politely, then jumped from the car and disappeared round the corner of the fish and chip shop and towards the steps to her flat. Dave sat in his car, knowing that to follow her would only make matters worse. He also knew that it wasn't going to work out for them. With a deep sigh he started the engine and drove slowly home.

Meanwhile Josie let herself in and closed and locked the door behind her. Leaning on the door, tears began to run down her cheeks. She knew her friendship with Dave was over, and because she was fond of him, it upset her to realise how much she had hurt him. But he had known how she felt from the beginning, and she had done nothing intentionally to make him think differently. Drying her eyes, she carefully hung up her dress and prepared for bed. Sleep was a long time coming, however, as the events of the evening went round and round in her head.

The next morning as she was ironing a few things, her recently acquired phone rang.

"Hello?"

"Don't put the phone down, Josie, please. It's Dave. I just want to say sorry about last night."

"I'm sorry as well, Dave, but although I like you a lot, I don't want a romance, so it's best if I don't see you again."

"Don't you fancy me at all, Josie? Couldn't you grow to love me, perhaps?"

"No, Dave, and it's not fair to raise your hopes. I just look upon you as a brother, that's all, so it's not going to work, is it?"

"OK, I'll see you at the nursery, then. Goodbye, Josie."

Later that morning, Josie rang Stella, needing to talk about the previous evening.

"Stella, it's all over between me and Dave."

"Oh, what happened, did you have a row?"

"No, but he started to get all serious and he kissed me, Stella, and I didn't like it one bit. Anyway, he rang me this morning and we decided to finish. I'm relieved really, but I didn't want to hurt him by carrying on any longer."

"Well, Josie, if you don't fancy him, you've done the right thing. Were you scared when he kissed you?"

"No, I wasn't, actually, and I'm glad about that. It means I'm getting over my fear of men, so maybe someday I'll meet someone special. Who knows?"

"Oh Josie, I hope so. I'm really fond of Brian – I know he feels the same about me. But I'm that bit older than you so there's plenty of time. Thought any more about Spain?"

"Oh yes, I'm definitely going back next year, probably the same time but a different place."

"Who are you going with? You know it won't be me."

"I know, I'll go on my own, I don't mind. I've just started Spanish lessons, by the way. It was actually Sue who noticed them in the local paper, so I signed up straight away. The first lesson is tomorrow night. I just can't wait."

Josie was still helping at the King's Head when she could, and keeping the garden tidy. Now it was October and there was nothing to do in the garden, but the pub was doing well and Doris and Bill were glad of Josie's help. It was also busy at the nursery, preparing for another Christmas. Over the last few years, Doris and Bill had become very fond of Josie and looked upon her as another daughter. Josie felt she could talk to them if she was worried about anything and they would be there for her. So it came as no surprise when she was asked to spend Christmas with them again. As she was helping Doris prepare the vegetables she told her about her plans to go back to Spain, and how she was enjoying her Spanish lessons.

"So when are you going, dear?"

"The same time, at the end of April. But Doris, can I tell you a secret?"

"Course you can, dear."

"Well, I'm thinking of getting a one-way ticket and staying for a while."

Doris looked at her in amazement. "What?! How can you afford to do that?"

"I'll get a job. I've got it all planned. I'm going to Benidorm. I think there are lots of English people in Benidorm with businesses, and if I go early in the season, I should be able to get a job."

"You are taking a big chance, Josie. What if you can't get a job?"

"I'll always make sure I have enough money to get home if it doesn't work out, so don't worry. But I really love Spain and I want to give it a try."

The door swung open and Bill came in with some glasses. "What are you two hatching up between you?"

"Nothing, just girls' talk," Doris said.

She looked at Josie and they grinned at each other. But Doris felt uneasy about Josie's plans.

As soon as Christmas and the New Year were over, Josie went to the travel agent and bought a one-way ticket for the middle of April. Heart thumping, she passed over the money and tucked the receipt away safely. Well, she had done it, and would be counting down the weeks on her calendar. She told Doris and Bill, who was now in on the secret. She must now tell Bob and Sue, and the sooner the better.

The couple looked at her in disbelief.

"You're what?! Josie, please tell us you are joking."

"Sorry, I'm not joking, I'm really going and I can't wait."

"But Josie, on your own? You're too young to be

138

doing something like that. If you were going with a friend it wouldn't be so bad. Please tell us you will reconsider."

Josie didn't know what else to say, so she just shrugged and looked from one to the other in silence.

Bob was the first to speak. "Well, Josie, it seems you're determined, so we are just going to wish you luck, and I think you're going to need it. When do you go? And where? Are you going back to the same place?"

"I'm going in the middle of April, that's three months away and I shall fly to Alicante again, but I'm going further up the coast to Benidorm this time."

She went on to explain that there were lots of Brits already living there and a job and accommodation should be easy to find, although she had booked a self-catering flat for the first week. Now she just had to get through the next few months and make preparations.

CHAPTER 9

"Ladies and gentlemen, we will shortly be making our descent into Alicante. Please return to your seats and fasten your seat belts."

The hostess switched off her PA system and several minutes later the pilot's voice told them that the weather in Alicante was fine and sunny and about 19 degrees, but with a cool breeze. Josie felt excitement course through her. She was here at last. The past three months had not been easy. Everyone, without exception, had been against her moving to Spain; even Mrs Reynolds had tried to dissuade her. But once Josie's mind was made up virtually nothing would change it. The Spanish lessons had gone well and she could get by as long as things didn't get too complicated. This was the start of a new life for her.

The plane touched down and people began to sort out their belongings. Then the doors were opened and everyone shuffled forward. Oh, that wonderful aroma of airplane fuel and hot tarmac. Josie smiled to herself at her sentiments. Then it was collecting suitcases and climbing onto the coach taking holidaymakers to Benidorm. Josie gazed out of the window, looking at the views she remembered so well from eleven months ago. The blue seas at El Campello, the orange and lemon groves with the perfume of the blossom reaching inside the coach, through Villajoyosa and then in the distance the first glimpse of Benidorm. The driver dropped people off outside various hotels and apartment blocks and finally it was Josie's turn. She stepped down with four other young people who were obviously all together, and they made their way to reception. An elderly man, with very little English, checked their papers and handed out keys.

As they went up in the lift one of the girls asked Josie, "Are you all on your own?"

Josie nodded.

"Gosh, you're brave," the girl continued. "I'm Janice and this is my sister Kathleen. These two ugly blokes are Paul and Pete."

Josie laughed and the ice was broken.

"Don't be lonely. We're in room 226 if you want some company."

"That's really nice of you, thanks," Josie responded.

"How long are you here for?" Kathleen asked.

"I'm not sure. I'm hoping I can get work and stay."

"Wow! How exciting. Let us know how you get on."

The lift arrived and the two couples got out, leaving Josie to go on to the next floor. As with the last visit to Spain, Josie was surprised by how big the room was. She had a balcony again overlooking the sea, and a beautifully tiled bathroom. It was now just after

3pm. Impatient to be outside, she hurriedly unpacked, then went down in the lift and outside into the warm sunshine. She soon found a café with seats outside and ordered a cup of coffee and a pastry. As she sat there it gave her a chance to look around and get an idea of the area the apartment was in. It also made her realise that she could not have coffees out every day, lovely though it was; nor could she afford to eat out. The apartment had very basic cooking facilities in one corner and she would have to make full use of them. She finished her coffee, paid and walked along the front, taking note of all the cafés, bars and shops; then went up one of the side streets to find a supermarket. An hour later she was back in her room trying to cram as much food into the tiny fridge as possible. She had decided, as she was alone, not to go out after dark, but to eat in the apartment and if she wanted to treat herself to a meal, to do so in the middle of the day.

After a good night's sleep, Josie was up bright and early. She sat on the balcony with a bowl of cereal and a cup of tea and planned her day. She decided the morning would be spent exploring and the afternoon relaxing on the beach. She discovered there were many streets in Benidorm, although from one side to the other it wasn't very far. Going into a newsagents, she managed to find a street map and used this to locate some interesting buildings and plazas. She sat in one of these and ate the sandwiches that she had prepared earlier, and then slowly made her way to the beach. The two young couples were there and invited her to spend the afternoon with them, although the young men were not so enthusiastic, hoping to have their girlfriends to themselves. Josie spent an hour or so with them, and then went back to the apartment to study the map a bit more and plan the next day, before cooking herself a simple meal.

Monday morning dawned bright and sunny and after toast and tea, Josie set forth to explore Benidorm again. Map in hand, she took the first road away from the sea to find some gardens marked on the map. These were entirely different to anything in England. Many of the plants were succulents or cacti and the trees were mainly palms, but here and there mimosa and jacaranda were in full bloom. Although so different, it was lovely just the same and well cared for. A young man was busy watering and called out a cheery *Buenos días* to her as she wandered by. She walked on and found the next place of interest, an old church, but it was locked, probably because it was still quite early in the morning. She had discovered on her last visit that many Spanish stayed up late at night, sometimes into the early hours, and then would rise quite late in the morning compared to English people. Josie turned right and headed back towards the sea, gazing in the shop windows. Outside one stood a rail of clothes, mostly brightly coloured, traditional Spanish dresses, ranging from adult sizes right down to the smallest, cutest little dresses she had ever seen. She smiled and moved on. Taking a bottle of water from her bag and finding a seat overlooking the sea, Josie slaked her thirst, and then munched her way through a pastry bought the day before in the supermarket. Then she continued to explore, stopping at lunchtime to eat her sandwich.

As she set off again, she realised most places were closing for the siesta, so she made her way to the beach, where once again she saw Janice and Kathleen. They beckoned her over.

"I don't want to become a nuisance," Josie said.

"Please stay and chat, the boys have gone off to explore, but we wanted to stay here and sunbathe and swim," Kathleen replied.

"I'll look after your things if you like," Josie offered. "I'm not swimming today. You go off for your swim, but be warned, it's going to be very cold."

The shrieks coming from the sea proved that she was right, and she chuckled as she watched their antics.

Some time later, as the girls dried off, the boys came back and soon after Josie left them, saying she needed to buy some milk. As she left the beach she noticed a narrow road that had not been explored, and this led to another small square, shaded by mimosa trees, and quiet and peaceful. To one side were two shops and a café. Suddenly realising how thirsty she was and finding the water bottle empty, she made her way towards it. Loud voices could be heard from inside, but Josie took no notice, having discovered already that the Spanish like nothing better than a noisy argument. However, she paused in the doorway and took in the cluttered tables and unswept floor.

A blonde-haired woman came out of the back room

with a smile firmly fixed on her face and said, "*Hola*."

Feeling rather embarrassed, Josie replied, "*Hola. Café por favor?*"

"*Si, si.*" The woman indicated a table which was clear of dirty cups and Josie sat down. The woman began to speak Spanish, but Josie raised a hand to stop her.

"I'm sorry; I only speak a little Spanish."

"Don't worry, love; I thought you were English and so am I. I was just apologising for what you have heard."

She glanced towards the back room, and as she did so, a young girl came out, eyes flashing, and with an angry toss of the head said, "I've had enough, you can stick the job. Scrub the sink, clear the tables, sweep up, that's all I hear. You can find somebody else to slave for you for a pittance, 'cause it isn't going to be me!"

With that she hoisted her bag onto her shoulder and stormed out.

"Oh dear, I'm sorry, you can have a coffee and a biscuit on me."

"Just a minute," Josie said. "If you are English I bet you can make a decent cup of tea."

"You bet I can. Shan't be a tick."

The woman proceeded to prepare the tea, casting worried looks at the state of the café. As she brought it over to Josie, two couples came in. She hurriedly cleared a table by the window, wiped it down and then served the customers. Josie drank her tea and nibbled at the biscuits. Before the foursome had sat down, more people had come in. Josie's kind heart and desire for order and cleanliness came to the fore, and before she could stop herself, cups and saucers and rubbish were being piled onto a tray and tables wiped down. From the corner of her eye she could see the woman watching her as she was serving, but nothing was said. Taking the loaded tray to a shelf behind the counter and grabbing another tray, she continued clearing the tables, and more people came in. In fifteen minutes everyone had been served and all were sitting at beautifully clean tables. The woman beckoned Josie over to the doorway, which led to the back room.

"I don't know what to say. I'm just so grateful. Melissa leaving like that really gives me a headache; mind you, she was pretty hopeless anyway. I'm going to have to close until I can find somebody else. As you can see, I can't manage on my own." She sighed. "And that won't do the business any good – people will just go elsewhere and they probably won't come back."

Josie realised here was a chance she couldn't ignore.

"I'm looking for a job. I've worked in a pub before and I'm a hard worker – would you consider taking me on?"

The woman's face broke into a big smile. "I certainly would – you could be just the sort of young lady I'm looking for. My name is Lily, by the way. What's yours?"

"I'm Josie."

The two shook hands.

"It's 5.30pm and I close at 6pm; would you help me till then and then once we're closed we can discuss money and what your job would entail?"

"Yes, that's fine," Josie said.

She went back out to the café, said, "*Adios*" to some people leaving and cleared their table. Soon everyone had gone and Lily turned the sign to *Cerrado*, and turned the key in the door. She and Lily worked together tidying the coffee shop itself, but Lily said they would leave the kitchen till the morning. Milk was put in the fridge and the cake covered and put away.

"Right, Josie, if you don't mind we'll sit on one of the seats in the square, otherwise people will keep trying the door."

She locked up and they found a seat under the trees. Lily took a pad and pen from her bag and began to write.

"Josie what?"

"White, and I'm nearly nineteen."

"And your address, Josie?"

"Well, you see, I only arrived from England on Saturday. I've got an apartment till Saturday coming, and then I'm homeless." She grinned at Lily. "Will you help me find some cheap accommodation, please? You probably know the best place to try."

"I do indeed. See that brightly painted office on the corner? That's George, he does short-term or long-term lets. He's been over here ten years so he's very familiar with the area. He doesn't close till 8pm, so shall we pop over and see him?"

"Oh, I am so excited! Yes please, can we?"

Josie did a little dance, much to Lily's amusement.

George was busy on the phone, talking to a customer in another language, which Josie didn't know, but Lily mouthed 'German' at her. George put the phone down.

"Hello, Lily, what can I do for you?"

"Oh George, that awful girl has left, I'm glad to say, and this is Josie. She's starting immediately but she needs accommodation as from Saturday. Something reasonable, George, if you please!"

"Well, I've got a nice little apartment on the front vacant now, if you want it."

He named a price and Lily gasped.

"Hang on, George, I said reasonable. How much do you think I pay my staff?"

George checked his book, muttering to himself. "Well, if you want somewhere around here or on the front it's going to be dear. Look, I've got a flat up the top near the main road, much cheaper. Bus goes right past the door to the bus station. That's only five minutes away. What do you think?"

"Is it respectable? And is the area OK? She's only a young girl, George."

"Yes, it's fine, mainly Spanish, of course. Do you speak Spanish, love?"

"*Si, un poco*. Is that right for 'a little'?"

"Yes, very good," Lily said, and chuckled.

"I've been having lessons in England but I need to carry on with them here."

"Don't worry about that for now, Josie, we'll sort something out." Lily patted her arm. "Right, George, when can we see this apartment?"

"Well, when I'm closed for siesta, you're at your busiest, Lily; we might have to say 9 o'clock in the morning. What do you think?"

"That's OK with me. How about you, Josie?"

"Yes, that's great, shall I come here?"

Everything was arranged for the next morning and they said goodbye to George and sat down again on the seat in the square.

"Everything is happening so quickly, I shall be too excited to sleep tonight. Thanks for everything, Lily."

"If you're not doing anything this evening, we'll get a takeaway and go back to my apartment and you can meet my other half. What do you say?"

"That would be lovely. I have to admit, I'm starving. It must be all the excitement."

Josie was amused when they picked up fish and chips from an English-run establishment.

"Where are we?" she asked Lily. "Spain or England?"

"Well, there are quite a few Brits here now," Lily replied. "But I think in twenty years' time there will be a lot more. I mean, you can't beat it, can you, all this sunshine and everything is so cheap. Mind you, wages are much lower than in England, so you have to take that into account. Here we are. This is where I live."

She unlocked the outer door and propelled Josie through and up the stairs. A door to the first floor opened and a man looked out. Josie could see by his dark complexion that he was probably Spanish.

"This is Juan. Juan, this is Josie. I'll explain

149

everything in a minute. I'll just pop some plates under the grill."

Josie smiled shyly at Juan and said, *"Hola"*, and he shook her hand; then busied himself putting cutlery out, and salt and pepper. Half an hour later as they sat over coffee, Lily told Juan the events of the day, speaking sometimes in English and sometimes Spanish.

"I can't tell you how glad I am to get rid of that awful Melissa, and now Josie is going to work for me and I know already she's a good worker. I think we're going to get along just fine."

"Does Josie speak Spanish?" Juan asked.

"Well, a little." Lily smiled at Josie. "I'm going to sort out some lessons for her with Gwen Thomson, and I'll help her in any quiet moments we get."

Josie finished her coffee and made to leave.

"I'll walk you back to your hotel," Juan offered, and Josie didn't argue because it was now quite dark. But on the way Juan patiently waited while Josie bought some postcards and stamps.

Dear Bob and Sue,
Well, I have been here two days and I have a job already, working in a café with an English lady called Lily. And I'm going to look at an apartment in the morning, which sounds as if it will suit me fine. Lily is arranging more Spanish lessons for me and the sun has shone every day so far, so everything is great. I will send you a proper letter next week.

150

Hope you are all well.
Love Josie xx

Then she wrote a similar card to Stella, stuck stamps on and placed them on the table ready to post the next day.

Josie had guessed correctly about not sleeping. Her brain was going round and round thinking about all that had happened that day, so it was the early hours before sleep took over and it was only voices from the corridor that woke her at 8.15am. She leapt out of bed and ate her cereal as she was getting ready and just made it to George's office by 9am. Lily was already there, and they climbed into his car and set off towards where the apartment was situated. George gave them more information on the way.

"It's a small estate, with different sizes of villas. One, two and three bedroom, but as you drive in, there are two small blocks of flats, one either side. Eight flats in each, on four floors, so two flats on each floor. It's basically furnished, Josie, but I don't think there's much in the way of linen or kitchen equipment, so you'll have to go shopping. I don't let this one for holidays, you see. I had a Swedish girl in there for a year, but she went home a couple of weeks ago. And I can tell you, she left the place absolutely spotless. I didn't have to do a thing to it."

By this time they were approaching the urbanisation along a road running parallel to the main road. The entrance was very grand, with a large, ornate archway decorated with colourful tiles, and just beyond were the two blocks of flats. George parked outside the left-hand one and opened the car door for Josie and Lily.

"Right, follow me. The flat is on the top, Josie, and there's no lift, so I hope you're fit!"

He used a key to get in the main door, then stepped to one side and with a sweep of his arm indicated for them to go ahead. Josie ran all the way to the top floor; then leaned over the stair rail to grin at them.

"Come on, you two, not much further."

"Cheeky madam," Lily responded, but she exchanged a smile with George. "What it is to be young and full of energy."

George let them in and Josie and Lily looked around silently. Lily was the first to speak.

"It's a bit small."

"How can you say that, Lily? It's much bigger than the one I had in England."

"Yes, but English accommodation is always smaller. By Spanish standards this is small."

"Well, I like it," Josie stated.

The entrance to the flat consisted of a small hallway with cupboards. The bathroom was straight ahead, with the bedroom alongside, both looking out over the town and the sea shimmering beyond. The living area was quite large and looked over the two roads to the hills and the mountains behind. Although the room was spacious, it was sitting room, dining room and kitchen rolled into one. There was also a small window looking out to the side, letting in more light. As George had indicated, there was just enough furniture to get by and the windows were all fitted out with blinds. Josie opened some cupboard doors in the kitchen area to find some rather tatty saucepans, a well-used frying pan and several bits of unmatched crockery. George came over and looked over her shoulder.

"Mm, that doesn't look very good. I'll give you a few pesetas to replace some of them, Josie, you can't use them in that state."

"Thanks, George, I need all the help I can get." Josie gave him a grateful smile.

"So you think this will suit you?"

"Yes, I like it," Josie repeated.

They went back to the office and everything was sorted out to everyone's satisfaction, then Josie and Lily hurried away to open up the café. Lily sorted out the coffee machine for the first customers and Josie cleaned the two sinks in the kitchen and swept up from the night before. Lily darted in and out, putting pastries from the freezer into the oven, explaining that she would usually be in at 9.30am to do that, before the café opened. For the next couple of hours, whenever there was time, Lily explained more to Josie and Josie tried to take it all in. At 12.30pm, a Spanish lady came in and Lily introduced her.

"This is Maria, Juan's sister. She helps over the lunch hour, for two hours, mainly doing hot snacks and sandwiches, but we all help each other if necessary."

Josie was shown how Lily liked the washing-up done, and was then left in charge of that and keeping the café neat, clean and tidy. It was a busy lunch hour and at one point Josie was sent out to a local bakery for more bread and rolls. She was also allowed a few minutes off at 12.30pm for a sandwich. Maria left at 2.35pm and as the café was quiet, Lily and Josie sat down for a much-needed cup of tea.

"I always sit out here for my breaks," Lily said. "People are reluctant to come in a café that's empty. They think there must be something wrong with it."

At that, people came in and Lily got up to serve them, motioning for Josie to stay and finish her drink.

At 6.15pm, as Josie plodded back to her apartment, she thought, *I might be young and energetic, but right now I'm exhausted.* In her bag were some pastries left over from the day, one savoury and one sweet. With a little salad they would do for an evening meal.

The next day, Josie soon got into the swing of things and didn't feel quite so exhausted. She intended to buy a kettle that evening. Most of the shops closed for three or even four hours for a siesta in the afternoon, and then opened around five o'clock until eight or nine o'clock, so it all worked out well for Josie to equip the flat. She went to a shop recommended by Lily not too far away and bought the electric kettle, and then on to the supermarket for some cleaning materials. She had brought her own linen from England, so that was one expense less. George had agreed to buy saucepans, a frying pan, some china and cutlery. He had also replaced the fridge, as the door was falling off. When she got back from the shops Josie wrote a long letter to Stella, telling her everything about the café and the flat, and saying how much she missed her, and inviting her to come and stay, if she could pluck up the courage to face the flight.

As the season progressed, the weather got hotter and the café busier. Fortunately the kitchen and café had air-conditioning, so the heat was bearable. Lily, Maria and Josie were a good team and worked well together. Lily had put tables and chairs outside on the pavement and a few more under the trees in the square. Business was good.

The week Josie turned nineteen, the schools broke up for the summer holidays and the world went mad. The three were kept busy all day. Maria's younger sister, still at school, came in during the holidays and helped over the busiest times. At the end of each day, Josie got the bus back to her flat and just collapsed. There was no air-conditioning in the flat, but Josie took Maria's advice to leave the windows and the blinds closed during the day. Then when she got home she would open the windows on the shaded side of the building and hope for a cooler breeze. With the help of a fan, the flat wasn't too bad.

The urbanisation, although small, had its own shady square, and it was pleasant to sit there amongst her Spanish neighbours. She would practise her Spanish, which was coming on well, and she was getting to know several of the locals by name.

Finally the holidays came to an end, and families

were replaced by middle-aged and elderly couples. The heat lessened and things became less hectic. The café was always closed on Saturday; otherwise nobody would have a day off. Saturdays were changeover days for holidaymakers, and therefore the quietest day of the week. Josie also finished at three on Wednesdays and Maria stayed on to cover her.

It was a Wednesday afternoon at the end of September, and Josie was meandering slowly in the general direction of the bus station. As she passed through one of the numerous plazas, her heart gave a huge leap and she stopped in her tracks.

"Manuel!" her voice was barely a whisper, but it was as though he heard her. He turned his head and his eyes met hers. For several moments they stared at each other in silence, then Manuel leapt up, his chair tumbling to the floor.

He ran across the plaza calling, "Josefina, Josefina, it's really you." He gripped her arms and kissed her on both cheeks and looked at her again, a big smile on his face. "What are you doing here?"

They both spoke together, then laughed.

"Have a coffee with me. I remember how you like Spanish coffee."

"How can you remember that when you meet so many people?"

"Come, sit down and I will tell you."

Manuel called to the waiter for two coffees and they sat down.

"I remember a lot about you, Josefina, because I like you a lot. I remember you came in May last year with your friend Stella. I think about you every day, Josefina. I thought I would never see you again and I was very sad."

Josie's heartbeat was now almost back to normal – but not quite, and her hands were shaking. She rested them on her lap, out of sight of those warming black eyes.

"I bet you say that to all the girls, Manuel." She gave him a shaky smile.

Manuel just looked at her for several minutes, causing her to blush. He was not smiling now. "So you think I remember this much about all the people I meet? How could I? There are too many. But if you do not believe me…" He shrugged.

Josie sipped her coffee; then said, "So what are you doing in Benidorm, Manuel?"

"My *madre* and *padre* moved here and I have to come here too, to keep my *madre* safe. Do you remember my father is not good with my mother, and she was in hospital a few months ago? He broke her arm."

"Oh Manuel, that's awful." Josie looked at him, aghast. "For a religious man that's wicked. God would not expect her to put up with that. We call him a merciful God in England, and I'm sure He would understand if your mother moved away somewhere safe."

"She won't listen to me or my sister and she won't talk to the *Policia*, she would be too ashamed." He was silent for a few moments; then said, "My father has been ill. It is the drink. He will die soon."

His voice was full of hate and bitterness. Josie sat silently. What could one say? Suddenly Manuel gave a huge sigh, straightened his shoulders and smiled at Josie.

"So, *mi amor*, why are you in Benidorm? On holiday? Are you with Stella? When are you going back?"

Josie laughed at all the questions. "You won't believe this, Manuel, but I live here."

"You live here? I don't understand."

"Well, when I was here last year, I just fell in love with Spain and so I decided to come here and see if I could find work and stay for a few years. I came in April and within two days I had a job and an apartment. I've just finished work and I was on my way to the bus station, or perhaps I should say *autobus estacion*."

"So you are learning Spanish, Josefina?"

"Yes, and I'm getting quite good, but the lady I work for is English, so that's what we speak. I work in a café and a lot of our customers are English, although we do get quite a few Germans and Spanish as well."

Manuel shook his head slowly, still trying to believe that this was Josie sitting here with him, and that she had been living here for nearly six months. He couldn't drag his eyes from her, and started to pluck up the courage to ask her out. When they had met the previous year, he had the strong impression that she was wary of him and he didn't want to frighten her away.

"Josefina, would you meet me again here and we can talk some more? I would like to know about your family and what you did in England." He looked at her quizzically. "I think perhaps you were a model, wearing beautiful clothes."

To his delight Josie threw back her head and laughed heartily. "Modelling wellington boots, maybe," she said, still chuckling.

"*Que?*" Manuel clearly didn't understand.

"I worked in a *centro de jardineria* and wellington boots are waterproof boots that come up to here." She indicated an area just below her knee. "In England we get lots of rain, so we have to wear them for much of the time. I also helped some friends in a pub, so I was very busy."

She glanced at her watch, and then jumped up. "I must go, I've already missed one bus and I've got things to do this evening."

"I will walk to the *autobus* with you," Manuel said.

They set off together at a brisk pace and duly arrived at the bus station.

"Will you meet me again?" Manuel repeated.

"OK, same time next week, Manuel, but I must get on the bus now."

Quickly Manuel kissed her cheeks; then watched as she boarded the bus and sat down. He waved as the bus pulled away, and Josie waved back. She looked back several minutes later and could just see him in the distance, still watching the bus.

The next day at the café, she waited for a quiet moment, and then said to Lily, "I need to have a chat to you in private. Could you spare me half an hour or so sometime, please?"

"Of course I can. Have you got a problem? You're not going to leave me, are you?"

"Oh no, nothing like that. I just need to talk to you about a man I met yesterday on the way home. I got to know him last year and now I've bumped into him again."

"Tell you what, Josie, we'll close really promptly tonight and we'll sit in the square for a while. I'll phone Juan and let him know I'll be a bit late."

"Thanks, Lily, I'm sorry to be a nuisance."

"You're not a nuisance, love. You're very young to be here on your own, and any time you want someone to talk to, I'll always be around."

Later on that day, Josie and Lily sat in the square. It was already dusk, but the air was warm. Sparrows chirruped noisily in the trees and people wandered past, going about their business. Lily knew about Josie's past and how nervous she was of men, so she had a good idea what this was all about.

Josie told her about Manuel and how they had been drawn to each other the previous year, and how Manuel had seemed to be very fond of her. She went on to tell Lily all about their meeting yesterday, how delighted he was to see her and how keen he was to see her again.

"And then, Lily, when the bus drove away, he watched it till it was out of sight. He genuinely seems to like me and I like him, but I'm scared. Is he just after 'you know what', do you think, or does he like me in a nice way?"

"Well, Josie, it seems like he really likes you a lot. Look, if you're nervous about meeting him, always go where there are people around; you'll be quite safe then. Would you like me to meet him next week, so he knows you've got someone watching over you?"

"Yes, that's a good idea. I'm probably being over-cautious, but that's just me." She rolled her eyes and pursed her lips, then grinned at Lily. "I'm meeting him next Wednesday after work, is that OK?"

"Yes, that's fine." Lily paused; then said, "I've never told you how I met Juan, have I? I came over here on holiday with a friend, just like you, but I was twenty-two. Me and my friend, we just used to lie on the beach, in fact my friend got sunburn. These boys were kicking a ball about on the beach; well, they were men, really, in their twenties. They were smashing. We'd never met Spanish blokes before and we were impressed, I can tell you. But anyway, being good girls – don't look at me like that, we were good girls." Lily grinned; then continued. "Suddenly one of them kicked the ball really hard and it hit me here." Lily touched her face, just under her left eye. "It nearly knocked me out. They all came running over. It was Juan who'd kicked the ball, and he was distraught. He insisted on taking me to the hospital to get checked over. My friend Amy came with me and I was glad because we had a bit of a wait. The doctor had a quick look at me when we arrived and obviously could see I wasn't about to die, so we had to wait our turn. Well, the three of us chatted…" Lily laughed. "We spoke about ten words of Spanish and he spoke a little more English, so there were a lot of arms waving about and sign language. Then I went in to the doctor. He poked my cheek about and it really hurt, then sent me in for an X-ray. So then we had to wait again. Anyway, to cut a long story short, nothing was broken, just badly bruised. Quite spoilt my beauty for the rest of the holiday."

"So did you see him again?" Josie asked.

"Course I did, I'm married to him, aren't I? We saw him on the beach next day. He was sitting on the wall waiting for us. Oh Josie, he was so sweet. He asked me how I was and he looked at my face, which was going a lovely shade of red and black, and asked Amy and me out for a tapas lunch. He paid for everything and couldn't do enough for us. And, well, we just saw him every day after that."

"But always the three of you? Didn't you ever see him on your own?"

"Well, it got to the Thursday, and Amy suddenly seemed to find other things to do. I never realised she liked museums and art galleries, but she couldn't see enough of them, bless her, so Juan and me were on our own quite a lot those last couple of days. Enough to fall in love, anyway."

"So then what happened when you had to go home?"

"Well, we wrote to each other and I saved like mad so I could go over again, which I did three months later. I stayed with his elder sister, who was married, so I didn't have to pay for a hotel. For two years, that's how it was. Either I would come here or Juan would come to England. When we decided we wanted to marry, I had to become a Catholic. That was a bit stressful, I can tell you. And here I am, ten years later and still happily married. The only sad thing is we've never been able to have children, but Juan has got four nephews and three nieces, so we spoil them instead."

"So you think Spanish men are quite good to women?"

"Yes, if it's offered they will take it, but if they know you're not that sort of girl they'll treat you with respect. You meet Manuel next week and I'll have a look at him and let you know what I think!"

"Thanks, Lily, I feel better about it now."

The next week seemed to drag by, but finally it was Wednesday and Josie and Lily locked up the café and set off to meet Manuel. Josie was nervous and excited, and not sure she was doing the right thing.

Manuel was sitting in the square at the same table. On seeing them, he stood up and raised a hand in greeting, then pulled out chairs for them to sit down. He seemed unbothered by Lily's presence, and Josie introduced her straight away.

"This is Lily, the lady I work for. Lily, Manuel, my friend from last year."

The two shook hands, then Manuel ordered coffees.

"So have you been busy in the café today, ladies?"

"Well, not bad, but it's getting quieter now the

163

holidays are over," Lily replied. "So where do you work, Manuel?"

"In the Panorama Hotel, Wednesday is my day off. It's so good to see Josefina again."

He seemed to sense that Lily was here to size him up and wanted to reassure her, in fact both of them, that Josie would be safe with him. They chatted easily about the summer just ending and the pros and cons of working with holidaymakers. Then Lily finished her coffee and stood up.

"Well, I must be off. I've got a hungry man at home. Goodbye, Manuel, nice to meet you. Bye, Josie, see you tomorrow."

She looked at Manuel as though she was going to say more, then smiled and turned for home.

"She is a nice lady, Josefina; I think she is like a mother to you, yes?"

"She's been very good to me. I'm very fond of her. I can talk to her about anything and she doesn't laugh at me."

"So Josefina, *mi amor*, tell me about your family and your life in England."

Oh dear, Josie thought, *where do I start?*

"First of all, Manuel, can I ask you to call me Josie, not Josefina? Do you mind?"

"No, I don't mind. If you want me to call you Josie, I will. Please tell me everything."

So Josie did. From the moment she was left at the door of St. Anne's as a day-old baby, through her childhood, her love of gardening, the incident with Mr

Shenstone and running away. She told of her working life and her friends and the unpleasantness with Richard. And she finished by telling him of her fear of men and how she was trying to conquer it. Apart from a few questions, Manuel listened to her in silence.

"So, Manuel, if I seem nervous with you, perhaps you can understand why."

Manuel still said nothing, but took her hand in both of his, then raised it to his lips. His eyes were full of understanding and affection for this badly treated young lady. Finally he said softly, "Josie, I promise I will never treat you like that. I hope one day you will trust me, because I would like you to be my girlfriend. I think you know that. Will you, Josie?"

At that moment, as Josie looked into his eyes, she would have promised him anything, he was so gorgeous, but she just gave a small nod and a smile.

They arranged to meet again on Saturday, which was Josie's day off. Manuel was given a few hours off between lunch and the evening meal, which was about 4pm till 7pm. He took Josie to the old part of Benidorm and they wandered happily whilst Manuel pointed out places of interest. Six o'clock found them sitting in a large paved area overlooking the sea enjoying an ice cream. They had talked and talked until they were hoarse and an ice cream was the only cure! Josie felt completely relaxed with him and was quite happy to hold hands as they were sightseeing, feeling a tingle of excitement at his touch.

They slowly made their way back to the bus station, and with a great reluctance they said goodbye. Manuel gently kissed her lips and turned away to head for the Panorama and another evening's work. They waved as Manuel reached the corner of the street, and then he was gone. Josie climbed on the bus and settled down for the short journey home. The date had been so good. Manuel had been the perfect companion and Josie herself had not shied from physical contact. To others it might have only been the holding of hands and a small kiss, but to Josie it meant huge progress in her feelings towards the opposite sex. *Stella would be pleased with me*, she thought.

Dear Stella,

You are never going to believe this, but I have got a boyfriend! Do you remember Manuel? Well, I bumped into him here in Benidorm and things started to happen. He knows how I am with men and we are taking it slowly. But Stella, he is so gorgeous and I think I am falling in love. I'm pretty certain he feels the same, or he is an amazing actor! He works in a hotel here now, doing the same thing as last year. My job is still OK and I'm enjoying it. Things are a bit quieter now but there's always plenty to do. Are you seeing anyone at the moment? Please write soon and tell me all the gossip. With lots of love from Josie xx
PS: Please, please visit next spring!

Dear Josie,

Thanks for your letter. I'm really pleased you are managing to put the past behind you and enjoy life. You're only young once! Yes, there is someone for me too. His name is Brian and he's twenty-four years old. He works in a bank and is quite clever, but also lots of fun. We are planning a big party for my twenty-first in a couple of months' time. It would be just great if you could come, although I know it's not likely to happen. Margaret is expecting a baby! So you are missing that as well. I really do miss you, Josie, and hope it won't be too long before we see each other again. Look after yourself.

Lots of love, Stella xxx

Over the next few months, Josie and Manuel's friendship grew into something much deeper. Manuel had confessed his love for Josie on their fourth date and soon Josie told him she felt the same. Their embraces became more ardent, and although Josie was determined not to go 'all the way' she welcomed and returned his kisses with a passion that surprised even her! She had met his sister Angelina, and the two had become good friends. But Manuel would not take her to meet his parents.

"You would not like my papa, Josie, and he would be rude to you."

"But couldn't I meet your mama, then? We could have a coffee somewhere."

Manuel was silent for a few moments. "Josie, let

me tell you what my mama is like. She is not frightened and er… quiet like you think. Sometimes I think when she shouts at my papa that is why he drinks too much. How you say in English? She asks for it?"

"Oh, well yes, I am surprised. So does she shout at you? Would she shout at me?"

"Yes, she would, I think, because you are not a 'good Spanish Catholic girl' but a bad girl from England."

Manuel took her hand and looked into her eyes. "Josie, *mi amor*, you know how much I love you and would like very much for you to be my wife, but my mama and papa would make big trouble, it would be impossible! I will try and talk to my mama, but I don't think it will be easy. Perhaps next week when it is Christmas, she will be happy and I can try then."

They met again on Christmas Eve and exchanged presents. Manuel had bought Josie a beautiful gold chain with an amber pendant, and Josie had bought Manuel a silk shirt in dark navy with a matching tie.

"Oh, Manuel, you will look so handsome in it. Have a lovely Christmas with your family."

Manuel grimaced. "Who knows, maybe it will be OK with my sister there and the little ones. But I will see you in two days, which is the most important thing, *mi amor*."

He took her in his arms and they clung together for several minutes, then kissed before reluctantly parting to go their separate ways for Christmas apart.

Lily and Juan had asked Josie to join them for Christmas. That would have been good, but then at the last moment as they closed the café on Christmas Eve, Lily told Josie of the change of plan.

"We are going to Juan's parents' house tomorrow. There will be about twenty people there and it will be lots of fun!"

Oh no. Josie was horrified. How would she cope with a house full of Spanish people all talking Spanish at ninety miles an hour?

"They won't want me there. I'll feel the odd one out. Sorry, Lily, I just can't come."

Lily put her hands on Josie's shoulders and looked at her fondly. "Josie, not all Spanish people are like Manuel's parents. Juan's mama and papa are lovely. They will make you very welcome. Please come."

"All right, but I'll be very nervous."

"We'll pick you up at 12pm. We will probably eat about 3pm and the meal will be huge. I'm warning you in advance! But we take our time and the meal will probably go on for several hours. It's amazing how much gets eaten when there's no hurry." Lily laughed and patted her tummy. "See you tomorrow then love. Bye."

The next morning Josie agonised over what to wear. Would it be warm in their villa or cold? Should she wear dark clothing or something bright and cheerful? In the end she put on a pretty green dress with long sleeves and a full, lined skirt. Green had always suited her, and she felt confident in it. She slipped a t-shirt on underneath in case it was cold in the villa, with the knowledge that she could always go to the bathroom and slip it off. She was ready by 11.30am, and found herself pacing the floor nervously and looking out of the window frequently to see if they had arrived. In the end, impatient with herself, she sat down and did some Spanish revision, although she seemed to be reading the same words over and over again. Then when her door buzzer went, she nearly leapt out of her skin. She ran down the stairs, clutching her handbag, coat and a bunch of flowers for the hostess. Lily gave her a quick hug, told her she looked lovely and held the flowers while Josie climbed into the car.

Josie's eyes widened as they approached the villa. It sat on the very edge of the town in large grounds which seemed to be occupied mainly by olive, orange and lemon trees. Near the front of the house, ornate stonework and huge plant containers, still filled with late flowers, gave a colourful welcome. The villa itself was fascinating. The main central area was obviously the original building, but over the years bits had been added. Little attempt had been made to match them to the main building, but somehow the whole effect was utterly charming.

The door opened and a smiling Maria ushered them in, giving them a warm hug and wishing them a happy Christmas.

A short, plump, elderly lady came out of the kitchen with a welcoming smile, hugged and kissed everyone and said, "*Bienvenido*, Josie." And immediately Josie did feel welcome. She was introduced to the guests already there and tried hard to remember names.

The villa was equally charming inside, with rooms going off in all directions, often with floors at different levels. Sometimes there was one step up or down, sometimes three or four. Lily gripped her arm and Josie realised she was still holding the flowers.

"For you," she stuttered in English, handing them to the smiling lady.

"Come," Lily said. "Follow me." She led Josie to a bedroom where she left her coat, then told her where the two bathrooms were. Already delicious aromas were filling the house and making Josie's mouth water.

Over the next few hours, it seemed everyone came to have a chat to Josie. Most spoke some English, but it gave Josie an opportunity to practise her Spanish.

Then Maria came up to her and said, "You must meet our *abuela* – our grandmother. She is eighty-nine and she will love it if you say a few words to her in Spanish. Come!" She led Josie to a small, somewhat quieter sitting room, where the old lady sat with Maria's daughter, Anna-Maria, keeping her company.

"*Abuela, la presenter al Josie.*"

The old lady held out her hand and Josie took the frail hand in hers and shook it gently.

"*Encantada señora, como esta usted?*"

"*Bien, gracias.*"

Maria's daughter told Josie that her great-grandmother didn't hear too well and that Josie had spoken clearly enough for her to understand her query about her well-being. Just then Juan came up to them

171

and handed the old lady a glass of wine, and he gave one to Josie as well.

At 3pm on the dot everyone was called to the huge dining room table, eighteen people in all. Then the feast began. After Juan's father had said grace, everybody helped themselves to the plates and dishes of starters in the middle of the table. Everyone could take as much or as little as they wanted, or nothing if they did not care for a certain dish. It meant there was no waste, and seemed a good idea to Josie. She was seated next to Lily, who explained what the dishes were. Over the next three hours, dishes were taken away and more brought in, accompanied by as much wine as you cared to drink. The voices grew louder as the meal went on. One of the main courses appeared to be meatballs.

"Believe it or not, Josie, these meatballs are minced turkey." Lily laughed.

Josie made her wine last; she didn't want to make a fool of herself in front of everyone. Gradually people left the table, starting with Abuela. Lily leaned close to Josie and spoke quietly.

"People will have a siesta now; the old lady has gone first, then the men. The ladies will wash the dishes and the children will tidy up. Then the children will probably read or do something quietly for a couple of hours. When the ladies have finished in the kitchen they will rest for a while. Let's go and sit in the garden, Josie."

"Can't we help in the kitchen?" Josie asked.

"Oh no, we are guests. They wouldn't expect us to

help. Come on, I know a nice little corner in the garden that catches the winter sun."

They made themselves comfortable on some garden chairs and in no time at all Lily was asleep. Josie smiled fondly at her and rested her head on the back of the chair. The next thing she knew, music had started up and she realised she had been asleep too. She looked at her watch in the lights from the window and was surprised to see it was 8pm and quite dark.

"I'm glad you're awake, Josie. I'm dying for a cup of tea. I bet you are too!"

"Ooh, yes please."

"They allow me to make the tea because they know how fussy us Brits are about it. Let's go in now."

Josie thought they would soon be going home, but no, at 9pm more food was brought out, mainly cold tapas and nibbles. Despite claiming to still be full, Josie and Lily managed to sample a few things. Then someone started playing guitar and Grandmother and Grandfather got up to dance. Others sat around and clapped their hands and stamped their feet. Josie was enthralled: for two people in their mid-sixties they seemed to have a lot of energy. Other people got up to dance, and the fire and the excitement in it was something Josie would never forget. People began to leave at midnight and Lily, Juan and Josie left at 12.30am and made their weary way home. Josie had thanked her host and hostess, in her best Spanish, for a truly wonderful day.

Josie was glad of a quiet day on Boxing Day. Her head seemed to be full of music, talk and laughter, and her stomach full of food. She went for a walk in the afternoon sun, then came home and wrote Stella a long letter, describing the most amazing Christmas Day: the company, the house and garden, the food and the dancing.

The café was closed for another day, and then up to New Year's Eve it was open from 10.30am to 3.30pm. On the first day back Lily sat Josie down at a table and brought two coffees over.

"While there's nobody here, Josie, I have to tell you that I must cut your hours down for a few months until things pick up. I'm sorry about that. I thought I would leave it till after Christmas before I told you. I didn't want to spoil your Christmas."

Josie just stared at her for a few minutes. "How much will I lose? Will I have to give up my flat?"

"Well, probably about a third. But you have got a little saved, haven't you? Do you think you can manage? I don't want to lose you, Josie; you're such a good worker."

"I'll sit down and work things out tonight. Oh dear, I do hope I haven't got to go back to England."

They got up as four people came in for coffees. At 3.30pm on the dot Lily turned the sign round to closed and put the lights out. They said goodbye and Josie made her way to the bus station. She was just nearing the area her bus left from when she heard running feet, and looking over her shoulder she saw Manuel rushing towards her.

"Josie, thank goodness I am here in time, I must talk to you. Is it OK?"

"Yes, what's the matter?"

"Come."

Manuel took her arm and led her to a nearby park. They sat on a bench and Manuel took her hand.

"It's my papa." He paused. "He's dead, Josie."

Her hand flew to her mouth. "What happened, Manuel?"

"Well, on Christmas Day, Angelina and me, we hide most of the drink. Papa was a bit angry but we calm him down. But yesterday he find the drink, and he just drink and drink. He didn't listen to us. Not me or Angelina or Mama. He just kept on! Then Mama just looks at him – such a look! And that was it. He was going to hit her, and Angelina and me, we hold on to him to stop him. But then, Josie, he look so angry and then he go a bad colour and fall down. He looked dead straight away. I call an *ambulancia* and Angelina tried to help him, but he dead."

Josie laid her hand on his. "How is your mama?"

To Josie's surprise, Manuel leapt up, and waving his arms about, exploded.

"My mama is heartbroken, she cry and cry, she call him her beloved husband. I will never understand her. He beat her and drink all the money away and she call him her beloved."

"Well, maybe she did still love him, Manuel. How about Angelina?"

"She doesn't hate him like me, but I don't think she love him like Mama. I don't know how she feels."

"Oh Manuel, what a horrible Christmas you've had. Do you know when the funeral is yet?"

175

"No, but in the next two days. So I will see you in a few days, Josie, but I'm not sure when."

They hugged and held each other close for several minutes, and then Manuel left to sort out the funeral arrangements. Josie climbed on her bus, deep in thought. Poor Manuel, he'd had a dreadful Christmas and she had enjoyed a fantastic one, but how could she tell him about it now? And how could she worry him about her hours being cut?

The following Saturday Manuel came to her flat in the afternoon and pressed the buzzer. As Josie let him in, she could see how tired and strained he looked.

"Sit down, Manuel, and tell me how you are, and your mother and Angelina."

"We are OK. The funeral is over and things are being sorted out. But Mama, she surprise me. She is going to live with Angelina and she tell me I am old enough to have my own home, so I am looking for a flat or small villa. Of course I had my own flat in Alicante, so she is right."

"Does Angelina mind having her?"

"No, no, they get on well. Mama will help with the children and the housework, they will be fine. Josie, you never tell me about your Christmas Day. Was it good?"

"Oh Manuel, it was wonderful."

She went on to tell him all about it, and how they had welcomed her into their home.

"Then when I saw you a few days ago, Lily had just

cut my hours down and I'm worried about how I'm going to manage. My savings won't last long. I feel I must keep enough in my account in case I have to fly back to England."

Manuel looked horrified. "Don't leave me, *mi amor*. We will think of something."

"Well I'm all right for a couple of months anyway, so please don't worry."

He pulled her into his arms. "I couldn't bear to lose you now, Josie, I love you so much."

He kissed her and Josie responded ardently, wishing, but not saying, that he would ask her to marry him. She wanted him so much and knew he felt the same, but to give in now, and maybe become pregnant, would not be a good thing. She gently moved out of his arms and went to put the kettle on, telling herself that something would turn up and things would sort themselves out.

Josie now finished work at 3.30pm, and one day the following week Manuel was waiting for her as she left the café.

"I've got a villa, Josie, and I want you to see it."

"Where is it, Manuel? Fancy – a villa, not an apartment. How lovely."

"Oh, it is needing a lot of work, it's not lovely now and it is on the hill on the other side of the motorway. It is very cheap, and Mama is helping me to buy it. She has been saving money for years without my papa knowing. Will you come and see it, *mi amor*?"

"Yes, I'd love to, can we go now?"

They set out on foot as the villa was only a short distance away. Holding hands, they took the path under the motorway and joined a rough road on the other side. After about a quarter of a mile, they passed through a gate hanging off its hinges. On either side, neglected orange and lemon trees grew, and further on, a few olive trees. The track was stony underfoot and Josie, busy watching where she was going, didn't notice the villa at first.

"There it is, Josie. You see, it is very bad."

They stopped and looked silently at the building ahead of them on raised ground. It was small and square, its roof a lovely terracotta, but obviously needing repair. The walls looked sound but desperately in need of paint. The glass in one window was broken and the tiles on the steps leading to the door cracked and uneven.

"Very bad," Manuel repeated.

They walked up the steps and Manuel produced a key from his pocket and unlocked the door.

Inside there were just four rooms: a living room and kitchen at the front and a bedroom and bathroom at the rear. An attempt at adding a second bedroom had been started, but had got no further than a foot from the ground. Everything was damp and mouldy, except in the bedroom, where due to the broken window, air had got in and prevented damp and mould forming. There was virtually no furniture, just a couple of old wooden chairs and a rusty oven. Josie suddenly found her voice.

"Oh, Manuel, there's so much to do. How will you manage?"

"Pablo, Angelina's husband, he is very good with building and 'do it myself'. He will help."

Josie couldn't help smiling. "It's 'do it yourself', not 'myself'. We just call it DIY in England." She paused. "Anyway, Manuel, I'll help. I did my flat in England so I can be some use."

"The first thing I must do is mend the roof. I'll try and do that this Saturday and Sunday, and Pablo said to put air bricks in all the rooms, then it won't go damp." Manuel's face shone with enthusiasm. "Pablo said he will do the broken window soon, and I will borrow a truck to take away the oven and chairs and any other rubbish."

They stepped outside and looked back over the town towards the sea.

"Surely this is not all yours." Josie's arm swept from left to right, taking in all the trees.

"Yes, all mine, but the trees need work before they will have fruit. I don't know about trees. I will have to find someone to do it for me."

"Mm, perhaps we can get a book from the *bibliotheca* on gardening, that will tell us how to prune them. That way it won't cost you anything."

"My clever Josie, that is a good idea."

During the next two months Manuel, Pablo and Josie worked on the villa whenever they had spare time. Manuel had another key cut for Josie because she had the most time off. As she worked alone, painting and scrubbing, she had plenty of time to worry about how her savings were fast disappearing. As March gave way to April, things became dire. Tentatively she asked Manuel for a loan, to see her through till things picked up in the café. What she really wanted was a proposal, but unless Manuel's mama suddenly softened, that wasn't likely.

"*Mi amore*, you know I can't marry you yet, but why don't you move into the villa with me? It's good enough now."

Josie asked for time to think about it, but their need for each other and the lack of money hurried along a decision. The following day she went to the clinic and asked to go on the pill. She had to lie and say she was getting married, but finally the doctor agreed. Then she met Manuel from work and told him she would move into the villa in two weeks' time. Manuel was over the moon and just couldn't stop smiling.

"Are you going to be my woman properly, Josie? If you are you should go on the pill."

Josie looked at him from under her lashes. "I already have."

Manuel held her close. "I love you so much and we are going to be so happy together, you will see. Come, there is something I must buy you."

He led her down several streets and despite her pleas, refused to say what he had in mind. Then he stopped in front of a jewellers.

"I have only a little money, Josie, but I want to buy

you a ring so you know I really mean to marry you, and everyone else will know it as well."

Jewellery was not displayed in the window but in glass-fronted counters inside. The doors were locked, which was not unusual, and a middle-aged man was busy in the shop. He looked up as they rang the bell and studied them for a few moments, then having decided they looked honest, he unlocked the door and let them in. Once inside the door was locked again, but now the man was all smiles and listened politely as Manuel explained what he wanted and how much he wanted to pay. Then he took a ring sizer from a drawer and measured Josie's finger. Josie had quite long fingers, but they were slender and the jeweller said in halting English, "Such elegant hands." He smiled and lifted a tray of rings from the display in front of them and placed them on the counter. He spoke rapidly to Manuel, and Manuel nodded.

"You can choose any one of these, *mi amor*"

While Josie was looking the jeweller found another tray, removed two rings and put them to one side, then placed the remainder in front of Josie.

"Oh dear, they are all so beautiful. I really like the solitaire, and this one with three diamonds."

The jeweller placed them on her finger one at a time and this helped Josie to make up her mind.

"I like this one best, Manuel." She gazed at the three diamonds sparkling on her finger. "Please can I have this one?"

"Of course you can. It looks really nice, Josie. Do

you want to keep it on, or the *señor* will put it in the box
for you?"

Josie decided to have it in the box so that when they
were alone, Manuel could put it on her finger and they
could seal it with a kiss. Josie wandered to the other
side of the shop and looked at the other jewellery on
display, so that Manuel could pay and have the ring put
in a box and wrapped.

When they were outside on the pavement again,
Manuel took her hands and said, "Go home, *mi amor*
and put on your best dress and I will take you to a nice
restaurant and we will celebrate. Come, I will walk you
home, and I will be back in one hour to take you out.
Will that be enough time?"

"Oh yes, plenty of time. Oh Manuel, I'm so happy!"

One and a half hours later they were sitting in a very
posh restaurant, sipping champagne. Josie had on her
best cream dress, which she hadn't worn since moving
to Spain, and after some difficulty had managed to pile
her hair up on top. Manuel's eyes were full of love and
admiration as he gazed at Josie. Then he took the box
from his pocket and opened it. The ring sparkled in the
lights of the restaurant. He reached across the table and
took her hand.

"Josie, *mi amor* will you marry me?"

"Yes, oh yes, Manuel."

It was what she wanted more than anything else in
the world. They gazed at each other for a long time,
unable to quite believe that they were engaged and

would soon be moving to the villa together. As they ate their meal, Josie's eyes were drawn to her ring many times and then she would look up at Manuel and smile.

And so on a bright, sunny morning at the beginning of April, Josie waited, her belongings packed and ready for Manuel to arrive with a borrowed van. Nothing Josie had was heavy, as all the furniture belonged to the flat, but still, two suitcases and six cardboard boxes were waiting by the door. Manuel arrived and rang the buzzer. He already had almost a vanload of his own things, all his clothes and personal bits and pieces and some small items of furniture. But they crammed everything in and headed for the villa. Josie felt a mixture of excitement and nervousness. She kept pushing down the old fears and told herself that they loved each other and everything would be all right. They unloaded the van, then went straight off with a shopping list. The list was long and money short, so the most important things like a bed, kettle and saucepans were highlighted. As they drove towards the shops, Josie's curiosity got the better of her.

"Do you mind if I ask you how much you paid for the villa, Manuel?"

"Well, they were asking 800,000 pesetas. I said no way, I will give you 600,000. We argue and argue and in the end I pay him 675,000. I am pleased. Mama is pleased. Everyone is happy."

"Gosh, Manuel, that's about £3,500 – that's so cheap, with all the land as well. I can hardly take it in, and when we've finished the work on it, the value will go right up."

"I know." Manuel smiled at her. "And if we build the second bedroom…" He smiled and spread his hands. "Who knows, we will be rich, Josie!"

He pulled into a car park behind a big furniture store and they went first to the bed department. They chose a reasonably priced bed and bought bedding to go with it, as all Josie's sheets were single size. Then they moved to the housewares department and chose the minimum to keep them going until a little more money had been saved. Manuel was very businesslike as they shopped and Josie liked that. It felt very reassuring somehow. The bed was secured in the van and the other purchases squeezed in around it.

Back at the villa everything was unloaded, and then they sat down for their lunch.

"I am going to get my electric heater from home and warm it up a bit for you, Josie. I can see you are shivering."

"Thank you, Manuel."

Best not to tell him the shivering was mainly nervous anticipation. It was such fun unpacking everything. The things for the kitchen had to sit on the sink unit, as there were, as yet, no cupboards. The only things in the kitchen were an old fridge and an even older cooker. Josie made up the bed and hung their clothes on hangers from doorways, and from the picture rail in the lounge. Her mind kept going back to what would be happening tonight, and she was trying desperately to push down the fear, knowing that it was totally irrational. When she felt a light touch on her arm she leapt out of her skin.

"Josie, why you…?" Manuel aped her startled jump.

"Sorry, so much to think about. I was miles away."

"You want to be miles away?"

"No, no, Manuel. It's what we say in England. It just means thinking of other things." She put her arms round him and kissed him. "My mind is back here now. Did you want me for something?"

"I am just going to fetch the heater, can you think of anything else we need?"

"Yes please, you could rob a bank and bring me a million pesetas!"

They chuckled together, then Manuel climbed in the van and disappeared down the track.

When he was gone, Josie gave herself a good talking-to. *You are stupid, Josie, you are insane. You love Manuel. You fancy him like mad; love him tonight, as he deserves after being so patient. Now, no more nonsense.*

But that evening she could not eat. They sat down on an old settee that Lily had given them and Manuel took her in his arms and kissed her gently and stroked her, telling her over and over how much he loved her and trying to encourage her to relax. There was nothing demanding in his caresses and slowly she relaxed; then began to respond. Manuel's kisses became more urgent and his eyes darkened. He pulled her to her feet and led her towards the bedroom.

185

Josie had confided all her fears to Lily, and Lily, bless her, had tried to understand. Many times that day and evening her thoughts turned to the young couple and she found herself willing Josie to forget those fears as well, and just enjoy herself.

Josie awoke at dawn. She lay there for several minutes while her mind went over the hour last night when her life had changed. She had let Manuel down, crying and telling him to stop. Fortunately he hadn't stopped and she was a virgin no longer. But the experience for her had been terrifying and painful. Her eyes were heavy with weeping that had continued long after Manuel had fallen asleep. She looked at him, still sleeping peacefully beside her. She wanted to hold him and tell him how sorry she was, but that might lead to something else, and she couldn't bear the thought of that, not yet.

Creeping out of bed, she slipped on her dressing gown and went from the room, closing the door quietly behind her. She put the kettle on and put coffee in the mugs, then went to the bathroom. *I'm not sorry at all, not one little bit. How strange. Manuel said I would be all right today and I didn't believe him.'* She hesitated; then stepped under the shower. Ah, that felt good.

There was a gentle knock on the door.

"Are you OK, Josie?"

"Yes, Manuel, I'm fine. I'll be out in five minutes," she called. "The kettle is on."

As soon as Josie came out of the bathroom she ran to Manuel and flung her arms round him.

"Oh darling, I'm so sorry about last night, I feel so ashamed."

"Don't worry, *mi amor* it will be all right next time. You were very brave."

"No, I wasn't, I was awful." Josie shook her head in despair at her behaviour.

"Just forget it now and have some breakfast. Shall I do some toast?" Manuel asked, and Josie suddenly realised how hungry she was.

"I want more than toast, I'm starving. Shall I fry some eggs?"

Ten minutes later they were tucking into breakfast with gusto.

"Oh Manuel, I wish we could buy baked beans in Spain, a big helping with these eggs would have been yummy."

"I've heard this many times from English visitors, it must be liked a lot."

"Oh it is; we love our baked beans. I think England would grind to a stop without them." Josie laughed. "If Stella ever visits I'll ask her to bring us a tin."

They spent the day happily together. Manuel had bought some curtain wire which was very cheap, and fixed it above the windows. Angelina had found some old curtains she no longer needed and Manuel hung them in the bedroom. The villa was slowly beginning to look more homely.

Josie explored the garden, enjoying the April sunshine and making plans. Several old terracotta pots lay amongst the weeds and she took them back to the villa and brushed them off. They would look nice with some geraniums in them. She wandered back amongst the olive trees and then on to an area of lemon trees, where a few of last year's crop hung, wrinkled and rotting on the branches. She gazed out towards the sea and felt very happy and content.

That evening Manuel cooked paella, and proved himself an excellent chef. That night there were no tears from Josie, but she didn't enjoy the lovemaking and was relieved when it was all over. Manuel had assured her it would all come right and she was not to worry. In every other way their life together was idyllic. They worked on the villa and Manuel and Pablo started on the second bedroom. The book on pruning had been borrowed from the library, and while the men worked on the villa Josie worked on the trees, taking off dead wood and weeding round the base. She managed to cope with the orange trees, but the olive trees, they had decided, needed an expert. However, Josie was going back to full-time with Lily in the next few weeks and then there would be spare cash to pay for this.

As summer approached, Josie was thrilled to get a letter from Stella to say she would be visiting in June with her fiancé, Brian.

"I just can't wait, Manuel. I'm so looking forward to seeing her again. It's been a year and letters aren't the same as a good chat."

They arranged to meet the day after Stella and Brian arrived, at a popular coffee bar along the front. Maria had agreed to stand in for Josie for the whole day, and at 11am Josie was impatiently pacing up and down outside the bar, when she spotted Stella's dark hair in the distance. Unable to wait, she ran excitedly towards her, waving her hand in the air, and then they were hugging and laughing and poor Brian was being completely ignored. Josie felt her eyes fill, so happy was she to see her dearest friend.

"Oh, sorry, Brian, how are you?"

"I'm fine, thank you, but I'll see you later. I'm going to buy some t-shirts and leave you girls to catch up. Shall we meet back here in a couple of hours?"

"Yes, then we'll have something to eat. See you later." Stella gave him a quick kiss and he wandered off to some beach shops to see what he could find.

"That's very thoughtful of him, Stella."

"Well, he would soon be bored listening to us droning on. Anyway, I might want to talk about him and I certainly want to hear all about Manuel."

"Mm, then let's get a coffee to keep our voices lubricated."

They sat at one of the tables outside and Josie ordered two coffees and some pastries, while Stella listened in admiration.

"You speak Spanish really well now, Josie, I'm most impressed."

"Thank you. I can deal with most situations now and I like the language, I think that helps. Well, Stella, how's life treating you?"

Stella told her she was still enjoying her job at the builders' merchants, where she was now in charge of the office. Brian worked in a bank and was earning good money. They were saving hard and hoped to marry in September and put a deposit down on a house.

"Brian can get a mortgage through the bank at a good rate; otherwise we wouldn't be able to do it for at least another year. Will you come to the wedding, Josie, and be my bridesmaid? Please, please say you will."

"I have to see if we can afford it, but I would love to, Stella. I'll let you know as soon as possible. How exciting."

"Yes, it is. But how about you, Josie, have you overcome your fears now you are with Manuel?

"Well, Stella, it was pretty ghastly to begin with, but Manuel was so patient with me. Now I just accept it. But enjoy it? No, I'm afraid not. And I don't know why. Sometimes I think there must be something wrong with me."

"I'm sure there's not, Josie; it's only been two or three months. But are you still a bit scared?"

"Not really, it's difficult to explain. I just feel it's an invasion of my body and it shouldn't be happening."

"An invasion? I think I know what you mean. Don't give up, Josie; I'm sure it will come right. I can tell you, when two people love each other it's wonderful."

"I'm sure it is, and I won't give up. I don't want to lose Manuel."

The girls fell silent, then Josie paid for the coffees and pastries and they left the bar and walked towards the town.

"I'm going to take you to meet Lily and Maria and

show you where I work, then we'll come back and meet Brian and I'll take you to my home. Manuel finishes at 3pm today and he's managed to get the rest of the day off, so we can perhaps do something this evening?"

The café was quite busy, so the girls sat in the square until a lull allowed them to go and say hello to Lily and Maria.

"So this is Stella. I've heard so much about you, dear, and it's lovely to meet you at last. Maria, leave the dishes for a moment and come and say hello to Josie's friend."

Maria dried her hands and shook Stella's warmly. "*Bienvenido*, Stella."

They sat down and Josie said, "We'll just have a *cortado* please, Maria, as we've already had a coffee on the front."

Maria placed a small coffee in front of them and they were soon chatting away happily. But after only ten minutes, more customers were coming in and they hurriedly made arrangements to meet Lily later in the week. They were still rather early to meet Brian, so Josie took Stella round her favourite shops and plazas.

"I've been thinking, Stella, do you remember when we had that talk at St. Anne's about growing up? I think it was Mrs Reynolds who gave it, as far as I can remember."

"Goodness me, what a memory you've got, Josie. No, I don't remember it at all. Why?"

"Well, one thing sticks in my mind and that probably hasn't helped the way I am with men," she said. "'I know how girls love to flirt, but I want to warn you, some men may lose control if you flirt too much and then they can't stop. They may persuade you to do something you shouldn't, or may even force you.'"

"I don't remember that at all," Stella said.

"Well, I've never forgotten it. It's always been at the back of my mind. I know Mrs Reynolds meant well, but she frightened me."

Stella gave Josie's arm a squeeze. "Oh, that's so sad. Just don't give up, Josie; like I said earlier, I'm sure everything will come good in the end. Oh look, there's Brian waiting patiently."

After a simple lunch, Brian and the girls set off for the bus station. The bus dropped them off and they walked under the motorway and along the track to the villa. It was a lovely day, hot but not oppressive, with a pleasant breeze. The crickets were chirruping in the grass, competing with the sparrows flying amongst the orange trees. The scent from the orange blossom hung on the air. Stella was enthralled.

Then they walked round a bend in the track and there was Josie and Manuel's villa, freshly painted with cream paint and a new wooden door finishing off the effect. Josie felt rather proud. It was tiny, but perfectly respectable. The bathroom was completely finished and looked really good. The lounge and the bedroom were painted, but rather bare. It was difficult to decide which was most important: bedroom furniture or things for the lounge. But the kitchen was probably most vital to Josie. They had some cupboards now and the fridge was behaving, but the oven was very temperamental and there had been a few burnt offerings, and on other occasions, food not cooked! Thank goodness for the microwave. Most food could be finished off in there. However, Stella and Brian seemed impressed.

Josie showed them where the second bedroom was going to be and then brought some chairs outside so they could sit in the sun and wait for Manuel. Shortly before 4pm, Manuel appeared round the bend, his work bag on his shoulder and a bottle of water in his hand. His face broke out in a big smile and he waved cheerily. He kissed Josie; then hugged and kissed Stella, before shaking Brian's hand.

"It is good to see you again, Stella, and good to meet you, Brian. Are you enjoying your holiday?"

"Oh, it's lovely, Manuel, and what a gorgeous day. We love your villa. When I go home and I think of Josie, I will think of her here."

"We have much to do, but perhaps by this time next year everything will be finished. That is what we hope, isn't it, Josie?"

"Would you like a coffee, Manuel?" Josie made to rise from her chair.

"No, no, I will have a shower first. Excuse me please."

He smiled and went inside.

"He's just as nice as I remember him, Josie. No

need to look at me like that, Brian." Stella grinned at him. "You're quite safe."

The girls chuckled.

That evening the four of them went to a tapas bar and thoroughly enjoyed the food and each other's company. As Manuel and Josie walked back to the hotel with their friends, Stella hung back a few yards behind the men and said to Josie, "How can you not fancy Manuel? If I didn't love Brian, well…" She left the rest unsaid.

"But I do fancy him, Stella, and yet I don't want the other thing. Can't you understand?"

"No, frankly I can't, Josie. I'm surprised he hasn't packed you in. He's a very patient man, that's all I can say."

Josie sighed. "He did say it was like making love to a plank of wood the other day. I think he is getting fed up with me."

She shrugged and took Stella's arm and they caught up with the men, who were too busy talking themselves to notice the girls whispering behind them.

The week flew by, with Josie and Stella meeting up for a couple of hours on the Tuesday and Thursday. Then on Friday they all decided to go back to the tapas bar because they had enjoyed it so much. As they said goodbye, the girls hugged each other and both had tears in their eyes.

"Let me know about being a bridesmaid, Josie, and write to me soon."

"I will, have a good journey back."

Life settled down into its normal pattern. Manuel was very busy at the hotel and put in extra shifts. Josie was also very busy at the café. Both were too tired to work on the villa and things came to a halt, although they did purchase a new oven and other furniture during the summer, and when things started to quieten down in early September and the weather was slightly cooler, Manuel and Pablo began working on the second bedroom again.

But then in the middle of September, things happened which drastically changed Josie's life. Manuel came out of the shower late one evening and took Josie in his arms.

"Come to bed, *mi amor.* I need you."

"Oh, Manuel, not tonight, I've got a thumping headache."

Manuel pushed her away roughly. "Oh, it's a headache tonight. Last night you were too tired, before that, the wrong time of the month. It's three weeks now. I'm tired of waiting." He glared at her. "And when you agree you lie there like a dead body and can't wait to get rid of me. I've had enough. I'm going out. I don't know when I'll be back."

He stamped out of the villa and strode off down the track. Josie stood for some minutes staring at the door, and then flopped down in a chair. She knew she was to blame and yet felt unable to change. When Manuel still hadn't come home at midnight, she went to bed, but couldn't sleep. It must have been about an hour later when she heard him singing as he made his way home

195

and let himself in. She knew straight away he had been drinking and her heart plummeted. He came into the bedroom and put his face close to hers.

"It's all right; I shall not be needing you tonight."

He pushed her roughly to the very edge of the bed and collapsed fully clothed beside her, the reek of drink on his breath, and very soon he was asleep.

Josie lay awake for a long time, listening to his drunken snoring and sobbing with despair. He had tried so hard to stay off drink and not become like his father, but she had pushed him too far.

The next morning, neither spoke unless necessary and Josie went off to work with a heavy heart. She felt quite unable to talk to Lily about it, so ashamed was she. So she stitched a cheery smile onto her face and prayed for a busy day.

That evening Manuel didn't come home for his meal, and Josie couldn't eat. At 10pm she threw the food away, had a shower and went to bed. She was so exhausted that sleep claimed her almost at once. The next thing she knew, someone was shouting and shaking her. She put out her hand and switched on the bedside light. Manuel was swaying above her, his face contorted with anger and shouting abuse at her. Although he was using Spanish, she had a good idea what he was calling her. She could say nothing; it seemed impossible to speak or to move. Incensed by her lack of response, Manuel lost it completely. His hand struck her hard across the face, knocking her partially out of the bed. Then as she cringed and waited for another blow, he swore and stumbled out of the room. He crashed into the bathroom, then into the lounge. She heard the sound of the settee feet skidding on the tiled floor, and he flung himself down. Then the snoring started again. Josie turned her head into the pillow and sobbed as though her heart would break. Her face throbbed from the blow and she was terrified to go to sleep, but in the early hours, she fell into a deep sleep and only woke when Manuel came in for clean clothes.

When he saw she was awake, he came over and sat on the bed. Josie cringed, expecting him to hit her again, but instead he awkwardly patted her hand, and not meeting her eyes, muttered, "I'm sorry I hit you, Josie, but you have made me drink like my father, and then I am angry like him. You are to blame, Josie, but I shouldn't hit you. We will try again to be friends, yes?"

Josie nodded, and then swung her legs out of bed.

"I'll make some coffee."

For a week, there was an uneasy truce. Manuel made love to her once and Josie, in despair, pretended to enjoy it, but Manuel wasn't fooled. And then the following weekend, after a strained day at home, Manuel went back to the bar.

"I will only have two drinks, I promise," he said.

But the hours went by, and Josie finally went to bed. But this time she took a stick with her, she was so frightened, and lay in the darkness waiting for him to come home. As before, it was about 1am when she heard his noisy approach. The front door crashed open and slammed shut, then the bedroom door opened. Josie reached down for the stick just as Manuel turned on the bedroom light. For several moments they stared at each other, Josie sitting up in bed, terrified and shaking, the stick clutched in her hand; Manuel hanging onto the door for support, his eyes like a madman's. He roared and lurched towards her and wrenched the stick from her hand as though she had the strength of a baby. He flung it to the floor, then began to beat her. He dragged her from the bed and slapped her around the head, this way and that way, till she thought her neck would snap. The last slap sent her flying across the room, where she landed with a crash on the floor, her head just an inch from the wall. He looked at her for several minutes, then flung himself from the room.

Josie barely slept that night. Her head and arm throbbed painfully and she couldn't stop shaking. All was quiet in the living room, except for loud snoring from time to time. When the snoring was its loudest, Josie crept back into the kitchen and made a mug of coffee and took it back to bed. The sun was up and it was a lovely day, but Josie was oblivious to the weather – to everything. All she could do was sip her coffee and stare unseeingly at the wall. When, half an hour later, the door opened gently and Manuel entered the room cautiously, Josie barely looked his way. His shocked gaze took in the sight in front of him. Josie's eyes were swollen and nearly closed; her face black and blue and her hair in a tangled mess. Manuel sat on the bed and buried his head in his hands, sobbing uncontrollably.

He couldn't speak for some time; then he raised his head and looked at Josie in anguish.

"I'm so sorry, *mi amor*. How could I do this when I love you so much? Can you ever forgive me?"

Josie didn't reply because, no, she couldn't forgive him, but was too frightened to say so. She had been moved by his tears, however, and knew he was genuinely sorry. He was like two separate people, one gentle and loving; the other like a wild animal, completely out of control. Now he sat at the foot of the bed, an expression of hopelessness on his face.

"I have the weakness of my father, Josie, but I will see the doctor next week and see if he can help me. I don't know what else to do."

He looked at her, then looked away quickly, the sight of her injured face too much to bear. "Let me get you some breakfast, Josie, would you like some scrambled eggs?" He knew it was one of her favourites.

"I couldn't eat anything, but I would like another cup of coffee, please."

"Are you sure, *mi amor*"

"Yes, quite sure, I think food would make me feel ill."

Manuel nodded and left the room. Josie ate nothing that day and didn't get up or get dressed; she just felt too ill.

She slept a little better that night, and woke late. Manuel was on split shifts this week, from 7 to 11am and 7 to 11pm. She had an hour or so before he arrived home, so carefully showered and washed her hair, using her one good hand and arm, then feeling refreshed and suddenly very hungry, cooked herself some bacon and eggs for a late breakfast. Knowing that Manuel would soon be home, she made a pot of coffee and sat down in comfort on the settee to drink it. She heard his footsteps on the path and the door swung open. He came over to her, a huge bunch of flowers in his hands. He studied her face, and his eyes welled up with tears again.

"How do you feel today?"

"A little better, thank you," Josie said politely. "I have had some breakfast, but everything is still so painful." She touched her arm and her cheek with her fingertips. "If it's no better tomorrow you will have to take me to the hospital for X-rays, in case my arm is fractured, or my cheekbone."

Manuel looked really worried. "What will you say to them? Will you tell them that I beat you?"

"No, but they will probably guess, especially if they remember your parents."

Manuel was silent. What could he say?

That afternoon, Manuel couldn't do enough for her, bringing her food and drink, helping her outside to sit in the sun for a while, and making sure she had everything she needed, before going back to work for the late shift.

After he had gone, Josie sat thinking for a long time. She wasn't sure how she felt about Manuel anymore, and couldn't really see that there was any future for them. Suddenly, making a decision, she eased herself out of the settee and pulled open the left-hand drawer of the sideboard. This was where they kept all their paperwork. Lifting it all out and taking it back to the settee, she went through every single receipt, form and leaflet. There wasn't really anything of any importance to her personally, except her birth certificate and passport. Finding a loose elastic band, she put them together and tucked them at the back of the drawer, then piled everything back untidily as it had been before. She stood thinking for a moment, then found a notepad and a biro and started a list:

- *Passport*
- *Birth certificate*
- *Photos*
- *Money*
- *Pad and pen.*

She moved around each room of the villa, adding to the list and making brief notes. The photo of Stella and herself, but not the frame, she wrote. The list was surprisingly long. By this time she was beginning to feel very tired and achy, so after tucking the list into a drawer under her underwear, she prepared herself for bed.

The next morning, Manuel left as usual at 6.30am. Josie pretended to still be asleep, but as soon as she heard him walk away, she eased herself out of bed. She'd had a much better night and had even slept for a short time on her left side, the side with the worst bruises. As soon as she got up, she knew there were no bones broken or fractured, thank goodness. After she had eaten some breakfast, she did some washing and hung it on the line. As yet, they hadn't managed to save enough for a washing machine, so dirty clothes would be soaked in a bucket the night before and then washed and rinsed and hung to drip, and finally dry, outdoors. She was just hanging the last thing out when she was aware of someone coming round the bend in the track. To her dismay she realised it was Manuel's sister, Angelina. There was no time to hide; she just had to stand there and wait for Angelina to approach. Angelina's eyes widened with horror when she saw Josie's face, and for some minutes she seemed unable to say anything. Then realisation dawned.

"Oh Josie, Manuel, he do this?"

"Yes, I'm afraid so. Don't blame him completely, Angelina, I have not been good to him and it has made him drink, and well, you know from your papa what happens next!"

"He tells me, Josie has flu, and I think I come and see how you are and maybe help you."

The young ladies walked inside and Josie put the kettle on.

"It is very bad, what is he going to do, Josie?"

"He says he's going to the doctor, but I don't know what he can do."

They sat sipping their coffee, but Angelina was ill at ease and obviously didn't know what else to say. She would have liked to ask Josie in what way wasn't she good to her brother, but didn't feel she could. She got up to leave.

"I not say anything to Manuel. I not tell him I been here." She gently kissed Josie. "Take care. I see you soon."

With that, she left and Josie began to prepare lunch. As she worked, her mind went over the last few days. For the first twenty-four hours after Manuel had attacked her, she had felt incapable of even thinking. But since then, her mind never seemed to rest. She had decided almost at once that she wasn't going to allow herself to be beaten over and over again, as Manuel's mother had. *If he comes home drunk like that again and threatens me, I'm off, even if he doesn't actually touch me*, she had thought. *I've heard say the longer you put up with it, the harder it is to leave.* Easier said than done, though, with so little money of her own, and absolutely no chance of paying for a flight home to England if that's where she wanted to be. She decided the best thing she could do was take as much as she could carry and get as far away as possible.

So engrossed was she in her thought and plans that she didn't hear Manuel until he came in the door. She jumped, startled, her eyes wide. Manuel had the grace to look ashamed. They spent an uneasy few hours together, then Manuel went back to work. Josie spent the evening going through every cupboard and drawer, adding to her list, and making decisions about what to take and what to leave behind. Everything had to go in her backpack, and maybe to begin with a couple of carrier bags with food. The backpack had been purchased from the market some months ago to carry groceries from the shops up the hill to the villa. It was very roomy, with two extra pockets in the main bit, another smaller zipped compartment on the outside, and another zipped pocket inside. There was a netted piece on each side for carrying water bottles and some straps with buckles, probably meant to hold a small tent in place. Also, another pocket for maps. Manuel had laughed at her when she'd bought it, but it was going to be so useful now… if Manuel continued to be abusive.

Josie had always been a bit of a tomboy with her clothing, and her wardrobe and drawers were full of practical items such as trousers, shorts and t-shirts. So now she decided what she would take. Jeans were too heavy and too difficult to wash and dry; cotton trousers were best. Things she decided to take went on the right and the remainder on the left. She had one pair of trainers which were beginning to get scruffy, and another new pair to take. She sorted out four t-shirts, two jumpers three pairs of trousers and one anorak. Next she went through all the drawers again, putting stuff to the right and left as before. She looked in the kitchen as well, deciding to take a set of cutlery, a sharp knife and a pair of scissors; also a mug and plate. There were some plastic ones that would do nicely. Finally she went to Manuel's clothes drawers. She wasn't too sure why, but it was the last place to check and maybe something of hers might have been put there by mistake. Taking care not to move things from their allotted place, she searched thoroughly through the three drawers. In the bottom one, were several jumpers which Manuel rarely wore. Josie glanced in, and then closed the drawer. But something was catching. She pulled it open again and reached to the back. Her fingers closed round a roll of paper.

Ah, old receipts, she thought. Pulling it out, she gasped. It was a roll of peseta notes, all different values, from small 50s to 500s. Straight away, without any feelings of guilt, she knew she would, if possible, be taking some of that with her. Satisfied with her evening, she showered and prepared for bed.

Wednesday began as every other day, with Manuel up and gone by 6.30am, and as the day before, Josie got up as soon as he had left. She went into the bathroom and studied herself in the mirror. Her eyes were getting back to normal, but the bruises now were a lovely shade of yellow! Only her cheek was still black and blue, but less painful. After some toast and coffee, she went outside to the old outhouse, where everything that might come in useful was thrown. Cardboard boxes, bits of wood, spare tiles and bits of packaging, garden tools and half-used tins of paint. Josie's eyes soon picked out what she was looking for: the plastic cover that the mattress had been in. Clearing a space on the floor, she cut a big square from one side of it, then folded the remainder up and put it back where she had found it. Pushed inside a box was a roll of plastic foam, which had been round the new oven. She laid the plastic on the floor, folded it over, then folded the foam over in the same way and laid it on top, then rolled them up together. She found two pieces of string and tied a piece round each end.

"That's my bedroll!"

Tucking it away at the back of the building and out of sight, she went back into the villa for a cup of coffee. She decided that when Manuel came home, lunch would be ready and she would be innocently cleaning the bathroom. In the event all Manuel did was stare at her yellow face and look guilty.

Thursday was dull and cloudy, with light rain from time to time, and Josie spent most of the day watching TV and reading. Already the yellow bruising seemed to be fading, and Josie was young and healthy and recovering fast. She was cool but polite with Manuel, while he was crawling and couldn't do enough for her. The week seemed to be speeding by and tomorrow was Saturday. Josie's heart gave a great lurch every time she thought about it. How would Manuel be tomorrow? Would he stick to his word and not drink, or would he not be able to help himself? Josie was a realist, and she thought the latter. But she would be ready for him, ready to defend herself and ready to flee. Her plan for today was to clean the villa from front to back, make sure all the washing and ironing was up to date and tidy up outside. She also decided to bake some cakes. She would make sure Manuel couldn't fault her on her domestic skills. She also decided to be a bit warmer towards him, to maybe help him to stay off the drink. Although her feelings towards him had changed, she was prepared to give it another try.

Manuel was supposed to be off work on Saturdays, but he had offered to do overtime this weekend, probably to keep out of Josie's way. Josie made him a nice lunch when he came home and tried to behave in a more affectionate way, but Manuel was wary. He left before he needed to for the later shift, saying he had shopping to do.

"I will be seeing some friends after work, Josie, but only for an hour or so, and I won't be drinking, I promise."

"That's good, you have a nice time and I'll see you later," Josie replied with a smile.

For the rest of the day Josie couldn't relax. She sat down, then got up again, walked round the garden and amongst the orange and lemon trees, came back indoors and made herself a drink and wandered around the villa drinking it. The time dragged by, and at 10pm she showered, washed her hair and went to bed. Eleven, then twelve passed by; then one o'clock. Sleep eluded her and her heart thumped as she tossed and turned. At 1.30am a car drew up outside and there were loud goodbyes, then the car drove off. The door burst open and crashed shut. It didn't take much working out that Manuel was drunk again – very drunk. Josie leapt out of bed and grabbed her stick, a look of determination on her face. In her other hand she had an insect spray, which she fully intended to spray in his face if necessary, as she had intended all those years ago with Mr Shenstone.

The noise of Manuel's entry was followed by a short silence and then the sound of something falling and a chair going over; then silence again. How long Josie stood by the bed, she had no idea, but after some time had passed she crept towards the bedroom door and quietly opened it.

Manuel was curled up on the floor, completely out of it in a drunken sleep. Josie gave a long sigh of relief and her head dropped forward. For a second or two the world tilted and she sat down with a thump in the other chair. She took a few deep breaths; then stretched out her leg and gently nudged Manuel's arm. He didn't move. He'd broken his promise, as she'd known he would. If she hadn't triggered this weakness in him, something or somebody else would have done, and a part of her felt dreadfully sorry for him. Then adrenalin kicked in. She jumped up and fetched her backpack, and list in hand, began to fill it, aware that things were going in higgledy-piggledy, but not caring. She pulled her jacket on and stuffed things in the pockets. Then she found a couple of carrier bags, putting the rest of her clothes in one and food and water in the other. Bread, cheese, biscuits, a piece of cold meat, some chocolate – whatever she saw. Then she grabbed a torch and a tattered map of the area and pushed them in another pocket. In her haste she knocked a table mat to the floor.

Manuel stirred and mumbled, while Josie held her breath. Manuel flung out an arm; then was still again.

As Josie stared at him she noticed money sticking out of his inside jacket pocket. Very slowly and carefully she removed it and pushed all of it into her coat pocket, then felt guilty and left a couple of notes by the kettle. She hesitated; then slipped off her engagement ring and left it beside the money. She thought for a moment and checked her list once more, then remembered the money in his drawer. In no time at all, most of that was tucked snugly into her trouser pocket. Right, just the bedroll to go.

She cast a last look around the villa that had been her home for the last seven months, then stepped quietly from the house and walked over to the outhouse. With no spare hands she just had to take a couple of minutes to strap the bedroll onto her backpack, and then for some reason she wasn't sure of, she picked up a ball of twine and rammed that into her backpack. She stepped out of the building and closed the door. By the light of her torch, she could see it was after 3am. Now to put some distance between herself and Manuel was uppermost in her mind. She scrambled up the slope behind the villa until she found an animal track, and with the sea on her right, she headed north. Josie walked as fast as she dared along the rough track. Sometimes the track went over rocks and through scrub, and she had to slow down. Other times it was good and she could trot. After a couple of hours she sat down and rested. Taking two t-shirts from her backpack, she twisted them round the handles of the carrier bags, which were beginning to make her hands sore. After a quick drink of water, she set off again. The track led her onto a minor road, and this made for easier walking. Here the coast jutted out into the sea and she had already decided to cut that corner, so the sea was lost to view. So it was with some relief that she spotted the lights of a town ahead and knew she was on the right track.

The sky was lightening, and it was time to find somewhere to rest. Scrabbling up a hill to a rocky outcrop, she found a corner away from the road where she could curl up and maybe doze for a while. Opening up her bedroll and lying down with her head resting on the carrier bag of clothes and her backpack tucked safely behind her, she closed her eyes. *I'll never sleep* was her last thought, and then she slept!

The sound of a lorry on the road woke her some time later, and looking at her watch, she realised she had been asleep for about three hours. She was stiff and one arm was numb, but the sleep had refreshed her and now rumbles reminded her she'd hardly eaten yesterday. She sat up and rubbed her arm as the feeling returned. Using her knife, she cut slices from the cheese and made a chunky cheese sandwich. Never had anything tasted so good. This was followed by a long drink of water. She then rinsed her face and cleaned her teeth. It was now late morning and it was probably wise to stay out of sight.

Looking around at her possessions, in fact all she had in the world, it seemed a good time to repack her clothes more tidily and have a look to see exactly how much money she had. The spare shoes could go in the bottom of the backpack, then her undies, some tucked into the shoes. Next she carefully rolled up her spare trousers, trying to press out some of the creases incurred during the night. Next the fleeces, then lastly the t-shirts, also rolled up. This time, packed carefully, all her clothing fitted into the main part of the backpack. In the smaller compartment went her toiletries and sun cream and the spare carrier bag; also the torch and several other small items. Her passport and birth certificate and the photo of her and Stella went in the pocket of the main compartment. Her water bottle went in the net on the side. To even out the weight a bit, she put the biscuits on the other side with her mug. That left just the plate and cutlery, which just about squeezed in with the torch. Now she had just one carrier bag with food in it. She could swap that from left to right and one hand would always be free.

Satisfied with her packing, she took all the money out of various hidey-holes and weighed it down with a stone while she decided the best places to keep it. Perhaps 10,000 pesetas in the inside pocket of the rucksack, some more notes in the inside pocket of her jacket, and the rest in her trouser pocket. So it was with some surprise, after counting it, that she discovered she had much more than she thought , so she spread it around as best she could, deciding that in a few days when she was well away from Benidorm, a money belt might be a sensible purchase.

She leaned back and nibbled on the lump of meat, knowing that if it wasn't eaten today it would have to be thrown away. She got the tattered map out and carefully unfolded it. A lot of last night's walk had been uphill, and she was now wondering if she'd chosen the best route. Certainly it was longer round the coast, but at least it was mainly flat and she couldn't lose her way. But fear of being found by Manuel or the *Guardia*, as she had stolen his money, made her decide to stick to this route. She reckoned that in two or three days at the most she would be back at the coast. *But I need to alter my appearance*, she thought. She had a t-shirt that had never been worn, but her hair was rather an unusual golden brown colour and always in bunches – easily recognisable. Making a sudden, brave decision, she took her scissors from her bag and a small mirror from her make-up bag and propping it on a rock, started to snip away.

It took quite a time before she was happy, then taking the carrier bag from around her shoulders and shaking the hair away, she walked away from the rock and ruffled her hand through her hair until all loose trimmings were gone. She couldn't resist having another look in the mirror, and chuckled as she looked at her reflection. She looked a sight, but hopefully a wash would improve it. Also, as the sun-bleached curls had been cut away, at a glance her hair looked darker and this would help to make her look different. She sat back and tried to relax before the night-time walking, and did manage to doze for a while. As the sun went down, she finished off the meat in a sandwich and ate an apple, then brushed her teeth. She had read somewhere that if you neglected your teeth, they could become loose and possibly fall out, so cleaning them had become a priority.

Because of the climate, it was normal practice for the Spanish to have a long siesta during the afternoon, then work in the evening, eating late at nine; even ten o'clock at night. Things didn't quieten down till the small hours, and because of this, Josie decided that over the next few weeks her walking must mainly be done between midnight and daylight. It would make progress slower, but couldn't be helped. The time dragged until she felt ready to leave. As she thought, the going was tough, the road twisting and turning and mainly heading uphill. If a vehicle came along she hid in the bushes or behind rocks, but there were very few cars about for her to worry much. There was no noticeable track that she could safely use, so that was just asking to get lost.

She plodded on till the sky began to lighten, then found herself on the edge of a town high up in the mountains, with magnificent views over the countryside. Here the countryside was wooded in some areas, so scrambling through the undergrowth, she managed to find a good place to spend the day. The biggest problem now was the shortage of water. A walk into the town was unavoidable, and sooner rather than later. So after having something to eat and a rest, she dropped down the quarter-mile or so into the town and purchased two bottles of water and a loaf of bread, then returned to her resting place amongst the trees.

CHAPTER 10

Three days later, she was back at the coast, but very wary. Using minor roads, tracks and paths wherever possible, she came to the town of Gandia. Here the River Serpis made its way to the sea, but as most of the water was diverted for irrigation, it was only a trickle, about three feet wide. Josie followed the river inland and into the countryside. There she rested for three days and two nights, washing clothes out and hanging them on bushes overnight to dry, and washing herself from top to bottom. It was a delight to wash her hair, now so short, run her comb through it and leave it to dry into tight curls close to her head. Her base for the two nights was a tumbledown building, probably used for storage many years ago, but now swallowed up in the undergrowth and hidden from view.

At the end of the third day, rested and clean, she set off once more. Again travelling mainly by night and resting by day, she followed the coast, sometimes making use of toilets in bars and buying food and drink when necessary. The miles slowly went by. The roads were now mainly at sea level and very flat, so easy walking, but with very little vegetation it was hard to find somewhere to sleep. One day she slept on the beach amongst some dunes; another day behind a caravan in a campsite. Then in the distance, she could see a big city, Valencia. Not confident enough to walk through the city at night, she rested and waited for the dawn. Still staying as close to the sea as possible, she walked right through the city, on edge and hating every minute of it. She desperately needed a few days' rest, and so she walked inland a little, knowing that there were plenty of abandoned buildings that would be good enough, preferably by a stream or river, and two days later she found the ideal place.

Once more she stayed two nights, and then walked on. The money was slowly diminishing, but by eating simple food, bread and cheeses mainly, and fruit, it was lasting well. A bag of chips was also a very welcome change of diet once or twice a week. Passing through large and small towns and villages, there were often street markets where she could buy things even cheaper. In one market she purchased a money belt and a pair of socks to replace a pair that had developed holes.

On the first day of November, Josie came to another big river and once again had to follow it inland for several miles before coming to a suitable area to camp for a few nights. She had a small bottle amongst her belongings, which she kept filled up with liquid soap from various service areas and toilets. She used this for everything – washing herself and her hair, and washing clothes. She spent the next two days making full use of it. It was now getting cooler and washing in cold water was not very pleasant, but needs must. She walked back to the coast and through a large town, resting that night under a motorway bridge.

The next day the road led her towards a village and she looked for a bakers, needing some more bread. In the centre of the village there were half a dozen shops and a bar restaurant. One of the shops was a bakers, but as she approached the door, a woman came out, looking flustered. She closed and locked the door behind her.

"I'm sorry," she said, "I have to close for half an hour to pick up my children. My mother is ill and cannot manage the shop for me today."

"I'm not in a hurry," Josie replied, thankful that she now spoke good Spanish. "I'll wait till you get back." She smiled at the lady and sat down on a low wall, easing her backpack off her shoulders and placing it on the pavement. Soon the young woman reappeared, holding onto a child's hand on each side; a little boy of about six and a girl about two years older. They smiled shyly at Josie as their mother unlocked the shop door again. They all stepped inside and Josie waited patiently while they were given a drink and a biscuit.

"I'm sorry to keep you waiting. What would you like?"

"I'd like a small loaf, please, and one of those lovely pastries."

The transaction was completed and Josie turned to leave the shop, then turned back and smiled at the young mother.

"I am staying locally for a few weeks and I'm looking for work. Can I be of any help to you?"

"Oh, I can't afford to employ anyone, but thank you anyway."

Josie hesitated, then said, "I wouldn't want much money, just some food at the end of the day – whatever is left over. I'm honest and hardworking and I have been working in a café until recently, so I know a little about the food you sell. Please, let me help you tonight, then if you aren't satisfied, I'll just move on."

The young lady suddenly flopped into a chair and closed her eyes for a few moments, a look of desperation on her face. "I really am in need of some help. I don't know you, so I must ask you not to use the till, but I can certainly find you plenty of other things to do. Are you English?"

"Yes, I am, but I've been living here for some time so I'm familiar with how things are done and I'm fairly good with Spanish."

"You are very good with Spanish, and my name is Isabella, by the way. Please take your bags out the back and I will find you an apron."

Josie did as she was asked, thankful that she and her clothes were clean. Three days ago it would have been a different story!

"I'm Josie, and I'm taking a break and doing some walking and exploring other parts of Spain, but I'll be glad to have something different to do for a few days."

She slipped on the apron and Isabella asked her to wash up some tins while she put some pastries in

218

the tiny oven. Customers came and went regularly, all enquiring after Isabella's mother and obviously knowing the family well. In the quiet moments Isabella explained how she kept everything clean, and also how much she baked to make sure it was all fresh. She also had a little sideline – local housewives would bring along their bread dough in tins ready to bake and Isabella would bake them to be picked up later. There was only a small charge for this, but it all helped.

By the time the evening was halfway through, Josie and Isabella were quite relaxed with each other. Isabella was visibly easier in her mind when she could see that Josie was hardworking and good with the customers. The children were as good as gold, the little boy Sergio, playing with his cars and his sister Donna, with her crayons and colouring book.

"So where are you staying, Josie?"

"I haven't found anywhere yet. I'll have a look round when we close. Can you recommend somewhere? It will have to be very cheap."

"Well, I only know of one place in the village and I wouldn't recommend it." Isabella gave Josie a worried look.

"Oh, don't worry, I'll just camp. I'm used to doing that. And would it be all right if I have a wash out the back?" She waved her hand in the direction of the toilet.

"Of course, but how have you been managing?"

Josie went on to explain how she coped with personal hygiene and doing her washing, omitting to tell Isabella that this only happened about every four or five days! Isabella was obviously horrified, but made no comment. Josie had already learned that Isabella's husband had been killed in a car crash two years earlier and his insurance had enabled her to start up the bakery and to keep her own little home going. She told Josie she lived in a small terraced, two-bedroomed house, and that she was worried about what she would do when the children got older and wanted a bedroom of their own.

"Maybe I will marry again, but at the moment I can't bear the thought of another man." She gave a little shiver. "I loved my husband very much and I still miss him and so does Donna, although I don't think Sergio remembers him."

She sighed as she lifted some pastries from the oven. Josie was surprised how many people came in during the evening, but at 9pm Isabella closed the blinds and cashed up, while Josie did the last-minute tidy-up and sweep. The children were getting tired and miserable, so their mother quickly locked up and set off for home with Josie alongside. Isabella let herself into her home, smiled at Josie and wished her *"Buenos noches."*

Setting off towards the edge of the village, Josie looked for somewhere to spend the night. Once away from the streetlights it was very dark, and she was just beginning to get desperate when she saw a house with a large carport to one side. Two cars were parked there, side by side, and there was plenty of space behind for her to spend the night. But lights were on in the house, and people's voices floated out. Best to wait a bit, Josie thought. She walked further up the road and sat on a rock and ate some leftover food Isabella had given her, then brushed her teeth and settled down to wait.

The bakers opened at 9.30am and Josie was waiting outside when Isabella arrived. They greeted each other and went inside. Isabella immediately put on the oven and took some uncooked baguettes from the freezer. Meanwhile Josie slipped into the toilet and washed and brushed her teeth, before returning to help. Isabella smiled at her.

"I hope you found somewhere to camp."

"Yes, I did, thank you."

But Josie wasn't going to say where. Very soon the first customers began to trickle in, and they were kept busy. At 1pm Josie was told to sit out the back and have some lunch. Isabella toasted some of yesterday's baguettes and Josie ate the bread with some of her own cheese.

"As I'm only paying you a little, Josie, I would like to give you a proper meal in the evening. I'm sure you can't be eating properly if you are camping, and I don't see any camping stove."

This was just what Josie was hoping for, and then the small amount Isabella was paying her could mostly be put aside for when she continued her walk. Isabella explained that the children finished school in the early afternoon, and yesterday a neighbour had picked them up and taken them to her home to play with some friends. Then Isabella had picked them up from there while Josie had waited outside the shop. In the meantime, for the three hours the shop was closed, Isabella had hurried home to do some chores and put her feet up for a while. Today, though, she would be picking the children up from school after she had closed and taking them home for some lunch and a rest, then bringing them back with her when she reopened. Not an ideal situation, but it couldn't be avoided.

"What are you going to do for three hours, Josie?"

"Oh, I'll just explore the village and the area."

Isabella laughed. "That won't take you long, it's only small." She waved and walked briskly down the road to pick up the children.

First of all, Josie walked towards the sea, which was about half a mile away. It was a beautiful beach, long and straight, stretching away into the distance. To her left, as she faced the sea, was an almost deserted campsite with caravans, mainly closed up for the winter, and one or two tents that were obviously in use. A small group of buildings at one end appeared to be a toilet and shower block, with a small shop and café nearby, both closed up as far as she could see. To her right were miles of sand and dunes. Josie retraced her steps to where the village began and walked down the narrow streets with their small terraced houses, then turned and crossed over the road she had come in on. The villas on the other side were larger and most of them detached, but by no means luxurious. She walked briskly, as though she had a purpose and somewhere to go. No way did she want to appear to be loitering, but still taking in everything. Then she turned inland towards the busy coast road. Here there were a few industrial buildings and a garage, but nowhere suitable to spend the night. Walking back, she explored the other end of the village. There were some abandoned greenhouses, the ground covered in broken glass and weeds, but to one side a shed, its door open and hanging awkwardly. This was the only shelter she had seen, and from here there was no guessing what may be inside it. A sudden sharp longing for a comfortable bed and a hot shower assailed Josie, and she sighed and began to make her way back to the shop.

I'll probably have to go back to the carport tonight, she thought, *but what about washing clothes? I can hardly have knickers hanging about at the back of the shop! I'll just have to wash them there, then drape them over the cars tonight and hope they dry.*

She sat down on the wall outside the shop and waited for Isabella, Sergio and Donna to appear.

It was quiet in the shop that evening, and Josie was able to spend some time getting to know the children better. She pretended she could hardly speak Spanish and they must help her. She purposely said things wrong and misunderstood what they were saying to her. The children were highly amused by this, and Isabella smiled as she listened to the laughter coming from the back room. At 9pm on the dot, the door was locked and they set off down the road.

"Are you camping in the same place tonight, Josie?" Isabella asked.

"I'm not sure. It wasn't ideal, and the campsite on the beach looked all closed up. But don't worry about me. I'll be all right."

They walked on for some minutes; then Isabella broke the silence.

"If you don't mind sleeping on the sofa or on the floor you can stay with me, Josie. I don't like to think of you out there alone, sleeping goodness knows where. If you stay with me you can have nice showers and I can put your clothes in the washing machine with mine. What do you think?"

Josie couldn't answer for some minutes, and was glad of the darkness so that Isabella couldn't see her tears.

"How kind you are. I would really like to do that. But promise me you will say if you want me to leave."

"I will, but I'm sure we'll get along fine, and the children love you already, otherwise I wouldn't have suggested it. Come with us now, and I will show you my little home and we'll have something to eat."

The front door opened straight into the living room, which was a reasonable size, being the dining room as well. Through the back was a small kitchen with a small patio to one side, with a rotary clothes airer full of clothes, blowing in the breeze; then a small, rather rough piece of ground with some plastic garden chairs and a small table, and some toys lying about. Isabella had switched the oven on as they came through the kitchen, and taken a large pizza from the fridge. Then she took

Josie upstairs, where there were two bedrooms and a bathroom. Everything was neat and tidy, and the house had a nice atmosphere. Isabella took a spare blanket and pillow from a cupboard and they made their way back downstairs. She popped the pizza and some chips in the oven; then they all sat down and waited for the food to cook. After they had eaten, Isabella took the children upstairs and bathed them, read them a story and tucked them up in bed. In the meantime, Josie washed up and said a prayer of thanks for her good fortune.

"Thank you for washing up, Josie; you must say when you are ready to shower. Do you mind showering in the evening, and then I can shower in the morning? I can see you are very tired, so just go to bed when you are ready. I have some paperwork to do in my bedroom – I use it as an office as well, so you can sleep whenever you like."

"You are right, Isabella, I'm exhausted. I will go and shower straight away."

"You can call me Bella. All my friends do, and I prefer it, really."

They walked upstairs to the bathroom and Bella explained how to get the best out of the shower, then giving Josie two towels, she disappeared downstairs. Oh, the bliss of a hot shower. Josie enjoyed every second, and was almost reluctant to step out of it. Then she partially dressed again in clean underwear and a clean t-shirt, and went downstairs, a big smile on her face.

"That was wonderful, thank you, Bella."

"I'm going up now, Josie. *Buenos nochas*; sleep well."

The sofa was rather short, so Josie used her bedroll, opening it out on the carpet, then laying the blanket on it. She then lay down, pulled the other half of the blanket over her, nestled into the soft pillow and was almost instantly asleep.

It seemed only a short time later when Josie was woken by whispered voices and the sound of running water. For a few seconds she lay there, confused. Where was she? What was happening? Then she remembered. She stretched and opened her eyes to see two pairs of eyes smiling back at her.

"*Hola*, Josie." Donna smiled, while Sergio hung back, just a little shy again this morning. "Why have you got your clothes on in bed, Josie?"

Bella swung round from making the coffee. "Don't be rude, Donna."

"It's OK." Josie chuckled. "You see, Donna, I haven't got room for pyjamas in my bag, so I have to sleep in a t-shirt."

Donna seemed satisfied with this answer and stepped back as Josie tidied up her blanket and bedroll and tucked them away behind the sofa. Then she grabbed her clothes for the day and ran upstairs to the bathroom to dress and freshen up.

And so the four of them slipped into a routine. Josie did all she could around the house, and did most of the ironing. She also shared the cooking. They decided to have their main meal in the afternoon and just a snack in the evening, and this worked very well. Several days passed by, then Bella came back from seeing her mother and told Josie that she was to have an operation in three weeks' time. She tried to explain what for and indicated that it was quite serious, but not life-threatening. From what she could gather, Josie thought it might be a hysterectomy. Her mother was to take it easy before the operation and for several months after.

"So, Josie, do you think you could stay for another few months?"

"I would be delighted to, Bella."

"My mama wants to meet you. She will worry until she does."

Bella's mother was not old, as she and Bella had both married and had their children while still young. Bella was now only twenty-eight and her mother, Adella, was going to be fifty on the 26th December. Hopefully she would be out of hospital in time for Christmas.

It was with some trepidation that Josie, along with Bella and the children, set off the following Sunday morning. But Josie need not have worried. After a few minutes of awkwardness she seemed to be accepted. Bella's parents even insisted she called them by their Christian names, much to her surprise, so Adella and Gregorio they became, and over the next few weeks, Josie was to become very fond of them. They lived in one of the detached villas she had walked past when exploring the village. It was nicely furnished but homely inside, and the garden simply landscaped but tidy. They drank coffee and ate pastries and chatted, then left for home so that Adella and Gregorio could have their meal and then rest.

Soon, Josie was helping with the baking and using the till. She felt really well, and barely gave Manuel a thought. That part of her life was over, and now, although she was quite content, the thought of England and home, and the distance she had to cover, was never far from her mind.

In mid-November, Adella went into hospital for her operation. Now Bella was helping to look after Gregorio as well, and it was a hectic time for her. Josie would look after the children when she visited, and try and do most jobs so that Bella only had paperwork to think about when she got back from the hospital. One evening, when she got home and had put the children to bed, she told Josie that she wanted a chat.

"I haven't said anything yet to Mama and Papa, but I wondered how it would be if you agreed to move in with them when Mama comes out of hospital," she began. "I'm sure we could work something out with work and the children, and it would only be for a few weeks, I'm sure."

"Well, yes, I wouldn't mind. But I'm not sure how they will feel about it."

Josie was a bit doubtful. They sat and discussed it for the next hour, trying to work things around the shop, Gregorio's work hours and the children, until finally they were ready to put the idea to Bella's parents.

"They have two spare bedrooms, so that wouldn't

be a problem, but although they are my parents, I'm not sure what they will say!" Then she chuckled. "They will try to make you fat, you can be sure of that! When you first came here, you were so thin, you looked ill."

Josie remembered the first time she had used Bella's bathroom, and how horrified she had been on catching sight of herself in the mirror. It made her realise that her diet when she was walking was totally inadequate. Bread, cheese and an apple several times a day at best was just not enough. But still, no point in worrying now. She was going nowhere until the New Year.

As December arrived, Adella came out of hospital and Josie moved into their villa. There had been no opposition from Adella, but Gregorio thought he could manage. Bella soon put him right.

"What's going to happen with Mama while you are out at work? She will be trying to do the things she normally does, and then she will make herself ill. Please, Papa, let Josie come here, just for a few weeks till Mama gets her strength back."

He had to agree it made sense. Now Josie settled into her bedroom, while Bella and the children went to pick up Adella from the hospital. She finished putting her clothes away and then put the kettle on. Sitting on a chair where she could watch the road, Josie waited for the family to return.

It was Christmas, and the villa was filled with music and laughter and the excited cries of the children. Was it really only a year ago that Josie had spent Christmas at Juan's parents' home? It seemed much longer than that – so much had happened, and now her life had changed and would change again in a few weeks' time. Part of her wanted to stay here, but a bigger part wanted to move on, northwards and towards home.

Towards the end of January, that time arrived. Adella was making a good recovery. Josie had stayed there as there was more room, and so still helped around the house. Adella was managing a few hours in the shop, and also having the children sometimes. Bella felt they could now manage. The friendship between the two women had deepened, and it was a sad parting as Josie set off again, backpack full and with carrier bags tied on either side with food – enough to feed an army! They had promised to keep in touch and Bella had given Josie four stamped addressed envelopes and a writing pad, so there was no excuse. If Josie had other breaks in her journey to work and earn some money, she would forward her address so that Bella could reply. Bella had made Josie a more comfortable bedroll and bought her a tin opener as a parting gift. It was not possible to carry a stove for hot food and drink and all the other items necessary to use it, but Josie had promised to buy tinned meat and vegetables and just eat them cold.

CHAPTER 11

Josie walked for a week, stopping every three or four days to wash herself thoroughly and also wash her clothes. Sometimes she would sleep in deserted campsites, sometimes in abandoned buildings and sometimes under motorway bridges. In that respect, everything was as before. The food she had been given lasted for almost a week and then she had to buy more. A tin of meatballs was cheap and would last two days, and vegetables the same. Most days this would be her main meal, with bread and cheese for her breakfast and in the evening. It certainly made her feel better, and more energetic. Now always travelling in daylight and sleeping at night, fifteen to twenty kilometres a day was the norm. Then one night, the sky darkened and rain threatened. There was no shelter ahead, so turning inland seemed the only option.

After walking for half an hour a huddle of buildings appeared amongst the hills. Maybe there would be shelter there. It was now early evening and getting dark. As she got close to the village, a feeling of uneasiness settled over her. There were no streetlights as far as she could see, and then, she realised, no lights in the houses.

The village was eerily quiet, and nothing stirred. No people about their daily business, not so much as a dog or stray cat. The village had been abandoned and nature was taking over. Along the cracked roads, weeds were sprouting and trees were growing up against house walls. Windows were broken in some of the houses, and doors hanging off their hinges. It began to rain, and Josie ducked down one of the side roads and began to try doors and windows to gain entry. Finally at the end of the street, she found a way in through a rear door. Pausing in the doorway, she flicked on her torch. The room was almost completely empty. Just an old table stood against one wall, and a dining chair with three legs. The house was just a single storey so it didn't take long for Josie to investigate. It was tiny, with only one bedroom, totally empty, and a small kitchen. A battered saucepan appeared to be the only item left, and a half-empty box of matches. Josie looked around for something to burn and her eyes fell on the chair, and in a corner behind the table, a newspaper – perfect!

It took a long time to get a fire going in the fireplace. Everything was slightly damp, but after half an hour there was enough heat to warm up some water in the saucepan. When it was good and hot she opened the tin of meatballs and lowered it into the water, then did the same with a tin of veg.

The small room warmed up slowly, and as the food was heating through, Josie dragged the table across the back door for security and laid out her bedroll. The rain was now thundering down and one or two leaks appeared in the roof, but nothing to worry about. The meal was delicious, but then Josie was very hungry. She washed her plate and cutlery in the still-hot water, then got her map out and studied the route she would take; where she would be tomorrow or in a few days' time, she wasn't sure. But just in case she decided to stay and wash some things through, more water would be needed and there was plenty coming down outside! Dragging the table away from the door, she pushed the saucepan outside to gather water and then dragged the table back.

Josie stretched and yawned; she'd had a really good night's sleep and felt refreshed. The rain had stopped and the sky was blue once more. She relit the fire and put the saucepan on. While it was heating up there was time for some bread and cheese and a long drink of water. Then clothes were washed in the sink and rinsed, then hung on the bushes outside to dry in the sun. But now the water was all gone, so there was no chance to wash herself. She decided to walk the mile or so back down to the coast, find a shop and buy some water for drinking and some provisions.When she returned she filled two empty water bottles from a small stream. By lunchtime she was clean and fresh, and the clothes on the bushes almost dry. *One more night here*, she thought, *and I'll be on my way*. It was very sad to think that these houses had been abandoned, but very lucky for her.

Three days later, she sheltered around a castle for two nights, then in another few days in a gazebo in the grounds of a very posh hotel, but only for one night. At the end of one hard day's walking and with darkness quickly descending, Josie looked for somewhere to sleep. After another mile or so, she saw the ideal place: a small, abandoned villa fifty yards above the path. She plodded up the overgrown track and looked inside. It was totally black. She reached into her pocket for the small torch she kept there, but then froze. From a dark corner came a rustle and a grunt. For a few seconds more, Josie remained frozen to the spot, then she was hurtling down the track and back onto the path. Tiredness forgotten, she raced along, stumbling over stones, weeds and small bushes tearing at her clothes, until gasping for breath, she slowed and looked behind. She could see a few hundred yards and the path was empty. Sighing with relief, she slumped down on a rock, and waited for her pounding heart to slow. Gradually she regained her breath and looked for the hundredth time, it seemed, back along the path. It was clear. Taking a deep breath, she set off once more, but was now desperate for sleep. In the end she laid out her bedroll behind some bushes and was asleep in a few minutes.

By the middle of February, she had reached the Delta de l'Ebre. This area fascinated Josie. The Ebre was a huge river, and the delta many miles across. She spent a few days exploring and managed to find a tumbledown shed to camp in. The area was used mainly for growing rice, and was low-lying and crisscrossed with water channels. A week later she was in Tarragona, and by the first week in May she was in Barcelona. Here she intended to look for work. She camped in municipal gardens, in old buildings and anywhere she could, as she looked for work. Up and down roads, into cafés, bars and restaurants, even shops, desperate to find employment somewhere. Cleaning, gardening – anything would do. Money was running out, and trying to keep clean and tidy became more difficult as the days passed. Finally, when she had been in Barcelona a week, a visit to an agency was successful. A cleaner was needed in a large hotel, just off La Rambla.

Josie tidied herself up as best she could, put a bright smile on her face, and went for an interview. A rather stern, middle-aged woman frowned.

"So, you are not Spanish?"

"No, but I speak good Spanish and I've been living here for some time and working in English and Spanish establishments. I can give you the address of the Spanish lady I worked for, if you would like a reference."

Josie kept her voice quiet and spoke in her best Spanish. The lady, whose name was Señora Garcia, asked her a lot of questions, some of which seemed irrelevant; probably, Josie thought, to test her knowledge of Spanish. Finally, much to Josie's relief, she gave her the job.

"Thank you very much. Can you recommend some cheap lodgings for me, please?"

"There is a small room on the top floor you can have. Other staff are up there, and there is a shared bathroom. The money will be stopped out of your wages."

She mentioned the figures and Josie could see it wouldn't leave her with much to live on and to save for her ongoing journey, but she dare not complain, and anyway, it was good to have a room. Señora Garcia went on to explain how staff could do their washing in the basement, and how they could prepare food if they wanted to. No food was allowed in the bedrooms. She then took Josie on a tour of the public rooms, the kitchen, which was huge, the basement and finally up to her room.

"You will start at 7.30am tomorrow. I hope that's all right." She gave Josie a hard look.

"Thank you, that will be fine."

"Come down to the basement and I'll tell you what needs doing each day." She seemed to soften, and gave Josie a small smile. "It's 5pm and Chef will find you something to eat. The rest of the day is yours."

As Josie turned towards the door, Señora Garcia said, "You can leave your bags here. They will be quite safe as your door will be locked." She gave Josie a key attached to a key ring. "I advise you not to lose it. I have a spare locked in my office, but I'm not always here, so you could find yourself sleeping under the stars."

Josie felt she ought not to tell her that that was what she had been doing! They went down in the lift to the basement, which was huge. It was one big room, taking up the whole area underneath the hotel, with pillars here and there, supporting the floors above. Two small

236

windows at the back let in the only natural light, but it was well lit with high wattage bulbs. At one end stood two large washing machines for the hotel linen, and alongside, a rather battered smaller machine for the staff. There was also a tumble drier, but this was not to be used for staff washing. Washing lines crisscrossed the room, some with sheets, pillowcases and towels, all hanging up to dry.

"We wash every day. In the season, both machines will be in use. We often leave the fire escape door open, and those windows at the back to bring in some fresh air. I'm sure I don't need to tell you that they must always be closed and locked when work is finished for the day. As you can see, the ironing is done in that corner over there. We have two boards and two irons. The floor where you work must be washed every night in case any linen is dropped. Right, follow me."

She led the way up a flight of concrete stairs, which came out near the kitchens. Once again the sheer size of the room made Josie gasp. Everything was stainless steel – ovens, grills, worktops and sinks – and everything sparkling with cleanliness. The chef was sitting at a worktop with a plate of food in front of him. He looked up and smiled as Señora Garcia led Josie into the room.

"This is Inyake, our main chef. Inyake, can I introduce Josie, who will be helping us through the season?"

She turned to Josie. "Chef will find you something to eat, and then I would advise you to unpack your bags and relax. Tomorrow will be a busy day!"

She left the kitchen and Inyake indicated for Josie to sit down.

"I eat whatever is left over from the *menu del dia*. It is good, although I say it myself!"

He brought half a dozen dishes to the table and told Josie to help herself. Feeling almost faint with hunger, as it was now 6pm and Josie had eaten nothing since some bread and cheese at 8am, she didn't need persuading. She set to, trying something from each dish, while Inyake checked his menus for the following day, turning to smile in her direction from time to time. When Josie sat back, replete, he remarked, "Well, you have a good appetite, and yet you are so slim."

"That was absolutely delicious, Inyake. Don't worry, with food like this, I shall soon be as fat as a little pig."

"I don't think so. You will find it hard work, and Señora Garcia expects a lot from you. But she is fair, I have to say."

"So what will I have to do about food normally?"

Inyake beckoned for her to follow and led her to a small room off the kitchen. Here, a lot of spare stock was stored in cupboards, but against a wall stood a Formica-topped table and several chairs.

"A lot of the staff go home for their siesta and eat at home, or maybe they are finished for the day. Others start at 7pm and have already eaten, but some eat here. They just have whatever is left over. Sometimes there is a good choice, sometimes not so much, and sometimes nothing; then you will have to go out and buy something. But the wages are not very good, so I advise you to eat here when you can. If you want breakfast you must be down by 7am, and then it's mainly just toast and coffee. I'm afraid there is nowhere you can cook for yourself. It's just not allowed. When you have finished eating and drinking, wash your china and cutlery, then put it in the steriliser. Make sure you leave everything clean, wherever you are. Señora Garcia is very fussy." He paused and looked at Josie. "And so am I!"

He put a cup of coffee down in front of her, and as soon as Josie had emptied the cup, she thanked the young chef once more, and then made her way back up to the top floor.

Now she was alone, and could explore. The top floor seemed to be divided in two. One half was possibly a self-contained flat; there was no way of knowing. The other half consisted of four tiny bedrooms, obviously once two larger rooms, with a good size bathroom at the end of the corridor. Cleaning materials were kept in a cupboard there, and a notice stated that everyone must clean the bathroom after use, and not to spend too much time as other people were probably waiting. On the landing was another cupboard with a vacuum cleaner and other cleaning things to do the bedrooms. It all seemed well organised. Josie let herself into her room and closed the door behind her. There was one small window looking out over the back of the hotel to a small garden area with tables and chairs, and beyond that, to the backs of some shops. As she looked, someone came out of the rear of a shop, leaned on the wall and lit up a cigarette. Then two guests, a middle-aged couple, came and sat in the hotel garden, and a few minutes later a waiter brought out coffee.

Josie turned and surveyed her room. It was about seven feet wide and approximately eight feet from door to window. The furnishings consisted of a single bed with a cupboard alongside, and a small wardrobe with hanging space and shelves. The only other furniture was a wicker chair. A tiny rug was the only floor covering. There didn't seem to be any heating, but this didn't bother her. Sleeping rough through cold weather had hardened her. Just to be in this tiny room, in a proper bed with a bathroom down the corridor, was luxury indeed.

Unpacking her bag didn't take long, and the bedroll went on top of the wardrobe. She searched through her pockets for any loose coins and emptied her wallet; then looked at the pathetic little pile. Fortunately she would be paid weekly, but still, these few pesetas had to last the week. She would have to eat in the hotel or not at all for the first week. She would need some soap powder and a toothbrush for a start, and that would leave her practically penniless. She smiled to herself – or pesetaless! Exhausted, she walked down to the bathroom and showered and washed her hair, and as soon as it was dry enough, fell into bed, drew the bedclothes up and was asleep in seconds. She woke once at midnight when girls' voices sounded outside her room, then doors closed and all was quiet once more.

The next thing Josie knew, there were voices outside

her door again. She looked at her watch – gosh, 7am; she would have to be quick or there would be no breakfast for her. Hastily pulling on some clean clothes, she dashed to the bathroom, then down in the lift to the kitchen. Two girls looked up as she entered the room and smiled at her.

"*Buenos días*, are you new here?"

"*Buenos días*. Yes I am, and I'm late."

One of the girls stood up and put some bread in the toaster. "There you are. It'll only take a minute. You must eat, it's changeover day on Saturdays and there's loads to do."

Josie was relieved that the girls she was working with seemed very nice. She hastily ate her toast and helped herself to coffee from a jug sitting on the table. Just as she was finishing, Señora Garcia came into the room.

"Ah, Josie, I see you have met Margarita and Connie. You go and help in the kitchen, Connie. Margarita, I want you to stay with Josie for the morning and show her what to do. There are twelve rooms to do today." She handed Margarita a list, and added, "Now hurry along, there's lots to do."

The girls did as they were asked, and for the next two and a half hours they changed beds, cleaned bathrooms and vacuumed and dusted. Then they had a quick break before going back and finishing the last few bedrooms. Guests could book in from 12pm onwards, and they were finished with fifteen minutes to spare. Then it was down to the basement to put the washing in the machines. They took the linen that was already dry down off the lines, and folded it up neatly, ready to be ironed.

"We'll make a start on this," Margarita said as she prepared the ironing board and plugged the iron in. "I finish at 1pm. What hours are you doing?"

"Well, I'm off for lunch at 1pm till 4pm, then I've got to come back and do some more. But Señora Garcia said my hours will vary this evening. I may have to work till 6.30pm or I may finish earlier, and I will be paid accordingly."

"Don't forget to come down about 3 or 3.30pm and see what Chef might have left over." Margarita grinned at her. "I've heard you ate quite well yesterday."

"Yes, I did. I was starving and the food was so tasty. He's a good cook isn't he?"

"Yes, he is. Señora Garcia thinks a lot of him."

Margarita folded up a sheet and put the ironing board away. "There, I've made a start, so there's not too much for you to do later. I'm off home now, and you had better go and rest and make the best of the next hour or two. I bet you're tired, aren't you? It's hard when you first start!"

Without waiting for an answer, she asked Josie what days she was doing.

"I've got Monday off and I don't do Wednesday or Friday evenings. I've quite enjoyed this morning. The bedrooms look nice when they are all clean and tidy, don't they? Thank you for showing me what to do. I'll see you tomorrow."

"No, I don't do Sundays, so I'll see you Tuesday."

The girls bid each other goodbye and Josie plodded up to her room. Throwing herself down on her bed, she reflected how lucky she was, always managing to find work when she desperately needed to. And providing she worked hard, she could see no reason why this job shouldn't be hers until summer was over. She drifted off to sleep, but woke after an hour, stretched and walked down to the bathroom to freshen up. Then she meandered down to the kitchen. Inyake was still busy, so Josie helped herself to some coffee and sat leafing through a magazine someone had left on the table. Suddenly she was aware that Inyake was leaning on the doorway, grinning at her. Josie smiled back.

"*Hola*, have you been busy today?"

"*Si*, very busy, but suddenly they have all gone to their rooms to unpack. Hungry, Josie?"

"Mm, I've been working hard too."

She was too embarrassed to actually ask for food, but didn't need to. Inyake went back to the food preparation area and quickly made up a plate of salad with tuna and quartered hard-boiled eggs; then a small bowl with potato salad and some crusty bread. He placed them on the table with some cutlery, then sat down opposite Josie and watched her attack the food with enthusiasm.

"I'm off in a few minutes, Josie; my kids are waiting for me. We look forward to some time together on Saturday and Sunday. I only have a couple of hours with them, so I make the most of it!"

"How old are they?"

"The boy is five and my daughter is nearly seven."

"That's nice. Thanks for the food, Inyake. I'll leave everything neat and tidy, so don't worry."

"OK. There's cold rice dessert in the fridge. You can have that as well. *Adios*."

He grabbed a bag and disappeared.

I don't care if anyone thinks I'm greedy, Josie thought. *I'm going to eat as much as I can, as often as I can, and if it's free, all the better!* She hoped to put some weight on and build up her strength during the summer, because she now knew what her plans were for the autumn and winter.

She was just rinsing her lunch things and stacking them in the steriliser when Señora Garcia appeared.

"Ah, Josie, I'm glad I've caught you. I'm pleased with your work this morning. You did well for your first morning. If you come back at four, you can finish off any ironing, then tell Gina on reception what time you finish so we can keep a track of the hours you do."

She bustled away and Josie went down to the basement to iron. It took her an hour to finish; then it was up to reception, where she waited for Gina to finish with some new arrivals. Once she had introduced herself to Gina and told her she'd finished for the day, she ran back up to her room once more, slipped her shoes off and sat on her bed. She had been keeping a diary since leaving Benidorm, but she had a bit of catching up to do, and now seemed a good time. She settled down and began to write.

As the weeks went by, Josie got used to the work and with Connie and Margarita they made a good team. The hotel got busier as the season went on, and the weather hotter, but most of the hotel was air-conditioned, so this was no problem. The basement seemed to keep fairly cool too, which was helpful when there was a mountain of ironing to tackle. Sometimes, if the girls were all off at the same time, they would meet up and stroll up and down La Rambla, enjoying the lively nightlife that Spanish cities, and indeed towns and villages, enjoyed. They were joined sometimes by other young people, boys and girls, of a similar age. Now and again, a couple would pair up and go off together, but mostly they stayed in a group, which Josie was pleased about. It was also good to be accepted even though she was English. When questions were asked, she would just say that she was travelling round Spain and working when necessary, and this seemed to satisfy them.

Then it was July 15th and Josie's twenty-first birthday. With the help of Margarita and Connie, an evening out was arranged. Twelve of them, eight girls and four boys, descended on a tapas bar, where they ate an enormous amount of food, drank a lot of wine and had a good evening, staggering back to their rooms at 2am. It was three bleary-eyed young ladies who dragged themselves out of bed five hours later, but all agreed it had been a great night.

On the following Friday, Señora Garcia called them together before work.

"Now, girls, as I'm sure you know, the next six weeks are the busiest of the year. Every room is fully booked, mostly for one week only, so Saturdays are going to be hectic. There will be an extra person helping who is experienced, and you should cope. Any problem with the rooms, no matter how small, must be reported to me immediately, is that understood?"

The girls nodded, and Señora Garcia continued.

"If anyone is ill or injured, I must know straight away. Then I can find someone to help out. All right, off you go."

As they walked away to start their work, Connie whispered, "We got extra money last September because we did so well, so that's something to look forward to."

The next six weeks for Josie were just a blur of work, cleaning, washing and ironing, and sometimes even helping in the kitchen. She was never finished before 6.30pm and sometimes later. The weather was hot and sapped her energy. Her break in the middle of the day was spent sleeping, and any personal tasks were done on Monday mornings before the heat of the day. Then she would relax in her room and plan the next stage of her journey. She had made full use of the markets, buying cheap yet warm clothing and new trainers, because she was heading for the Pyrenees next and it would be winter and very cold. As Connie had said, they were given a bonus in September and Josie went back to the market and bought a thick, padded winter jacket with a hood, and a thick scarf. It seemed rather strange to be doing

246

this when the temperature in Barcelona was still in the 80s.

One last thing Josie wanted to do before leaving Barcelona was visit the Sagrada Familia. She had heard so much about it from her friends at work and from visitors to the city. The ornate cathedral had been started almost a hundred years ago in 1882. The architect was a man called Villar, but Gaudi had taken over a year later and continued until his death in 1926. It was called an expiatory church, meaning that the entire costs were met by donations. It wasn't expected to be finished until the next century. Josie set off one Monday, and it took her an hour to walk there. She gazed in awe at the intricate stonework and the sheer size of the building. Sitting on a nearby seat, she ate her *bocadillo* and just looked, trying to take it all in. She tucked her empty wrapper in her pocket; then wandered around the building wherever the public were allowed. She was so very glad she'd made the effort to see it. Then she walked back to the hotel. *Good walking practice*, she thought.

Things were quieter now in the hotel, and it was time to move on. Señora Garcia accepted her notice without any complaint, explaining that she would have sent her on her way at the end of September anyway. Josie and Bella had been exchanging letters whilst Josie was living in Barcelona, and now she wrote explaining that she would be on the road again and unable to receive mail, but promising to write again when she was settled in the Pyrenees. Her hotel wages had been paid into a local bank, and most of it had stayed there, accruing interest. Although the wages had been low, a very satisfying amount had built up. Josie closed the account and tucked the money into her money belt. She finished her last week, the third in September, packed her bags, said goodbye to everyone and set off on the next leg of her journey.

CHAPTER 12

Her first stop was a bookshop to buy a new map, which covered the whole distance to the Pyrenees, and gave quite a lot of useful detail. Her plan was to have bed and breakfast once a week, so that she could keep herself and her clothes clean. Maybe a hostel would be all right, and very reasonable. It was three or four miles to the outskirts of the city. Josie headed inland and was confronted by a small mountain. The road wound round and round this way and that to the village on the top, a distance of three or four miles again, but there was a funicular railway which took you there for a small charge. The temptation was too great, and Josie paid her fare and climbed aboard.

The views from the village were amazing. She could see right over the city to the sea. The Sagrada Familia was easy to pick out, but the hotel impossible to see, lost amongst the many roads and other buildings. It was possible to see some of the countryside, but the area was very hilly and restricted the view inland. Josie headed along the small mountain road that led towards the motorway, then ran alongside it for some way. It was along here that she managed to find shelter for her first night on the road. It was an old ruin with only three walls standing and no roof, but it was a warm, balmy evening so it didn't matter. She sat on a rock and ate some of the food Inyake had packed up for her, and then went through her routine of freshening up, brushing her teeth and preparing for the night. As she settled down later, the roar of the traffic on the motorway lulled her to sleep.

The hours of darkness were quite long, and Josie woke whilst it was still dark. She could see by the light of her torch that it was only five o'clock, but decided to make a start and stop for something to eat when it got light. Always trying to keep the motorway within view, she walked along roads and tracks and covered quite a few miles before the sun came up. Then she stopped for a well-earned breakfast of a rather dry *bocadillo* and some salad, followed by a long drink of water. Her food was now all gone, but there were plenty of towns and villages where she could buy more.

She followed the motorway for the next three days before coming to a large town, where she managed to find a hostel. She was able to take the room over at 12pm, which suited her very well. It gave her plenty of time to wash some clothes through and hang them over a chair on the balcony to dry in the sunshine. The room was basic but clean, and when Josie had finished her washing she slipped out for an hour or two to get some shopping and explore the town. She also treated herself to a cup of coffee. Spanish coffee was something she would never tire of!

The town was the usual mix of very old, ornate buildings and rather ugly new ones, with an attractive plaza in the middle, which was where Josie had her coffee. At 3pm she had a cheap but nourishing meal in a small bar, then made her way back to the hostel. Her washing was virtually dry and would air in the room overnight. Then it was time for a much-needed hair wash and shower. As soon as her hair was dry enough Josie climbed into bed and was soon asleep.

There was a tiny breakfast area downstairs with just orange juice, bread and various spreads. A toaster stood ready if anyone fancied toast, and there was a rather basic coffee machine. Josie tucked in, eating and drinking as much as she could, then went back to her room, brushed her teeth, grabbed her bags, paid at reception and was on the road again by 8am. The route she was using led in a northerly direction following the Río Llobregat.

Josie made excellent time, the weather was good and she felt fit and well. Four days later she was in the Pyrenees, but not quite able to believe it. She booked into a hostel and followed the same routine as before. The following morning she found a tourist information centre, and with fingers crossed, stepped through the door. All around the walls were books and leaflets about the area, and she began to look through them. A young lady came over to her and asked if she could help.

"I'm looking for work over the winter," Josie explained. "Maybe a ski centre or something similar. Where do you advise me to try?"

"There is a ski village just five kilometres away," the young lady told her. "They will be taking on staff in a few weeks' time, but I advise you to see them now because working there is very popular and the jobs go very quickly." She glanced at her watch. "There will be a bus going from the town hall in twenty minutes at 10.30am."

"Where is the town hall?" Josie asked.

The young lady stepped through the door and pointed up the street to a rather grand building. "Quite close, as you can see," she said with a smile.

Josie thanked her and wandered up the road to wait for the bus. She found a rather unusual tile-covered bench to sit on and idly watched the passers-by. Then her eyes fell on a man looking in a window opposite. He had his back to her and his face was just a blur in the reflection from the glass.

"Manuel!" she gasped. Her heart did a double somersault, and if she hadn't been sitting down, she would have fallen down. She began to tremble violently as different emotions swept through her. Fear, regret; maybe love? She tried to calm herself, and then the man turned and walked away. She could see his face – it was not Manuel. She bent her head and stared at the ground as tears of relief ran down her cheeks. For a few moments she thought she would faint, but taking deep breaths, gradually the feeling passed. The bus came and she stepped on board and paid her fare. Passing down the bus, she sat down and looked out the window till they passed the young man, and she looked again. No, the nose was too long, the eyes too close-set; it wasn't Manuel, thank goodness. Josie pushed it to the back of her mind and concentrated on the job in hand: to find work as soon as possible.

By now it was mid-October, and the weather was much cooler, partly due to the fact she was further north, and also at a much higher altitude. The bus wound it's way up the twisting, steep road till it came to the ski resort village.

The passengers all alighted and Josie looked around. Chalets, hotels and shops appeared to be the only buildings. The bus had dropped them at a crossroads and the village stretched in all directions, one street looking much like another. Josie began by walking down the street she had been dropped off at, walking up one side and down the other. There was only one hotel down this street and it appeared to be closed. She turned into the next street. There were several hotels in this one, of various sizes; the last one very large and three storeys high. When she looked around, it seemed to be the highest building in the village. She decided to try there first. Knowing nothing about skiing, it was difficult to know what to expect.

This hotel was open, but very quiet. A young lady stood at reception writing in a book. She looked up and smiled at Josie.

"*Buenos días*, how can I help you?"

"Well, I understand you will be taking on staff for the skiing season. Do you know if there are any vacancies?"

"We are not doing that for another month, perhaps you would like to come back then. Can you leave a telephone number so we can contact you?"

"No, I'm afraid not, I haven't even booked into a hotel yet, but I will come up and see you again if I may?"

"Yes, that's all right," the girl replied.

Josie noticed there was a small bar open to one side of the reception. "Is it possible to have a coffee, please?" The idea was to make the girl remember her, and hopefully to make a good impression.

"Yes, I will do that for you."

It was obviously so quiet that the staff were few and far between. Five minutes later a cup of coffee was placed in front of her.

"Do you have many guests at this time of year?" Josie asked.

"We have guests on the first floor, walkers mainly, and two men who are climbing, and we have a group of people looking at birds, I believe they are English."

The young lady seemed happy to chat. Probably bored, Josie thought.

"I've been working in Barcelona for the summer, as a chambermaid and kitchen assistant," she told her. "I have a reference in my bag. I'll give it to whoever interviews me. Have you enough staff at the moment?"

"Oh yes, plenty, but it might be worth you coming again next Wednesday. The man who owns the hotel is coming. I will tell him about you. You seem keen, and that's what he likes to see."

"Thank you very much." Josie gave her a wide smile. "Can you tell me how much your rooms are?"

But when she was told, it was too much. Getting up to leave, she promised to come back again in the next day or two with at least an address, if not a telephone number.

Later, back in the town, she found a hostel and booked in for a couple of nights, unsure what to do for the rest of the time. Although the money was lasting well, with possibly a month to go before she was earning again, care had to be taken. With the weather now so much cooler, the priority was a warm bed for the night, a hot shower whenever she wanted it and somewhere to wash and dry her clothes, so the hostel was a must. The big saving could be on food. She would find a supermarket and eat as she had before when on the road. She soon found a supermarket, but it was closed till 5pm and that was four hours away. So as a last treat for some time, she found a bar serving food and had Spanish omelette and chips and a cup of coffee, then wandered around looking in shop windows until 5pm.

Once in the supermarket, her basket was soon full. Bread, cheese and peach jam, something she had developed a passion for, then tins of meat, fish and veggies. But now it had to be taken to her room in the hostel, where food was not allowed. Twenty minutes was spent hiding a tin in one pocket and a packet in another, taking it out and trying again till finally it all seemed to be hidden, although she was rather a funny shape! Then back to the hostel for the evening.

The next day Josie decided to explore the town some more, and the surrounding area. There wasn't much more to see in the town so she walked along a path beside the river. Everything was quite different here. The rivers were wide and full, unlike the rivers on the Costa Blanca. There, the rivers were almost empty as the water was diverted for irrigation. The path took her along for about a mile, then crossed over a bridge and climbed up into a large wooded area. After some time, Josie came to a small area that had been cleared, and somebody had kindly put a seat there overlooking the town. She sat down and took in the view. The town, when seen from here, was quite small, and the hostel could clearly be seen. Then high on the hill opposite she could just make out the roofs of some of the buildings in the ski village. The hotel where she hoped to get work could also be clearly seen.

As it was now autumn, the leaves were beginning to turn on the trees. The contrast between the dark green of the conifers and the bright yellows and oranges of the deciduous trees was quite beautiful. Josie took out a tin of meat and one of peas and opened them. She sat there completely alone and ate half of each, then drained the remainder of the peas and tipped them in with the rest of the meat for tomorrow. A breakfast of bread and peach jam had been eaten that morning in her room and every last crumb thrown out of the window. The spare food was hidden at the back of her wardrobe. But now Josie wasn't sure which way to go. There was no way of knowing where the path led, so to be on the safe side she headed back the way she came.

An hour later, Josie was back amongst the shops, and suddenly longed for a cup of tea.

"*Té, por favor*," she asked in the first bar she came to. Thankfully it was better than tea she'd had before in Spain, probably because of the Brits visiting the ski village, but it came black and Josie had to ask for a little cold milk. She knew if she didn't say cold she would be given hot milk! By the time the tea was gone, the shops were beginning to open and Josie spent the next couple of hours wandering around from shop to shop before finally going back to the hostel. She missed the company of the girls in Barcelona, and the evening stretched before her.

The next day was a Saturday, and Josie knew from experience that it would be changeover day in the hotel and busy, so it was on the Sunday that she got the bus back up to the ski village. To her relief it was the same receptionist, and she smiled as Josie approached.

"*Hola*, could I have a coffee please?"

When the coffee was placed before her, Josie told her she was staying at the hostel and gave the telephone number. The young lady made a note.

"I still think if you come up on Wednesday morning about 12pm the owner may agree to see you. I'll have a word with him before you get here. By the way, my name is Carmen, what is yours?"

"I'm Josie White and I'm twenty-one."

They chatted for a few minutes more; then Carmen

left to help a guest. Josie drank her coffee, paid Carmen and left. Just three more days and then she would know if she had a job or not.

Those three days dragged by, as the weather was wet, cold and miserable. Walks were short and the hours long. But Wednesday arrived and Josie got the bus to the ski village, arriving at 11.15am. She walked slowly round the shops and finally at 12pm arrived at the hotel. A young man was at the desk and Josie was unsure how much to say, but before she could say anything he asked her if she was Josie White.

"I am," she said.

"Please sit down and I will bring you a coffee while you wait. Carmen is going round the hotel with Señor Vicente. She is going to talk to him and they will be back soon."

However, an hour passed before Carmen appeared.

"Señor Vicente will be here in five minutes. He has agreed to talk to you."

"Oh, thank you," Josie replied with relief.

When Señor Vicente arrived, Josie was surprised to see he was quite elderly, possibly in his sixties. A rather short, plump man with silver hair, he was however very dapper and had a kind face. He walked with small, quick steps to Josie's table, and she rose to greet him. His handshake was warm and he gestured for her to sit down; then produced a notebook and pen. He made a note of her name and asked her about previous jobs, writing the details down. He also asked her why she was living and working in Spain.

"Well, I came here on holiday several years ago and fell in love with it." She shrugged, then smiled. "That's it, really."

"Do you think you will stay in Spain?"

"Well, I think I will go home in the spring to see my friends, and I'm not sure after that."

"Will you see your family too?"

"No, I have no family. I'm an orphan. I was raised in a home. But I have lots of friends."

Señor Vicente continued. "You have good health? Are you strong?"

"Yes, I'm very healthy. I walk a lot and I have always had lots of energy. I find it very difficult to sit around doing nothing." She gave a nervous chuckle. "I sometimes get told off for not relaxing."

Señor Vicente smiled. "I understand you have a reference for me to see."

Josie delved into her bag and found the reference, but Señor Vicente didn't read it immediately.

"Can I take this away with me? I will bring it back next Wednesday when I come again, and I will confirm with you then whether you have the job. But at the moment it looks good, so don't look so worried."

He smiled and patted her hand, then rose and left the table, walked over for a quick word with Carmen; then with a wave he left the hotel, climbed into his car and was gone.

Carmen came over at once to Josie and said, "He likes you; I think it will be all right."

The next week dragged by and Josie went on a couple of trips to help pass the time. The bus fares were cheap and she took food with her, as always. On the Friday she went to Berga. It was not so high here and therefore not quite so cold, and although cloudy, the rain held off. Information was available from the tourist office, and she underlined all the places to visit that interested her and were free. This included old buildings and churches, municipal gardens and a walk partway up a very steep hill with wonderful views. She spent the weekend in an agony of boredom and impatience, walking up and down the river path and in the woods.

When Monday arrived she climbed aboard a bus again, this time going north. The bus rattled its way up a hill and then suddenly it was in a tunnel going through the top of the mountain. Weak lights came on in the bus and Josie hoped the tunnel wasn't too long; she felt rather uneasy, but looking round the bus, everyone else was relaxed and chatting happily, so she told herself not to be silly. However, the tunnel was several miles long and it was at least five minutes before they were in daylight again. She could tell straight away they were very high. To her left she could see towering, snow-capped mountains. To her right the hill dropped away and she could see for miles. Forty-five minutes later they arrived at their destination, a large town almost on the border of France. Her heart gave a little leap, and all of a sudden she felt nearer to home, although common sense told her it was many hundreds of miles away.

The town was interesting and Josie enjoyed looking

around, but it was very cold and twice during the day she was forced to go into a bar and have a hot drink and warm up. By mid-afternoon she had seen all she wanted to and headed back to the bus station, where a bus soon left to take her back to Camorno and the hostel.

Tuesday it rained all day, and there was sleet and snow in the rain. Josie spent most of the day in her room. She started letters to Bella and Connie and decided to finish them off when she knew the results of her second interview the following day. Putting pen and paper to one side, she walked to the window and looked out. The weather was horrible and yet, if early snow fell on the slopes above the ski village, it could be good news for her. Señor Vicente would be much more likely to take her on, and possibly earlier than she had hoped if a few hopeful skiers turned up.

It was mid-morning and Josie stepped off the bus and walked up the hill to the hotel. As she headed for the steps leading up to the entrance she noticed an elderly lady struggling with her luggage. Hurrying forward, she asked if she could help, and took the biggest case from the lady, leaving her with two bags and a briefcase. Josie leaned against the door and opened it wide, allowing the lady to pass through.

"Thank you so much." She said.

"You're welcome". Josie replied with a smile

"Ah, you're English, that's good. My Spanish is not good, so would you mind staying with me while I book in?" The lady gave Josie a hesitant smile.

"Of course I will, but I'm sure the receptionist will speak English," Josie reassured her. She smiled at Carmen and stepped back a pace. As she thought, Carmen's English was good enough and the lady was soon booked in.

"Is it all right if I help the lady with her case?" Josie looked at Carmen, unsure whether she was stepping over the line.

"No, thank you, Josie, Sancha, who you met yesterday, will do it."

Carmen pressed a bell and Sancha appeared, smiled at the lady and took her case and one of her bags. They walked away towards the lift. Carmen had already disappeared into the bar to make Josie a cup of coffee. Ten minutes later Señor Vicente appeared. Carmen greeted him and spoke quietly to him for several minutes, then prepared a coffee for him as well. He walked over to Josie's table, shook her hand and sat down.

"How would you be placed, Josie, to start straight away?"

Josie struggled and failed to stay composed. A big smile appeared and she let out a sigh of relief. "I can start right now if you want me to."

Señor Vicente chuckled. "Well, before you agree, let me explain the situation to you. Normally I would not visit the hotel so often, and I would not be interviewing you. I have a manager here, Sebastian, who runs it efficiently without much input from me. But several weeks ago he was involved in a car accident and injured.

He will make a full recovery, but I'm not expecting him back for four to six weeks. The staff have been coping well without him, but it's been hard for them. They have all put in extra hours. I know they would be glad of some help. I can't say what your job would be because I want you to help wherever you are needed. It may be in the bedrooms, in the kitchen or even" – he swept his hand towards the front of the building – "outside. If you are willing to do this, we will assess you over the next few weeks and decide where you are best suited when Sebastian comes back. Are you willing to do that?"

"Yes, I am."

"Good. Now we need to talk about your money and accommodation, and I will get Carmen to show you around."

He told Josie what her wages would be, and it was slightly more than in Barcelona. Then Sancha took over from Carmen on the desk and the two young ladies made their way through to the back of the hotel. Behind the bar and reception areas were the kitchen and stores, with a door leading out to the side for deliveries. To the right at the front was a large lounge area for guests. At the rear behind this area was a corridor, and leading off this, staff bedrooms and a small kitchen area and lounge.

"The bedrooms are very small, I'm afraid," Carmen said as she unlocked one of the doors.

They were indeed very small. A single bed was pushed against one wall, and there was a wardrobe and very little else. Then Josie spotted another area behind the wardrobe. It was a tiny shower room, probably measuring only about two feet or maybe a bit more. In it was a small shower, a toilet and a minute sink.

"Wow, my own shower, that's great, what a luxury."

"Well, it's very small, but you are slim so you should be fine. You like it, then?"

"Yes, I do. It's perfect." Josie was thrilled with her little room.

"You will be expected to keep it clean, and there are inspections from time to time. But don't worry, you will be warned in plenty of time. I will show you where the cleaning things are."

They left the room and Carmen locked the door.

"Breakfast is supplied, but it is very simple. The rest is down to you, but as you will see, cooking facilities are rather basic."

They walked into the kitchen where a young lady was eating a sandwich, and Carmen introduced them.

"This is Dilores, who helps us with the bedrooms. Dilores, Josie is joining us and will be helping out wherever she is needed for the next few weeks."

The young ladies smiled at each other; then Carmen pointed out a three-ring hob, a microwave, toaster and kettle. In a cupboard were cups and saucers, mugs and plates. In a drawer were some cutlery and cooking utensils; then saucepans and a frying pan in the bottom cupboard. A large fridge stood to one side. Carmen opened it and pointed to the shelves.

"There is one shelf each and your name will be put on your shelf. It looks like the bottom one is going to be yours – it seems to be empty. When the season gets going you will have to share a shelf, I'm afraid. Some of the girls put their food in a container and label it. It saves any confusion. There is a rota for cleaning the kitchen. Each member of staff does it for one week, but you will be expected to keep the tops and sink clean when you have been using them. OK?"

She then pointed to some comfortable chairs and a settee on the other side of the room. "You can relax there. The TV is not much good as reception is not very good here. Right, I'll take you to meet Chef now."

As they were walking back to the kitchen, Carmen touched Josie's arm and said in a hushed voice, "Last autumn an English girl came here to work, but she was very overweight. Her references were very good and she was really nice but Sebastian couldn't take her on. She would have struggled in the bedroom and it would have been impossible for her to use the bathroom. She couldn't afford a hotel room so she had to go straight back to England."

"What a shame," Josie replied. "Perhaps she has lost weight and will come back and try again."

"I don't know, it's not easy to lose weight. But we would hire her straight away if she did."

The kitchen was similar to the one in Barcelona, only smaller. Once again it was mainly stainless steel, and clean and sparkling.

"Diego, this is Josie. She is here to help, anywhere, while we are so short-staffed. Just shout if you need her and if she's free, she will help."

They shook hands.

"When do you start?" he asked.

Josie looked at Carmen, not sure when that would be. Carmen thought for a moment.

"I think if Josie brings her things here from the hostel and settles in today, then she can start tomorrow morning. OK?"

"*Si*, yes, that's fine."

Carmen smiled at him. "It's 2pm. I'm hungry, and I'm sure Josie is. Have you got any spare food, Diego?"

"Not really, but I've got plenty of eggs. Go to the bar and I'll bring something in about ten minutes."

"Thanks, Diego. Come, Josie, I'll take some details and explain some things to you while we wait."

October passed, and November arrived. Suddenly it was warm and sunny again, with no signs of snow. But there was still plenty to do. Guests mainly seemed to be English and elderly. They would go off in groups or just couples and be out all day. Carmen and Diego agreed to move the evening meal forward from 8.30pm to 7.30pm to suit them. They were quiet and polite, and appreciated everything that was done for them.

Josie spent her days helping Diego or checking off a delivery, sometimes helping in the bedrooms; even sweeping the front steps or watering the pots. Sometimes she would be sent down to the village on the bus to buy bits and pieces, and would be gone for a whole morning because of the infrequency of the buses. She was thoroughly enjoying the assortment of tasks and as they were coping better it was decided that Sebastian should have another couple of weeks off to get completely fit. Once the snow and the skiers arrived, it would be very busy and very tiring.

Josie loved her little room. Although the window only looked out over a concrete area with dustbins, then beyond a rocky hillside, she was warm and comfortable. It became quite normal now to see young people coming in for work. They would be British or German or Spanish, but all had to speak some Spanish and English, and be able to communicate with guests.

One morning in early December Señor Vicente arrived and Carmen disappeared with him into the office. Josie was checking off a delivery of food at the side door when another car pulled into the car park and a man climbed from it. Surreptitiously, Josie looked at him. He could have stepped out of a romantic novel – tall, dark and handsome! As he walked from the car and up the steps she noticed he had a slight limp. Could it be Sebastian? She finished checking the food and put it away in the fridge and freezer, being careful to bring the older stuff to the front, and then took the delivery note through to Diego.

"Could you help me prepare the salad please, Josie?"

Josie answered in the affirmative and began taking lettuce from the fridge. The two worked together in companionable silence until Carmen appeared at the door.

"Josie, could you come to the office please? Señor Vicente and Sebastian want to have a chat."

Although Josie was confident she would keep her job, she was still a little nervous, but the men soon put her at her ease. Señor Vicente introduced Sebastian and the two shook hands.

"Sebastian, Carmen and I have been having a chat about where we are to put you. It has been a hard decision to make, because you are so willing and useful wherever you are. How would you feel about carrying on as you have been? It seems to have worked very well. It will get much busier over the next few months and I think various areas will be fighting over you." He laughed. "Saturdays, of course, helping in the bedrooms, and two or three times a day helping Diego. I think we will make your hours 10am to 3pm, then 7pm to 9pm. Wednesday can be your day off, and Saturdays once the bedrooms are done. Are you happy with that?"

And so, once again, Josie had work. Some might have said, 'how boring, how menial', but not Josie. In fact she enjoyed the variety of her work, and rapidly opened a bank account in Camorno, offering some interest on her savings. Once again she needed to save as much as possible to return to her trek in the spring.

As Christmas drew near, the hotel filled up. Some guests came for the skiing, others to spend the festive season in the mountains. Special events were organised and menus discussed. Josie had sent Stella a birthday card in November, but she decided she owed her an explanation of her silence over the last fifteen months. Undoubtedly, Stella would have written to Benidorm and wondered why she wasn't getting any letters back. So Josie bought a nice Christmas card and wrote in it:

To my dear friend Stella,
I thought I ought to explain why I haven't written for so long. You see, I only stayed with Manuel for about six months, but it didn't work out. Things were bad between us and I had to leave, but as I had very little money, shanks' pony was the only way. I've found seasonal work in various places, which has kept me going, and I'm now in the Pyrenees! I'm working in a ski village and enjoying it. Come spring I'll be on the road again and heading north through France. It would be lovely to hear from you whilst I'm here, and I promise I will reply. Have a lovely Christmas.
With lots of love from Josie

Extra help was brought in over Christmas, and the regular staff had at least one day off to be with their families. To Josie, Christmas was like any other time, so she worked right through. There was a party, though, on the 28th December, to which all the staff were invited. At some time during that evening everyone that was able spent half an hour or so on reception. Then there was another party for guests on New Year's Eve, which went on till 2 in the morning! Overtime was offered for everyone, whilst everything was sorted, tidied and thoroughly cleaned.

The next three months were hectic. Young skiers arrived in droves, bringing noise, laughter and melted snow to the hotel. Josie seemed to be using a mop most of the day. The exercise meant huge appetites and Diego was kept very busy. Josie helped whenever she could and enjoyed her time in the kitchen and serving at the tables. It was lovely to speak to people in her own language, and very difficult not to stay too long with any group. She was longing to know what was going on back home, and she yearned to be back there.

Winter was hard but satisfying and seemed to fly by. Guests were generous with tips and Josie tucked most of it away in the bank. There were times when she was tempted to go down to the town and buy warmer clothes, but she was reluctant to spend the money. Instead she put on lots of layers, and her only purchase was warm boots.

As spring drew nearer, Josie began to make plans. She bought a map and planned her route. Having one night a week in a hostel had worked very well, and she planned to do that again. The thought kept coming into her head that a tiny tent for sleeping in would be a good idea. The weather was bound to be much wetter and rather cooler in France. The shops in the ski village were rather expensive, but maybe in the town things might be cheaper. So on her next Wednesday off, she walked down the hill to the town and looked around. To her delight the camping gear shop had an end of season sale on – 33% off most items! Josie got her tent; it was very lightweight and would be no problem to carry. It rolled up small and would tuck in with her bedroll. Happy with her purchase, she caught the next bus up to the village.

Although Josie had been at the ski village longer than with Bella or in Barcelona, she had not formed any close friendships with anyone. She got on all right with them, but that was as far as it went. So there were no feelings of sadness about moving on, only excitement. As things quietened down towards the end of March, several staff left: two English girls who were going home for a wedding and not coming back, and a Spanish girl whose contract had ended. So for Josie, the work never slackened and she hoped she could stay for a few more weeks until the weather improved. It was still very cold with lots of snow about, although the roads were always kept clear.

In the middle of April, Sebastian called her into the office and told her she must go in one week's time.

"I shall be sorry to see you go, *mi amigo* – you have been a great help to us. You will be receiving a bonus as all our staff do, according to their area of work, but as you worked in all areas I need to discuss with Señor Vicente how much it will be."

He smiled warmly at Josie, patted her arm and they left the office to go about their various tasks.

The following Wednesday, just three days before she was due to leave, Josie walked down to the town and joined the queue in the bank.

"I would like to draw my money out please, and exchange it for francs."

"Are you closing your account, señora?"

"Yes, I am."

The young teller looked at her balance. "Well, I have not got enough francs for you today, but I can get them for Friday. Will that be all right?"

Oh, dash it, Josie thought, but out loud she said, "I will try and get to you Friday, but it may be Monday."

"No problem," the teller replied.

Josie walked back up the steep, winding hill to the village to get herself fit for the walk ahead. As she walked, she mulled over how she could get to the bank on Friday. Their hours were 9am to 2pm and then they did not reopen. The first bus down was at 9.15am, so perhaps she could complete her business at the bank and get the 10am bus back, which meant she could be fifteen minutes late starting, maybe later – best to have a chat to Sebastian. When she approached him, he beckoned her into the office.

"I wanted a word with you, Josie."

They sat down and he told her, "I have spoken to Señor Vicente and we have agreed you should have 10,000 pesetas for your bonus."

Josie gasped – that would be about £50 in sterling. "Thank you, that's very generous, and I need to ask you a favour, Sebastian."

She explained about exchanging her money and how the bank hours made it difficult to collect the francs.

"So you see, I would be fifteen minutes late starting work."

Sebastian actually laughed. "I think we can spare you fifteen minutes, Josie, and I will phone the bank and ask them for some more francs to cover your bonus. Is that what you would like me to do?"

"Oh yes please, and Sebastian, when do I have to move out of my room? Midday on Saturday? Or can I stay till Sunday morning?"

"Please stay till Sunday, but if you can clean your room that would help."

It was Sunday morning and the time seemed to be rushing by. Everyone wanted to say goodbye and Diego insisted on packing up food for the day, which so far he hadn't done. Josie decided that day one would just have to be a walk down to Camorno with a night at the hostel and then set off first thing Monday morning, because she had a goal on the first full day, and that was the town on the border between Spain and France, Lugio, which she had visited last autumn.

Finally she was on her way down to the town. She was now carrying more weight, of course. She was wearing her boots because it was still cold in the mountains, and her trainers were in a cheap holdall purchased in the village, along with a few extra bits of warm clothing. On top, wrapped in foil and then in a plastic bag, was a huge *bocadillo*, probably a foot long and filled with tuna and gherkins, that Diego had given her. Fortunately, he had cut it into three manageable sized pieces. He had also given her a big bag of crisps and two rather battered bananas. These had also been crammed into the holdall, and then finally the tent strapped to her backpack along with the bedroll. Once in her room at the hostel she ate one piece of *bocadillo*, then went out for stroll and a last cup of coffee in Camorno.

The next morning, Josie was up early. She showered and ate breakfast in the hostel, wanting to save the rest of the *bocadillo* for the day ahead. She could see from the map there were very few villages and certainly no towns between Camorno and Lugio, and food was essential to keep her strength up on what was going to be a long, hard day. At 8am she was on her way, adrenalin lending wings to her feet. After several miles, though, she found the boots to be heavy and had to swap them for trainers. However, it was a dry, sunny day and the roads were free of snow, so this was not a problem. The route ran between high mountains, giving the impression that the road was at a low altitude. But this was not the case. At times the road was as much as six thousand feet above sea level; a fact that was almost impossible for Josie to grasp. Then she would turn a corner to find the road following the mountainside, steep grey cliffs reaching up towards the sky on one side and dipping away thousands of feet on the other; yet only a low metal barrier to stop cars careering over to the valley below. And it was on this side Josie had to walk, where she could be more easily seen by motorists.

As the day wore on, tiredness began to take over and it was with some relief that she saw Lugio in the distance, possibly, hopefully, only about two miles away.

She was also very hungry, and by the time she walked into the town her legs felt weak and her first priority was food. Very soon she came to a supermarket, but it was closed till 5pm, so the only answer was a bar. She staggered into the first one she came to, called out for a coffee and collapsed into a seat. The waiter brought her coffee and Josie enquired about food.

"We only have sandwiches and pastries," the waiter informed her, "or I might have some tortilla."

He went to a door behind the bar and shouted to a colleague, then turned back towards Josie. "Hot or cold?"

"Hot, please, and another coffee, please, and some bread."

Half an hour later, feeling much better, Josie paid and thanked the waiter and got directions to the nearest hostel. As she approached it, cold rain began to fall, and what a relief it was a couple of minutes later to be in the hostel, in the warm and dry.

Josie slept long and deep that night, and didn't wake till 7.30 the next morning. She hurriedly swung out of bed and looked out of the window. It was pouring with rain and sleet and the roads were awash. In fact it looked horrible out there. After dressing, she walked downstairs to the reception and asked the young man on duty if he knew how long it was going to rain for.

"All day," he replied, "and probably tomorrow as well, and then Thursday may be better."

Josie booked herself in for one more night, then

slipping on a pack-a-mac, left the hostel to find a supermarket.

She noticed a woman walking towards a large building, and realised it was a covered market. She spent a happy couple of hours there, looking, buying and eating. Her bedroll, tent, water bottles and holdall were all back at the hostel, but her backpack never left her. The next day the rain still poured down and Josie booked in yet another night, worried at the cost and annoyed and frustrated that she couldn't cross the border. The receptionist smiled at her when she returned from another visit to the market.

"It will stop raining soon," he told her. "Tomorrow will be much better, dry and warmer."

"Oh, thank goodness." Josie sighed with relief.

Whilst at the shops that day she had bought a Spanish/French phrase book and she studied it closely that evening, but French was a complete mystery to her.

As the receptionist had said, Thursday dawned bright and sunny and by 7.45am Josie was on the road again, eager to cross the border into France. It was unguarded, so no holdup there. Today was going to be another long one. Whilst in the mountains, she would have to use hostels or cheap B&Bs. It was far too cold to camp in her flimsy tent, so that meant walking to the next town or large village. Now she was over the border, she couldn't wait to be out of the mountains, to milder weather. Apart from some initial stiffness, the walk went well. There was no snow left – only on the mountain peaks, the rain had seen to that – and it did seem a little less cold, but the road was still at high altitude. As the afternoon wore on, Josie saw a sign pointing to Andorra only a mile away, but that was not her route. She took the road that was signposted Toulouse, and shortly entered a small town.

Eager to find accommodation, Josie went into a café and asked for a cup of tea. By the time the waitress brought her tea, she had referred to her phrase book and was able to ask slowly, and very badly, where she might find accommodation. When the waitress had difficulty understanding her, Josie repeated her request, first in Spanish, then in English. The young lady spoke a little Spanish, being so close to the border, and managed to send Josie in the direction of a hostel. As this area was very popular with skiers and walkers, there would always be hostels, which was a relief to Josie.

She found it and booked in, then went to find a supermarket, much relieved to find the opening times similar to England, and not closed for hours in the afternoon, as in Spain. She bought some tinned food for that evening and bread and cheese for the next day, and more water. Straight away she could tell things were dearer here, but there was nothing she could do about it, other than use large supermarkets if possible, where food should be a little cheaper.

A week after leaving Camorno, Josie seemed to have left the most mountainous area behind her and it was warmer and much more springlike. May had arrived, and all around her were signs of spring. Already many trees were in leaf and wild flowers were everywhere. She began to use her tent, struggling at first to erect it, but after a few nights it was up in no time at all. There was just enough room in it to sleep with her bags around her, and if she sat in the middle, her head was about two inches from the top. She used woods and commons and behind hedges, sometimes stopping early if she saw a suitable place, and as before, stayed at a hostel or B&B once a week.

Just south of Toulouse, she was turned away from a B&B even though it said vacancies were available. She was sure it was because she was English and couldn't speak much French. However, at this point she was close to many major roads, and near these were industrial areas with hotels ranging from really plush down to very basic. Going into the cheapest one, she managed to book a room at a very reasonable price. The room was small and basic, but with its own facilities, and it was clean. By now it was well into the evening and the first job was to wash some clothes and hang them in the shower to dry. Then she sat and wrote some letters, explaining that she was on the move, so had no address. In the morning she would buy stamps and send them off.

An interesting experience awaited her the next day as she walked through Toulouse. Needing to relieve herself, she found a public toilet and stepped inside, locking herself in a cubicle. It was very dark and she couldn't see a switch for a light. Inside the cubicle it appeared to be bare, with unpainted concrete walls and floor, and then in the middle a hole. Josie was horrified and stepped back, but her bladder was full, so with much manoeuvring she managed to do what she had come in for. Then she flushed it and water splashed out in all directions. Josie leapt back and let herself out. Quickly she washed her hands with the liquid soap, then hurriedly filled her little bottle with some of it before stepping outside and breathing in fresh air.

She walked until she came to a post office and explained as best she could that she wanted stamps for letters to go to England and Spain. The lady became more and more impatient, and Josie more and more embarrassed.

Then Josie felt a tap on her shoulder and the lady behind in the queue smiled at Josie and said, "*Excusez-moi*." She then proceeded to tell the assistant what Josie needed.

The transaction was soon accomplished and Josie stood to one side so that she could thank the lady when she had finished her business at the counter.

"*Merci, madame*," she said gratefully.

"I speak a little English," the lady told her with a smile. "I am pleased to help you. *Au revoir*."

She went on her way and Josie stuck the stamps on her letters and put them in the letterbox. She tucked the spare stamps away safely and set off once more. Soon she found herself in a square. Stalls were all around selling all sorts of things: food, clothes, kitchenware, tools and jewellery. As Josie wandered through, she noticed a small metal structure in the middle of the square. It was about six feet square and about four feet high, with a gap around the bottom of about a foot. What could it be? Josie soon had her answer as a man walked into it. Obviously from his movements, it was a men's toilet. His feet could be clearly seen below the wall and his head and shoulders above. Josie suddenly realised she was staring, and felt herself go hot. She moved quickly away and over to a stall selling bread. As she slowly calmed herself she became aware she was looking at some golden-crusted bread. Pity she had no hopes of slicing it with her tiny knife, so instead she bought some crusty rolls and a couple of croissants. At another stall, a man was selling cheeses, and Josie studied them for some minutes before choosing one. Then suddenly she had an overwhelming desire to be through this city of high buildings, hustle and bustle and strange toilets, and out the other side into the countryside again.

It must have been a good three miles before she left most of Toulouse behind and she found herself walking along a busy road, which fortunately had a pavement. Nearby, the motorway led north in the same direction. She walked for several more hours until the sun sunk low in the sky and then walked into a spinney and deep into the bushes and trees until she found herself a level patch of grass to camp for the night. She had a delicious crusty roll and a lump of cheese and croissant, then went through her nighttime ritual and settled down for the night.

Over the next two weeks, Josie passed through some

beautiful countryside, even camping for two nights in a wood carpeted with bluebells. There was a stream that she made good use of, washing herself thoroughly and washing her clothes, and generally relaxing before moving on to the next big town. The two weeks had been broken up by one night in a pleasant B&B, but now she was pleased to see a motel like the one in Toulouse, and booked in for the night. As she sat in her room, she emptied her purse and pockets and opened her money belt and took out the notes. She was very surprised and delighted to see she had plenty of money left. Reassured, she settled down for a good night's sleep.

Taking to minor roads over the next few days, she found herself on the edge of another beautiful area. With hilltop villages and spectacular scenery, she was tempted to explore further; after all, she might not get another chance. She found somewhere in a wooded area to camp and put the tent up. After a meal of tinned sausages and vegetables, she studied her latest map. She dare not spare more than three nights here, but was determined to see as much as possible. There appeared to be some caves, which had to be seen, although she didn't like the thought of being underground. Maybe she would just visit one cave, then spend the rest of the time in the pretty villages and countryside.

The next morning she decamped and headed in a westerly direction. She came to the first cave and walked through a car park to a small wooden building where fortunately the young lady spoke some English.

She advised Josie to wait till 2pm, when there would be a guided tour. It had taken Josie all morning anyway to walk this far, and as it was now 1.30pm there was just time to eat some lunch. The cave was certainly amazing and Josie gazed about her in wonder, almost forgetting her fear of being underground. The tour lasted one hour and then it was back into the daylight.

Walking north, a hilltop village came into view. Josie spent the next hour or so exploring and then sat outside a small café with a cup of tea, taking in the view. Suddenly it was 6.30pm and time to find somewhere to camp for the night. The next day, Josie continued to head north, looking at another two villages on the way, and wishing, not for the first time, that she had a camera.

It was now the month of June and as she headed for the next big city, the weather deteriorated. By the time she found a motel, she was wet through. The pack-a-mac had kept her top half fairly dry, but the rest of her was soaked, including her trainers, which was a real nuisance. With the rain came cooler weather, and being June, the motel was unheated. She had discarded her boots way back and had no other footwear. The only thing she could do was hope the trainers dried a bit overnight, and would continue to dry on her feet tomorrow. Not ideal! Still, there was something else far more pressing on Josie's mind, and that was a shower and washing some clothes. This accomplished, she draped the washing around wherever she could and climbed into bed.

Putting on very damp trainers the next morning

was horrible, as was folding all the still-damp washing and putting it in a carrier bag. She decided to buy herself a really cheap pair of shoes and headed for a large hypermarket in the next street. It was huge! She had never seen such a big store, and in the area just inside the door were other small stores selling all sorts of things. Also a tiny shop repairing shoes, and further along, a launderette. Josie sat down on one of the chairs placed for customer use and got out her phrase book. Then tearing a sheet of paper from her diary, she worked out a sentence she hoped would make sense, asking if she could just dry her clothes and maybe her trainers.

She walked over to the counter where a tall young man was in charge. She pointed to herself and smiled. "English."

He shrugged, obviously not able to speak English, so Josie handed him the piece of paper. As he tried to read it, she took her damp clothes out of the carrier bag and waited. He looked at her, then at her clothes and nodded his head. Josie slipped off her trainers and gave him a questioning look. He shook his head. Josie gave a rueful smile and handed over the clothing. He pointed to his watch to indicate to her not to come back until 10.30am. Josie smiled and thanked him before walking through into the supermarket and heading for the clothes department. After studying all the alternatives, she decided on another pair of trainers, which were a reasonable price and seemed to be quite good quality. Whilst there, she also got a good supply of food and some water, paid and sat down at a small café near the launderette for a coffee. About ten minutes later the young man leaned over the counter and caught her eye, beckoning to her to pick up her clothes. *Mission accomplished*, Josie thought as she left the store with her purchases and headed north through the town.

The continuous rain had passed over during the night and although it was cloudy, the rain stayed away for most of the time. It would suit Josie now to walk in the same direction as the big main highway, but this was not always possible. Sometimes she would be walking alongside it, sometimes miles away from it. In the end she found a road that was fairly direct and eventually ended up in the same place.

Now it was mainly countryside, and certainly no motels or hostels. Luckily the weather improved again and Josie found enough streams and lakes to do what was necessary and keep herself clean. For twelve days Josie trudged on, determined to eat sensibly to keep strong and healthy, but now her money was running out. She found very few places she could ask for work, and when she did she was immediately turned away because of her lack of French. Even in two garden centres the answer was the same, and at a farm she was almost pushed back onto the road. Josie took a road that led over a river, then a canal, a railway and three major roads, all in the space of two or three miles. Ahead lay another town with a name so long she didn't even try to pronounce it. On the way in was a hostel, and with relief, Josie booked in. It was only 2pm so she went straight up to her room and went through her usual routine. She had a tiny balcony, and so was able to put her washing near the open patio door to dry. She showered and put on clean clothes, and hoisting her backpack onto her back, set off to explore.

Rather nice residential roads led off the main road. The properties were old and attractive, and most set in large plots. Some had elaborate front gates, beautiful landscaped gardens and double garages; others were just neat and tidy, and a few gloomy and run-down. Josie walked fairly briskly, not wanting to appear to be loitering, but nonetheless taking everything in. It was a lovely day and people were out in their gardens, either relaxing in the sunshine or mowing the grass and tidying the borders.

Suddenly Josie heard a sharp cry. The house she was passing at that moment was rather shabby, and the garden overgrown. The house was substantial, probably four bedrooms and with a large garden, but no garage or drive, just a small wooden gate with a path up to the front door, and on this path stood an old lady with pruners in her hand. A climbing rose was hanging over the path and she was obviously trying to cut it back, but was now caught up in the thorny growth. Without hesitating, Josie pushed open the gate and ran up the path. Taking the pruners from the old lady, she slowly and carefully snipped through several pieces and removed them from her clothing, freeing her from the vicious thorns. All the time the old lady was talking, and Josie only understood the odd word here and there. She just got on with the job and then handed back the pruners.

"Ah, *merci, merci*."

"You must go and wash the scratches," Josie said, along with some vigorous miming of washing arms. The lady beckoned to Josie and they walked through the house to a large, old-fashioned kitchen overlooking the back garden. The old lady slipped off her cardigan while Josie ran some water. First she washed her hands as the lady pulled a clean tea towel from a drawer. Between them they cleansed the wounds, which once the blood had been washed away, didn't look too bad.

Josie rinsed out the tea towel and tipped the water away, then asked the old lady, "Are you all right now?"

"Yes, zank you."

This was said in English, and followed by much more in French.

Josie gave her an apologetic smile and said in French, "I'm sorry, I don't speak French." That much she had learned early on.

The old lady thought for some moments and then said, "I speak a little English. Would you like coffee?"

"That would be lovely, thank you."

Soon they were sitting at the kitchen table with a cup of coffee in front of them and some biscuits. Josie tried to tell the lady that she was on a walking holiday and camping at night.

"My name is Josie and I could tidy your garden in exchange for food, and camp in your back garden. Would you let me help you?"

"I don't know." The old lady shrugged. "I don't know you; you are a stranger to me."

They fell silent. It was so difficult to understand each other and Josie had to keep referring to her phrase book. But she told her she was staying at the hostel for one night, but didn't have enough money for any more nights there.

The old lady said, "I will share my food with you tonight. You go the hostel and see me in the morning and I will decide."

"Yes, thank you. Shall I start on the garden?"

The old lady nodded. "My name is Esmé. Please…"

She beckoned for Josie to follow her and they went to the front garden again. She indicated that she wanted all the shrubs cut back away from the path, pointed to the wheelbarrow, then took Josie's arm and led her to the back garden. She pointed to a small heap of twigs and greenery, and Josie could see by the ashes on the ground that this was where she had a bonfire, and where Josie was to empty the wheelbarrow. Then she disappeared inside to prepare a meal, and Josie took the pruners and attacked the shrubs enthusiastically. An hour later when Esmé came out to tell her the meal was ready she was obviously impressed by how much had been done. There was just another barrow load to be taken away, and the path to be swept. But that could be done later. Now, Josie needed to eat.

The food was delicious and Esmé was a skilful cook. She said to Josie, "Big meal, you are too small."

She meant thin, of course, but Josie understood. There was not much meat, but lots of potatoes and vegetables. Josie ate every last morsel; then thanked

Esmé and stood up, indicating that she wanted a broom. Esmé pointed to the shed and Josie fetched the broom, put the last few bits in the wheelbarrow, swept up and took the barrow to the bonfire heap. Esmé called her in again when she had finished and gave her an enormous piece of homemade cake and another cup of coffee. It was 8pm, and after helping with the washing-up, Josie headed back to the hostel.

As she showered that night she thought over the day. She was enormously relieved she had found somewhere to work, even if it was only in return for food. She had a feeling that Esmé would want her to carry on and bring order to the whole garden and employ her for some weeks. Hopefully with all the food she would put some weight on, all too aware that she was painfully thin again. And if she couldn't camp in the garden she would have to find somewhere else to camp. What a blessing that Esmé spoke a little English, and Josie now understood a little more French. Perhaps Esmé would help her a bit with French?

The next morning Josie ate the last of a stale piece of French stick and drank some water, then set off for Esmé's. She was there at 9am, but her knock on the door went unanswered. Slightly uneasy in case the old lady was unwell or had fallen, she knocked again. Still no reply. She was just about to get some tools out when she heard someone come through the gate, and with relief saw that it was Esmé. A bag with a French stick poking out from it was hooked over her arm and with other bits of shopping tucked in alongside, and in her other hand was a walking stick, which she waved at Josie with a smile.

"*Bonjour*, Josie. We will have *le petit déjeuner*."

She unlocked the front door and beckoned Josie inside. She explained as best she could that every morning she walked to the shop for a paper, some fresh bread and anything else she needed. Whilst she talked she took eggs from the larder and prepared scrambled eggs, asking Josie to toast some bread taken from the bread bin. The kettle began to boil and once it had stopped bubbling, Esmé poured water into a cafetière and put it on the table. Josie put out cutlery, and cups and saucers. Esmé pointed to salt and pepper and that went on the table as well. Then they sat down and ate. Josie had a huge pile of scrambled egg and Esmé about half the amount, but it was all soon demolished.

Josie worked hard all day, stopping only to eat and drink. As they were eating lunch, Esmé asked her to stay and finish the garden, maybe two or three weeks.

"Can I put my tent up in the garden?" Josie asked.

But Esmé didn't understand, so once they had finished eating, they stepped into the garden and Josie swiftly erected her tent in a private area between the house and a hedge. Esmé watched fascinated, and laughed as Josie crawled inside and pretended to be asleep.

"Is this all right?"

"Yes, yes, of course."

"Can I use your toilet to wash each day?"

"Yes, no problem."

So everything was arranged. Over the next few days Josie mowed and edged the lawn and tidied up another bed containing herbaceous plants. She had a bonfire and tidied up the shed, putting rotting garden chairs and old bits of wood on the bonfire to get it going. She also managed to explain to Esmé that she would help in the house. At first Esmé declined, but obviously thought about it and asked Josie to clean the stairs, which she found rather difficult, and to give the bathroom a good clean. And it certainly needed it! It took Josie over an hour, but it was transformed and Esmé was thrilled.

"*Merci*, Josie. You use it now."

"Oh, that will be lovely. Thank you."

Washing in the tiny downstairs toilet had not been easy, and washing her hair almost impossible. But Esmé didn't believe in bathing every day. She made it clear that twice a week was enough, and Josie had to be content with that. Although a little wobbly on her legs, Esmé was surprisingly active; walking to the shop each morning, pushing an ancient vacuum cleaner around and best of all, serving up lots of delicious food. She loved to see Josie tucking in, and after each meal Josie insisted on doing the washing-up. When Esmé wanted the vacuum cleaner upstairs, Josie took it up for her and brought it down again when she had finished. The bathroom and toilet cleaning became her regular job, and the two of them settled into a friendly routine. As they were having their meals, Josie would point at things and ask for the French word, and practise phrases from the book with Esmé's help. After their evening meal, with the clean dishes put away, Esmé would wag her finger at Josie and say, "No more work today", and Josie would smile and say "OK." On the evenings the bathroom was out of bounds, Josie explored the town and surrounding countryside. There was a river to walk beside and lovely public gardens to admire.

At the end of her first week with Esmé, Josie had her twenty-second birthday. To begin with she wasn't going to mention it, but that evening, much to her surprise and delight, Esmé put an envelope on the table next to her knife and fork and said, "A little money for the work." Then, as Josie opened her mouth to refuse it, Esmé held up her hand and silenced her. "You work hard, it is a little money, and I want you to have it."

Josie thanked her and couldn't resist saying, "What a lovely birthday present. I am twenty-two years old today."

Esmé gave her a big smile and wished her a happy birthday.

When in her tent that evening, Josie opened the envelope and took out the notes, then gasped. A hundred francs lay in her hand, about £10 in sterling, much more than Josie had expected and very generous when she thought of all the food she was eating, and the hot water she used when she showered or washed her clothes. But that wasn't the end of it. Esmé was longer at the shops in the morning, and when she came through the gate she had a gaily-wrapped parcel in her bag, which she gave to Josie, saying again, "Happy birthday, Josie."

"Oh Esmé, you shouldn't have done this, but thank you."

The parcel was unwrapped to disclose a very pretty blouse in soft cotton. It was pink with small white flowers and short sleeves, and it looked expensive.

"Put it on, Josie. Is it too big?"

Josie went into the toilet and pulled off her t-shirt and put the blouse on, doing up the buttons and tidying the pretty rounded collar. It was not something she would have chosen, but she was surprised how good it looked. And it fitted perfectly. She did a twirl in front of Esmé and they both laughed with delight.

Then Esmé said, "Tomorrow is Sunday, so no work, Josie. My son Louis is coming to see me, he wants to meet you. We will have *déjeuner* in a restaurant. He has much money, he will pay. You will wear your new clothes."

"Are you sure, Esmé?"

"Yes, it is OK, it will be good," Esmé reassured her. She had spoken of her son, living in Paris and with a good job, but Josie wasn't sure what that was. Esmé also had a daughter living in Limoges, married and with three children, but as far as she could gather Louis had never married. His work was all-important to him.

Josie was very particular with her toilette in the morning, bathing and washing her hair. She ironed her new blouse and pressed the most respectable pair of trousers she had, which were pale blue cotton, and applied a little make-up, something she hadn't done since leaving the Pyrenees. Esmé also looked very chic, putting on a dress which suited her peaches and cream complexion and silver hair. Obviously expensive when new, the silky fabric in pastel shades hung elegantly to mid-calf. Round her neck she wore a beautiful pearl necklace, and a dainty watch was strapped to her wrist. They admired each other with a smile and sat in the morning sunshine in the front garden, waiting for the arrival of Louis.

Just before 11.30am a sleek black car drew up outside and came to a stop. The door opened and a tall man stepped out.

"Ah, here is my Louis." Esmé stood up, and with her walking stick tapping on the path, walked eagerly to greet her son. Josie stood up but didn't move, feeling very nervous and shy. She watched as mother and son greeted each other. There was no likeness, Esmé being fair-skinned and Louis dark-haired and thin of face. But they were obviously pleased to see each other, talking rapidly in their own language and smiling at each other. Then Louis glanced up and saw Josie. He said something to Esmé and Josie heard her name mentioned. Esmé wagged her finger at him and replied, and they both laughed.

They walked up to her and Louis took her hand and said in perfect English, "How do you do, Josie? Mére has been telling me all about you."

His face was quite serious now and his eyes seemed to bore into her, no doubt wondering if she could be trusted with his mother. Josie met his eyes, and although quaking, managed to respond.

They walked into the house and Esmé put the kettle on and prepared coffee while they chatted happily. Then Louis turned to Josie.

"Forgive us talking in French, but my mére's English is a little rusty. She has been telling me how hard you have been working, and I can see how much better the garden looks. My mére tells me you have been helping in the house as well. She refuses to have any regular help, no matter how much I nag her. She will miss you when you move on."

"I like Esmé very much. She has been very kind to me," Josie replied, "and she is trying very hard to make me fat with all the delicious food."

Louis laughed, and his face changed and softened. "Mére is a good cook, I know, but today we will dine at the hotel. The food is very good there. Come, Josie, walk me round the garden and tell me what you have been doing."

They finished their coffee and then went out into the garden. Josie told him how she had discovered Esmé tangled up in the roses, and how she had cut her free and helped to clean her wounds. They walked round the side of the house and Louis admired the lawn with its neatly trimmed edges, then Josie told him how they had tidied the shed and had a huge bonfire.

"Next week I am going to put the vegetable garden down to lawn. It's too much for Esmé now."

They walked over to a large weed-filled plot. Here and there strawberry plants struggled to survive, and a couple of tomato plants had come up themselves from last year's seeds. Apart from that it was weeds, some several feet high.

"It will be hard work for you, Josie."

"Yes, I know. But I'm strong and I love gardening. I shall pull weeds out and rake it over and sprinkle it with grass seed, then all I've got to do is water it."

"You seem to know what you are doing, Josie. I'm impressed."

Josie smiled and said, "Thank you."

As Louis took his mother's arm and returned indoors, Josie found an excuse to stay outside to give them some privacy. Then half an hour later they left for the hotel, where they had a beautifully cooked meal. Josie kept to simple food, having heard of snails and frogs' legs and not fancying either. So she started with consommé, followed by *poulet chasseur* with delicious vegetables and ended with crème brûlée and finally coffee. During the meal, Louis did his best to find out as much as he could about Josie.

"So, Josie, what have you been doing before you arrived at my mother's?"

"Nothing really, just walking and exploring."

"Did you have to find work before?"

"Yes, here and there."

"Where did you start out from?"

"Spain."

"You've walked all the way from Spain?"

"Yes."

"That's quite a trek."

Then realising he wasn't getting very far, and aware of Josie's reluctance to talk about herself, he paused; then said, "Do you mind if I tell Maman what you have told me?"

"No, I don't mind."

Louis and Esmé then had a conversation in rapid French, of which Josie only recognised a word or two. But Esmé looked suitably impressed. Louis asked no more questions, but just chattered generally about the garden and the need for Esmé to have some help when Josie moved on.

It was a leisurely meal, and the afternoon sped by. At 4pm they arrived back at the house and Esmé unlocked the door. Josie excused herself.

"I will go for a walk now, then back to the hostel."

Esmé, who was standing just behind Louis, grinned and gave Josie a wink. They had decided not to tell Louis about the tent in the garden and the use of the facilities in the house. But Louis was far too astute to be taken in by this story. He took Josie's arm and propelled her through the door.

"Now Josie, my *maman* has told me how you arrived here a week ago, half-starved and begging for food in exchange for work, so how have you found the money to stay at the hostel every night?"

Josie felt herself blushing, and couldn't think what to say. Louis continued.

"And when I was upstairs I noticed Maman has two toothbrushes and two tubes of toothpaste." He raised one eyebrow and looked at her quizzically. "So are you sleeping here? Come on, Josie, I'm not cross, but I think I should know the truth."

"No, I promise you I am not sleeping in the house, but yes, I am using the bathroom."

It was obvious that Josie was speaking the truth.

"So explain, please."

Louis looked at her sternly. In reply, Josie took his arm and led him up the garden to the shed. Opening the door, she reached in and pulled out her rolled-up tent and bedroll. She took it down to the corner of the garden where she had been camping, and showing off a little, erected the tent and prepared her bed in four minutes. Louis and Esmé chuckled the whole time this was going on, and clapped when she had finished.

"Am I such an ogre, Maman, that you need to deceive me? Come, let us go indoors now. I would like a cup of tea and Josie is English, so I'm sure she would like a cup of tea as well."

Louis stayed until 7pm, then kissed his mother fondly and told her to take care. He then kissed Josie on both cheeks and wished her a safe journey onwards – wherever that might be.

Josie stayed with Esmé until the end of July. The garden was immaculate and the grass seed sown on the veg patch was beginning to come up fresh and green. She had painted the bathroom and the kitchen for Esmé during a week of wet weather, and they both looked much brighter. Esmé wrote her full name and address in Josie's diary, and her telephone number so that Josie could contact her when she got back to England.

CHAPTER 13

As Josie left early one morning, Esmé stood at the gate and waved goodbye. She looked very old and frail and rather lonely standing there, and Josie felt tears fill her eyes. She gave a last wave and turned the corner to head north along the main road of the town. She was loaded down with a bag of food and some francs in her money belt, which had been boosted by a gift of 200 francs from Louis. Along with the 300 francs that Esmé had paid her, it made a nice round 500 francs. It sounded a lot, but Josie knew it wouldn't get her very far. She pushed the thought of the approaching autumn, then winter, to the back of her mind.

Her first purchases before leaving the town were a map to take her to the coast and a reel of tape to repair a small tear in her tent. She knew that her nights in hostels were over and the next few months were going to be tough.

In four days she had reached Orleans. There were plenty of rivers to make use of, all full and running well, so Josie was keeping clean enough, but despite her best intentions, had no choice but to cut back on the amount of food she ate, and the variety.

The next night she camped north of the city, and before it became dark, took out the map and studied it with the idea of cheering herself up, but all that happened was a feeling of frustration because of the distance still to be covered. Also, it had suddenly occurred to her that she wouldn't have the money to cross the Channel. For foot passengers it was very cheap, but it was going to be impossible to find the necessary cash. Still, she couldn't give up now. The thought of going through Paris terrified her. It looked huge on the map. A jumble of hundreds – maybe a thousand – roads and lots of people, some kind, but many would be unsympathetic towards an English girl on the road, and there were always rough areas in any town or city where crime and violence were rife. No, she just couldn't face it. So although it would add miles and therefore days to her journey, she would stick to the countryside and skirt round Paris.

By the time she had left Paris behind, it was mid-September. Darkness fell by 6pm and the nights were cool. Her energy was lagging and she was getting thin again. The twelve miles or more a day had become eight, and her money was running out. She arrived at another town and walked through the residential area, walking round dustbins pushed to the pavement for collection. As she walked past one large house a man came out and threw what appeared to be half a loaf of sliced bread in the bin. It was growing dark and Josie walked a little farther, then stepped into a park and sat on a bench. *I can't believe I've sunk to this*, she thought, *but needs must*. As darkness descended, people came home from work, parked their cars and disappeared inside, back to their families. Josie walked slowly out of the park and looking to the left and right, headed back the way she had come. Then in a flash, she had the dustbin lid off, the loaf of bread was in her hand and she was hurrying back to the park.

That evening, she ate some of the bread, which was dry but edible, and then as the hours went by and the streets became quiet, she left the park again. Walking carefully down the road, she looked inside all the dustbins and took out anything that looked edible. There were plenty of bread crusts, also vegetable peelings, old cabbage leaves and apple peelings. She took them all to study in the light of day and eat what she could. She also found the rind off some cheese, which was a real bonus. Then making her way back to the park, she made camp under some trees.

The next morning, she washed some carrot peelings in a stream running nearby and ate them along with some bread and cheese, then finished up with apple peelings. Quite a feast! As it became lighter, people began to walk through the park on their way to work, so she packed up her belongings and surreptitiously moved out from among the trees and then walked on. Although aware she was getting thinner and weaker, it was no good worrying about it; she just had to keep moving north as best she could. Her road crossed a motorway, and across the fields she could see a service area, and hear the sounds of traffic. Suddenly it occurred to her here was another source of food. But the only way someone on foot could get there was probably across these fields and climbing a fence. It seemed worth the effort, though, but best to wait until dusk. It was already mid-afternoon and the days were shorter, so not long to wait. She found a place to sit on a log under some trees, and waited. The sun began to sink low in the sky and Josie set off, climbing over a gate and keeping close to the hedges. One field, then another, over a farm track, then through some rough, uncultivated land and she was within yards of the service area.

It was now quite dark, but her eyes were used to it and she moved round the edge of the service area, looking for a way through. There were small trees either side of the fence to keep it more private for the landowner. It was not difficult to find one to climb, step on the top of the fence and drop down on the other side. The trees and bushes were still full of leaf, and she was hidden from sight. Peering through the undergrowth, she seemed to be looking at the back of the building, where staff cars were parked and large bins stood to take the rubbish from the cafés and restaurants inside. As she watched, a member of staff came out and threw a bag of rubbish into one of the bins. After a minute or two she stepped out from the bushes and walked past the cars and to the front of the building. Here it was a hive of activity, with cars coming and going, and people walking to and from the building. Josie walked inside and made her way towards the toilets. The sign directed her to the left, but as Josie turned the corner her foot caught in a plastic carrier bag lying on the floor and she toppled forward. But before she went sprawling, two strong hands grabbed her arms and steadied her.

"*Oh, merci, monsieur.*"

"That's all right, love," said a cheerful voice.

"Thanks, that floor looks really hard. I'm glad you were there."

"I thought you looked English, not that it makes much difference, but I don't speak much French."

"Me either," laughed Josie; then went on her way.

It was lovely to use a proper, modern toilet and wash her hands thoroughly in hot water. Then she topped up her liquid soap container before going to a seating area not in a café, and eating some bread and cheese. As she sat there she made the decision to come in during the night when it was quiet and have a good wash, taking advantage of the lovely hot water. She wandered round a couple of shops, then went back outside to wait till things quietened down.

It was after midnight before Josie returned to the building. A fairly thorough wash was accomplished between a cubicle and a sink. A member of staff came in as Josie, feeling refreshed, was scrubbing her flannel and some underwear. She just nodded at Josie and disappeared into a cubicle. Josie dried her hands at the hand drier and as soon as the lady had returned to work, she partially dried her flannel and undies under the hand drier, before tucking them back in her bag.

Outside once more in the car park, she systematically

went from bin to bin and searched for anything edible, then went to the back of the building and quietly lifted the lid on one of the big bins. But someone was unlocking and coming out of the door. Josie ducked down and waited as the bin lid was opened and more rubbish thrown in. The footsteps went to the door, the person stepped back inside and the door closed with a bang. Josie inched out again, opened the lid once more and lifted out the top bag. It was almost certainly the one that had just been put there. The contents were still hot. She opened the bag. Hot, but rather dried-up chips – yummy! She grabbed as many as she could and put them in her food bag, stuffing some in her mouth at the same time. Underneath the chips were a couple of rather hard bread rolls and an empty margarine container – but when Josie opened it there was plenty still round the sides and on the bottom. It hadn't been cleaned out very efficiently! That went in her bag as well. Searching further, she found some individual packets of sugar and a tiny, half-used tub of jam. The rest of the rubbish was too low down in the bin for her to reach. She then went to the second bin, only to find it disappointingly empty. Still, very happy with her hoard, she made her way back to the trees to find a place to put the tent up.

This proved to be impossible as the bushes were all too close together, so she climbed back over the fence and found an ideal spot under the trees there. But before erecting her tent, she had to study her haul. Beside the things from the big bins, she had half a bottle of Coke and almost a whole bottle of water, half a round of sandwiches, which looked like cheese and ham, half a chocolate muffin and a few crisps – brilliant! She ate the sandwich with the crisps and drank the Coke, then got down to sorting the tent out and getting herself prepared for a few hours' sleep.

As she drifted off she thought of all the food in her bag – from today and from the bins yesterday – and decided this was going to be how she kept herself fed, and alive, over the next weeks.

Noisy rooks woke her the next morning. It was just getting light, but as the days were getting shorter it was after 7am and farmers would be up and about. So she hastily decamped and made her way through the fields and back to the road. Within a few hundred yards, she found herself walking alongside a field of cauliflower. It was just too tempting. She struggled through a gap in the hedge and pulled one, trimmed the root and outer leaves off and pushed them into the hedge, then buried the head in her bag under the bread. But for the next few miles she was very nervous in case someone had seen her. Now, whenever a village came in sight, her eyes were searching all the time for dustbins, public bins and anywhere she might scavenge food. At the beginning of each day, she would start walking briskly, but soon tired and would go slower and slower, resting frequently.

It was now October, and Amiens came within sight. Josie was losing heart and hope. If she could get to Calais, how would she find the money to cross the Channel? She saw the spires of the Cathedral de Amiens and although it was adding miles, felt a desperate urge to go there and pray. The next morning she approached the cathedral and entered through the huge, old doors. She gasped at the sheer height of the ceiling and the ornate stonework. Gazing about her, she made her way to a pew. As she knelt to pray, she felt a sense of peace steal over her. She prayed that she might survive and get back to England. She asked for forgiveness for stealing the cauliflower, but couldn't promise that she wouldn't steal again! She stayed there for an hour, then walked back outside into the bright autumn sunshine.

Her route crossed, or went under, many major roads before she was back near the motorway. Here there was a junction, and leading off it an industrial area with factories and warehouses, hotels and shops, and a garage selling fuel. The area seemed good for finding food. Wandering around, she noted where bins were and where she might camp for the night. As she passed the garage, a lorry pulled in and the driver put up his hand to her. Puzzled, she did not respond; then she realised it was the man she had bumped into some days ago, or was it a week or more? She wasn't sure. She did quite well that night from the bins, which was just as well because she had no food left at all.

It took her another week to get to Abbeville, when she would once have done it in two days. Then after scavenging in the town, which included picking up rotten fruit and veg from where there had been a street market, she headed out the other side. Very soon she saw another service area only a mile or so away. She found her way to the boundary fence, and summoning all her strength, heaved herself over it. As she landed the other side her knees gave way, and only the trees and the undergrowth prevented her from falling. She staggered through the trees, across a picnic area, now deserted on this overcast, cold and windy day, and collapsed onto a low wall surrounding the car park.

PART 2

CHAPTER 14

Another gust of wind blew more litter across the car park. A plastic bag flew across, inches from her head, and became tangled up in the hedge, along with a crisp packet and what looked like a receipt. It seemed to be impaled on a thorn or a piece of twig just underneath the carrier bag. Josie watched it being frantically twisted about in the wind, seeing it, and yet not seeing it; too exhausted and despondent to really take anything in. Then a small frown appeared on her face, and she screwed up her eyes in the dim light and stared at the 'receipt'. Surely it was a note, a franc note. Carefully she reached out and untangled it from the hedge. It was a 100 franc note. Josie stared at it blankly. Was it real? Was she seeing things? Had she passed out and started hallucinating? She smoothed it out and studied it carefully. Yes, it was definitely a 100 franc note. She looked around, expecting someone to run over and claim it, but nobody appeared.

For another ten minutes Josie sat there, staring at the note, turning it over, then back again. Then her brain seemed to kick in – *FOOD!* She thought of her time in the cathedral and whispered a prayer of thanks, then heaved herself to her feet. She went into the toilets and thoroughly washed her hands and face and combed her hair. She took off her scruffy, dirty coat and folded it, hiding the dirtiness inside, before heading out to the restaurant. She thought at first that the smell of food would make her faint, but steadied herself and walked to the counter. She pointed to the fish, chips and peas and asked for a hot chocolate as well. The girl gave her the food and drink, then moved along to the till to take the money. *She thinks I've stolen it*, Josie thought as she saw the suspicious look on the girl's face, *or I've got it for favours*. She shuddered at the thought. She held her hand out for the change and sat down at the nearest table. *Now I must eat this slowly, or I will have terrible stomach ache and probably lose it*. She nibbled delicately on a chip, then a small piece of fish covered in crispy batter. She chewed slowly and thoroughly, then had some peas. Oh, this was good.

She closed her eyes in bliss, then opened them and started as a voice said, "Hello again, do you mind if I sit with you? There is something I want to say to you."

So shocked was Josie that she didn't answer, and the man, the lorry driver, pulled a chair out and sat down. He placed his own plate of food on the table, smiled at Josie and took a mouthful.

"Mm, their fish and chips here are always good. I come here most weeks and this is what I have."

Josie made no reply, just took another mouthful of fish and stared at her plate. He started to talk.

"I'm going to tell you a bit about myself, then I have

a suggestion to make. My name is Phil and I'm married to a lovely lady called Pammy. We live in Essex, and as you probably know, I'm a lorry driver. I come over to France twice a week with a load of cartons to be used in a factory for packing, mainly food stuff, then my lorry is reloaded with stuff to go back to England."

He paused, but Josie remained silent, concentrating on eating the food on her plate.

"I've seen you several times, slowly making your way north, and at a guess I would say you're heading for Calais. Am I right?"

Josie glanced up at him and nodded.

"It's also my guess that you've run out of money, and you are struggling."

Josie made no comment.

"Look, tell me to go away and mind my own business if you like, but you remind me so much of my eldest daughter that I almost feel I know you, and I would like to help you."

Now Josie looked up and snapped, "I'm not getting in your lorry, if that's what you think. I'll walk, or die trying."

Phil didn't seem to know what to say. He cleared his plate of the last bits of fish and chips and wiped his mouth on a napkin. "How far have you come?"

"From Benidorm in Spain," Josie replied.

Phil's mouth dropped open. "Benidorm? My goodness, that's some feat. How long has it taken you?"

"Oh, ages. I've had to stop and get work so I had money to carry on, but since I've been in France I've only managed to get one job because my French is so bad."

"What about Spain, then? Do you speak Spanish?"

"Yes, I'm quite good with Spanish and I lived there for a while."

Thoughts of Manuel sprang to Josie's mind, and tears filled her eyes.

"Don't get upset, I didn't mean to pry. Look, can I tell you my other suggestion?"

Josie shrugged.

"Well, I know a woman who lives just over there in a pretty little village." He waved his hand vaguely in the direction Josie had come from. "She has a couple of spare rooms and she does B&B."

Josie opened her mouth to say she hadn't the money for a B&B, but he put up his hand and stopped her.

"Hear me out. She's a lovely lady, very kind and she speaks a little English. Why don't you let me take you there? You could stay a couple of nights, sleep in a proper bed, have a bathroom for your use and I'm sure she would do some laundry for you."

Josie was just looking at him and frowning.

"She's very cheap, she only does it for the company," Phil continued. "I've always got spare cash in my lorry for emergencies, and if this isn't an emergency I don't know what is. Then I'll give you a little cash to get you to the coast. Then you can finish your walk. What do you say?"

"Why would you do this? Spend all this money on

me? You don't even know me. You don't even know my name. How do you know I'd pay you back?"

"I don't know, really. I think it's just because you're so like my Emma and you look as though you're at the end of your strength. I'd never forgive myself if…"

His voice trailed away. They were silent for a few minutes. Josie was still eating her fish and chips, which were now quite cold, but she didn't care. *He thinks I'm going to die*, Josie thought, *and I think so too, unless I accept his help*. She started to speak.

"Well, I went to Spain for a holiday with my friend Stella – I'm Josie, by the way – and I fell in love with the place. So I went back the next year and found work. I got to know this Spanish man and we fell in love and I moved into his villa with him. But because of my past history and things that had happened to me… well, it all went wrong. I had very little money so I couldn't fly home, so I started walking, and here I am!"

Phil finished his cup of tea and watched silently as Josie wrapped the chips she couldn't manage in a napkin and put them in her bag.

"It's a difficult decision I know, Josie, but I've got to be on my way. Will you do what I've suggested? I'll give you a little more cash and an IOU, because I can tell you'll want to pay it back. Then I'll give you my name and address and telephone number in Essex and wait to hear from you. Or better still, we can meet up in Calais and you can come over the Channel with me as a hitchhiker. Believe me, it will be easier that way. I know a lot of the men at the docks; I've been through so many times. I can make it easier for you. I don't want to be rude, but if you go through on your own, as you are, you'll have no end of trouble – they'll search you and question you and you'll be there for hours. Yes, it will be much better if you come through with me. Look, I know a nice little café in Calais. I'll show you where it is in my atlas."

Without waiting for a reply, he got up and left the building. A few minutes later he was back. He opened the atlas and found a street map of Calais.

"Look, you'll be coming into the town around here, I would think." He pointed to a place on the outskirts of Calais. "Make your way to here, where there is an industrial area. I top up with diesel there 'cause it's cheaper, and if you go round the corner there are a few shops and a café called Mirabelle's. Wait for me there, either inside or outside. I'll find you, OK?"

Josie nodded. Phil continued.

"Any idea how long it will take you to get there?"

Josie thought as she studied Phil's atlas. "Well, I can't walk very far each day now, I'm too tired. But I would think about a week."

"You must eat, Josie, or you'll never make it," Phil stressed. "Shall we say a week today, then? That's next Tuesday, if not, next Thursday. If I don't see you by then, try and phone me or Pammy at home and we'll sort something out. Now come on, I really must make a move."

Still, Josie hesitated.

"This woman won't want a scruffy person like me in her house."

Phil rolled his eyes. "I'm going, are you coming or not? We'll think up a story when we're driving there."

He got up, took his jacket off the back of the chair and began to walk away. Suddenly panicking, Josie got up, grabbed her bag and followed.

Phil had to help her into the lorry, she was so weak, and the lorry so high, but finally she was sat in the passenger seat with her seat belt done up and Phil was starting the engine.

"Now, I'm just going to drive a couple of miles up the motorway, then come off at the next exit. Then I'll double back for a few miles till I'm virtually where you left the road to get to the services. That's where Mimi's house is. Now let me think, what are we going to tell her? I think we'll say that we know each other from the past and you were on a walking holiday and you got robbed. How does that sound?"

Josie couldn't help smiling. "Very good, you ought to be a writer," she said.

Phil indicated and turned off the motorway. Ten minutes later they stopped in a layby near a substantial house. It was now completely dark, but two outside lights lit up the house.

"Wait there." Phil jumped out of the lorry and trotted up the path to the front door of the house. He rang the bell and waited. Then the door opened and a tiny elderly lady stood there. As Josie watched, a big smile spread across her face and then she kissed Phil on each cheek and ushered him in the door. Five minutes went by and Josie began to worry; then the door opened and Phil hurried back to the lorry.

"It's OK, I've explained and she can't wait to look after you and make you feel better. Come on now."

He helped her down and took her rucksack and her arm and walked with her back to the house. Mimi took one look at her and made horrified noises before pulling her inside. Josie had no idea what she was saying, but her face said it all.

"I'm going, Josie. Good luck," Phil said, and then to Josie's surprise, he kissed her lightly on the cheek, then he kissed Mimi and bid them both goodbye.

"Come in, welcome," Mimi said. "Phil gave me francs, and francs for you."

She handed Josie a wad of notes and put a similar amount in her pocket. She beckoned to Josie to follow her and led the way up a grand staircase; then along a corridor to a door, which she opened with a flourish.

"This is your bedroom," she said slowly. "Put your bag 'ere and I will show you the bathroom."

She walked to the end of the corridor and opened another door. Inside was a large bathroom with clean towels hanging by a radiator. She walked back to the bedroom with Josie.

"I give you this." She handed Josie a towelling robe and matching slippers. "You bath and you give me your clothes. I wash your clothes. Tomorrow, dry for you. When you finish bath you come to me and I give you food and drink."

Josie felt completely overwhelmed, and tried hard not to cry. "Thank you, thank you so much."

Mimi left her and Josie went into her bedroom and closed the door. Weeping uncontrollably, she dropped to her knees beside the bed. Silently she prayed.

Thank you, Lord Jesus, for giving me the chance to live. Bless all the kind people who have helped me on my journey, especially Phil and Mimi. Thank you that I was always able to find work in Spain, and for getting me so far through France. Please help me through this next week so that I can get home. Amen.

She reached into her bag and pulled out a long piece of toilet paper and wiped her eyes and blew her nose, then staggered to her feet. For the first time she looked at the room. The drapes at the window were cream with red roses, and the bedspread matched. A brown and beige carpet covered the floor and a wardrobe stood against one wall. Alongside this was a small chest of drawers with a mirror standing on top. Josie looked at herself. She saw a dreadfully thin young woman with thin, dull hair, dressed in dirty, ragged clothes, and she hardly recognised herself as the young lady with the shiny, golden brown curls who had left Benidorm just over two years ago. But now hope was back in her heart, with some of her natural determination. She picked up the robe and mules and walked down to the bathroom.

Forty minutes later, with her body thoroughly washed and her hair in clean, damp curls, Josie walked hesitantly down the stairs to find Mimi. She had no idea if there were other guests or if Mimi had a husband, and she felt rather embarrassed in just pants and a robe. But it did seem too quiet for there to be other people. She had her clothes stuffed into a carrier bag and her coat over her arm. Mimi must have heard her coming down the stairs, because she appeared from a room at the rear of the property. She beckoned Josie to join her, and this appeared to be Mimi's private quarters. The door led straight into a large kitchen/diner, and another door led, probably, to Mimi's own bedroom and bathroom, and possibly sitting room.

"Sit down, Josie, it is warm here. Phil says you have good food in the services, so I make you just cheese with toast. You like this?"

Josie didn't know how much she would be able to eat, but knew she must try. "Yes please, Mimi."

The snack was started and Mimi disappeared with the washing. After a few minutes she returned. "I do this colour first." She pointed to her dark trousers. "Next I do this." She pointed to her white blouse. "Come and see, Josie, when you have eaten."

The food slowly disappeared. It may have been simple but was delicious nonetheless. Then Josie followed Mimi through the door. To the right she pointed out her bedroom, bathroom and sitting room, and to the left a door led to a large utility room with a washing machine, sink and tumble drier. An ironing board stood ready on the other side. Pulled up to the ceiling was an old-fashioned pulley, and linen was airing up there. The room was heated so things would air quickly. Mimi looked rather anxiously at Josie.

"Your clothes, they are old. I don't know…"

"Don't worry, Mimi, if they fall apart I can mend them," Josie reassured her, hoping that Mimi had something to mend them with, because she certainly didn't.

"I will make a hot drink for you."

They returned to the kitchen and Mimi made tea. When it was drunk, she sent Josie upstairs to bed, but when Josie turned off the light, the room was plunged into total blackness. She put the bedside light back on and went over to the window and pulled back the drapes. But behind these were some thick silver coloured curtains to help keep the cold out. Josie pulled these back and was confronted with shutters. She knew she was being silly, but could feel panic sweeping over her. With some difficulty she opened the shutters. At least now she had a little glimmer of light from a new moon. She was completely unable to open the window, but stood for several minutes taking deep breaths till her panic subsided, then pulling the robe snugly round her body, she climbed into the bed and pulled the covers up. The sheets were cold, but in a short time warmth stole over her and she slept.

After what seemed a very short time, a bright light in her eyes woke Josie. It was the sun streaming through the window, and her watch said it was 9am. She stared at the sunshine and her watch, hardly able to believe she had slept for eleven hours. The biscuits Mimi had given her in case she was hungry in the night sat untouched on the plate, and the glass of water was still full. She picked up a biscuit and swung her legs out of bed, then stretched and yawned. Then nibbling hungrily, she wandered to the window. The view which met her eyes made her gasp; then burst into tears. It was the English Channel. She was nearly there. How she wished she could wave a magic wand and find herself on the other side of the water. Ashamed of herself for the tears, she managed to stop and blow her nose before her face became all blotchy and her eyes red. Slipping her feet into the mules, she made her way to the bathroom and then down the stairs. Mimi opened the kitchen door with a big smile on her face.

"Good morning, Josie. What a good long sleep you've had."

Josie smiled and returned the greeting, and took the plate and glass to the draining board.

"Sit down, Josie. Do you like eggs?"

When Josie said she did, Mimi handed her some orange juice and went to the hob to begin breakfast. Josie had scrambled eggs on toast, and then after a pause and a cup of coffee, she managed to eat a croissant, then another cup of coffee. Mimi disappeared for few minutes, then came back with a dry and ironed pile of washing: Josie's trousers and coat, and a dark t-shirt.

"White washing is ready in ten minutes," she told Josie.

"Oh thank you, Mimi. Mm, they smell lovely."

Mimi took Josie's coat from the top of the pile.

"Is still good," she said with a smile.

The coat had come up really well, as had the other things. The blue trousers needed a button on the waistband but otherwise everything was good. And when Mimi brought her pale things through a few minutes later, these also looked good. Her green t-shirt had become faded with the sun, but that didn't matter. Josie told Mimi her delight at seeing the Channel, and the elderly lady seemed to understand.

"Phil says you must eat every two or three hours, but I will give you only small meals. It is sad you have to go tomorrow. I like you to stay one week. I make you fat."

Josie laughed, remembering how other people on her journey had said the same thing.

"It would be nice to stay, but I have to meet Phil at Calais next week and I mustn't miss him."

Mimi was true to her word, and food was on the table at regular intervals: a meaty broth at 12pm, tea and cake at 2.30pm, then chicken casserole at 5.30pm. Then as they sat in the kitchen that evening watching a small television, Mimi got up and put several different cereals on the table and indicated for Josie to help herself. It took a long time to eat each meal, and Josie felt she had been eating all day without a break. She bathed again that night and was in bed again by 10pm.

She was soon asleep, but woke early the next morning before it was light. She repacked her bag and dressed, then stripped the bed for Mimi.

After a good breakfast, Josie packed the food Mimi

had given her for the day, hugged and kissed her and after thanking her again, set out. The route she was taking would gradually draw nearer to the coast, and she hoped to be spending her first night near the sea. Thirty-six hours of good food was not going to make much difference to her weight, but the nourishment and two good nights' sleep had made her feel better, and her face looked less grey.

She was able to get to an inlet where a river emptied into the sea, and camped for the night amongst the trees and bushes there. All that day she had eaten well, but still had nearly as much left over for the next day. The small wad of notes in her money belt reassured her that she wouldn't go hungry. As she drifted off to sleep she thought how nice it would be to have one night in a hostel in Calais before meeting Phil, just to feel clean and look respectable, but food was more important.

She slept fitfully, for the night was cold, and woke at dawn. If she could walk the same distance as the first day, about eight miles, she would be quite near to Calais by Wednesday, then maybe she would have the night in the hostel. With excitement and adrenalin keeping her going, she was successful, and Wednesday evening found her in a coastal resort two or three miles from Calais. With only food for three days to buy, she had used very little of Phil's money, so decided to look for a hostel. But as it was in a popular resort, it was the most expensive hostel so far. She turned away and walked up and down the streets, enquiring at small B&Bs and hotels, and finally on the outskirts of the town and on the main road she found somewhere reasonable. It was shabby but reasonably clean and warm. Josie booked in and was shown to her room. It was now 7pm, so she washed some underwear and a t-shirt and draped them over the radiator. She bathed and washed her hair, rubbing it as dry as possible, then sat near the radiator until it was time for bed.

In the morning she refused breakfast and just paid for her bed for the night, buying bread from a baker on the way out of town. By lunchtime she was in Calais, and celebrated with a cup of coffee and a gooey cake. The weather was overcast and cold, but at least dry. Now to find the café Phil had described to her. It took her over an hour to find the industrial area, and then another fifteen minutes to find Mirabelle's. But there were still at least two and a half hours before Phil arrived, and she couldn't sit in the café all that time. Wandering off, she found a supermarket. It was huge! If she walked very slowly up each aisle, at least an hour would go by. She studied all the clothes, holding things up against herself; went to the book section and pretended she knew what the titles were, then slowly up and down each food aisle. Putting a small pack of ham and two bread rolls in her basket, she then studied all the wines and spirits before finally going along the aisle with soft drinks and water. She popped a bottle of water in the basket, then walked slowly back to the tills. After joining a queue, it became obvious there was a problem at the till with a customer's credit card. Good; that would kill a bit more time.

By the time she stood outside the supermarket, it was 5pm and dark. She found a seat and broke open a roll, filled it with several slices of ham and chewed slowly. Suddenly it was 5.40pm and she needed to find Mirabelle's. After a wrong turn and a bit of confusion, she found herself outside the café. A wind had sprung up and it was very cold, so she didn't wait outside but went straight in and bought a cup of tea. She found a table near the window and sat down to wait.

Her feelings were in turmoil – excitement to be going home, worry in case Phil didn't turn up and terror at the thought of going through customs. After all, she did look a bit like a hippy and although she had no experience of drug-taking, she probably looked like a drug addict. But then an idea flashed through her mind and she took her few bits of make-up from her bag, and with a rather embarrassed look around, carefully applied it. A little bit of blusher, some powder and eye shadow, then a hint of lipstick. Any more would look strange with her thin face. But it did make her look and feel better. She tidied everything away and gazed out of the window, then at her watch – 6.45pm. *Oh do hurry up, Phil, before I go mad with worry.*

It was difficult to see much outside the café window, but the road taking the lorries and cars back onto the main road was only about thirty yards away, and she could see the lights and the rough outline of the vehicles, but it was too dark to see anything clearly. She bent down and checked for the third time that her passport was handy, then heard the café door open.

"Phil," she cried, leaping up and rushing over to him. "Oh, am I glad to see you!"

Phil laughed. "And I'm rather relieved to see you too. Come on, grab your bag and let's go."

As they sat in the lorry heading to the port, Josie admitted to him how scared she was.

"Just relax, and if they do question you, just tell the truth. You've got nothing to hide. You've done nothing wrong or broken the law. You'll be OK."

He patted her shoulder and pulled in behind some other lorries.

But ten minutes later Josie found herself sitting in a small room with a customs officer. He asked her lots of questions and Josie answered honestly, as Phil had advised.

"So you are telling me you have walked from Spain? Explain to me how you have managed that."

So Josie did.

"Well, I was working in Spain and living with my Spanish boyfriend, but it didn't work out. He began to knock me about and I had to leave in a hurry one night when he was passed out with drink. I didn't have much money, so I had to walk. I just needed to get as far away from him as possible. Then after some time I got a job for three months, then I moved on and got a job in Barcelona for the summer. Then I walked to the Pyrenees and got more work in a ski resort. Then I got quite a long way through France before I managed to get work with an old lady. But she couldn't pay me much, and I soon ran out of money. Because I don't speak much French, I couldn't get another job. I started taking food from rubbish bins and I was getting very thin and weak. Then Phil, that's the lorry driver I'm with, came up to me and said he'd seen me several times and realised I was heading back to England."

By this time Josie was crying and finding it hard to continue. "He was so kind, he has… loaned me some money and…" She wiped her eyes and blew her nose. "And he's going to take me to his home. His wife is a nurse and she'll be able to help me."

The officer looked at her for several minutes. "Well, that's an amazing story. Can you give a phone number for one of these people you worked for so I can confirm your story?"

Josie thought carefully. "Well, if you speak French, you could ring Esmé, the old lady I helped. She speaks a little English, but over the phone she may get confused."

"Yes, I speak French, have you got her number?"

Josie got her notebook out and opened it on the page where she had written everyone's address and phone number, and pointed out Esmé's details.

The next few minutes of a rapid French conversation were lost on Josie, but the officer seemed satisfied. He put the phone down, stood up and told Josie she was free to go. Then as she sighed with relief and picked up her bag, he smiled and said, "Good luck."

She went back outside and found Phil, and they walked to the lorry and climbed aboard.

Half an hour later they were on the ferry and walking up the stairs.

"Now, I shall go into the lorry drivers' café, but you are not allowed in there, I'm afraid."

He reached into his pocket and pulled out some money.

"Oh, I don't need any money, thanks, Phil, I've got some left. Where shall I meet you?"

"Go back to the lorry. Can you remember what deck we are on?"

Josie assured him she could, and they parted company. She went straight to the restaurant and bought chicken, chips and peas. It took her forty minutes, but she ate it all and drank a bottle of water, then walked to the very front of the ferry, wondering if she would be able to see the lights of England. She was amazed how close they looked. Once more, tears filled her eyes and ran down her cheeks. She just couldn't stop crying. The relief of being almost back home after a gruelling journey, and her weakened state of health, had left her very emotional.

"Are you all right, dear?" A middle-aged lady looked at her sympathetically. "Are you ill?"

"I'm all right, thank you. I've been away a long time and I'm just so glad to be nearly home."

"So it's tears of happiness then, dear?"

"Yes, and thank you for being so kind."

Josie blew her nose again and managed a watery smile. She walked slowly back to the stairs and waited until a voice over the tannoy said they could make their way back to their vehicles.

As she sat beside Phil heading out of Dover, she told him about what she had eaten and about the kind lady finding her in tears – again!

"I just keep on crying, Phil." Her voice wobbled as she spoke.

"You're just very run down, Josie, don't worry about it. My Pammy will soon sort you out."

They drove steadily onwards, not speaking much. It was now nearly 10pm, and Phil said they should be home soon after 11pm. It was a dark night and Josie could see very little through the lorry window. But just road signs in English or a Tesco store or a roadside pub, lit up to encourage would-be diners, were enough to start the tears again. Phil said nothing, he just handed her a tissue and let her cry. Then later she slept, exhausted, and only woke when Phil stopped and turned off the engine. He reached out and touched her arm.

"We're home, Josie, and here's my Pammy to meet us."

He leapt from the lorry and hugged and kissed his beaming wife, then hurried back round the lorry to help Josie down.

"This is Josie, I told you about her on the phone. Josie, Pammy, my wife."

They shook hands. Pammy shivered.

"Come into the warm, it's a cold wind today. I'll put the kettle on."

She was a lady of about fifty, with dark curly hair and like her husband, slightly overweight. She had what Josie called a smiley face. She was either smiling or looked as though she was about to. They were obviously very fond of each other, and glad to be together again. Phil helped Josie off with her jacket and pushed her gently into a chair.

"What would you like to drink, Josie?" Pammy looked over her shoulder as she filled the kettle.

"A cup of lovely English tea, please," Josie said with a smile. She reached into her bag for the roll and ham. "And I'll use this up while it's still reasonably fresh."

Pammy gave her a plate and a knife, and put a tub of butter on the table. Butter was rarely used in Spain, and although Esmé had used it sometimes, it still seemed like a treat. Pammy watched with satisfaction as Josie spread it on the roll, thinking that it would do her good, but not saying anything. As yet she wasn't sure whether Josie's weight loss was due to lack of money or whether she may have an eating disorder. She put a mug of tea on the table by Josie and handed another one to Phil, then sat down opposite and sipped hers. Phil looked at Pammy.

"You ought to be in bed, love. You've got an early start tomorrow."

"No, I'm OK, Phil. I swapped with Elana. I'm doing 12 to 4pm tomorrow, so Josie and I can get to know each other. And Josie, when you've finished your roll and tea I think you should go to bed. You look exhausted. Have a shower or a bath first if you like, but if you're too tired it doesn't matter."

Josie swallowed the last bit of her roll. "Well

actually, I had a shower last night and washed my hair, so I'm fairly clean, so I think I'll go straight to bed."

Phil looked at her with astonishment. "How come you managed to have a shower, then? I thought you were camping!"

"Well, Mimi gave me so much packed food it lasted me two days, so I only had to buy food for two more days. That meant I had enough money for a cheap B&B last night."

"Well I never, that's good," Phil said.

Pammy put the dirty crockery on the draining board, picked up Josie's coat and bag and beckoned her to follow. They climbed the stairs and Pammy opened a door to a small bedroom.

"This is our Emma's when she's home, but she'll be delighted for you to borrow it. The bathroom is next door. I'm going to leave you now and let you get your head down. Get up whenever you like in the morning. Time is not important."

Josie thanked her and wished her goodnight. She slipped into the bathroom and washed the remnants of her make-up off and brushed her teeth with the well-used and almost useless toothbrush, then undressed down to her t-shirt and pants and climbed into bed. Her feet found a hot water bottle as she wriggled down, and she pulled it up and cuddled it. She was not aware of Phil and Pammy coming up to bed; she was already fast asleep.

Josie opened one eye. It was morning. She picked up her watch and squinted at it: 10.15am, but where was she?

The room was strange to her and it took several moments to remember. She lay there and tried to remember the events of the previous day. Slowly everything came back to her, although the journey to Phil's home was a blur of weeping and darkness and later sleeping. She had no idea of the area where Phil and Pammy lived or what the house looked like outside or inside. She vaguely remembered sitting in the kitchen eating and drinking, but what it looked like, she had no idea. She slipped out of bed and peeped through the curtains – just houses and gardens; obviously a modern housing estate. She let the curtains fall and went next door to the bathroom. When she came out, Pammy called up the stairs.

"Morning, Josie, are you ready for some breakfast?"

After pulling on some trousers, Josie walked down the stairs and found the kitchen and Pammy.

"Well, love, you've had a good long sleep, but now we need to get some food inside you. How about scrambled eggs on toast? That's nice and easy to digest."

"That will be lovely, thanks," Josie responded, then added with a smile, "That's what Mimi gave me for breakfast. It must be good for poorly people."

Pammy broke a couple of eggs into a saucepan and stirred vigorously, then put two slices of wholemeal bread in the toaster.

"Yes, eggs are good for you. Once you have eaten this and had a drink, I want to talk to you about your diet for the next few weeks." She glanced at her watch. "I've got an hour before I leave for work, so I'm all right for time."

Josie swallowed a mouthful of egg and said, "Let's talk now; I'm very slow at eating."

"Yes, you need to chew thoroughly and eat slowly. While I waited for you to wake up, I've made some notes." She pushed a piece of paper towards Josie. "These are all the things we would probably avoid if trying to lose weight and I want you to eat them, you lucky thing!" She laughed and continued. "Lots of dairy products, cheese and milky drinks, full fat yogurts and then meat, mainly chicken, and lots of fish. Do you like fish?"

After a nod from Josie, she went on.

"Plenty of carbohydrates like bread, pasta, potatoes and rice, and of course plenty of veggies and fruit, and you can snack as much as you like. There's ice cream in the freezer and crisps and biscuits in the cupboard." She grinned. "There's even chocolate somewhere, in the cupboard, I think. Eat and drink whatever you want while I'm at work. I'll ring when I finish and you can tell me if the cupboards are bare and I'll shop on the way home."

"It sounds to me like I've died and gone to heaven," Josie said. "Please, Pammy, leave me a list of jobs to do. I may have time when I'm not eating."

They laughed together. Josie felt completely at ease with Pammy, as she did with Phil, and suddenly hope for the future flooded through her.

"I don't know whether Phil has told you, but I want a record kept of everything I owe you and when I'm fit I'll get a job and pay you back."

"Oh, don't worry about that, Josie. It will be a pleasure to help you back to full health."

Josie sat silently for a few minutes, then said quietly, "Pammy, you must allow me to pay you back or I'm afraid I shall be on my way. Promise me now or I'll go today."

"Yes, OK, I promise. If that's how you want it, I can understand."

"Shake on it, then."

Josie thrust out her hand and Pammy solemnly shook it, then they smiled at each other.

"When you've finished your tea, Josie, come upstairs with me. I may be able to find you some clothes."

As they stood in front of Pammy's open wardrobe door, Pammy said, "I've put on a bit of weight over the last few years and I've got clothes I can't get into anymore. I keep meaning to take them down to the charity shop. I'm glad I didn't now. They are a bit untrendy, but apart from that they are in reasonable condition. The only problem is that I'm shorter than you, so the trousers may be a bit short. Let's have a quick try-on, then I must shoot off to work."

Josie tried on a pretty check blouse and a t-shirt. They were a bit loose, but as Pammy said, hopefully she would grow into them. A skirt was the same, and would need the button moving over. The trousers were too short, but there was a decent hem on the bottom which when let down would make them just about long enough. There were also a couple of jumpers, and as winter weather was here, that would certainly be useful.

"I know they are second-hand, Josie, but they will help till you can get some new things."

Josie hugged her. "Do you know, Pammy, I'm just as thrilled with these as I would be with new. Thanks ever so. Can I wear them now?"

"Of course you can. Now I must get ready and go. Are you going to be all right?" She looked worriedly at Josie.

"Yes, I'll be fine. Don't worry about me."

When Pammy had left for work, the first thing Josie did was to make herself a milky coffee and nibble a couple of digestive biscuits; then she explored the house. The kitchen was large and served as a dining room as well. There was a lounge, small but cheerful, and off the hall, a downstairs toilet. At the back a door led to a small utility room with a washing machine, tumble drier and sink. Standing against the wall was an ironing board, and when she looked in the sink cupboards she found an iron, along with washing powder and other cleaning products. A door opened into the garden. It was simply landscaped, with a patio, lawn and a few shrubs. Josie turned to go back into the kitchen and noticed a pile of neatly folded washing waiting to be ironed. *Right*, she thought, *job number one!* The front garden was just a small lawn with a few roses and a drive leading to the garage. The front of the house looked out over a narrow band of trees, with countryside beyond. She ran upstairs and had a quick look round, but the only room she hadn't seen was another bedroom, so making her bed and tidying the room, she grabbed some grubby clothes and ran back downstairs.

She ran some nice hot water in the sink in the utility room and put some soap powder in, whisking it about to dissolve it, then pushed the clothes in and left them to soak. The milky drink had filled her up and she didn't feel ready to eat, so she did the ironing, then took it upstairs and put it in the airing cupboard. Now for lunch! Feeling a little guilty, she rummaged through all the drawers and cupboards and had a good look in the fridge. But the thing she fancied most and hadn't had since leaving England three and a half years ago was baked beans. That good old standby so loved by the British, and there were a couple of tins in the cupboard. Josie put a slice of bread in the toaster and heated up half a tin of beans – heaven!

After the lunch things had been tidied away, Josie surprised herself by sitting in the armchair and falling asleep. But the nap did her good, and she felt refreshed. She decided to shower and wash her hair before Pammy got home. She would also clean the bathroom when she had finished.

An hour later, clean and respectable, Josie was sweeping the kitchen floor when the phone rang.

"Hello, Josie speaking."

"Hello, Josie, how are you?"

"I'm fine, thank you."

"What do we need? Milk, I suppose. Anything else? Have you used anything up?"

"No, not really. Only the chocolate."

"You've eaten all the Kit-Kats? Gosh, Josie, I hope you don't feel sick."

Josie giggled. "Only joking, I just had one, there's still four left."

"You monkey; I can see I'll have to remember you've got a wicked sense of humour. I won't be long then, I can get milk from the local shop."

She rang off and Josie finished the kitchen floor, then sat down to wait.

Pammy gently told Josie off for working when she should be resting, but Josie told her she liked to be busy and had rested. She had written out the food and drinks she'd had that day, to show Pammy, and Pammy was pleased, but said she should try and eat more tomorrow. They both agreed the milky drink before lunch was a mistake as it had taken the edge off her appetite.

On Friday evening, Phil was home in good time and the meal was started when he came in the door. He hugged Pammy, then Josie, and asked about their day, then disappeared upstairs to change and freshen up. Pammy cooked them a lovely meal consisting of fish pie with cheese grated on the top and browned under the grill, and fresh vegetables. Then rice pudding, which Josie had to eat later because she was so full. As they sat down with coffees after the dishes had been done, Pammy had something to say to Josie.

"I hope you don't mind, Josie, but I begged and

pleaded with my doctor and I've got an emergency appointment for you in the morning at 10am." There was a long pause, then Pammy said, "You're not happy, are you? Oh dear, I've done the wrong thing, I can see by your face. I'm sorry, Josie."

"I'm not keen on seeing a doctor and I would refuse to go into hospital, no matter what anyone said."

Josie knew she was being rude and ungrateful, but couldn't help herself.

"You must realise, Josie, that without seeing a doctor some of the responsibility for your recovery rests with me, and that's not really fair, is it?"

Josie made no comment.

"Look, sleep on it and we'll talk about it in the morning."

"All right. Sorry, Pammy, for being awkward."

They smiled at each other, and Josie excused herself, said goodnight and went to bed. As she lay there, she knew she was being unreasonable and she would see the doctor tomorrow.

Dr Rogers was a man in his fifties with a kindly face and a twinkle in his eyes. He seemed quite unruffled by the painfully thin young lady sitting in front of him. He asked for details of how Josie had become so thin and listened without interruption until she had finished.

"So this has come about through lack of money, then, not because you want to be thin?"

"That's right – I usually eat well, but I'm naturally

slim anyway. I can assure you I haven't got some eating disorder."

"Right, Pamela has told me she will give you the right diet and do her best to get you back to full health. Now tell me, are you having normal periods?"

"I haven't had one for months, probably two or three in the last year. Will they come back?"

"It's hard to tell, but I must warn you that should you want children at some point, you may find it difficult to conceive."

"Oh, that's all right, I've no intention of ever marrying, so having children is not an option."

When Dr Rogers gave her a hard look, she continued.

"I've had some bad experiences with men, and I'm afraid it's put me off for life."

"Well, I always say, 'never say never,'" the doctor said with a smile. "Now, make an appointment for three weeks' time and I shall expect to see you at least half a stone heavier – over seven and a half stone would be good for a start. With your height you should really be at least nine stone."

He stood up and shook Josie's hand, and she thanked him for seeing her. On the way home in the car, Josie told Pammy everything that had been said and how relieved she was that he hadn't mentioned hospital.

"Now, Josie, do you need anything from the shops before we go home?"

"Yes, I… No, thank you."

"Come on, Josie, yes or no?" Pammy chuckled.

"Well, you see, I haven't any money. Not a penny."

"Oh, sorry, Josie, how thoughtless of me."

Pammy indicated and pulled into a car park alongside a small parade of shops. She took Josie's hand and spoke gently.

"I know how independent you want to be, dear, but I think we will have to give you a small loan. There's bound to be things you need and we know you will pay us back when you can. Will you accept £20 for now?"

"I think I shall have to, Pammy. When we get home I'll show you my toothbrush, or what's left of it."

They laughed, then got out of the car a walked into a small grocery store. A toothbrush, toothpaste and flannel went into the basket and were paid for, then they walked next door to the newsagents and Josie bought a writing pad and envelopes and some stamps. That was £5 gone out of the £20, but it was all important to Josie.

Dear Stella,

Guess what, I'm back in England. But I am not well at the moment so cannot visit you yet. I have loads to tell you. I hope you and Brian are well. I am staying temporarily at the above address, probably for a few months. Write soon.

Love Josie

Next Josie wrote to Lily, then Bella and Esmé. Not long letters, but promising to write again at greater length in a few weeks' time.

Over the next three weeks, Josie ate well and walked every day, starting with a short stroll, then gradually going further and walking quicker. Three days before Christmas, she kept her appointment with Dr Rogers.

"Well, I must say you are looking much better. Slip your shoes off and hop on the scales."

Josie obliged.

"Very good, seven stone nine. I am very pleased. Keep up the good work."

"Will I be able to get a job now, Doctor? I really need to be earning."

"Just leave it until the New Year. Nobody will employ you over the holidays. That will give you another two weeks to get stronger. Did you say you were walking every day? That's good too. It will all help. Come and see me again in six weeks."

"Thank you, Doctor. Have a good Christmas."

That evening it was decided that Josie should move into the spare room for the rest of her stay with Phil and Pammy. Emma was coming home for two weeks over the Christmas period and it was only fair that she should have her bedroom back. The two young ladies got on well, and the two weeks were a happy time. Josie had Christmas cards from Lily and Stella and a letter from Bella, much to her delight.

Emma went back to her nursing job in Cambridge and things got back to normal. One bright but cold January day, Josie walked into town and began to look for a job. As she had done all those years ago in Plumbford, she walked up and down each street as she came to it, trying in almost every shop, and although it really wasn't her type of job, also trying in offices, but to no avail. Some shops had taken on extra staff for Christmas and some of those had been kept on as permanent staff. Josie covered about half the town and then at 4pm made her way wearily home. On the way she called in the grocers on the parade for milk and stopped to chat to one of the staff there.

"You look weary. What have you been up to today?" The plump, middle-aged lady was quite happy to stop filling shelves and chat.

"I've been looking for a job, but no luck today. I'm going to try again tomorrow."

The woman smiled sympathetically. "It's not easy after Christmas. Everything's a bit quiet. The boss here was looking for someone to do 12 till 2pm each day to cover lunchtimes, but nobody is gonna want to do that. Just two hours, and it breaks up the day. I said to him, 'You'll be lucky.' But then, what do I know?"

"I'll do it." Josie almost grabbed the woman in her enthusiasm. "You probably know I've been ill, and this would just get me going gradually. Do you think he would consider me?"

"I'm sure he would. I'll give him a shout, he's checking off a delivery."

She bustled out the back and Josie heard her voice and a deep voice answering, although it was too faint to hear what they were saying. The lady reappeared.

"He's nearly finished, can you hang on?"

"Of course I can," Josie replied, thinking Pammy would just think she'd been held up in town.

Five minutes later, a grey-haired man came through, probably in his late fifties but looking slim and fit. He smiled and shook Josie's hand.

"Good afternoon, I'm Mike and I like to think I'm the boss around here, but I think Marilyn has other ideas."

He grinned across the shop at the lady, who was back to her shelf-filling. He then went on to explain how two people could keep the shop going most of the time, but he needed someone to cover lunchtimes.

"Marilyn tells me you have been ill. It can be very busy here at times and there is a bit of heavy lifting if I'm not around. Do you think you could cope with that?"

"Oh yes, I'm stronger than I look and I'm just longing to get back to work. My doctor says it's OK for me to work and he doesn't want to see me again for another month, then I'm 100% certain he'll sign me off."

Josie didn't want to tell him what her problem had been, and hoped he wouldn't ask. And to her relief, he didn't.

"I'd like you to start as soon as possible. How are you placed?"

"How about tomorrow?" Josie said with a big smile.

So it was all arranged and Josie left for home. As she walked she thought about the money soon to be earned. Not enough to be independent, but enough to give Pammy housekeeping and stop her debts getting any bigger.

344

"Where have you been? I was just beginning to worry."

"Sorry, Pammy." Josie slipped off her coat and hung it up in the hall. "Here, let me do those potatoes. I expect you've had a busy day."

"Yes, I have, and I don't like these extra hours. I'll be glad when my colleague is better and back to work. Successful day, Josie?"

So the day's events were told, and Pammy was pleased for her.

"That's perfect, Josie, just a few hours a day to start you off, then you can keep on looking for something better. Did you ever think of going back to a garden centre? You told me you liked that sort of thing."

Josie put the potatoes on the hob and lit the gas. "Yes, that's what I'd really like. Perhaps if I wait a few weeks till spring is in the air, then I'll try. Where are they?"

"There's one in the town, actually. You go down that small road by Woolworths and it's about two hundred yards down there."

Josie was surprised. "Well, I never knew there was a garden centre down there. Is that the only one?"

"That's the only one here, but there's several more on the main road into the city. But I don't know what the public transport is like."

Pammy lifted the remains of a casserole from the fridge and popped it in the microwave, then put some broccoli on to boil. Ten minutes later, they were sat at the table eating their meal. It was a Monday, so Phil was in France.

345

"I'm really glad about the job, Josie."

"And I'm really glad I can give you some money for my keep now, Pammy."

They looked at each other and smiled, then Pammy said, "I know how stubborn you are, Josie, but please keep a little for yourself and get yourself some clothes. You must admit, you desperately need them."

To her relief, Josie agreed. The clothes she had walked in were falling to pieces and she was mainly wearing Pammy's castoffs and a couple of things Emma had grown tired of.

It was mid-March and spring was in the air, and things had moved on for Josie. She was fully recovered and now had a full-time job at the nursery in town, Braithwaite's. Her hours varied as she had to do some weekend work. She had started a month ago and was enjoying it. She had done as Pammy suggested and bought lots of clothes, including new underwear, and thrown lots away. In her spare time she kept Pammy and Phil's garden tidy, and also the old lady's next door. She was also doing evening classes to learn a little more about gardening and planned later to do a course on decorating. It all kept her pretty busy, but that suited her. Then out of the blue, things happened that took her completely by surprise.

On her own one day in the house, the front door bell rang. Josie put down the iron and opened the front door. A young man in a smart suit stood there.

"Good morning, I'm sorry to disturb you. I wondered if I might have a word?"

"Yes, what do you want?" Josie didn't intend to invite him in.

"Are you Josie White?"

Josie nodded.

"I'm from the *Essex Chronicle*. I understand you have accomplished an amazing trek. I wondered if you would be prepared to talk about it?"

"No," Josie said.

The young man ignored her. "It would make a wonderful story, please reconsider."

"I don't want my name in the paper, thank you very much, and have reporters here snooping around and people pointing at me in the street. No is the answer. Now goodbye."

She stepped back indoors and closed the door with a bang. She ran upstairs and watched through the window as the young man slowly walked back to his car. He reached into the back and pulled forward a file and began to write. Then a few minutes later, he got out and put a folded-up piece of paper through the door before returning to his car and driving off.

Dear Miss White,

Please believe me, I know exactly how you feel. Forgive me for saying this, but the things you fear may happen, will happen, but then very quickly you will become old news and something else will happen to catch people's interest. I think it's only fair to point out that you would be paid for your story; a sum to be decided between us and the editor. I hope you will think again

and share your adventure with our readers. If I may,
I will call again, maybe next week at the same time.
My name is Tony Williams and I can be reached at the
Chronicle most weekday mornings up to 10am.

He had written his work phone number and his home number on the bottom of the page. Josie wandered through to the kitchen, the piece of paper still clutched in her hand, somewhat dazed and confused. Thank goodness Pammy would be home at 12.30pm today. She needed to talk to someone. Giving herself a mental shake, she put the kettle on for a cup of tea and then continued with the ironing. Pammy listened as Josie told her of the young man's visit, then read the letter. She looked at Josie.

"Well, to tell the truth, I'm surprised this didn't happen months ago. Phil and I haven't said anything, but things have a habit of getting around. He's right what he says; it will be a nine-day wonder. Did he give you any clue how much they would pay you?"

"No, I just couldn't wait to get rid of him."

Pammy looked thoughtful. "You could probably bargain with him, and let's face it, Josie, the money would be useful no matter how much or how little."

"Yes, even though I've nearly paid you back, if I want my own little flat I'll probably have to pay a month's rent in advance. Goodness knows how much that will be."

"Well," Pammy said, "I'm on afternoons next week, so I'll be around if he calls. Would you like that?"

"Oh yes, please. We can tie him to a kitchen chair and only release him when he offers me lots of money."

They laughed together as they let their imaginations run riot.

"Oh, Josie, you do make me laugh." Pammy wiped her eyes as she tried to control her giggles.

When Tony Williams called the next week, he was met with a stony-faced young lady.

"I thought I'd told you no," she said as she stood on the doorstep.

Pammy appeared behind her. "Let him in, Josie. Let's hear what he has to say."

Josie stepped back and glared at him as he walked into the house. She pushed down a giggle as she followed him through to the lounge. She and Pammy had planned everything, right from the cold stare on the doorstep, through to the reluctant agreement and negotiation of payment. Now she just had to call on all her acting skills.

"Sit down." Pammy indicated a chair near the window.

An hour and a half later, a somewhat dazed Tony Williams climbed back in his car and drove away. Goodness knows what the boss was going to say. He'd given him an upper limit and he'd gone over it. But boy, after just one short chat, he knew he had a good story.

The plan now was to come back over a few days and get a good story as soon as possible. It would possibly be ready for next week's issue, or if not, the week after.

349

Meanwhile, Pammy and Josie were dancing round the lounge, laughing and cheering, not quite able to take in the amount they had squeezed out of him. Plenty for Josie to pay back Phil and Pammy and pay a month's rent on a flat, and still with a reasonable sum to put in the bank for a rainy day.

The next few weeks were not easy for Josie. There were some things she could never talk about. She had to just tell enough to make it interesting. So there was no mention of why she and Manuel had parted, and she would not give any names of people who had helped her. In the end, pseudonyms had been used. The paper was duly released and all hell broke loose. There were reporters outside the house, with local television crews, and at work it was not much better. In the end they closed up the house and went away for a few days. When they got back it was a little better, although the TV crew were still there. Josie made a statement, composed by herself with Phil and Pammy's help while they were away.

"What I did was nothing special. I merely walked home because I had no money to fly. Now I would ask for some peace to get on with our lives."

After that she refused to talk to anyone and in the end they were, as she asked, left in peace.

The next few months were frantic at work, but Josie still had every fourth weekend off. When the next one came up in the middle of June she decided it was time to make the journey to go and see Stella. Her suggestion had been eagerly taken up by Stella, who said she must go for the weekend. So on the Friday, Josie hurried home from work, washed and changed, grabbed her already packed case and leapt into the car. Phil drove her to the station, where she got a train to London and then another to Sandacre, where Stella was to pick her up. By the time she got there it was 8.30pm, but the sun was still shining as she left the train. And there was darling Stella! The girls squealed and rushed towards each other for a big hug, both unashamedly crying with delight.

"Oh, Stella, it's so lovely to see you."

Josie took her arm as they walked to the car. They looked at each other, taking in the changes. Stella was now a mature young lady, married for several years and, Josie noticed, with a baby on the way. Josie had also matured. The events of the last few years and the long walk had changed her. She still had her feisty nature and wicked sense of humour, but there was a serious side to her now, when she would become quiet and thoughtful. She would tell nobody what was going through her mind at these times; those thoughts were for her alone.

They arrived at Stella and Brian's neat three-bedroomed semi-detached house, and Stella hustled her in. Brian appeared with a big smile on his face.

"Josie, welcome. How are you?"

"I'm very well, thank you, and you?"

"Yes, we're fine. Gosh, you must be exhausted – all that travelling after a hard week at work. Come through and I'll make a cup of tea, you can unpack later."

As they sat drinking the welcome cup of tea, Josie told them about her job and evening classes and Brian said he was getting on well at the bank and was hoping for a promotion next year.

"And that will come at just the right time," Stella said. "I've only got a month to go before I leave my job and wait for the happy event, so a few extra pennies will help."

At 10.30pm Brian went upstairs for a shower and Stella showed Josie to her room.

"It's our smallest room, I'm afraid, Josie, and we're in the middle of decorating the other one for baby."

"Oh, this will do me fine. It's a lovely little room, Stella."

The next morning Brian went off at 9.30am to play golf and the friends were left alone to chat and catch up to their hearts' content.

"So what went wrong between you and Manuel, Josie? You seemed to be getting on so well."

"It was the same problem, Stella, I just don't like lovemaking and Manuel got really fed up with me. I don't know whether I told you but Manuel's father was an alcoholic and he died just before Manuel and I got together. Manuel never drank because he thought he probably had the same weakness, and, oh, Stella, I drove him to start drinking."

To Stella's distress, Josie burst into tears and it was some time before she could continue.

"I just made excuses not to do it, then Manuel would get angry and go out and get drunk. Then like his father, he would get violent and knock me about."

Stella gasped. "Oh, Josie, how horrible. Did he hurt you much?"

"Well, it just got worse and worse. In the end I had to take a week off work, I looked such a mess and my arm hurt so much I thought it was broken – but it wasn't, just really bruised."

She went on to tell Stella about her plans and escape from a hopeless situation, and about her journey home and the places she had worked, and finally how she had nearly died of starvation, until Phil, darling Phil, had saved her. Stella sat enthralled as Josie told her story, just interrupting with a question now and again, and keeping the coffee coming.

"But Josie, I never thought Manuel was so horrible."

"He wasn't really horrible. It was just the drink. And it's my fault he started drinking. I'll never forgive myself."

She fell silent, trying hard not to cry again. She took a deep breath and then told Stella, "So I will never, ever get involved with a man again. I don't want to and it's not fair to them. I'm just going to be a wrinkled old spinster like you told me years ago." She gave a shaky laugh. "So, Stella, it's time I stopped talking. Tell me what you've been up to."

"Oh, my life must seem terribly dull and uninteresting beside yours, Josie. I'm still working at the same place, just in a better position. Brian is still at the bank and this is the only house we've lived in. End of story."

They laughed.

"But I must tell you, Margaret is married with three children."

"Three? Goodness me, that's quick work. Has she plans for any more?"

Stella gave a wry smile. "No, she went to Family Planning last month and she's on the pill."

"I'd love to see her again, but maybe next time. And do you keep in touch with Mrs Reynolds?"

"Yes, we meet from time to time and she always asks after you, Josie – I think she was a bit concerned about you. You were always a bit special to her. Try and get to see her sometime."

"Yes, I will. One day I hope to have a car and I can get here much quicker then. By the way, did you know I'd been in the paper and on the telly?"

"No, you're kidding me?!"

"No, I'm not."

Josie reached into her handbag and pulled out the article she had taken from the paper, and handed it to Stella. There was silence in the kitchen as Stella read it.

"I'm glad you have been discreet about Manuel," she said. "That should just be between him and you – and me, of course," she chuckled. "I don't know about you, Josie, but it's 12.30pm and I'm starving."

They had some lunch, then Stella had a rest while Josie read the weekend paper, then later Stella took her on a gentle walk down to the park. When they got home Brian was back triumphant from his game of golf and suggested they had takeaway fish and chips later. He put a bottle of white wine in the fridge and they sat and talked about their day.

354

Sunday was sunny and warm as the previous day had been. Brian pottered in the garden while the girls prepared a roast dinner and apple crumble. They chatted non-stop all morning, and when Brian came in to wash his hands and open the wine, they were still at it. Soon it was time for Josie to start her journey home. As it was a Sunday, the trains were not so frequent and Brian took her to the station at 4pm. It had been such a lovely weekend and it made Josie determined to learn to drive and get a car – or, of course, move back to Plumbford or Sandacre. She had plenty of time to think about the options on the way home. How lovely it would be if she could go back to her old flat and be close to her friends and the area she had grown up in. She decided to pursue that idea, and not get a flat in Essex. She now had a full week at work, then a Monday and Tuesday off. She would go back to Sandacre then, not to see Stella, but to look at flats in the area, and jobs. The only problem she could see was that rents were a little higher there than in Essex.

Now that a decision had been made, she couldn't wait to go back and the week seemed to drag. She wrote to Stella and thanked her for a lovely weekend and told her about her possible plans. To her surprise, Stella wrote back by return post and told her to give her notice and come back soon. She and Brian would be delighted to put her up until she found a job and a flat. So on Friday, Josie gave two weeks' notice, and one week before her twenty-third birthday, she moved back to Sandacre. There were lots of hugs and a few tears as she said goodbye to Phil and Pammy, and she promised to come back and see them soon.

CHAPTER 15

It was now July 1984, and Josie's twenty-fourth birthday. So much had happened in the last year. Her stay with Stella and Brian had been short as she'd soon found a studio apartment in Sandacre; it was very small but adequate. Her old flat was occupied, as she thought it would be. She got a job in a supermarket, Monday to Friday, and set about finding another job for the weekend; also enrolling on evening classes again to continue with her gardening and decorating courses. She went back to see Doris and Bill, who greeted her like a long-lost friend, and by the time she left them, she had a job to help at lunchtimes on Saturday and Sunday, and to keep the garden tidy. It was as though she had never been away.

Now she had enough money saved up to start driving lessons and buy a vehicle. In the spring she had put up a sign in a local newsagent, advertising her gardening skills and offering competitive rates, and she now had two more gardens that she tidied every other week, using the customers' own tools. Stella and Brian now had a dear little nine-month-old daughter, and Josie saw them often.

As October arrived, and the cooler weather and shorter days, Josie began what she hoped would be her last winter at the supermarket. She found the work boring, and sitting on a till all day didn't suit her at all. But no matter how much she pleaded to be allowed to do something else, nothing happened. But one good thing had happened. She had passed her driving test on her first go and was now the proud owner of a small blue van. She was now quite determined that gardening was going to be her career, with some decorating, hopefully, to see her through the winter. The supermarket became busier and busier as Christmas approached and everyone was exhausted by the end of the day. But soon, it seemed, Christmas and New Year were behind them and Valentine's cards were in the shops and snowdrops coming out in gardens. Josie advertised again, this time by having several hundred slips printed out by a colleague, and spent evenings pushing them through letterboxes.

TIDY GARDENS
Lady gardener available to get your garden shipshape for summer. Competitive rates and a special rate for pensioners. Call Sandacre 18288 – evenings only.

February was mild and things were happening in gardens, and so there was an immediate and satisfying response from the leaflets. But now Josie panicked. She still had a full-time job and the job with Doris and Bill, and no garden tools. She told customers she could fit them in but it would be in about ten days' time, and then as more enquiries came, two weeks. She took particulars and promised to ring them when she could give them a definite day and time. Then the next day she gave a week's notice at the supermarket. When the personnel lady, Maureen, asked her why she was leaving, Josie told her of her love of gardening and working outside. She explained about the evening classes and her diplomas, presented to her at the end of each course. Maureen listened with interest, then stunned Josie by asking if she would do her garden on a regular basis.

"My husband hates gardening and to be honest, so do I. It's an awful mess; it needs a good spring tidy-up."

Josie said she would be delighted to do it, but she would have to let her know when. That evening she drove round to the King's Head gave Doris and Bill a hug and asked for an orange juice and lemonade. She sat on a stool sipping her drink and waited until Doris had a quiet moment.

"What brings you round here on a Friday night, Josie?"

So Josie explained. "And I've got no mower and no tools," she finished by saying, "so I may be a little late getting to work tomorrow, 'cause I must get everything I need so that I'm prepared. And do you think I could try out the mower on your back lawn? We've had a dry week or two and the grass is growing."

"Course you can, love, and we'll manage until you get here, don't you worry."

After things had quietened down in the pub on Saturday afternoon, Josie and Bill went into the back garden and unpacked the mower. After tightening a few bolts, all was ready. It was a petrol mower, but started easily, and Josie was off up and down the lawn, leaving neat, straight lines. Then with Bill's help, the table and chairs were lifted back onto the grass, ready for drinkers and diners in the spring. Doris was very impressed.

"That's made a much better job of it than our old mower. It looks really smart."

After the first week of gardening, Josie had earned more in three days than she had earned in five at the supermarket, and it was so much more satisfying. Gardens had been tidied up after the winter, shrubs cut back and roses pruned. *Not bad for early March*, Josie thought. She couldn't wait to tell Doris and Bill how she had got on. She parked the van in the pub car park and went in the back door to start work. In between serving customers and wiping tables Josie told them everything, her eyes sparkling with happiness.

"When I've finished here this afternoon, I'm going to see Mrs Reynolds. Just a social visit, you know." She giggled. "Then I'll just happen to mention I'm a gardener now – I'd just love to do the garden at St. Anne's."

Later, with her van parked at St. Anne's, Josie rang the front door bell. The door opened and Mrs Reynolds stood there with a beaming smile on her face.

"Josie, how lovely to see you, come in."

They walked up the stairs to the flat and Mrs Reynolds made a cup of tea while Josie sat on a kitchen stool and chatted. Then they went through to the lounge and made themselves comfortable.

"Have some sponge, Josie. Cook made it for me when she knew you were coming."

Josie happily accepted a piece of Cook's delicious sponge. "Mm – this is lovely. She's such a good cook."

"So, Josie, how's the job going in the supermarket?"

"Oh, I'm not working there anymore."

"What are you doing then, dear?" asked a surprised Mrs Reynolds. "Don't tell me you are going travelling again?"

In reply Josie gave Mrs Reynolds one of her leaflets and waited, smiling as she read it.

"You've started your own gardening business. Oh, you must be thrilled to bits!"

"I am. I've only done one week, but I'm really enjoying it."

"What a pity I've already got someone, Josie. I'd love you to do St. Anne's." She waved at the leaflet. "Can I keep this just in case?"

"Yes, that's fine; just give me a ring if you need me."

They spent the rest of the afternoon chatting happily, then Josie left for home, happy in the knowledge that sometime in the future she may be keeping the garden tidy in the place she'd been cared for and educated whilst a child.

During the next year, Josie worked most days of the week, either gardening or decorating, and also as a temporary assistant in a toyshop for the six weeks leading up to Christmas. January was a little quiet, but she filled any free days with visiting friends and soon things picked up. Being Josie, she spent little and saved hard, hoping to buy her own house. Prices were rocketing and even the smallest house would probably be too much for her.

On her twenty-sixth birthday, Stella invited her to come for a meal. There was now another member of the family, a chubby, contented six-month-old son, Luke. His big sister Gemma was now a lively two-year-old and never stopped talking.

"Excuse the mess, Josie; we're having the bathroom redone. We found a plumber who's really good. In fact, he'll be calling in when he finishes work to drop me off some brochures."

She picked up Luke from the playpen. "I'll bath this little scallywag and put him to bed. Do you want to come and help, Josie?"

Everyone went up the stairs and into the partly demolished bathroom.

"Still useable, thank goodness. Andy is going to change the bath, basin and loo on Friday. He's promised he won't leave us without facilities for more than two days, so if he doesn't finish Friday, he'll come back Saturday morning."

She undressed Luke and lowered him into the bath.

"I want to go in with him, Mummy."

Gemma already had her shoes and socks off, and after a nod from Stella, Josie helped her off with her dress and pants and popped her in the bath with her brother. Josie watched them splashing and playing in the bath and felt a sharp pang of regret, before pushing it down. No point in regrets – even if she married, there was a good chance she wouldn't be able to conceive. At that moment the front door bell rang.

"Oh, that's probably Andy. Do you mind dealing with him, Josie?"

"Course not." Josie ran down the stairs and opened the door. A startled young man stood on the doorstep.

"Am I confusing you?" Josie laughed. "I'm just a visitor; you have come to the right house."

A tall young man smiled back at her. Fair-haired and blue-eyed, he was rather good-looking. He had his work clothes on, though: a pair of old and grubby jeans and a t-shirt with *Florida, USA* printed on it. He handed Josie several brochures.

"Give these to the lady of the house, please, and tell her I'll see her Friday at 7.30 or 8am, OK?"

With that he turned and walked down the path, climbed into his van and with a cheery wave, drove away. Josie dropped the brochures on the coffee table and ran back upstairs. Luke was wrapped in a towel on Stella's lap while Gemma continued to have fun in the rapidly cooling water. Then Brian arrived home from work and ran up the stairs.

"Daddy!" Gemma held out wet arms and Brian lifted her out of the bath, wrapped her in another towel and gave her a cuddle. Soon, both children were tucked up in bed and the three adults were downstairs, each with a glass of wine, while Stella finished off the vegetables.

"It's just a chicken casserole, Josie. It's easier to prepare it earlier and then just pop it in the oven."

"You are so efficient, Stella. You always were. I do admire you and the way you cope with two little ones."

"I enjoy it, and I think that helps," Stella replied. "And Brian's a great help."

She gave him a quick hug, then took the warmed plates from the microwave. The casserole was very tasty and it was followed by trifle, also made by Stella. The evening rushed by and soon it was time for Josie to make her way home. It had been a most enjoyable evening.

One evening several weeks later, Josie's phone rang. Putting her paperwork to one side, she lifted the receiver.

"Hello, Tidy Gardens, Josie speaking."

"It's only me," came Stella's voice.

"Everything all right?"

"Yes, everything's fine, but Brian said I should ring you. Do you remember that lane that goes off by the new estate? There's a row of houses down there, built just after the war, I think. Well, there's one on the end that's for sale and Brian said you might be interested.

"Oh, Stella, I haven't got enough money for a house. Maybe a small flat, but that's all."

"Well, you see, for some reason, lack of space probably, the end one is smaller than the others and it's in a terrible state. An old man lived in it and I shouldn't think anything's been done to it for at least twenty years. Brian thinks it may be auctioned and you might get a bargain. It's worth a try."

"What do I do about finances, Stella?"

"Brian says to find out who can give you the best rates and get everything in place before you go to the auction. The building society will tell you how much you can go up to."

Josie felt her stomach churn with excitement. "I'll come over after work tomorrow and have a look, though when I'm going to find time to go to the building society I don't know!"

"Just go in your work clothes one day, Josie, and apologise for the scruffy clothes – just tell them you are too busy to go home and change. They'll be more inclined to give you a mortgage if they know you've got lots of work."

"What a good idea, I'll do that. But I must see the house first. Oh, I'm so excited."

"Come tomorrow then. Brian will come with you. He'll be home before 6pm."

"OK, and thanks, Stella, you're a star."

So the next evening found Josie and Brian driving up the lane towards the row of terraced houses. There were six identical ones with three bedrooms and two upstairs windows looking to the front. Then on the far end, as though it had been added as an afterthought, a tiny little two-bedroomed house with just one bedroom window looking towards the road. There were just a few feet down the far side for access, then a hedge, completely overgrown and blocking the path, then fields and countryside. They stood looking at it in silence. Tiles were missing from the roof, guttering was hanging down in some places and in other places, plants were growing, blocking the way for rainwater to get to the downpipe. The paint on the doors and windows was peeling and the wood obviously rotten. The front garden was completely overgrown and the gate hanging off the hinges.

"Oh my goodness," muttered Josie, "there's some work to be done here."

"In my opinion," Brian mused, "you just need to get the roof done and the gutters, then the rest when you can afford it."

"Hang on, Brian, it's not mine yet." Josie laughed. "But I'm already in love with it." She sighed. "Oh Brian, I don't know what to do – please help me!"

They struggled through the undergrowth to the front window and tried to peer in, but the windows were so dirty it was almost impossible to see through them. Dirty, ragged curtains hung at the window and one of the panes was cracked.

"Let's see if we can get round the back."

Josie struggled past the front door towards the side path. They snapped twigs and branches and beat down nettles and finally got to the rear of the property. The back garden was narrow, probably about fifteen feet wide, but seemed to go back some way, although with all the trees and overgrown bushes, it was hard to see. They could just make out the kitchen through the window. Not a bad-sized room, with space for a small table and chairs.

"Yuk," was all Josie could say.

They struggled back to the car and drove back in silence, but Josie's mind was going at ninety miles an hour! Stella let them in.

"Come in, Josie, and eat with us. I've got enough."

During that evening, they sat down and worked out a plan of action. Brian made out a list:

* *See estate agent for a viewing and date of auction.*
* *See building society.*
* *Get a surveyor in to check the house is sound.*
* *Cross fingers and hope.*

"I recommend you try the Sandacre Building Society, their rates are good and they are sympathetic towards first-time buyers. I'll back you up, which may help a little."

Brian wrote a letter for her to hand to the building society and said he would keep Saturday free so that he could view the house with her.

"It's in a bit of a state, I'm afraid." The estate agent unlocked the door and led them inside.

"Phew." Josie covered her nose with her hanky. There was an overpowering smell of damp and dirt and other unpleasant things.

"We've been in, obviously, and looked round and

made sure that floors and stairs are safe. We don't want prospective buyers falling through."

The young man grinned at them, then took them into the small, square sitting room. There was an old-fashioned fireplace, a stained carpet covered the floor and a sagging settee was pushed up against one wall, but most of the furniture seemed to have been removed. The kitchen looked as though it hadn't been cleaned for years, and it was difficult to tell whether it could be cleaned up enough to be used temporarily. There was a built-in larder, and beside it a door leading out to the side path. Upstairs the front bedroom was big enough for a double bed, with a recess suitable for a wardrobe. There was a small bedroom at the rear and alongside it, the bathroom. It looked as though it was the original bathroom from the 50s and was, like the rest of the house, old-fashioned, falling apart and filthy. They trooped back downstairs again.

"As you can see, there is a damp issue, which I would think is due to the bad state of the roof and gutter, but I would advise you to get a surveyor to have a look at it. It's been empty and closed up for two years and that doesn't help."

The estate agent led them from the house and before driving away, he told them it definitely would be auctioned, but they had no date as yet.

"So, what was it like?" Stella asked as soon as they got back.

"Well, rather you than me," she said when Josie and Brian had described the state it was in.

Josie made an appointment with the Sandacre Building Society the following Wednesday, then spent an hour at home, on the phone, rearranging her jobs for the week. Then, as Stella had advised, she turned up in rather grubby work clothes.

"I'm sorry I'm in my work clothes. I'm just so busy at the moment, I didn't have time to go home and change."

"That's all right, please sit down."

The bank manager was a man, probably in his late fifties and with years of experience in financial matters and a good judge of character. He listened as Josie explained about the house and told him about her job, then asked her how much she earned and whether she already had any loans or hire purchase commitments. He told her someone from the bank would want to see the house and the surveyor's report, then he would come up with a figure they were prepared to go up to. Josie had to be satisfied with that for now.

Brian recommended a surveyor and Josie took him to the house five days later. He made no comment as he walked around the house, looking at it closely inside and out – tapping walls, lifting the carpet and looking at the floors and examining the wiring – all the time scribbling notes on his clipboard.

Then he smiled and said, "I'll drop a full report through your door in a couple of days."

"Can't you give me any idea now? Is it worth doing up or just pulling down?"

"Oh my goodness, I hope it won't be demolished, but there's a lot of work to be done, that's for sure."

Later the same day, a man from the building society came. He also made no comment, but the expressions on his face were in turn amusing and worrying. The date for the auction was announced. It was to be in two weeks' time on a Friday. In those two weeks, the surveyor's report came and Josie studied it with a small frown on her face. The next morning she phoned the bank for an appointment. She wanted this little house so badly, but wasn't hopeful. A couple of days later found her sitting in the building society manager's office. He had studied the reports from the surveyor and from his member of staff. He steepled his hands and looked at Josie, a serious expression on his face.

"It seems that a new roof and guttering are needed urgently if more damage to the inside is to be avoided, and a complete rewiring is also needed. Those things would have to be done before you can even think of moving in, and have you the funds to do that?"

"Well, it depends on how much deposit I have to pay. I have got reasonable savings."

And so figures were discussed, as was the surveyor's report.

"The structure of the house appears to be quite sound. There is damp, of course, because of the roof and guttering, and the house being closed up for such a long time, but once the work has been done, it will soon dry out. There is no sign of dry rot or anything like that, I'm glad to say. Now, I am willing to give you a mortgage, but your savings won't cover the deposit and the urgent work as well, so what do you say if we add another £5,000 to your mortgage, so you can get the work done?"

"You mean you will give me a mortgage?" A huge smile of relief spread over Josie's face. "Oh thank you, thank you, thank you."

They discussed the auction and Josie admitted to him that she was very nervous about it.

"Find a friend to go with and you'll be fine," he reassured her.

That evening Josie went to Stella and Brian's and told them everything. They were very pleased for her and agreed with the building society manager that she should ask someone to go with her to the auction, preferably a man.

"I can't get time off, I'm afraid, Josie, but why don't you ask Andy?" Brian said. "He's a really nice chap and he's his own boss, so it's easier for him to get time off."

"But I don't really know him. It seems like an awful cheek."

"Well, at the worst he can only say no, and you may need him to work on the house, so you could bribe him with that."

Brian grinned at her.

"Tell you what; I'll ring him if you like."

"Oh, would you, Brian? That'd be great. If he says no, I'm just going to have to be brave."

Brian looked Andy's number up and dialled. "Oh, hello, Andy, it's Brian Sawyer." There was a pause. "No, Andy, the bathroom's great, no problem there, but a friend has a problem. Do you remember briefly meeting our friend Josie when you brought the brochures round?"

Josie listened with a smile on her face as Brian made the most of the situation – girl on her own, nervous, no one else to turn to, etc., etc.

"Yes, next Friday at 4.30pm, so it won't take all your day." There was another pause. "Oh, really? Nothing too painful, I hope."

Brian laughed at the reply, then after a bit more chat, put the phone down. "You'll never believe this, Josie – he's having the afternoon off because he's got to see the dentist at 2.30pm and he said he would be very interested to come with you. He went to an auction years ago with his father, so he can vaguely remember what happens."

Josie thought she would never forget the auction, she was so terrified. She had arranged to meet Andy at the front of the auction rooms between 3.30 and 4pm. He wasn't sure whether the dentist would be on time or how long the treatment would take. It was just 3.40pm when his van pulled into the car park and Josie was so relieved to see him.

"How did you get on, Andy?"

"Just one filling, and not too big. That's it now for another six months!" He gave her a lopsided smile.

"Let's go in so we can watch for a while till yours comes up."

They found there were plenty of empty seats as the sale was almost over for the day, and sat several rows back from the front. There appeared to be a break in proceedings as nobody was on the auctioneer's stand.

"Just having a cup of tea, I expect. They must get very dry," Andy said.

Ten minutes later the auctioneer returned. "Right, ladies and gentlemen, just two more lots to go."

He then proceeded to sell a semi-detached bungalow, and Josie and Andy watched with interest until the gavel came down and delighted buyers held up their number. Then it was Josie's turn. Andy, after much persuading, had agreed to bid for Josie, and so it began. The starting price was ridiculously low. If only nobody else wanted it, that would be great. But one other person was bidding. However, they soon dropped out, but the reserve price had not been reached.

"Come and see me in ten minutes," the auctioneer said.

Which Andy and Josie did. After another little haggle in the office at the back, between Josie, the auctioneer and the owner of the property, a price was agreed at £2,000 below the reserve. Details were taken and Josie and Andy left triumphant. She could now easily do the work needed in order to move in and have a little money left over. She thanked Andy sincerely for his support and told him she would be in touch when plumbing jobs needed doing. Then that night she left six bottles of wine on his doorstep, before ringing his bell and hopping smartly back into her van and driving away.

He rang her the next morning bright and early to thank her and she asked him if he could recommend a roofer. He gave her two names, telling her they were both good, but the latter quite a bit cheaper because it was just two brothers working alone, so their overheads were low. He also gave her the name of a good electrician, but warned her he was very busy.

It was a long eight weeks before Josie moved into her house. It was now October. The days were cooler and shorter. The gardening work had slowed up a little, but there were a couple of decorating jobs in the pipeline and the Christmas job started at the beginning of November. In every spare minute, of which there were few, Josie was at the house. As the roofers worked on the roof, Josie was inside scrubbing the kitchen and bathroom, which she couldn't afford to replace yet. And while the electrician worked in the house, Josie cleared the front garden and the side path, so at least people could get to the front and side doors.

Although she was very busy, she was very happy with her life, and then one cold but sunny day, she moved in. Stella had loaned her a fan heater and it was the only heating she had. There was an open fire but the chimney needed work doing, and she dare not light it. So she put on loads of clothes and carried the heater around with her to try and keep warm. By the New Year she should have enough money for central heating, and in the meantime she just had to manage as best as she could. She decided to ring Andy and book him because she knew he had lots of work on. He agreed to start installing her heating in the middle of January.

The next two months were as busy as ever. It was a rush to get her decorating jobs done by November, and then the toyshop was very busy. Every night Josie collapsed into bed exhausted and fell instantly asleep.

Christmas was spent with Stella and Brian and Brian's parents, at their insistence.

"No way are you spending Christmas alone, Josie. Anyway, we love to have you here and you're so good with the children," Stella told her.

Josie made up a food hamper for their Christmas present full of small luxury items and toys for the children. She also bought a box of chocolates and a bottle of wine for Brian's parents.

January was quiet as usual, with just two more decorating jobs and one large garden to be cleared and tidied ready for landscaping in the spring. It was also cold, with frosts and snow, and it was a relief to get a phone call from Andy to say he would be starting on the central heating in the third week in January. Being a typical workman he left all the doors open and the cold didn't seem to bother him. Josie was glad to go and decorate a neighbour's lounge and kitchen in the warmth and leave him to it. If he finished before she got home, he left the key in a prearranged place. Knowing how desperate Josie was to get the heating in and working, he came in for a few hours on the

Saturday morning. It was the first time that they had been in each other's company for any length of time, and they discovered a shared sense of humour and the same strong work ethic. Josie sat in front of the fan heater and did some paperwork, then some ironing. Mid-morning she made them both a cup of coffee, and they sat at the kitchen table and chatted about all sorts of things, but neither of them mentioned their personal lives.

"Do you want to stay for a sandwich, Andy?" Josie asked as the time crept round to 1pm and Andy started to clear up.

"That would actually be a great help. I've got to do an estimate for someone at 2pm and it'll save me going home."

They sat at the table eating their way through a pile of cheese and pickle sandwiches, then Andy just had time for a cup of tea before leaving to do his estimate.

"See you on Monday then. Another two or three days should see it finished."

"Great, have a nice day off tomorrow," Josie replied.

Andy laughed. "Yes, I will, doing my washing, ironing and housework."

Josie grinned and gave him a wave, then closed the door on the icy wind.

On Wednesday she came home from work at 5pm and Andy had gone, but as she let herself into the house, the warmth hit her. She walked from room to room and everywhere was warm – it was heaven! There was a note from Andy with a few tips about the gas boiler and how to bleed the radiators and adjust the temperature of the rooms and the hot water. He advised her to keep it on night and day for a few days to warm the house right through.

It was lovely that evening to sit and read and not be cold, to undress in a warm bedroom and bathe in a warm bathroom. As she lay in the warm water, she looked at the state of her surroundings. This would be the next job: to have a nice bathroom. But the money was all spoken for, put in the bank to pay Andy, and until spring arrived and work picked up, there would be nothing spare to save. For the next two months or more, she would be living hand to mouth.

During the first week of February Andy's bill came and Josie paid it promptly. It was a pleasant February and March, and spring came early. Work began in earnest; the grass was growing fast, as were the weeds. New fence panels, replacing those blown down in the wind, needed staining. Also, the large garden Josie had cleared earlier needed landscaping. She marked out lawns and spread grass seed and dug over the areas for flower borders and vegetable plots. Young fruit trees were planted and roses at the front of the property pruned back. She found herself having to start earlier and finish later to keep up with the work, and her time at the pub was a welcome relief. Although she loved her work, she was exhausted at the end of each day.

It was Stella who suggested she should take a holiday. They argued about it until Josie agreed to have

377

a long weekend, Friday to Monday, and go and see Pammy and Phil – and she was glad she did, because she had a lovely time, walking and talking and catching up on the gossip. The big garden had been finished before the weekend away, so its maintenance was not so hard. The break had come at a perfect time.

She was now in a position to book Andy to do the bathroom in July. He came round to look and give her an estimate. It was good to see him again, and Josie felt quite relaxed in his company. He didn't flirt with her and never probed into her private life.

Over the winter months and early spring all the rooms had been given a quick coat of cheap emulsion, until time and money allowed a thorough redecoration. She had also ripped up the old, stained carpets, finding old floorboards underneath. A few remnants of carpet had gone by the side of her bed and by her chair in the sitting room. In January and February when work had been short she had also attacked the back garden, having bonfires right at the back when the wind was in the right direction to blow the smoke across the fields. It was a long, narrow garden, fifty-five feet from the back of the house to the back hedge. Although she was attached to the house next door, to the back and other side it was just fields, and opposite, a small wood. Josie could not have asked for more.

Everyone in the row of cottages was friendly, although some would just give a quick nod of the head. Right next door to Josie were an elderly couple. The woman had retired from her job as a school cook and her husband was doing part-time work in a builders' merchants. They were very nice and obviously delighted to have the house next door lived in and being tidied up.

In July, Andy duly arrived to do the bathroom. He had already been round to discuss the fitments, so work could commence straight away. Josie had rearranged her schedule for the day so that she could stay around for an hour or so and make sure Andy knew everything she wanted for the new bathroom. She had gone for a simple white suite and chrome fittings, including a heated towel rail. The tiles she was going to endeavour to do herself to keep costs down.

"Do you want a cup of tea or coffee before you start, Andy?"

"A good workman never says no to a cup of tea."

Andy grinned at her. They sat down at the table with their mugs of tea and went over the plans to double-check everything, and all seemed to be straightforward. Andy smiled at Josie a little ruefully.

"You don't know how good it feels to work for somebody who is friendly and well… normal."

"What do you mean, Andy, was your last client a bit difficult?"

"I would describe her as predatory. He was a really nice bloke, but then he'd go off to work and then she would start fluttering her eyelashes at me. I can't be doing with all that. I can tell you, I dreaded going each day."

"If she had a nice husband, why did she do that, I wonder?"

"Bored, I would think," Andy replied. "Some women are like that. They just want a bit of excitement and don't care who they hurt." A bitter note had crept into Andy's voice. "And some men are easily tempted."

Josie looked at him. "You sound as though you've experienced similar things yourself."

"My best friend is an electrician." Andy paused.

"Don't stop there, Andy." Josie grinned, but the smile soon left her face as Andy continued.

"He came to do some work for me and my wife Paula. Next thing I know, they've run off together."

"Oh, Andy, your wife and your best friend, how awful! So you've lost both of them?"

"That's right. Paula and I were divorced nearly two years ago and I understand they are now married. I was shattered at the time, but I guess I'm virtually over it now. But it's completely put me off having another serious relationship. I've had a few dates, but nothing more. I don't know why I'm suddenly telling you this; I've never really spoken about it to anyone before."

"Well, maybe you sensed I have similar feelings," Josie told him. "I've been unlucky with men and I haven't even had a date for, gosh, it must be five years."

"Aren't you sometimes tempted if a nice guy asks you out?"

"Yes, I must admit I am, but I just think back to my experiences and I can easily manage to say, 'thanks, but

380

no thanks.'" Josie stood up. "Anyway, enough of this baring of the soul, we've both got work to do. I'll see you later, maybe, Andy; if not I'll see you tomorrow morning. I hope you get on all right."

Josie grabbed her sandwiches and van keys and with a cheery smile, set off for work.

Andy's plans for the day were to remove the old bathroom suite and tiles and begin putting the new suite in, much as he had done for Stella and Brian; then hopefully he would finish the job tomorrow. He said he would seal everything and put the bath panel on as soon as he could, then box the pipes in.

Josie had no time to start the tiling until the quieter winter months, but she was learning to be patient. Earning money and paying the mortgage were more important. She was very happy in her little house and would hate to lose it. As she walked up and down behind her mower she had time to think about Andy and the shocking events that had happened in his life. In fact she couldn't get him out of her mind. Later, as she sat on a seat in the garden and ate her sandwiches, she was still thinking about him – poor Andy, what a devastating thing to happen. But, she thought with a wry smile, they were two of a kind, both with unhappy experiences and both still a little bitter.

She was late finishing that day, and it was 6.30pm when she got home, so she was surprised to see Andy's van still parked outside. He was just tidying up for the day when she went in.

"Hi, Josie, late start and late finish for both of us, then?"

"Hello, Andy, how's it going?"

"It's going well, but your bathroom had been here since the 1950s and it was reluctant to come out, but it's out now. Tell me: some people like to keep old baths for herbs – are you interested or do you want me to take it away?"

"Oh, take it away please, Andy; it's such a horrible old thing."

"Would you mind giving me a hand with it? If it's too much for you, I've got a friend I can call on to help. It's such a heavy old thing."

They just about managed to manhandle it down the stairs and out of the front door, through the garden and into the van.

"Phew, that was heavy." Josie took several deep breaths.

"Thanks, I'll be off now. See you in the morning."

Josie would have been surprised to know that Andy had been thinking about her as much as she had about him!

As Josie stood at her kitchen sink that night, giving herself a strip-wash, Andy once more came to her mind. She began to mutter to herself.

"Just watch it, girl, you're getting to like him too much. That way leads to heartache. The sooner he's done the job and gone the better."

She rubbed herself hard with the towel, a frown on her face.

"Just be sensible: you don't want romance and neither does he. He's just the plumber, nothing more."

But she wasn't sure she had convinced herself. She used the plumbed-in toilet and made her way to bed, but it was some time before she fell asleep, and then she dreamt of Andy telling her to get lost because he didn't fancy her one bit!

The next day the bathroom was fully connected and sealed and the bath panel on. It was beginning to look really good. Andy would be doing one more day, when he would box in the pipes and finish off. As Josie thanked him over a cup of tea, Andy gave her some tips on tiling.

"Some are easier to use than others. Do you want me to come with you on Saturday when you choose them?"

"Oh yes, please, and you can help me with the glue."

"Adhesive, it's called." Andy chuckled. "OK, I'll see you inside the tile shop at 10.30am, how's that?"

Saturday came and Josie arrived a little early and began to look at the numerous tiles, looking up from time to time to see if Andy had arrived. She found a design that she really liked. It came in half a dozen shades and she studied them closely. Then she glanced up and saw Andy standing on the other side of the shop, obviously looking for her. She looked at him through the stands of tiles and other customers milling about; then he saw her and their eyes met. Josie's heart gave a big lurch and for several seconds they just looked at each other, then he made his way towards her. She stood there, unable to move.

It's happened, she thought. *It's too late, I can't stop it – oh, help!*

Andy walked up to her; his hand reached out and touched her arm, then in a strange, rather wooden voice he said, "Have you found anything you like?"

Josie dragged her eyes away from his and looked unseeingly at the tiles. "Yes," was all she could manage to say. She pointed at the tiles. Andy was the first to regain his normal voice.

"They should be fairly easy for you to manage. Which one do you like the best?"

Josie pointed to the three she liked the best.

"Well, I wouldn't have that one, Josie." Andy pointed to a green one she had picked out. "You'll always be restricted on paint and towel colours. I'd have either of the other two, they are more neutral."

When Josie still remained silent, he continued.

"I'd have the lighter one. It's quite a dark bathroom and it'll brighten it up." He looked down at Josie and was stunned to see two big teardrops running down her cheek. "Come on, let's get out of here."

He took her arm and hurried her from the shop and back to his van. He helped her in, then climbed in himself and started the engine. Then he drove out of the town and parked in a gateway to a field, then switched off the engine. There was no resistance from Josie as he gently took her in his arms and stroked her hair. Josie took a few deep breaths, then pulled away from him to wipe her eyes and blow her nose.

"Did I do something to upset you?" Andy asked. "That's the last thing I'd want to do."

Josie sniffed and sat silently for some minutes. "I don't know what to say," was all she managed. "I'm sorry, Andy; could you take me back to the tile shop, please? I want to pick up my van and go home."

Andy didn't move, just continued to look at her anxiously. "I think we need to talk, Josie. We need to be honest with each other. Now, what did I do or say to make you cry? I need to know."

"You didn't do anything, Andy." She still wouldn't meet his eyes. "I just suddenly felt all muddled up."

Andy took her hand between his. "You mean your feelings felt all muddled up?"

Josie nodded.

"Well, if it's any consolation to you, mine are pretty muddled up as well. The truth is, Josie, I think I've fallen in love with you, and I didn't want that to happen."

Finally Josie looked up at him. "It just happened so quickly, one second I just liked you as a friend, and then like a flash…"

Andy looked down at her, the love shining from his eyes. "So you feel the same – oh, darling."

He pulled her back into his arms and held her close, then pulled away a little so he could look at her. Then their lips met in a long, very satisfying kiss.

"I love you, Josie, and there's nothing I can do about it." He smiled down at her.

"And I love you too, but I'm frightened I'm going to break your heart – I've not got a good record."

Andy kissed her again. "Let's just take it slowly. We'll have a few dates and see how we go. What do you say?"

Josie could only say, "OK."

With difficulty Andy dragged himself away from her and started the engine. "How about we meet this evening and go for a meal? I'll pick you up and we'll go to a pub I know by the river."

"All right." Josie smiled at him, and he smiled back.

"I'll have to be in the van, I'm afraid. It's the only vehicle I've got."

"I don't mind, but brush the seat off, please, it's disgusting!"

"So, nagging already, I can see I'm in for a hard time."

They laughed together and Josie suddenly felt herself relax.

CHAPTER 16

An hour later she was sitting in her kitchen eating a sandwich and trying to absorb the events of the morning, from the moment when Cupid's arrow had pierced her heart, through the feelings of denial, fear and subsequent tears, to the magical moments in the van.

Please don't let me hurt him, she prayed.

That evening she took a lot of trouble with her appearance. Her usual routine was to pull on some respectable trousers and a clean shirt, comb her hair and maybe a dab of lipstick. But this time she put on a dress, which was much more suitable for the hot, sunny weather. The dress was a soft green in a satin-type fabric with a flowered border on the hem and cuffs. She slipped into some white sandals and ran her fingers through her almost-dry curls. Then a little subtle make-up and she was ready. It was still only 6pm, but she couldn't sit still; in turn nervous, excited and emotional. She stepped out of the side door and wandered up the concrete path that went right to the back of the garden. Many years ago there had been a vegetable plot here and the edges were still just about discernible, although completely covered in weeds. She was looking forward to digging it over in the autumn and growing her own vegetables next year.

She glanced at her watch for the twentieth time – 6.20pm – and then very slowly walked back down the garden, through the door, which she locked, then into the sitting room. She picked up her handbag, then put it down again, then ran up the stairs for a cardigan in case it got cooler later. As she slipped it round her shoulders, she heard the sound of a vehicle stopping outside and the slam of a door. Looking out of her bedroom window, she saw Andy walking up the path. Oh, he was so gorgeous! She ran down the stairs and opened the front door, and they stood and smiled at each other, before moving into each other's arms. Andy kissed her gently.

"Ready, then?"

"Yes, I'll just get my handbag."

She climbed into the van. "Wow, what a clean van!"

All the empty Coke cans and crisp packets had gone. The seats and floor had been vacuumed and the dashboard cleaned. Andy grinned at her.

"Well, I was scared, you see. I thought you might not come out with me unless I cleaned it."

Josie gave him a cheeky grin. "Well, you could just be right."

Andy drove them to a quaint old pub overlooking the river. He parked and they walked towards the pub.

"Shall we get a drink and sit in the garden? It's such a lovely evening."

Josie nodded. "Yes, let's."

Andy ordered a shandy for himself and an orange juice for Josie, and they took them into the garden and found a table close to the river. Andy looked at her thoughtfully.

"Josie, one day I would like to know what has happened in your life to put you off men. In fact I know nothing about you – where you were born, about your family, what you have been doing for the last twenty-seven years."

Josie sipped her drink. "Well, it's a long story and not quite, well… not quite normal."

They were interrupted by a waiter. "Ready to order, sir?"

"Yes, we're both going to have sausages in onion gravy, please, and another shandy for me and an orange juice for the lady."

The waiter disappeared back inside and Andy looked at Josie.

"It sounds like you've had an interesting life so far. Do you feel ready to tell me?"

Josie laughed. "Well, I'll have to condense it or we'll be here all night. To start off with, I was left as a newborn baby outside a children's home, so I don't know who my parents are. I was raised and educated there and it was a nice place. I had a happy childhood. How about you, Andy?"

"I was born in Sandacre, my mum and dad live on the estate off the Oxford Road. I've got a brother two years younger than me. He's married with a baby and lives in Australia."

"Gosh, Australia, do you ever see him?"

"I haven't since he left, but Mum and Dad went over last year just after the baby was born. I'd like to go one day. So, Josie, how old were you when you left the home?"

So of course, Josie had to tell him about Mr Shenstone and running away. Andy listened, shocked.

"Do you know, I seem to remember about that Mr Shenstone. It was in the papers. Didn't he commit suicide?"

"Yes, he did and his family moved away. It must have been awful for them as well."

She paused as two plates of steaming food were placed in front of them.

"Drinks are coming in a minute, sir."

"Just tuck in, Josie; it'll cool quickly out here. We can talk later."

Half an hour passed and the plates were scraped clean. Both had declined desserts, but decided to go inside for coffee.

"So have you always been a gardener?" Andy asked.

Josie told him about her plot at St. Anne's and her friendship with Mr Copcut; then working at the pub before joining Bob and Sue at the nursery – which meant telling Andy about Richard.

"You poor darling, you have been unlucky." Andy took her hand and raised it to his lips."

"I'll give you the second instalment the next time I see you." Then she blushed. "That's if you want to see me again."

He gazed at her lovingly. "What do you think? Course I want to see you again." He laughed. "How about tomorrow?"

"Yes, that'll be nice. How would you like to come to me for lunch and I'll cook you a Spanish meal?"

"Spanish! Josie, you are full of surprises. I'll bring some wine – what time would you like me?"

"About 1pm – is there anything you really don't like?"

"No, I'll eat anything. My mum calls me a human dustbin!"

They chatted happily until Josie looked at her watch and realised it was 10.15pm and she was very tired. Andy took her home and kissed her goodnight. He watched until she had let herself in and closed the door securely behind her.

As preparations were made for bed, she was so glad she'd given up the weekend job at the pub. At the time it was because the jobs in the house and garden that she could only afford to do herself were just not getting done. Two weeks had gone by, and she had filled in the Saturdays with gardening, which was much more lucrative than the pub, then spent the Sundays doing her own garden. Now things had ground to a halt again, but was she complaining? She climbed into bed with a smile on her face and was soon fast asleep.

Josie had opted for a cold starter, mixed salad with tuna and quartered hard-boiled eggs, served with a crusty roll, followed by paella, then to finish, cold rice with cinnamon sprinkled on. It must have been all right because it all disappeared.

"That was really lovely, darling – you are a clever girl."

They washed up together, then took a coffee into the sitting room. Sitting together on the old settee Josie had bought second-hand, they relaxed and sipped the hot drinks.

"I hope you don't mind, Andy, but I'd like to tell you about Spain. It's something you need to know about me before we go any further."

"Carry on then, Josie, it all sounds intriguing."

So Josie did. From the moment she first arrived in Spain with Stella, through to moving in with Manuel, then it got really hard to continue. Andy looked at her with concern as her head dropped and she fell silent. He waited patiently for her to continue.

"I loved him, Andy, and I fancied him, but I was terrified of what was to happen that night. You see, I was still a virgin and I found men intimidating in that way. I knew I had to conquer my fear and let Manuel make love to me, but it took all my willpower not to push him away. He was very gentle with me and I thought it would all improve, but it didn't. He didn't ever drink alcohol because his father was an alcoholic and violent with it. But as the months went by and I got even more reluctant he just lost it, Andy."

Josie began to cry, and it was some minutes before she could continue.

"He started drinking and then hitting me, and I

felt so guilty because it was my fault. It just got worse and worse and I thought he would kill me, so I made preparations, then one night when he was out cold, I left and started to walk home."

She wiped her eyes and blew her nose, while Andy sat stunned by her side.

"Walk home? What, back to England, you mean? All the way? You walked all the way?"

"Yes, every single mile back to Calais. It took me over two years because I had to find work on the way to keep me going. I was OK in Spain because I speak Spanish pretty well, but once I got to France I had problems and I nearly died of starvation. You've maybe heard me talk of Phil and Pammy – well, Phil saved my life by loaning me money, even though he didn't know me – isn't that amazing?"

Andy nodded. "But no, I haven't heard of Phil and Pammy. He sounds like a great man."

"Yes, you must meet them sometime. But Andy, the outcome of the starvation is I may never be able to have children. It's sad, but I've sort of got used to it now."

"I'll say one thing, Josie: my life story seems pretty dull now."

Josie laughed shakily. "That's what Stella says! Yuk, I've let my coffee get quite cold. Would you mind going for a stroll, then we'll have a nice hot cup of tea? There's a footpath that goes through that wood over there." She waved at the trees on the other side of the road. "Then through a couple of fields and back on the road about half a mile away. It takes about an hour at an amble."

Andy agreed and Josie slipped on some comfortable shoes and they set off.

The wood was in dappled shade and lovely to walk through. As they strolled hand in hand, Josie suddenly said, "It's my twenty-seventh birthday next week. I'm getting old."

"Well, I'm thirty-two, Josie, so I'm ancient."

They smiled at each other.

"I'm hopeless at choosing presents, darling, what would you like?"

Josie looked up at him cheekily. "Do you know what I'd really like? Did you notice my struggle with the taps when I was washing up? They have really had it, Andy – would it work to put new ones in that would still be all right when I have the kitchen done? Do you know what I'm trying to say?"

"I'm not sure without looking at it properly; I'll do it when we get back."

"Oh, would you, Andy? I can't afford to have the kitchen done until the end of the year and I don't think the taps will last till then."

Andy squeezed her hand. "Don't worry, darling, I'll sort something out."

They wandered on, sometimes chatting, sometimes silent, but relaxed and at ease in each other's company.

Over the next few months their love became deeper and they spent more and more time together. Josie cooked for them several times a week, and Andy would sometimes cook for her. She became familiar with his

394

house, a semi-detached on a small estate. Andy kept it clean, if a little untidy, and the dining room table, when she visited, was covered in paperwork. He was a good cook and seemed to enjoy it.

In November he began her kitchen. Josie was out all day at the toyshop doing her usual temporary Christmas job. Andy had a friend, Paul, who helped with big jobs and they promised it would be done in a week and a half; then Josie could paint the kitchen and hang the tiles in good time for Christmas. The day the men finished, she brought home some beer and wine and a takeaway Chinese, and they toasted the new kitchen. When they had finished eating, Paul left for home and Josie and Andy relaxed in the sitting room.

"I'm thrilled with the kitchen, Andy; would you like to have Christmas dinner here?"

Andy rubbed his chin. "Well, I always go to Mum and Dad's so it's a bit awkward. How about Boxing Day?"

They agreed on that, but the next day Andy said his parents had insisted she go there for Christmas Day. Josie had met them several times and got on well with them, so she was happy to accept.

One day, a week or so before Christmas, she came home from work and showered, then put on a new pair of tailored black trousers and a glamorous electric blue blouse and stood at the bedroom window, waiting for Andy. As she stood there, she thought how much she had grown to love him. Life without him now wouldn't have been worth living. He was in her thoughts constantly and in her dreams at night. Their time together was spent chatting and laughing and loving. Not fully loving – that hadn't happened. Andy was gentle and thoughtful and never pressed her into anything she wasn't ready for. Now Josie found herself in the situation of wanting him so much, yet feeling unable to let him know, and frightened it would all go wrong again.

She was jolted out of her reverie by the headlights of the van coming up the road. Andy was taking her out for a Christmas meal with Paul and his wife Val, and two other friends, George and Emily. They had a good evening, the food was delicious and they were all in a happy mood as they left the restaurant. Paul invited them back for coffee, but it was already 10.30pm and they declined. Andy took Josie's arm as they walked back to the van.

"Your chariot awaits, madam."

Josie giggled; she had drunk more wine than normal and felt wonderfully relaxed.

"You'll have to help me up into the van."

Andy obliged, causing Josie to squeak.

"Sorry, my hand slipped."

Andy climbed in his side and grinned at her. He leaned over and cupped her chin in his hand and kissed her passionately; then pulled her close and kissed her again. Josie gave a little groan as his lips nuzzled her ear and then her neck. Andy gazed down at her.

"I love you so much, Josie White, but it's time hardworking girls were tucked up in bed."

He started the van and they drove home in silence.

"Come in for a few minutes, Andy. It's been such a good evening; I don't want to go to bed yet."

"OK, just for a few minutes."

They let themselves in and Josie slipped off her coat.

"You looked gorgeous tonight, Josie."

He pulled her close again and kissed her, one hand in her hair, the other pulling her close. Josie knew, could tell, how much he wanted her, and she felt the same.

Relaxed from the pleasant evening and the glasses of wine, she looked up at Andy and said, "Why don't you stay?"

Andy's eyes darkened as he looked at her. "Are you sure, my darling?

There was no hesitation.

"Yes, I'm sure."

The alarm woke her and she rolled over to silence it, and nearly fell out of bed. Two people in a single bed was cosy, but not safe. She rolled back into Andy's arms and they smiled into each other's eyes.

"Morning, my woman, how are you this morning?"

"I'm fine, and how's my man?"

"I'm fine too."

He pulled her closer, but Josie reluctantly resisted.

"I'm sorry, I have to shower, have some breakfast and get off to work. Mrs Thomas likes us in at 8.30am prompt to fill up before we open."

"She's an old slave driver; doesn't she know my needs are more important?"

Josie giggled, but swung herself out of bed and ran into the bathroom.

Later, driving into work, her mind was full of those magical hours last night; the urgent loving, over too soon, and later the long, unhurried hour of rapture. After all her worrying, it had been all right, very all right – no fear, no pulling back, just eager anticipation.

With a week to go before Christmas, it was hectic in the shop and some of the year's favourite toys ran out. It was a relief when Mrs Thomas locked the doors and they could tidy up, sweep and go. Josie was to go home, freshen up and change, then go to Andy's where he had promised he would make her a simple omelette, after the richness of last night's meal. Josie unashamedly hung around him while he was preparing it, until he took her arm and gently pushed her into a chair.

"Eat first, my darling, you've had a busy day."

But his eyes told her he felt the same.

The next day at work, a rather harassed Stella came to get a few last-minute gifts. Josie helped her and they discussed their plans for Christmas.

"So you're going to Andy's parents', that's nice. How are things going with you and Andy?"

Josie looked at her friend, her face alight with a radiant smile. The next minute she was engulfed in a big hug.

"Oh, Josie, you don't need to say a word, I'm so happy for you."

"It's all right, Stella, everything's all right," Josie responded breathlessly.

"Well, you couldn't pick a nicer man," Stella said. "Just have a wonderful Christmas."

"I will, but can I pop in with the children's presents tomorrow after work?"

"Course you can – I'll see you then."

Andy came round to Josie's that evening and she cooked a simple meal; then Andy pressed her into a chair while he made a coffee. He placed the coffee on the small table at Josie's side and his own on the floor, ready to drink when it had cooled a little.

Then to Josie's surprise, he dropped onto one knee in front of her, took her hands in his and said, "Josie, I love you so much, I want to spend the rest of my life with you. Please, will you marry me?"

His face fell when there was no immediate response. "Josie?"

She took a deep breath. "I feel the same, darling, but don't you want children? There's not much chance with me, I'm afraid."

"It would be nice, I don't deny it," he replied, "but I'd rather be with you and have no children, than with someone else. Please say yes, Josie."

Her face softened. "I would love to marry you, Andy."

He was off his knee immediately and she was in his arms.

"Let's go into the town tomorrow and look at rings. It's Saturday and we are both free."

So that's what they did. Josie chose a diamond

solitaire and they walked to the local park, where Andy slipped it on her finger. It was wonderful to arrive at Andy's parents' home on Christmas Day and see the delight on their faces at the news. Josie wanted to shout if from the rooftops, but had to be satisfied with phoning or writing to her friends to tell them the news.

The hectic last few weeks of Christmas and New Year were over. It was January and things were quiet, as always, for Josie. She had a bedroom to decorate next door but one, and Doris and Bill wanted their private lounge done. But she was determined to dig over the vegetable plot at the end of the garden. It was hard work and slow. Andy didn't know, or he would have helped, but Josie wanted to do it herself. He was cross with her when she took him up the garden path to show off the neatly dug-over plot.

"But I enjoyed doing it, Andy. I'm stronger than I look."

He patted her gently on her behind. "You're also a very independent young lady!"

As they walked back into the warmth of the house, he asked her to come and sit with him on the settee, because he wanted to talk to her. They sat close to each other, his arm around her and her head resting on his shoulder.

"I want so much for us to be married. I want to cuddle up to you at night and wake with you beside me in the morning. Can we be married soon?"

"Yes, darling, how about tomorrow?" She giggled.

"No, I'm serious, Josie. How soon do you think we could arrange it?"

"Well, I don't want a big, fancy do, Andy, just a simple affair with close friends and family, so it wouldn't need much sorting out. But is it going to be church or registry office? What do you think?"

"The problem is, I'm divorced, so church is probably out. Personally, I'd be happy to get married in Sandacre Registry Office. It's a nice building and the room they use is quite posh, actually. I had a friend who got married there last year, so I've seen it."

Josie lifted his hand and pressed it to her lips. "Let's do it, then. Shall we see if they've got a date in late March or April? The weather shouldn't be too bad then."

"Yes, we'll go down one morning – you're not too busy now, are you? And I can take an hour or so off."

So it was decided, and the very next morning they entered the rather grand front entrance of the registry office and soon found themselves in a small office with a middle-aged lady smiling at them from behind a desk. She took their particulars, then pulled a large diary towards her.

"End of March, you say? No, sorry, can't fit you in then – how about the second Saturday in April? We have 11am available, how would that suit you?"

"Yes, that would be wonderful, thank you."

Josie smiled at the lady and then at Andy; the arrangements were all complete and they left the building and hurried back to Andy's house. He changed into his work clothes, dropped Josie off at her house, and went off to work, leaving her to do some household chores.

Later, as they sat down to a tasty chicken casserole, Josie told him of the ideas that had been running round her head all day.

"What would you think, darling, to a fairly long trip to Spain for a honeymoon?"

Andy chewed and swallowed a delicious mouthful of food. "I have a feeling this is not going to be a one-week, run-of-the-mill package holiday."

"No, it's not. Tell you what – there is so much to say, let's finish our meal and I'll spill the beans over coffee."

He looked at her. "I love you, Josie White."

Half an hour later they took their coffees through to the sitting room and sat down side by side on the settee. Andy gave her his undivided attention.

"OK, I'm ready, spill the beans."

"I would like to drive to Spain," Josie began. "It would take two or three days. Then we can go and see Lily, then drive back slowly, see Bella, then maybe stop for a couple of nights in Barcelona, all the time following the route I took. Next stop would be the Pyrenees, then up through France; maybe calling to see Esmé, but I'm not sure about that, then maybe Mimi."

She looked uncertainly at Andy, but she needn't have worried. His face lit up.

"What a fabulous idea, I'd really like that. And I'll

take my camera and we can take lots of photos. Yes, it will be really interesting, and probably quite emotional for you, darling."

"Mm, it will be, and I'll never stop talking, I'll drive you nuts."

"Never, it will be fascinating," Andy reassured her. "Shall we book or just take a chance?"

"We'll just take a chance; there are plenty of hotels and motels," Josie told him. "We'll just book the ferry."

They looked at each other and smiled excitedly, both looking forward to the wedding, then the holiday.

The next few months were very busy for both of them. Andy always seemed to have plenty of work, and while Josie was going through her quiet time, January and February, she had time to book Doris and Bill for a buffet reception, send out invitations and buy herself an outfit. Stella left the children with Brian's mother and came to help. Josie wanted something nice that she could wear afterwards, but had purposely kept an open mind. They went to Oxford and wandered round a large department store, looking at the clothes in different departments, some quite reasonably priced, others with famous labels and very expensive. Then they looked at the wedding clothes. By this time it was 12.30pm and Josie felt thoroughly confused.

"Let's go and eat something and have a break," Stella suggested. "I don't know about you, but I'm starving."

They both chose a sandwich with a side salad and a

fruit juice and thought over what they had seen.

"That cream suit would look nice on you, Josie, and they had it in apple green as well. Those colours look good on you."

Josie nodded. "Yes, I know, but how about that silky dress with the full skirt? That was cream and a lovely soft green, here and there. That would look nice with a cream jacket. And crikey, I suppose I'd better look at hats."

She pulled a face and made Stella laugh.

"Come on, Josie, we've done lots of looking; now we need to do some trying-on."

"Oh, I don't like this – I always look awful in anything posh. I'd much rather be in old jeans and a t-shirt."

"That's rubbish, Josie, you're tall and slim and your hair is so pretty. You'll see, we'll make you look gorgeous."

They set off back to the department where they had seen the suits and Stella hooked a cream one off the rail.

"How about the green one as well, Josie? The skirt's different. Do you want to try that one on too?"

Josie nodded and they took them to the fitting room. The cream suit fitted perfectly, but they both felt it was too formal. The green one with the pleated skirt looked awful.

"It makes me look like a granny," Josie said, which made Stella laugh.

They gave the suits back to the sales lady and said

they needed to think about it, then went to find the dress. Nothing else had taken Josie's fancy, but she had a good feeling about the cream-and-green creation. Then minutes later, Josie did a twirl in front of Stella and the sales lady. Stella gasped.

"Wow, Josie, you look fantastic. It fits perfectly and that soft green is lovely. Turn around slowly."

Josie obliged, and all three agreed.

"This is the one – now for accessories."

Cream shoes and bag were chosen, and a green wide-brimmed hat that perfectly matched the soft green in the dress. Satisfied with her purchases, Josie got out her chequebook and paid. Everything was carefully wrapped and taken back to Stella's car.

"Right, let's go home. Do you want to leave them at my house, Josie?"

"No thanks, Stella, I'll take them home and put the dress in an upside-down bin bag, just in case Andy goes nosing in my wardrobe, but I don't think that's likely to happen."

Stella looked puzzled. "A bin bag? You're going to put this lovely dress in a bin bag?"

"Haven't you ever done that, Stella? Make a small hole for the hanger to poke through in the bottom of the bag, turn it up the other way and slip it over the dress."

Stella still looked puzzled. Josie rolled her eyes.

"I'll show you when we get home."

And she did. Stella was impressed.

"Why did I buy expensive dress bags, tell me that?"

They laughed, then after a big thank-you from Josie, Stella left to pick up the children from her mother-in-law.

March arrived and work picked up. Josie warned all her customers that she would be away for at least two weeks in the second half of April, and without exception, they wished her well. Andy came round to see her one evening in early April and instead of arriving in the van, he parked a shiny black car outside. Josie ran to open the door.

"What's this, then?" she asked.

"Well, we can't drive all the way to Spain in the old van, can we? It's too scruffy and it uses too much petrol. One of my customers who changes his car every two years offered it to me. I hope you don't mind, Josie, but he wanted to get rid of it straight away. I would normally talk it over with you first."

Josie didn't mind at all. She had been a little worried about going in the old van.

CHAPTER 17

Josie opened her eyes sleepily, and stretched. Today was her wedding day and it all seemed a little unreal. After all the years of excluding men from her life, now she was about to be married. But she had no regrets. Andy was a wonderful man, thoughtful and kind and hardworking. And he loved her as she loved him. What more could anyone ask? But Josie hated being the centre of attention; that aspect of the ceremony she wasn't looking forward to.

Nerves took her appetite away, and she had to force down a slice of toast. Stella and Brian were going to be witnesses and they would get ready, then come round and help Josie before leaving in Brian's car for the registry office. George was good with a camera and said he would take some photos and put them in a nice album as part of their wedding present. Everything was organised; all Josie had to do was get ready.

When Stella and Brian arrived at 9.45am, she was about to slip the dress over her head. She laid it carefully on the bed, put her dressing gown on and ran downstairs to let them in. Half an hour later, she was ready, but there was no need to leave for another twenty minutes at least.

Brian looked at her shaking hands and said, "I've got some wine in the car, would you like some to steady your nerves?"

"No thanks, Brian, I might get hiccups during the ceremony and that wouldn't do!"

They all laughed, and suddenly Josie felt calm. As they left the house, the elderly couple next door, Alice and Des, came out and gave Josie a lucky horseshoe and a small parcel, which Stella put in her handbag. They kissed Josie and wished her happiness and told her she looked beautiful.

As she walked into the wedding room, Andy turned and looked at her and his face said it all. As she walked to his side, he took her hand and gazed down at her.

"You look amazing, my darling. What a lucky chap I am."

The ceremony was simple but moving, and soon the registrar was pronouncing them man and wife. Everyone clapped, the camera flashed and it was all over. Doris and Bill had laid on a magnificent spread in the big room they kept for that purpose, and the twenty-two guests mingled happily, helping themselves to food and sitting down at one of the tables arranged around the room. Then speeches were made, toasts were drunk, and the cake was cut. Suddenly Josie was very hungry. She filled her plate and sat down, followed by Andy.

"Hello, Mrs Matthews, are you OK?"

He smiled at her lovingly.

"Yes, I'm fine, just rather hungry."

She took a mouthful of sausage roll and looked around. Not many guests, but all of them were special. Most of them had stopped eating and were just sipping drinks. Josie chuckled.

"I seem to be the only one still eating, what a little pig I am!"

They had the use of the room until 6pm, so everything was leisurely, but people started to leave soon after 3pm. Josie and Andy left at 3.30pm, went back to Josie's house, changed, grabbed their suitcases, already packed the day before, and left soon after 4pm. They had a hotel booked for one night near Dover, and were getting an early ferry the next morning. As they drove down, they talked about their plans after the holiday. Andy would move in with Josie, his house would be sold, and they had lots of plans to improve Josie's house. Andy had been keen to do it that way. His house held unhappy memories of his first marriage and he just wanted to get rid of it. The miles went by and it became dark.

"Soon be there, darling." Andy looked across at his quiet and rather sleepy wife.

"It's such a comfortable car," was the reply, "but I won't go to sleep, honestly. I'm too excited."

They arrived at the hotel at 7pm and booked in.

"I'm hungry again, Andy. Can we eat soon?"

"Yes, I'm hungry too. There's a restaurant next door, will that do for you?"

They quickly unpacked their toiletries and clothes for the next day, and then went to find the restaurant. It was busy, but a table became available after a ten-minute wait. After they had eaten, they went back to their room and looked at the atlas, wondering how far they would get the next day. Suddenly Andy closed the atlas and took Josie in his arms.

"Are you going to shower, or am I going to make love to you right here and now?"

Josie gave him a saucy smile and disappeared into the bathroom.

Later, as they lay sated and blissfully happy in each other's arms, Josie touched his cheek.

"My darling Andy, you are the best thing that's ever happened to me. I know we'll always be happy."

Andy kissed her and agreed wholeheartedly.

Josie was quiet as the boat left Dover, remembering the last time she had crossed the Channel.

"Penny for them, darling."

"I was just thinking about coming back from France after the walk. I was so thin and so weak. I'm lucky to be alive and healthy now." She squeezed Andy's hand. "And to have a lovely husband to share my life with."

She talked of the crossing with Phil, and how he had helped her to get through customs. Andy asked her lots of questions and listened, fascinated, to the answers, then fished in his bag and pulled out the camera.

"Right, a few on the ferry to begin with."

Josie obligingly smiled, then took the camera and

returned the favour. They had coffee and looked at the fast-approaching French coastline.

It was a long day's drive and they decided to have their main meal en route around lunchtime. The service areas supplied tasty meals at a reasonable cost and with no delay. Then it was easy just to pick up sandwiches from the shop for later. So by 7.30pm, when they finally stopped for the day, they could just relax in their room and eat the sandwiches. Pleased with the progress they had made, having almost reached Lyon, they sat on the bed and studied the atlas again. Both agreed that eating at lunchtime had worked well, and they decided to do the same on the next two days. The plan was to get into Spain the next day, and then to Benidorm the day after. Everything went well, and mid-morning on Tuesday found them bypassing Barcelona.

"The rest of the day will be more or less following the route I took. It will seem strange." Josie stared out of the car window. "Oh yes, I recognise that bit – that's when I left this road and headed for the Pyrenees."

Andy slowed. "Do you want me to pull off?"

"No, we'll do all that on the way back. I just want to get to Benidorm now and get booked in somewhere. Don't you agree?"

So they pressed on, and as the skyscrapers of Benidorm came into view, the clock on the dashboard said 4.30pm. Josie knew a couple of smaller hotels from her time in the area and wanted to try for a room there first, before going to one of the skyscrapers.

It was early in the season, and they were lucky. A

411

room was available in the first hotel they tried, which happened to be only a couple of streets away from Lily's café. Josie had kept in touch with both Lily and Bella and they knew she was getting married and hoping to visit whilst they were on honeymoon. Although the plan was to see Lily the following day, Josie couldn't wait.

"Let's go and have a coffee in the café, please, Andy, can we?"

"Yes, why not? I'm looking forward to meeting her anyway."

They left the hotel hand in hand and made their way to the café. As they were approaching, Josie could see Maria wiping some tables. She pushed open the door and Maria looked up, a delighted smile on her face.

"Josie! Lily, its Josie."

She rushed over and hugged Josie as Lily came out of the kitchen at the rear. Now it was a big hug from Lily, and she seemed close to tears.

"I can't believe you're here at last. It's lovely to see you, and this must be Andy." She gripped Andy's arms and kissed him on both cheeks. "You want a coffee?"

"Yes please. You don't know how much I've been looking forward to one of your coffees."

Maria had already got them on the go, so Lily took two plates and filled one with savoury pastries and the other with sweet ones. She picked a table near the window and five minutes later, the four of them were seated eating the delicious nibbles and drinking the coffee, and talking nine to the dozen. Fortunately nobody else came in for twenty minutes, so they were uninterrupted, and then Maria got up to serve.

"You must come for a meal with Juan and I," Lily said. "I know he will be pleased to see you. Will you have time to do that? How long are you here for?"

Josie looked at Andy, who gave a small nod.

"Well, we've booked in for three nights at the Lemon Tree Hotel, but we may stay another night, and yes, we would love to come for a meal, either tomorrow or Wednesday. We've got no definite plans, although there's lots we want to do."

"Shall we say tomorrow, then? Come round to me about 7pm and we'll eat at 7.30pm."

"Lovely, now we must go and let you get cashed up. Do you want me to help?" Josie asked with a grin and a twinkle in her eye.

Lily just laughed and pushed her gently towards the door.

On Tuesday, Josie took Andy on a tour of Benidorm. She pointed out the flat where she used to live, and showed him, from a distance, the villa she had shared with Manuel, and then pointed out the rugged hills where she had started her walk. At lunchtime they sat at a café overlooking the sea, and Josie ordered two *bocadillos*, with tuna filling. Andy was impressed by Josie's Spanish. Considering it was quite a few years since she had lived here, it was still very good – well, to his ears it sounded good, anyway, and everyone seemed to understand her!

That evening, Lily and Juan made them very welcome, and they had an enjoyable evening. The men volunteered to wash up and leave the ladies to their gossiping.

"So, Lily." Josie spoke quietly. "Do you see anything of Manuel?"

"Yes, didn't I tell you? I meant to when I last wrote. He's settled down with a nice Spanish girl. They are married and they've got a baby."

"Oh, how lovely. I am really glad, I always felt it was my fault things went wrong, and I felt really bad I made him start drinking."

"Well, you need worry no longer. He looks really well and I feel sure he's not drinking."

"Does he still live in the villa I lived in with him?"

"No, he improved it, and then sold it. They've got a flat in Old Benidorm now, I think. Ah, here are the men. All finished then, guys? Thank you for doing that."

Andy and Juan seemed to be getting on really well, and had even made tentative plans to meet up again in the autumn. The evening flew by, and with promises to call in the café once more, Josie and Andy took their leave and headed back to the hotel.

Andy closed their room door and took Josie in his arms.

"My lovely wife, I've been looking at you all day and all evening, and I just want to love you."

He kissed her and Josie responded, melting into his arms. How lucky she was, and how happy she was with her life.

Andy turned the car into the hills. It was Thursday and Josie wanted him to see Guadalest and was looking forward to seeing it again herself. Just after 11am, Josie pointed to the right.

"There it is; you can pull in here."

Andy did so, and then looked where Josie had pointed and gasped.

"Gosh, that just doesn't look real."

He got the camera out and took several photos, and then they climbed back into the car and continued to their destination. Parking the car, they agreed a cup of coffee was the first priority, and then they would explore. They climbed to the top, looking at everything on the way up, taking photos when they got there, and then slowly headed back down.

"I must get a postcard to Stella while I'm here, and a little present or two," Josie decided.

She bought Stella's children a cute little t-shirt each and Stella a plate to hang on the wall, all depicting Guadalest. They found a table in a restaurant, both agreeing it had been a wonderful day.

Their last day in Benidorm had soon come and they went to the café for a last coffee with Lily and to say goodbye. Josie made sure Lily had her telephone number so she could ring when they arrived in England for their holiday. Lily's family lived in Devon, some way from Josie and Andy, but they agreed to spend their last couple of days in Sandacre and then Andy would take them to the airport. There were lots of hugs, and then Josie and Andy set off to spend their last day in Alicante.

Josie showed him the hotel she had stayed in with Stella on her first visit to Spain, and then they climbed the castle of Santa Bárbara, before descending back into the town. They found a small restaurant that did a good selection of tapas and only just managed to find a table. The place was packed out, always a good sign, Josie thought, that the food was good. They ate and then headed back north to Benidorm and their hotel.

"We'll do a bit of packing when we get back, shall we, Andy?

"Yes, good idea – we don't want to be too late leaving in the morning."

The first section of Josie's walk had been through the hills to the west of Jávea, and that's the way she directed Andy in the morning, even managing to find the places she had slept those first few nights. But once they were back near the coast, they got onto a better road and were soon heading north at a faster pace.

They arrived at Castello and booked into a hotel. They were now quite close to where Bella lived, and after settling into their room, went down to reception and asked where the nearest public telephone was. The receptionist told them that if it was only a short call they were welcome to use the hotel phone. Andy listened with a smile on his face as a voice answered the phone and squeals of excitement came from Josie, and a torrent of Spanish and English. Josie put the phone down and thanked the receptionist; then turned to Andy with shining eyes.

"We are to go straight to the shop tomorrow morning and she is going to arrange something so that we can see the children, although they won't remember me, and see her mama and papa as well. Isn't that great? Oh, you'll love Bella – the whole family are lovely. I just can't wait! And we are to stay with her mama and papa tomorrow night."

"Have they got room for guests?" Andy asked.

"Oh yes, plenty of room. They live in a lovely bungalow. Bella's house is very small; there wouldn't be room for us there."

Josie had been right about the children. They obviously barely remembered her, but after some initial shyness they were soon chatting away, Josie translating when necessary. Bella was teaching them some basic English, but they soon became confused when Josie or Andy tried to speak to them in English. They were both nearly as tall as Josie, and she kept having to do a double-take! The meeting that morning with Bella in the shop was a happy one, and later, after the shop was left in the charge of a young Spanish girl, they had gone back to Bella's house where the children had let themselves in ten minutes earlier. Now they were going to have a meal at Adella and Gregorio's.

The two elderly people still looked fit and healthy, and coped very well with cooking a meal for five adults and two fast-growing children. The meal was delicious and when they had finished, they retired to the lounge, collapsing into comfortable chairs, while the children sat on the floor. Bella stayed in the kitchen to load the dishwasher, and promised to bring coffees.

"You relax, Mama; you've been working hard preparing all that food."

Josie chatted in Spanish to Adella, who seemed a little concerned about Bella.

"She is young, she should marry again, but no, she is not interested. She doesn't listen to her mama."

"Perhaps she just hasn't met anyone she can love as much as her husband," Josie suggested.

"She is too fussy, the children need a father." Adella shrugged. "What do I know? I'm just her mother."

"Now, now, Mama, please don't start that again." A voice came from the doorway.

Josie thought it might be a good idea to change the subject, so she told Adella and Gregorio about their visit to Guadalest.

They sat around chatting well into the evening, as Josie knew they would, remembering how the Spanish would happily stay up till 1am or later. Not so hard when a two or three-hour siesta had been enjoyed in the afternoon! But Josie could see Andy's eyes beginning to close.

"Do you mind if we retire now, Adella? We've had a busy day."

Adella immediately got up and led them into the bedroom she had prepared for them. Josie and Andy turned and called, "*Buenos nochas*" to Bella and Gregorio and the children, and then thankfully prepared themselves for bed.

In the morning, they walked around the village and Josie showed Andy where she had slept in a carport, then when Bella closed for the afternoon, they went back to her house and relaxed in the garden. That evening, Bella and Josie prepared a meal and Adella and Gregorio came to join them. The five adults just managed to sit up to the small dining room table, while the children ate off trays on their laps. They spent the evening playing silly games with Sergio and Donna, before Bella sent them off for an earlier night.

Once again, it was a late night for the grown-ups and Andy whispered to Josie, "I couldn't keep this up for long, I'm shattered." They made time the next day to buy some flowers for Adella as a thank-you, and pop into the bakery to say goodbye to Bella, and there were a few tears as they hugged. But Josie knew Andy was keen to get on the road so they could reach Barcelona in good time and find a hotel.

As they drove out of the villa, Andy patted Josie's knee comfortingly.

"We'll see them again one day, darling, don't be sad!"

Josie sniffed. "I really like Bella. I hope you're right."

"Yes, the whole family are lovely. Exhausting, but lovely." Andy chuckled.

Things didn't go according to plan, however. Andy was fascinated by the Ebre Delta and what was supposed to be a short break became lunch, which turned into an afternoon exploring. Then when it became obvious they were not going to reach Barcelona, Josie suggested they head for Tortosa, just a few miles inland. She had never visited it herself, but had heard about it from Spanish friends. It was spectacular, and when Andy saw the Parador Hotel within the castle, no other hotel would do. They stayed there for just one night, but it was an experience they would never forget.

"Nothing is going to be quite the same after that," Andy said as they drove away the next morning, rather later than they hoped.

With only one quick coffee stop en route, they were in Barcelona by the early afternoon in time for lunch. Andy parked in an underground car park and they walked to the hotel where Josie had worked. Lunch was still being served, and they were shown a table.

"Would you like a drink?" the waiter asked.

Andy chose a beer and Josie a fresh orange juice, and when they came, they ordered their meal.

Josie could not resist asking, "Does Inyake still work here?"

"*Si, si*," the waitress replied.

"Tell him, please, Josie sends her regards."

All this was said in Spanish, so Andy had no idea what had passed between them. He took a long drink from his glass of beer and then began, "So what…"

At that moment a young man, obviously the chef, appeared at the table with a big smile on his face. "Josie, how are you? Still hungry all the time?"

420

Josie leapt up and hugged him. "I am well, thank you. This is my husband, Andy."

The two men shook hands.

"And yes, I am very hungry."

"Then I had better go and prepare your food. I will speak to you later."

With a chuckle he hurried back to the kitchen, leaving Josie to translate the conversation for Andy.

"Shall we stay here tonight, darling?" Andy asked.

"If they have a room that would be nice. I was a chambermaid here, of course, so I remember the rooms. I wonder if Señora Garcia is still here?"

The meal was as delicious as Josie had expected, and they finished off with a cup of coffee in the lounge. Whilst there, who should walk in but Señora Garcia. They greeted each other, and Josie introduced Andy. After chatting for a few minutes, Josie asked if there was a room available for two nights, and was told there was. Señora Garcia bustled away, and after they had finished their coffees, they went to reception and booked in, went to their room and rested for a while and then left to take a stroll up and down La Rambla. The weather was balmy and warm, but as the evening drew nearer, it cooled down and Josie was glad of her cardigan.

Andy had already been told he must see the Sagrada Familia. He told Josie he wasn't really that into churches, but went along with her suggestion. And he was certainly glad he did! He was completely fascinated and took lots of photos, and bought a couple of postcards just in case the pictures didn't come out well. They found a little restaurant down a side street and sat outside for a sardine lunch and a glass of wine, then looked round some gardens before returning to the hotel. They had a light meal that evening, and a much-needed early night. Inyake was not on duty the next morning, but Josie left a message at the desk to say goodbye and thank you for the lovely food.

As they headed for the Pyrenees, Andy found himself on a road they hadn't used before. There were not so many miles to cover on this part of the route, and they were able to take their time and enjoy the countryside and views. Andy suddenly swung into a layby and switched off the engine.

"Just look at that view, darling. Everything is so much greener here. Let's stop for a while and eat our sandwiches."

They opened the car doors and began to eat, gazing at the countryside around them. Suddenly Andy pointed to a track fifteen or twenty yards away. In an open patch of sunlit ground, five birds were hopping around.

"Look, Josie, what are those birds? Look at the colours, they're beautiful."

Josie looked to where he was pointing. "Oh, they are bee-eaters. Pretty, aren't they?"

Andy gave a small smile. "I take it you've seen them before?"

"Yes, loads of times. I remember the first time

though. It was at the villa one day when I was sitting quietly on the veranda. I was full of it when Manuel came home. I think they were nesting nearby."

"Gosh, I wish I had some binoculars," Andy said. "I'd be able to see them even better."

They sat watching for some time, then a tractor pulled into the track and the birds flew away.

"How was this part of your journey, Josie?"

"It was good. I was really fit after summer in the hotel, and I had money to buy good food and have the odd night in a hostel. And you are right; it is very beautiful here, and not too hot for walking. This was probably the best bit of the whole journey. Come on, let's go, then we'll be there in good time."

It was actually just after 3.30pm when they drove into the car park at the ski village. As they walked into the reception area, Josie looked around. A young lady was tidying the tables in the snack bar area, but her face was not familiar. Neither was the young man at the desk. They booked in, and Josie told him she had worked there several years ago. She mentioned Señor Vicente and Carmen, but he shook his head.

"The hotel changed hands last year. It's all new staff now."

"Oh." Josie didn't know what else to say.

They took the key and made their way to the room on the first floor, where Josie drew back the curtains and pushed open the windows. Andy looked at her.

"You're disappointed, aren't you? We can move

423

on whenever you like. We don't have to stay for three nights."

"Perhaps just two nights, then; there's not much to see up here anyway. We could wander round Camorno, and there's a nice walk in the wood above the town."

They agreed on this plan, and two days later found them driving into France.

"I was so excited when I walked across the border into France, Andy; it felt like I was nearly home. How silly was that?! France was so much harder, and so big."

"Just as well you didn't know, darling. Why didn't you fly home? You must have had enough money."

"Because I'm stubborn and stupid. I'd started walking and I wanted to do the whole thing. In fact, I was really looking forward to it. I think I just pushed the lack of French to the back of my mind. I got a French phrase book and thought I'd be OK." She shrugged. "How wrong I was!"

Andy reached over and patted her leg. "But you made it, darling, didn't you?"

By lunchtime, they were approaching Toulouse.

"I don't really want to stop here, if you don't mind, Andy."

"We should be able to bypass it."

She then told him of her experiences with public toilets, which caused him much amusement.

"Well, as you know, I've been to France on several occasions, and I do know they are different to ours, but it never bothered me that much. They always seemed clean enough to me."

"Mm," was all Josie had to say.

That night they found a motel in Brive-la-Gaillarde, and then moved on to the area of the caves and hilltop villages.

"I really wished I had a camera when I was here. Can we have a good look round, and will you take lots of photos for me?"

"Course I will, darling. Here, why don't you have the camera? I'm sure you'll be just as good as me at it."

They had lunch in the area, but Josie was impatient now to get as near to Esmé's as possible. Maybe they could find a hotel fairly near and go and see her tomorrow. She was so looking forward to it. As always, Andy was happy to go along with her suggestions and that night they were only about fifteen miles from where Esmé lived.

The next day they had a little trouble finding the road, and Josie had almost given up when suddenly there it was! Andy drove slowly down it, but Josie failed to locate the house. Andy turned the car round and drove slowly back.

"Stop!" Josie called.

She stared at the house they had stopped outside, but it was barely recognisable as the one she remembered. Gone were the creaky gate and the path leading to the front door. All the flower beds and roses were gone too. Now an extension had been built on one side of the house, and a double garage. The front was all paved, with only two flower tubs either side of the door showing any colour.

"I don't have a good feeling about this, Andy, but I'm going to ask anyway."

She climbed out of the car and walked to the front door, hesitated, then rang the bell. After a long pause, the door was opened and a pretty lady, possibly in her thirties, stood looking at her. She looked questioningly at Josie and spoke, but Josie had no idea what she was saying.

"I'm sorry, I'm English and I don't speak much French. A lady called Esmé used to live here. She was a friend of mine."

"*Ah, Esmé, oui.*"

By her expression and from what little Josie could understand, it seemed Esmé had passed away. Josie felt tears fill her eyes and impatiently brushed them away. The lady indicated to Josie to wait while she fetched something. After a few minutes she came back with a piece of paper. On it was Louis' name and address in Paris.

"*Ah, merci, mademoiselle.*" Josie smiled and said, "*Bonjour*" and went back to Andy in the car.

"Well, any luck?"

"Oh, Andy, she's passed away. She was probably in her eighties anyway, but I feel quite upset."

"That's a shame, but what's that piece of paper?"

"That's Louis, her son's address in Paris. He speaks perfect English. I can write to him and say I'm sorry and hopefully he'll write back and tell me what happened."

"Oh dear, let's move on. We could get near Mimi today if you like?" Andy said.

"Yes, let's do that. I know she's all right. Phil would have told me if she wasn't. Then the next day we can go home. It's been an amazing holiday, darling husband, but I'm looking forward to getting home."

Andy had noticed, as they were driving north through France, how Josie had become quieter and more thoughtful, obviously reliving her journey. Now he felt the next couple of days were going to be quite traumatic for her as she relived those hard few weeks when she had nearly lost her life. With this in mind, he found himself driving a little faster to cover as many miles as possible.

It was mid-afternoon when Josie touched his arm and said, "Stop at the next service area, please."

Andy glanced at her. Her face looked tense and her hands were clenched together. He pulled off and drove into the car park. As soon as he had stopped, Josie got out and walked towards the back of the building. Andy hurriedly locked the car and followed her, slipping his arm around her shoulders. Josie walked to a low wall at the back and sat down. She was weeping, and for some minutes couldn't speak. Finally she blew her nose and gave Andy a watery smile.

"I sat here and thought I was going to die," she began. "It was November and nearly dark, and very windy. Rubbish was blowing across here" – she swept a hand from right to left – "into that corner. And a piece

427

of paper blew into that hedge; that was the 100 franc note."

She looked at Andy. "Well, you know all that, don't you?"

"Yes, but it's quite different being here and seeing the exact place it happened. So then you went in to the restaurant and bought food, didn't you? And met Phil?"

"That's right, dear Phil. How many men would have done what he did?"

They sat a few minutes more; then Andy held out his hand and pulled Josie to her feet.

"Come on, darling, let's go and find something to eat, and then find a hotel."

"I wonder if Mimi's got a room? Would you mind staying there?"

"No, if that's what you would like to do. How far away is it?"

Josie grinned and waved at the bushes behind her. "About thirty minutes' walk in that direction."

Suddenly Josie felt her spirits lighten. Now she had been to the corner of the car park where things had been so desperate, she felt her mood lifting and began to look forward to seeing Mimi. And she suddenly felt hungry and ready to eat.

An hour later, just at 7pm, they drew up outside the B&B. Josie hopped out and walked up the path. The door soon opened in response to the bell, and Mimi stood there.

"Can I help you? Do you want a room?" It was quite clear she didn't recognise Josie.

"Mimi, it's Josie, don't you remember me?"

"Josie, no, you look so…" She struggled to find the right word.

Josie laughed. "I'm really well now, Mimi, as you can see. This is my husband, Andy."

Andy shook Mimi's hand, and then Mimi put her hands to her face.

"I am sorry, come in, please, Josie and Andy."

They followed Mimi into the lounge and Josie looked around. It looked just the same as she remembered. Mimi disappeared to put the kettle on and Andy leant forward and took Josie's hand.

"Are you feeling better now, darling?"

"Yes, I'm fine now, but it was difficult for me, going back to that place."

Mimi came back in with a tray of cups and saucers and a teapot, with matching sugar basin and milk jug. Andy leapt up and took the tray from Mimi and placed it on the small table by the settee. Mimi couldn't keep her eyes from Josie.

"Sorry, I look too much. You look so… healthy. Is that the word?"

"Yes, Mimi, but how are you?"

"I'm good, but getting old! Are you having a room tonight?"

Josie and Andy assured her they would like a room for one night, but explained they had been away for a long time and needed to get home tomorrow and back to work. Mimi asked if they had eaten, and Josie thought she seemed relieved when they told her they had eaten already.

After a pleasant evening and a good night's sleep, they were both eager to be on the road again, and on the way home. Once again, Josie was a little emotional on the ferry. They sat where they could see the English coast getting nearer and Josie talked quietly of the other crossing, while Andy listened silently. As they drove off onto English soil, Josie sat quietly, trying not to be upset again, but it was hard. She looked at Andy.

"You may not think this is the right thing to do, but I want to stop and say hello to Pammy and Phil, if he's around. I just want to give them a big hug!"

She bit her lip and Andy could see she was still struggling. He pulled into a layby and pulled her into his arms. He didn't know what to say, and could only hold her.

After a few minutes he said, "Shall we find a phone box and phone them?"

"Yes, perhaps we'd better, but I only want to make it a quick visit." She blew her nose and tried to compose herself. "Phil's home Wednesday nights, so we should see him as well, that's good."

Andy turned off into an area of housing and shops and found a phone box. "Do you want to speak to her, or shall I?"

"Do you mind doing it, Andy? I don't want to start crying again."

She gave him a shaky smile. They squeezed into the phone box together and Andy dialled the number, glancing at his watch. It would be about 4.30pm by the time they got there. They could stay just long enough to see Phil and then go home.

"Hello?" a familiar voice said.

"Pammy, it's Andy, Josie's husband. Do you think we could pop in and see you for a few minutes, at about 4.30pm?"

"Of course, is everything all right?"

"Yes, everything is fine. I'll explain when we get there."

"All right, see you about 4.30pm."

Andy rang off and they walked back to the car.

Josie was quiet as they drove to Pammy and Phil's, but there were no more tears. Although it was only two and a half weeks since Josie had seen them at the wedding, she was looking forward to seeing them again. They would always be special to her. It was 4.15pm when they pulled up outside. It was a little earlier than planned, so they sat outside for a few minutes, until suddenly the front door opened and a smiling Pammy was beckoning them in.

They hugged and Josie asked, "What time do you expect Phil home?"

"He's hoping to be home at about 5.30pm. He phoned this afternoon and I told him you were calling in, so he'll try and get home a bit earlier than usual. Will you stay for a meal?"

"Do you mind if we don't, Pammy? We've just got back and to tell the truth, I feel exhausted."

"You look tired, love – no, I don't mind. You just stay and say hello to Phil, then get off home."

With Andy's help, Josie told her about the last few days and how she needed to see her two friends and 'round things off'. Then they talked about the rest of the holiday, and Andy said how fascinating it had been.

The time flew by, and then the front door opened and a voice called, "Hello, where are my two favourite girls?"

He came into the room and gave Pammy a kiss, then held out his arms to Josie, She rushed into them and promptly burst into tears again. As Phil stroked her hair and tried to comfort her, Andy explained and Phil nodded, understanding now. Finally, Josie calmed herself and gave a shaky smile.

"Sorry about that; it's been such an emotional few days. I've never cried so much in all my life."

Pammy made a big pot of tea and they all sat round the kitchen table with steaming mugs in front of them.

"Pammy will tell you all about our holiday, Phil, when we're gone," said Andy. "But what I didn't tell you, Pammy, is that Josie's friends Lily and Juan are coming over in the autumn and you must come over and meet them. They are really nice and easy to get along with!"

"That'll be nice; thank you," Phil said. "We look forward to it."

Half an hour later, Andy stood up. "I'm going to take my wife home, she looks exhausted. Come along, darling."

He pulled Josie up from her chair, she hugged

Pammy and Phil, and then they left, with promises to get together soon.

Then they were home, and the car was unloaded and the front door closed soon after 9pm. Josie threw a load of washing in the machine, had a shower and was in bed by 10.30 and asleep by 10.35pm.

Andy went back to work the next day. He had so much to do and catch up on. Josie took the morning off, then mowed a couple of lawns in the afternoon and felt tired and lethargic, even after over nine hours' sleep. But after another good night, she felt back to normal on the Friday. They were up early and put in a long day, and both worked Saturday as well. Sunday was spent with Stella, Brian and the children. They told them all about the holiday, but there were no more tears. So everything settled down, and they both worked hard and caught up. Plans went in to the council for a garage on the side of the house, with another bedroom over it.

On Josie's twenty-eighth birthday in July, they met Stella and Brian at a nice pub just outside Sandacre, and enjoyed a meal there together. It had been a lovely summer's day and the evening was warm and balmy.

"Let's eat in the garden," Stella suggested.

They ordered drinks and took them outside. After a few minutes, the waitress came to take their order. The men both decided on steak, Stella had fish and chips and Josie had a salmon and prawn salad. The food was good, and they all managed a dessert. Then they went back to Stella and Brian's for coffee. It was nearly midnight before Josie and Andy got home, and they were soon in bed.

CHAPTER 18

The alarm went off at 6.30am the next morning, and after a quick cuddle they both got up to begin the day. As Josie left the bedroom she suddenly felt quite nauseous. She hurried to the bathroom and was immediately sick. As she came out, ten minutes later, she was met by an anxious Andy.

"Have you been ill, darling?"

"Yes, it must have been the prawns, although they tasted OK. Are you all right, Andy?"

"Yes, I'm fine, but I didn't have the same as you. I must say, I'm really surprised; they've got a good reputation. Are you feeling a bit better now?"

"Yes, I am, I'll just have a piece of toast and see how I go."

As the day wore on, Josie began to feel better, which was a relief, because she knew food poisoning could be very unpleasant.

That evening, she ate almost as much as normal, without any problems. But the next morning, the same thing happened. She was rather glad that Andy had already left for work. It was all rather embarrassing. She sat at the kitchen table, nibbling a dry piece of toast and feeling rather sorry for herself, when suddenly a thought struck her.

"No, I can't believe it," she muttered.

For some minutes, she sat there, stunned, then leapt up and ran upstairs. She hurriedly brushed her teeth and grabbed her handbag and van keys and left the house.

Parking in town, she walked briskly towards the chemist, made a purchase, and then drove home. Twenty minutes later, a stunned Josie left the bathroom and sat down on the edge of the bed. She just couldn't take it in. Pregnant – she was actually having a baby! She was roused from her dazed state by the phone. It was a customer.

"I'm just checking, Josie, that you are coming this morning. You are usually here by 9am."

"Yes, sorry, I'm running a bit late this morning. I'm leaving now; I'll be with you in fifteen minutes."

The day passed in a daze. She kept doing silly things. She missed a piece of lawn in one garden, put a plant in the wrong place in another and finally went home without being paid from her last job of the day, even though that particular lady always liked to pay her on the day. As she unlocked her front door and stepped inside, she couldn't help but giggle.

What a state I'm in, she thought.

She put the kettle on. Andy would be in soon and she just couldn't wait to tell him the news. Running upstairs, she pulled off her work clothes, freshened up and put on some shorts and a t-shirt. She heard the front door open and close and ran down the stairs.

"Is that my hubby?"

"Well, I hope so, unless some other chap's got a key!"

Josie giggled. "Kettle's boiled. I'll make tea."

It was their little routine. They would have a mug of tea, talk about their day, and then Andy would go upstairs to wash and change, while Josie started the meal. Andy sat down and took several sips of the hot tea.

"For goodness' sake, Josie, sit down, you're acting like an overexcited five-year-old. What's going on?"

Josie sat down and reached over the table to clasp Andy's hand in hers. For several moments she just gazed at him with a big smile on her face, then she said, "Darling Andy, prepare yourself for a surprise. I've got some rather good news for you."